Miss Iona (Bula!) -
Thank you for
your support & compan
I wish you long life
speedy recovery. ♡

Ruby

Jennifer Harris

[signature]
5·8·19

Copyright © 2018 Jennifer Harris

All rights reserved.

ISBN: 1539188019
ISBN-13: 978-1539188018

Dedication

Thank you to God from whom all blessings flow.

Thank you to my husband, Phillip Harris, whom reminds me daily of my talents, gifts and abilities.

Thank you to my father, Richard Bush, whom was a far better storyteller than I will ever hope to be.

Thank you to my mother, Bessie Bush, whom gave me the gift of words and the worlds books contained.

Thank you to the cities of St. Louis, New Iberia and Memphis which allowed me to paint with words everything my mind saw.

Also, I dedicate this book to those whom were fortunate enough to have the love of their lives—twice over.

Prologue

May 31, 1996

Dear Diary,

I thought of him again. On my birthday of all things. I thought about St. Louis, and what it meant to me. I came to St. Louis on accident. Accidents change people's lives, shug! Remember that. They come unexpected, out the blue, over yonder. Under the Master's control. I wanted to go to Chicago. I wanted to go to New York. I don't know how I managed to stay in St. Louis as long as I did. Being there sometimes felt like I was living in God's muddy footprint in the middle of the world. I felt like nothing was changing, nothing was happening fast enough. I mean, my cousins were here. I had family. But I wanted to be an actress, I wanted to dance. I wanted life bigger than New Iberia land and water would bring me. I wanted more light, colors and sound. I couldn't get that being someone's wife before I was twenty.

What life would that have been? I couldn't imagine being someone's anything when I was nineteen or twenty. My Daddy, Oliver, thought it would be a good thing for me to get married. I would have 'protection' he said. I wouldn't have to worry about taking care of myself. The man he had picked out for me was Moses. He was already twenty-one, was working and his family owned a hog farm. He also lived three houses down from my parents' house in New Iberia. Before I left, the last I heard of him he was working at the sugar mill, across from a fishery.

What did I think about Moses? Well, he was tall, a boy my grandma, Mother Oscella, would have called a 'big red boy', and brown-eyed. I didn't even like him. My mother would always remind me that he made nice money, but I didn't care. Moses was not what *I* wanted. I told my mother about what Daddy told me one day while she was snapping pole beans in her kitchen, watching the noon sun at her kitchen table. She didn't look up at me, her eyes on her bowls and cold water. I told her Moses had gotten another girl pregnant. I told her I could have sworn he walked past my window at least two nights a week. She didn't acknowledge my worry or observation.

My mother, Mae-Reavis, was a midwife and a nursemaid. She told me this girl's name. She delivered that baby, a baby boy, and told me Moses was not the man my Daddy thought he was. "Ethie, you got tuh get outta here." I believed her, and was already wrote to my cousin, John, in St. Louis.

I'm so glad I had the Mama I did. My mother was a L'sana Creole. She still threw salt over her opposite shoulder when she cooked, and during Mardi Gras time around the porch to keep the rain away. She still made her bleach for her good linen with a little bit of lye. My mother could write and showed all three of us, my sister, Stella and big brother Franklin, the plantation in Lafayette where her great-grandmother was born. She always wanted more from her life, she said. She taught me and my siblings to read before we ever went to school. We had lessons in her sewing room, when the Klan burned our school down. My mama would tap my left hand when I tried to write with it. "The devil is left-handed," she'd whisper. A pencil or pen never did feel natural in my right hand. I taught myself to write with both hands: right at my lessons and left when Mama wasn't looking.

I went there as a pit stop. This wasn't supposed to be home. New Iberia is home. I was going to do Broadway. Imagine! I had heard of *Shuffle Along*, and all the other plays on Broadway and wanted to be a chorus girl. I was supposed to go in St. Louis to save money. I had got a letter from my friend, Wynette. She was in New York, in Harlem to be specific. Wynette told me she got a job at the *Savoy Ballroom* as a waitress, if I remember. She was making $40/week with tips. Wynette was staying in a spare room of a Madam's house, and we would talk about how I could live there too while I worked for whatever Broadway show was playing.

She would write me all the time. See, her family got threatened by the Klan because her father was squabbling with this boss, Mr. Walter, over land her Daddy, J.D., could prove he owned and wouldn't be tricked to sell. Wynette told me Mr. Walter tried to burn their store down, and they had to all leave—they were livings with her aunt, Lizzie, in Harlem until Wynette got the job at the

Savoy.

New York City. I so badly wanted to go. All I could see what could be in New Iberia was folk who wanted nothing more than to fish in Lake Fausse, Moses, and a bayou that couldn't carry nothing nowhere else. I wanted more-- just like Mama. I think that's why she made sure I went to school, more than a little forceful about me graduating from that small Jonas Boley High School. More was outside New Iberia. More was beyond Lafayette. More was in New York. I was going to be a chorus girl and learn the songs and dances. Wynette told me that sometimes the main girls got sick or too far to hide their babies in their bellies, and a girl would get called from the chorus to do their part.

But St. Louis wasn't supposed to hold me here as long as it did. Keys did that. He was my quiet place, my thunder and my new good thing. I loved Keys and I knew he loved me. I knew it like I knew God was real. Why else would he have done for me what he did? Keys knew how I liked my drink. He knew how I liked my shoulders rubbed and what my favorite flower was—calla lilies—he made them my favorite because he gave them to me so often. I even had some in my wedding bouquet to my husband, James Aaron Carter.

And all this time later, I'm still on his mind. After all this time, I'm still somewhere in his mind. I don't know why he's on my mind like he is, but it's comforting. My mother told me when someone you once loved is on your mind, they must be thinking of you. Hmph. What could Keys be going through to make him think of me? Or maybe, I never did leave his mind. My heart had to grow to keep him and James. I wonder if his did the same.

PART I-

Katherine Brigby Lewis

St. Louis, Missouri- 1996

Chapter 1- February 1996

It started with keys; he lost his house keys in early November. He lost keys to the four-bedroom red-brick house, with the manicured lawn, and lush green yard in back he'd help build. The house at 2721 Mayfair Avenue we had moved into when our oldest daughter, Carolyn, was born in 1964. The house he'd etched her name into on one of the lower brick of the back of the house, which lead to the cellar. The house which had the portico archway, because I had asked.

Reuben found them before Thanksgiving behind our hedges. He had gone to rake some leaves the morning before the holiday and knocked on the door, keys in hand. He looked at me, still handsome. Still tall, with gray sprinkled in his and dark brown hair. And his eyes? Always bright and blue, in the gray Washington University sweatshirt our son Brian gave him for Father's Day. He held them up, right in front of his face, and shook them. I looked at him swinging them like a child with a foreign or broken toy. He just stared at them as they shook.

I have been Mrs. Katherine Brigby Lewis for more than thirty years—since May 31, 1961. We'd gotten married while still in college. I was planning on being an elementary school teacher. He'd left college to begin to build his construction company with his brother, Nathan and sister, Barbara who loved for everyone to call her 'Babs'. We'd raised three children. He'd driven our oldest daughter to the hospital to have our oldest grandchild, with her banshee wailing in his then new black Chevrolet pickup truck. This man I married could handle anything. He had a space for everything, but he couldn't remember where his keys were, or then what they were for.

I kept the keys a secret from our children for months. I thought it was a fluke, y'know? He just forgot. We all forget from time to time. We all need our memory jogged. We all need that, it's human to get busy and forget. That day in early November Reuben forgot his keys, we'd been to Soulard Market, something we did every Sunday. We'd get our fruit for the week. It was November in the Midwest, so there was always a chill. He tugged at his dark red jacket as he drove home. I drove my red Mazda home and once parked in the driveway, I rummaged for my keys in my purse. I left the car, my keys in hand, he had begun to unpack the trunk.

I unlocked the front door and opened it, looked for him as he held the bags of green grapes, bananas and pecans making his way towards the dark maple door I held open. He had taken a nap that afternoon before we went out, but so did I. He didn't know he had lost them, until I asked where his where when I couldn't find mine the week of Thanksgiving weeks later. By that time, I had already had a duplicate set made. "Katie, I lost my keys." He had said in a low voice. That was November. It was now a new year and three months later.

I played that day back and the day he found the keys. Over our almost forty years together, everything seemed to hinge on a twenty dollar a set of keys: backdoor, front door key, garage, two car keys: his Chevrolet truck and my Mazda. And lastly, a freezer key. He forgot what they were, and what they were for. My years with Reuben came down to a set of keys. I remember him shaking the keys, almost in disbelief. Those eyes, these eyes I had investigated, told I would marry him, looked past me and asked, "Katie, whose keys are these?" I froze. He never did look back to me. I told him to just bring them in the house. I told him he we would find whose keys they were. I put my hand on the back of his sweatshirt, and we had walked in silence through our door.

I had left Reuben on the couch, covering him with a thick patchwork quilt I kept on the back of our black couch which sat against the wall right across from the stereo and television set. I took off his shoes, and tucked him in. I sat on the side of the couch, watched him get comfy with, the November outside and watched him sleep. I had my head in my hands, feeling my anniversary band against my cheek. I had no idea what I could do, who I could call, and what I would even say.

I had heard of memory diseases-- dementia, forgetting spells. A lady in my sewing class, Charlotte, a short gray-haired Chinese woman, told me that ginger was good for a forgetfulness. I got some from Soulard Farmer's Market before Thanksgiving. I started to cook with it, make it into teas, gave it to him to sleep. I was doing all I could. All through the holidays, Thanksgiving and Christmas, I held my breath. I watched him with grandkids, I watched him decorate our Christmas tree and play Santa. I double checked appliances, car gauges and the milk I bought. I watched everything.

The first warm day in February, like Lewis family tradition, we had a barbeque. My sister-in-law, Barbara, was over already. The kids had called, confirmed they would be by later. She and I were talking in the kitchen that afternoon, she in a khaki cigarette pants and a white shirt, with her white wine, and newly dyed blonde hair. Reuben insisted he barbeque as he always did. I had obliged, resigning to make my berry shortcake desserts.

Barbara sat at the glass-topped kitchen table, looking out of screened back door, remarking she liked my new blonde bob. I was at the counter between the sink and stove arranging my shortcakes on the blue platter, making sure everything was perfect before I added my macerated berries. My back was to the door, I hear it slam open and slam. "Katie, have you seen my tongs?" I stirred my berries, spooning them on the Cool-Whip topped shortcakes. "There's a pair outside by your grill, babe." The door opened again. I was praying as I topped my shortcakes. *Hail Mary full of grace.* The door opened again. "Katie, you see my tongs?" Shortcake. Cool-Whip. Berries. "They are by your grill, babe." Door shut again. *The Lord is with me.* I heard Barbara sip her wine, feeling her eyes on my back. I heard the back door open, and slam. Silence then. I steeled myself in case Reuben had come back. The door opened and slammed, quick footsteps towards me. There were hands on my shoulders. "Katherine, Reuben couldn't find his tongs. I went outside to find them. They had fallen on the ground. What is going on?"

The concern, the noticing, knowing tone in her voice triggered what I thought was a howl in my throat. I wailed and heard the shortcakes, fall to the floor. I felt sticky fruit all over my blue blouse and dark khakis. "Katherine? What's wrong? What is going on!" I didn't know how I got to the floor or how I got back up on my feet. I looked at my pants and my shirt, vision underwater. I kept sobbing. I couldn't hold tears back, her asking me what was wrong had broken the dam. Barbara took me into the study down the hardwood floor hallway from the kitchen. The room was just walls covered with pictures, trophies and bookcases. This was the room we, as husband and wife, had built our life in—the local service awards, photos and on mahogany bookshelf. I concentrated on the red labeled encyclopedias on the tall bookshelves giving me an anchor while my world spun from its axis.

She sat me on the cream-colored sofa across from the anchoring bookshelves. I had just bought this couch last year. I couldn't stand the cognac colored one Reuben insisted on keeping just because the grandkids had written all over it. "It's a good couch, Kate! It doesn't make something better for it to be new, dammit!" I held my head in my hands again, my new blonde hair matted to my face with tears. Barbara was talking but I didn't hear her. "Kat, you need to talk to someone." I heard myself say, "Who?" "A doctor." She countered. There was a handkerchief in my right hand then, I dabbed my eyes. "How long has he been like this?" There was a weight and warmth next to me, Barbara pulled me to her shoulder. "November. Before last Thanksgiving." I heard Barbara sigh. "It's February." I was crying again. "I'm aware."

"Have you talked to the kids?" she asked. "No! God, no!" I sniffled. What would I even say?" I sat up then. I looked at her, hard. She and I were almost the same age, it was because of her I had married Reuben. I saw the concern in her face, the fear. Barbara was studying my face, her blue eyes to my green ones. "You need to tell the kids. Something is going on with my brother." I looked away from her and to the grandfather clock opposite the bookshelf, watched the pendulum swing. "He sees the doctor in May." I stared at the clock's face, willing time to stop. "May 15, Friday." The tears were falling over my face. "That was the quickest they could see him." Barbara patted my hand. "Kat, this...this..."

"Might be Alzheimer's. I know. I know." Barbara squeezed my right hand, held it in both of hers. I thought I might break if she asked anymore. I needed air. "I have to change, Babs." I saw her stare up at me as I got up from the couch, sliding my hand from hers. I heard my bare feet go through the same hallway, towards my front door and upstairs. The kids, my grown children, would be there soon. I wouldn't let them see me in such a state, I had to look my best, no matter my desire to stop time or run away. My husband, my Reuben, needed me. By God, I was going to keep putting on the show.

Chapter 2- Early May 1996

I sat up in bed, the same bed Reuben and I have shared for more than half of my life. I looked out the window and watched the moon through the trees. I hugged my aching knees, putting my head on them as I did when I was a little girl to steady me. I was tired. I was too tired to sleep. I was too tired to do anything. I listened to my heart beating, I listened to Reuben breathing. I listened to the house settle. I got up, my bare feet on the cold floor. I remembered how I had asked Reuben to redo the floor two years prior. I wanted the floor redone, insistent about it. I needed a change in the house, and I was preparing to entertain more. The bedroom was first, and then he redid the living room before the dining room. I wanted the sun-bleached hardwood replaced by this dark red Japanese maple I had seen in a March 1994 *Southern Living* magazine whilst at my hair appointment. Right before my cancer diagnosis.

I went to the bathroom, smoothing my hair and long emerald green gown as I went. I looked in the mirror of our dual sink, felt the cool of the tile under my feet, with only my reflection for company. Where had the time gone? I began to cry against the sink. I felt my knees almost buckle under the weight of my tears. I started to remember the day I met Reuben. I remembered how handsome he was, how good he smelled, and his crooked smile. I had walked past him on the Washington University campus. I was going to register for classes, and he had asked me what time it was. I looked at my leather watch my mother had given me for a high school graduation present and told him. I was reliving him strong and sound, everything intact. Thirty-five years. Through children, houses, deaths, we had us. Now the us, this us, was just me.

Looking in the mirror again, I looked at the eyes which had looked at Reuben. I looked at the hands which held his, his children, and every dream I had. I had given up so much for Reuben. Now—now, I had to give up more! I have always had to give up things for him: my catering business, my teaching career. I didn't know how much more I was supposed to do. I ran water on my face, holding the cool water there. I felt it flow through my hands, over my wrists as I remained bent over the sink.

I turned the water off and sat on the side of the bathtub. I looked at this old woman in the mirror. She had my face, but I didn't see me. I looked at my face, its features and how they changed. I looked at my hands, the spots which had crept over them, and could only keep crying. It had been almost two months since Barbara had come to my house and seen what has happened to my husband, her brother. I couldn't protect Reuben anymore. I couldn't cover it up anymore. There was a suspicion through the family now, there was a *thing*---this phantom now visible to our family. In a matter of days, this phantom would have a name.

I heard Reuben stir. I heard him moan, and I wiped my face. I looked towards the Queen-sized bed where he continued to sleep alone. I heard him whimpering, almost crying. "I'm sorry, Ruby. I'll come back. I don't leave. Wait here." He started to moan unintelligibly, I wasn't sure if he was still speaking coherently or just babbling. Reuben had always talked in his sleep. As I strained my ears, I couldn't place the accent. Reuben was a lifelong son of St. Louis soil, and I was a daughter of the same city. But this accent, the timbre-- I couldn't place it. I couldn't place it. It was husky, it was rough. It—I wasn't sure where it was from. It didn't *sound* like Reuben.

I sat there on the side of the bathtub, pushed the dark blue shower curtain back, when it was already pushed back. I thought about the red shower curtain I replaced, thought it didn't belong there—I thought it didn't go with the scheme I had going in the bathroom. I sat there feeling, watching him, remembering to breathe, feeling much like a rabbit who heard a fox. I sat there in wait; waiting for it to be safe. I waited, wanting him to speak again, and not at all. I wanted him to be Reuben again, for—for just a while. Let sleep be a release for us both. I didn't have the strength to be brave now. I simply didn't have it. I needed to recharge. I was always told that wives were the keepers of all secrets, their hearts were vaults. This would be one more secret I would have to hold onto. This was one more thing to have to try to smooth over with charm and tears. One more thing, I would have to perhaps cry in the bathroom about. I, facing the latter rain of my life, had become a child all over again. Perhaps just like Reuben would be.

*****

I had scheduled lunch with Babs the day after Reuben's appointment on the 15th. The day after tomorrow. I wanted my feet under me again. I knew the kids would be so nervous when I talked to them, most of all Carolyn. She was so close to her father. She would demand to know what was happening to her Daddy. What *was* happening to their father? There was so much *going on* with him. I had started to drink the ginger tea with him in the morning; sometimes I told him it was coffee. I think he drank it to humor me, he had to know it wasn't coffee. I had honey-sweetened to go down easier.

When Babs called me at home the day before the appointment I had almost jumped out of my skin. I willed my heart to slow down as I answered the phone on my night table in our bedroom. "Hello?" "Hi Katie!" I shut my eyes, sitting on the unmade bed. "Hi, Babs." She already sounded happier than I would be as the week would progress. "I called to see how Reuben's was doing." I kept my eyes shut and heard echoing deep breathing filling the bedroom. It took me a moment to realize the echo I heard was my breathing. "He's okay. Mowing the lawn right now." I looked over towards the mirror on top of the dresser my mother had given me after our oldest daughter was born. I had asked Reuben to refinish and stain it just two years ago when he Reuben redid the floor. I thought it would be nice if it matched, and he knew I loved Cherrywood furniture.

I heard Babs talking, I heard nothing she said. I looked at my reflection with reddening eyes and water leaking from them. The aged brass handles blurred as Babs's voice rang unintelligible in my ear. "Katherine!" I tried not to cry, I had to be presentable for Reuben and movie night with my oldest friend, Ruth. "That's it, I'm coming over!" With that, there was a loud clang in my ear with the beeping of a dial tone. I stared at my hand and the gray cordless receiver in it. She was coming over. I was in shambles. I heard the low roar of the lawn mower closer to the under our bedroom window.

I got up, still in my gown and went to the window sitting in the cushioned sill. I watched Reuben finish the lawn and surveying his work. I tucked my hair behind my ear and wiped my face. I watched Reuben as if I were watching ants. I watched him take his red towel and wipe his damp graying brown hair and face. *What was wrong with their father?* I wasn't prepared to answer this question. Every time I thought about it, I was felt more and more out of control.

I didn't know if I was relieved Babs was on her way over, but I knew that I didn't want to be alone. I didn't want to be alone in this feeling, this empty feeling. I had no idea how I would manage the appointment tomorrow. I had no idea what I would do with any diagnosis and what they would recommend I do about Reuben. He would be reduced to a folder, a number, a portion of a doctor's caseload or bookshelf. He would be on paper and reduced to ink. My husband would be inhuman after we left that office. I could not deal with that. I would not deal with that.

I began to go back to the bathroom where I stared into the mirror again, smiled at the old woman there, still not quite sure from whence she came. Not sure when I began to really see her there. She had no business there. I needed strength to get through the next few hours. I needed the strength of the young woman that bore three children in six years. I needed the strength of that girl who nursed an ailing mother while breast feeding her youngest child. I needed that young woman fought through her Elementary Education major at Washington University, shaving a whole year off her coursework. I needed her back. I couldn't find her. Without her strength, 9:30am the day after tomorrow would be hell. The wedding anniversary at the end of the month would be impossible. I didn't know how deep those wells ran for old women, but I would have to find out...or redig them. I had no idea if I had the strength to do so.

The phone rang again. My eyes leaked water once more. My feet were cement. I couldn't make it to the phone. I heard the answering machine sound with Reuben's voice echo weren't available. His voice sounded so certain. It was my oldest daughter, Carolyn. "Hey Mom! When you get in, call me back. I wanted to know if you wanted company this weekend. The kids are asking to bake with you and are so excited about the anniversary party! I talked to Aunt Babs. I want to know what's wrong with Dad." There was another click. Carolyn's voice added to Reuben's to be saved on the cassette. I heard the downstairs grandfather clock chime. Eleven o'clock in the morning. I watched him put the lawn mower away in the garage and get the edger. I smiled as he went along the lawn. I missed him so much then, he felt so far from me. I wanted Reuben to tell me it would be okay, everything would be okay. I wanted to know life wouldn't have to change. Nothing would have to be different--not at this point in life, my life, our lives together.

I sat against the wall of our bathroom, near the toilet, on the tile floor that Reuben had to have, but hated to mop. I closed my eyes and thought about our wedding day. This was the feeling I had almost forty years ago.

I smiled grimly feeling tears falling over my cheek. I remembered being in the bridal salon of Holy St. Michael's Church, and tearing up. I was scared out of my mind! I was in bare feet because I kept wobbling in the shoes I wore. I kept pacing in front of the brown cheval mirror. My sister kept trying to repin my then brunette bun. I was so nervous. So many things were running through my mind I laugh about now.

I was worried about the flowers wilting in the May heat, I was worried about my pregnant sister chasing me with pins. My grandmother, Ardelle, with her long, straight white hair, strength in a red pale red dress said, "Still, Tia," calling me to her, held me to her shoulder. Her scent of lilies steadied me, her accent coated with her lingering Greek accent. "It all will be okay." I remember I had sat down on the red settee and let my sister, Rose, finally repin my hair, then position the veil to my hair. I remember Rose's pin pricked my scalp and I cried more.

Anxious, uncertain, hot tears fell like they did on the cheeks of that twenty-year-old girl. I remember feeling out of control and helpless---uncertain but resolute. I was determined to get through the day and marry Reuben. I was going to make it! I had willed by body to an oak tree strength as I dabbed tears with my mother's blue linen handkerchief. I was determined make it through our life together, part of that was getting through this one day years ago. All I had to do was get through that day. The same advice I gave to my elementary school students, and my own children when they felt their days were insurmountable: just get through the day.

I wanted reassurance, I wanted strength and I wanted the resolve again to believe I could conquer anything. I wanted the anchor Reuben and I had formed: *we* were more than the world against us with nothing between Heaven and Hell to stop us. Now the *we* was a *me*. There was a warmth near me then. "Katie?" The warmth settled next to me then, smelled of vanilla. It was Babs. "Katherine?" she repeated. I didn't know how long I sat there, but I had no desire to move or open my eyes. I was still hunting for the twenty-year-old whom could tell me how to conquer the rest of the world—let alone the next twenty-four hours. "Are you okay?" the warmth said. I inhaled vanilla felt warmth in my hand, followed by Babs' voice. "How long have you been here?" I didn't answer the voice. "Reuben is on the back porch." I sighed. "He cut the grass."

"How long was he out there?"

"I don't know."

"Have you eaten?" I cracked an eye at the warmth and saw worry in Barbara's face and concerned green eyes. "I had oatmeal and ginger tea this morning." She was sitting next to me, in a white blouse and jeans. Her feet were bare. "Katie are you okay?" She was wiping tears from my face. "Katherine, I don't know what the hell is going on, what is happening, what is wrong with my brother, but you have to tell the kids. You have to tell the kids!" I rolled my head away from her hands and faced the tub, letting the cool of the bathtub settle me. I concentrated on the cream-colored towels hanging on the bar by the dual sink, and my slippers by the bathtub. So orderly, perfect and reliable. I sighed, heard myself say, "I'll tell them after the party."

"You still want to go through with it?" The vanilla was speaking again, and I kept my eyes closed. I felt my neck relax enough to nod. "I have to at least do that. If I do that," I opened my eyes, focused on the white wall behind the toilet. "I'll handle everything else. I'll handle everything else." I don't know when she began to hug me, but I melted in her hands, the vanilla she wore wrapping around me, quieting the screaming I knew was happening in my soul. I felt more tears then, more strength leave my body as I tried to pull myself out of the crying waves that started. I tried to tell Babs I was okay, Reuben was okay, nothing was wrong or going to change. The tears made me an abject liar. The tears broke into my strength and made me question everything. I wept and held onto her warmth. My whole life would change the day after tomorrow and I had no idea how I would keep the world spinning on this axis for one more day.

Chapter 3-May 1996

I had woken up to Reuben pacing around our bedroom. "I need my watch. I need my watch. I'm going to be late." There was that accent again. Rough and deep. "Reuben?" I heard drawers slam and open. I covered my head and felt the hot tears. "I need my watch! Rob, where is my watch!" There were closet doors slamming, then something shake and rattle and a crash. I lay there under a down pillow on the side of my bed. I had no idea what had broken, or what could be done to fix it. I knew that Carolyn would be there to accompany me to her father's appointment.

I began to sniffle and wish for her to get here as soon as possible. I began to wish I could have taken her up on the offer of staying over in the guest room downstairs. I told her to go home with the grandkids. They had baked lemon sugar cookies with me, there mother has taken pictures and Carolyn had taken them home at my behest after my break down in the bathroom with Barbara. I had kissed the brunette heads of Brice and Logan as they vanished into the night and her red Toyota minivan.

I heard the bedroom door slam, waking me from last night's memory. I lay there, listening to the small alarm clock on our dresser. I began to review what had just happened. I found myself recording everything he did, like a video camera. I remembered what he said, the inflection, the tone, whatever he was looking for. I didn't know of any watch he was looking for. He got a watch for Christmas from the grandkids, some digital cheapie they found a K-Mart. I didn't even know if he opened it, let alone where it was.

The shower ran as the phone rang. I sniffled and cried under the pillow as the cassette played Reuben's voice again, telling the caller we weren't available. "Hey Grandpa, it's Logan. I miss you. Bye." The chipper voice of our oldest granddaughter pushed me to roll over onto my side under the pillow. I concentrated on the water flowing. I remembered if I had put these dark blue mats outside of the tub, so he wouldn't slip when he stepped out of the tub. I tried to remember where his shaving razors where. I wondered if he remembered where they were. I felt glued to my bed. I didn't want to know what had broken, I already had.

My tears reached my ears when I heard the bathroom door open and shut again. I kept the pillow over my face. "Dear God." I muttered. I heard footfalls down the stairs and then silence. I hoped that he had fallen, and we would have to go to Barnes Hospital. There, they would be able to fix what has broken. They could see it, fix it and I could take Reuben home-- whole again. I sat up in bed, smoothed my emerald gown, stared at the clock on the dresser. I found myself wearing this gown more often to bed because I thought Reuben liked it, and on good days he would rub my hip, tell me how beautiful I was.

The red numbers jutted out from the black framed alarm clock reading 8:04 a.m. The appointment was at 10 a.m. Reuben had to have been up an hour before throwing his fit, and I was too out of it to try and keep him in bed with me longer. I was thinking starting on the wine Barbara had gotten me for Christmas last year, but the memory of my father coming home drunk from wherever kept me from opening it.

I looked around the room, wiping my face and counting any items I had hanging on the way that had glass in or on them. Window, fine. Mirrors, fine. I pressed my hands to my mouth when I didn't see our wedding photos. I had three of them in our room. One on the dresser we shared and the other two hung up on either side of the wall. I got up slowly, feet bare on the floor. I found the picture of Reuben and his brother, Nathaniel on the floor by the dresser.

They were so young in the black and white photo near the window outside their childhood home on St. Louis's southside. Reuben had to be a Senior in high school and Nathan was working for a Chrysler plant. I walked over, wiping tears and touched the frame. I looked at his dark hair, and Nathaniel's, same dark hair and broad shoulders. I cradled in and looked for the wedding day photo that was hung on the wall between the dresser and standing mirror. I smiled at young Reuben and Nate so strong and handsome. I smiled remembering how nervous he looked at the altar when I came in, looking like a struck deer. Nathan stood in back of him on the Holy St. Michael's Church's lawn. My mother had taken this picture on our wedding day.

Those Lewis boys were always so handsome. I caressed Reuben's silhouette, brushed the shards away. I held it in my hand and saw the other picture which had fallen from the dresser: picture of my bridal party, frame and glass broken. I felt the glass in my foot. "Shit!" I grabbed my foot and pulled it out. I dusted the glass onto the remainder of the frame and threw the remnants of both frames away in the bathroom. I took the pictures to my bed and held it as tears fell again. I tore the wedding photos, throwing them to the floor. I looked at my bleeding left sole and went into the bathroom to get dressed. Carolyn would be coming soon.

I went to the closet and stared into the walk-closet I made Reuben give me, smiling at the at the rack of clean clothes and shoes. I smiled musing what I told my children about getting dressed. *"The clothes aren't going to fly on your body. To meet the day, pick out clothes!"* I decided on khaki slacks, crimson blouse and those sensible white loafers the Maeghan had gotten me for my birthday last year. I got my outfit and shoes, I heard a tea kettle whistle and abandoned my items on the bed to rush downstairs. I grabbed red my robe from behind the door and smoothed my green gown under it. I pounded my feet over the wooden stairs to find Reuben at the coffee table, dressed and drinking out of his white mug. "I made coffee, shug." I looked at him. "Shug?" I repeated, sure I looked like a startled carp. He repeated it. "Yes, Shug. I made you coffee. Just how you like it." I walked closer to him, examining him.

I looked at him over the dark mahogany table. I looked at his white front button shirt underneath. He had barely combed his hair, the gray in evident on his temples. He replaced his cup on the table, and I made my way towards the table, watching him. I looked over at his cup, watched the coffee turn from mahogany to clay. "Reuben...um, thank you." I drank coffee on occasion. He knew that. I hadn't drunk coffee daily in years. He stood up, taking his coffee, and headed towards his study—still not looking at me. "I made you coffee, Ruby." I heard him lumber down the hall, I knew that gait happened when his hip hurt him. There was a fall at a site a couple years ago, and he had to have a partial replacement. I sighed thinking of something else to take care of.

He got his cup and got up from his chair. I hugged my robe, and sat in my chair, looking at this red mug of coffee. There was a ripple in my cup. I had begun to cry again. I was tired of hiding how I felt. I didn't know how much more I could take. I stood from the table, walked the cup into the sink, and tossed the coffee in the sink. My shoulders shook as I heard that same banshee wail, as I braced myself against the sink. I bit my lip and swore at God. "I can't God, I can't, not right now…" I heard the front door open, footfalls towards the kitchen. "Mom?" I heard my tears and felt them over my face. I felt myself slide to the floor. "Mom, where are you?" I was never so desperate and relieved all at once for one of my children to be nearby. I heard Carolyn closer to the kitchen, quicker footsteps. "Mommy?" I heard a bag rattle to the floor, something cracked, and arms surrounded me.

The arms shook me, held me again. "Mom, Mom! What's wrong?" She held me. She held me tight and rocked me. The same way I had done with her so many nights to fend off nightmares, break-ups and lost favorite toys. I pulled myself from her shoulder, stared into Reuben's eyes hidden in her face, my lips turned up, looking back at me. Carolyn wiped my face, her hands wrapped around it. She smoothed my cheeks. "Mom." She was searching my eyes again, giving me an anchor to come back to this reality. I couldn't focus. "Where is your father?" I heard my voice cracking. I sniffled and couldn't find my leg muscles to stand. My head felt so heavy, my eyes on the floor. She pulled me back to her, Reuben's eyes again looking back at me.

Pulling to my feet with my found leg muscles, I stood bearing up on the side of the sink. I heard rustling near me, seeing Carolyn by the door she bent in half near the kitchen door. I held the side of the sink. There were groceries she bought, sugar, flour and eggs—it was the eggs I heard breaking. She bought all the things Brianna and Logan had used making cookies days earlier. I saw Carolyn's brunette head bobbing, saw her body sway as she picked up the bag and set it on the kitchen table. I watched my oldest daughter, begin to be the strong one again as she began to put the groceries away like nothing happened—just like my mother did with my father. "You are so much like your Nan." I heard her snort. "Grandma Mae or Nana Zelda?"

I giggled. "My mother, Zelda." I watched her move from table to cabinet, to refrigerator while I found my sea legs found my sea legs against that sink. I sighed moving to the sturdy oak of the kitchen chair. My hands were in my hair, eyes closed. I saw my wedding day, I heard my mother's voice, remembered how she walked me to the door. She reminded me the Brigby women had all kinds of strength, "We are like cedar from the old world. We don't break, so neither will you." She walked behind me, praying and comforting me as the pins stuck my hair. I missed Zelda Brigby so much, needed her just one more time. *"You can do this, Kay. You can do it. Just breathe. Once step at a time."* She said. I heard the study door open and shut. "Carrie?" Reuben's voice then. I saw Carolyn traipse past me as I lowered my hands from my face, leaving the memory of my mother.

I heard Carolyn calling for her father.

Quicker footsteps, "Dad?" I heard her voice echo through the hallway like she was a little girl again, she always fearful of not knowing where her Dad was. "We were going to be late to this apportionment." I muttered, nesting my hands on my face. It might as well be the morning of my mother's funeral again, I was that helpless. I was swimming standing up. I heard the grandfather clock chime nine o'clock in the morning. We had to be at Dr. Miller's office in the next hour. I got up to go find the shower, and strength under the running water. I felt colder as grabbed the banister to head upstairs. My feet felt heavier, my mouth dry. I felt invisible as I passed my hall mirror and seeing that old woman again. Her eyes were watery and red. She looked scared, unsure. She looked more like the mother of that girl in the picture moons ago which had fallen to floor.

I figured I had about fifteen minutes to shower, and another ten to do my makeup before Carolyn began to look for me. I couldn't wrangle her father right now. I made it to the bathroom, I turned on the shower and shut the bathroom door. I had no desire to wrangle with him today. Carolyn was there, and she was always her father's favorite. She could fix him for the moment, calm him and make him better. In a matter of an hour, the life we put together, the one I was fighting to hold together, would be taken from me.

******

I looked in the vanity mirror again before we left Dr. Miller's office, on the tenth floor of Queeny Tower at Barnes Hospital. I took my red lipstick out of my purse, concentrated as I reapplied it. I looked over my reflection again, smoothed my hair in the vanity mirror. "Mom?" I heard the passenger door unlock. I looked at the mink gray floor with its mat. I smoothed my hair, tucked a section behind my right ear. "Mom are you hungry?" I shook my head, saw the worry in Carolyn's face, the confused look in her eyes. "I really don't want anything though, don't go out of you way for me." I saw Reuben get in the back seat of Carolyn's minivan. I looked at him, turned around in the front seat and put my head on the headrest. I heard the car doors slam, the car start. My mind replayed what had just happened to me.

My husband of over thirty years asked the doctor for the last ten years of his life if he knew when Ruby's next set was because he had to run something to Soulard. Height, normal. 6'1". Weight, okay. 200 pounds. Blood pressure a little elevated, no medicine needed. Then he asked for Ruby. He had stormed out when he couldn't find her and thought the doctor was lying to him. "How long has he been like this?" I couldn't answer and heard Carolyn's voice. "My mother said it's been going on about six months."

I saw Dr. Miller's face behind a clipboard adjusting his glasses, pen moving with automatic rhythm. He asked a series of questions to the room,

Reuben looking at his watch, Carolyn and I both silent. Before I could answer what, else Dr. Miller had to ask, Reuben got up and left! I left the sterile office, leaving Carolyn to speak to Dr. Miller to look for Reuben. I went through the short hallway, toward the waiting area, with its perfect white chairs, florescent lights while the black girl with the lavender shirt, starched blouse at the secretary desk with a serious pinned bob and bangs looked at me as if I was disturbing her. I caught her brown eyes, as she lowered her *Ebony* magazine. "Ma'am?" I said nothing, just looked at her.

I dashed past her desk and went through the heavy brown door of the office's practice. I found Reuben walking down the hall towards the elevators, looking at his watch and muttering. I jogged a little, calling his name. "Babe!" I yelled before he got to the elevator. He stopped, as if struck dumb. I caught up to him, hugged him from behind, groped for his hand. "Reuben." I whispered behind his ear. I smelled his shaving cream, his cologne. I breathed him in, deep, squeezed him tight.

He turned to me, slow, studied my face. "Deborah?" he said, looking at me yet past me. "No, love." I sniffled. "It's Katherine. Katie." He blinked, his eyes so blue then. He looked at me like he hadn't ever seen me. He kissed me, I concentrated on him and blocked out anything else. "Katie." He whispered, like he was hanging on to something, he started to pull me back into him. He said my name again like it was an anchor to him. "Katie. My Katie." Reuben took my hand and we walked back to Dr. Miller's office. I looked at the white marbled styled floor, remembered to breathe. I knew what Dr. Miller would say. My husband of almost thirty-five years, would, one day, not even know whom I am. Alzheimer's Disease was the phantom—my house, my marriage was haunted.

******

The banquet hall was so nicely decorated. Carolyn and her husband, Jason had done such a good job transforming the hall at Holy St. Michael's Church to 1961. I had my best friend, Ruth, to come over and get dressed, just like we had in college. I had called in Reuben's medicine to the Walgreen's in Richmond Heights pharmacy three days after the appointment. It would be ready Sunday. It was Friday. I was determined to enjoy this last night, this last weekend of freedom. I was going to be twenty again for one night. I needed everything to be perfect!

I sat in the same bridal salon I had thirty-five years ago. I sat in front of the vanity table, the red lamp off to the right side, saw smoothed the flyaway hairs in the updo I wore. I smiled and reapplied the Yves Saint Laurent 61 lipstick I had gotten from Plaza Frontenac that morning out with the youngest,

Maeghan. The sales associate, her name was, Ethylene, which I thought was strange, even with all my years of teaching. I knew there were some strange names out there—especially for black children. She had this red bob-length hair that was so nicely coifed and these big red librarian type glasses that sat on her pretty walnut brown face. I asked her where her name came from. She giggled, fanned me off, and answered, "Oh, there was this singer my mother knew, and she wanted a unique name for a baby." As she rung me up, she grinned as she told me to have a nice day.

Maeghan took her sales associate card, before we turned to leave. "Mom, really?" she hissed on the way to the car. I starred at my gold cased lipstick. Ethylene had said the color was something to "Surely get a woman noticed." I was hoping it would make me forget. Being pretty for an evening could only help. We got in my red Mazda, started the car to head home. Ruth would be at our house at four to get dressed in me—the party started at six. It was already three. "Did you really have to ask her where her name came from?" I didn't answer her. "All the kids you taught in St. Louis Public School District and you just couldn't wait to ask a someone who was African-American where their *name* came from?"

I took the exit towards I-64 and wished I had taken Carolyn shopping. Maeghan made everything an issue. Everything was a fight! Everything had to be debated! "I asked her what her name was because I never heard it before! Dammit, Maeghan!" I heard her suck her teeth and we continued in silence. "I think it was rude, Mom. Careful, God can hear you curse." I rolled my eyes and kept driving, snuck a look at the back of her brunette head. I thought how she had gone from my youngest daughter who cried when I left for work when she was a toddler when I left for work turned into this moody, dark twenty-six-year-old. "I guess you feel like this because you're still dating that black man?" She remained silent. "I wish you would find a nice guy and settle down. You're almost thirty!"

Meaghan huffed. "Say it, Mom! You would love for me to stop dating Anthony because he's black. Ugh! Why did I ever bother coming shopping with you!" As quickly as I drove back to my house, we were cursing at each other even faster. As we pulled into the driveway, Maeghan jumped out of my car, shrieking on her way to her blue Jeep Wrangler, "Don't fucking wait for me to come to this sham-ass event tonight!"

The door closed with Ruth on the other side of the door, looking simply stunning in her red boat neck dress. "Just like old times, eh?" I and my reflection laughed at her in the mirror. "Except this time, we aren't drunk in a car, trying to get home!" I turned to face her, happy to see someone whom still remembered me. "How's Charlie?" Ruth smiled. "He's amazing. I still wonder how I am still

Mrs. Bright after thirty years." I giggled. "I remember when you didn't even like him. You said he walked like a duck." We laughed again, riotous and full. She smoothed her dark black hair, her brown eyes twinkling. "He's still a sexy duck." I sighed.

I heard music through the closed door, looked at my gold watch Carolyn's husband Jason had given me for an early anniversary present. I sighed. "How is he?" I looked up at Ruth. "So far, so good." Ruth closed her eyes, sighed and walked over to me. I looked at her perfect round red nails. I envied that her life was so manicured, just like her nails. Healthy husband. Happy kids. Enjoying the rest of her life with a man she thought her soulmate. "Just get through the day." I nodded, stared at her right hand. "Just get through the day." Arm in arm, we left the bridal salon to be twenty again.

The dinner was catered by *Zelda's,* the catering company Carolyn and Jason owned. There were gold and cream-colored balloons, even though I told the grandkids didn't need gold balloons: those are for golden anniversaries. I'm glad they didn't listen. There was Elvis playing as Reuben and I bopped to music and traded cheek kisses at the head table. Carolyn, and her younger brother Brian Nathaniel, had arranged the banquet hall in such a way there was a screen at the front of the room, and the lead table was at the left side of the room. They were going to do a slide show about our life together. I saw the grandkids dancing to *Mr. Postman,* by the Marvelettes. Reuben hugged me close as he finished the roast beef and au gratin potatoes. "This was great, Katie. I'm glad we came. Where is Mae?" I studied his eyes, these oceans I kept falling into, wanted to stay in. "She said she may come by later. She had a busy day, you know how your Mayday is." He laughed, that laugh which anchored me. I wished that Nate had been able to come in from Florida, but his wife was will couldn't make it. He always found some reason to not visit St. Louis again. Barbara told me once this was because he didn't want to be in the last place their older brother, Robert, was alive in.

He stretched, his black suit jacket shortening around his wrists, I smiled at the lily he wore in his right lapel, the calla lilies I had in my bouquet thirty-five Mays ago. "You know Mayday." his arm draped around me, warmth flowed into me, steadied me. "I know." I sighed, kept breathing, and sipped the white wine in front of the empty black plate. I was glad Maeghan hadn't come. I was glad we had the argument before she had been contrary enough to come. I was going to have a good night, for God's sake! I was owed a good night. I was owed a good night with my husband, without my youngest daughter mucking it up with her bullshit and its accompanying attitude.

Brianna and Logan started the slide show, and gorgeous and brunette. Brianna wore her white ruffled dress and pigtails, every bit of an eight-year-old.

While Logan looked like such a young lady in her navy and high ponytail. Reuben whispered in my ear that Jason should get his gun ready because even at eleven, Logan was soon going to be 'Cindy Crawford pretty'. Brianna took deep breaths, speaking loudly into the microphone as the pictures scrolled behind them. "My Grandpa loves my Grandma, and they have been together forever!" Eight-year-old Brice said. The room filled with laughter. I looked around the room, saw the faces of Ruth and Charles at the end of the table. She gave me a thumbs-up. Logan took the microphone, walking the few steps to the podium, her back to the screen as she spoke.

She rolled her eyes at her little sister before she continued, "Reuben Michael Lewis-born August 18, 1935-- and Katherine Anne Brigby—born April 17, 1941--- got married in this church, our family church, on May 31, 1961." The slides continued, there were baby pictures of me and Reuben, our parents, even the baby pictures of Carolyn, Brian and Maeghan. I rested my head on Reuben's shoulder and exhaled. "Katherine, our grandmother, is a graduate of Washington University, and was a teacher before she became a full-time homemaker. Reuben, our grandfather, is the founder of Lewis Construction, Inc." There were cheers at the mention of the company we built.

"Aunt Babs, also known as Barbara Lewis Redding, keeps everything rolling!" More laughter then, as Barbara stood up and bowed. Her hair with her short blonde hair like a young Mia Farrow, all delicate and pretty. These two young men clad in their cater worker white wheeled out this three-tier cake on this stainless-steel rack. These white hatted, shiny faced young men smiled at us as they scurried away. Barbara walked to the forefront, happy and adjusting her glasses. She blew kisses at the lead table, before picking up the microphone from the podium where Logan and Brianna were. She wore this stunning navy V-neck dress, the weight she put on made the dress gorgeous, along with the gold heels she wore. It was so glad to see her getting out and doing things after Steven died two years prior. Like Ruth and I, she had been married for almost half her life. And his death rocked us as a family, and for a while we thought the spark which made her Barbara was gone. But she was slowly coming back to us. Maybe Reuben would come back to me too.

"Now, I know I have known Katie and my brother have been together almost half of forever," more laughter, even from Reuben, filled the room again. "And we thought it only right to make them cut this cake again!" She started to clap, and soon everyone in the room was clapping. I sat straighter in the plush white chair, feeling Reuben's hand slide to the middle of my back. "But first, we dance!" I stared at Barbara, bore into her, as she turned to nod to the long haired young man in the corner—I guess this was the surprise Brianna had told me about before I could even make it up the church steps. "Nana, Gramma, we have a surprise, a music surprise, but I can't tell you so bye!" She ran up the stairs in her white dress and matching shoes. I heard it, and almost screamed. I heard the first notes and heard Reuben laugh. "As Time Goes By!"

    He took my hand, and I heard Ruth and Charles cheering as we walked behind them to the middle of the floor. I saw Charles, and all his Steven Martin white hair, and blue eyes light up as he hugged and kissed his wife, my best friend of better than twenty years. "For those of you that don't know, *As Time Goes By* is the first song my brother and Katie danced to thirty-five years ago *tonight!*" Babs cheered into the phone and I shook while Reuben held me. He hummed he melody in my ear, kissed my forehead, as we swayed. "And when two lovers woo, they still say, 'I love you.' On that you can rely." I wrapped my arms around his shoulders, kissed him as if it were the very first time at Washington University. "Right now, babe." I said into his neck. He moaned. "All we have is right now." I raised my head, found the ocean in his eyes again, clear and calm. I kissed him, waited for his eyes to close, before I closed my own. I felt his warmth again. He could always steady me, and I needed the steady of the us again. Amidst roars, and laughter, I had my Reuben again, safe and whole. The cake would just have to wait.

Chapter 4- July 1996

I woke up at 2:14 a.m. I thought about my fifty-fifth birthday. I woke up thinking how quiet it had been. I thought about the fuss the kids made over me in the banquet fall at the. I thought about how Logan and Brianna made this collage for me, complete with pictures of my mother, my sister and my father, Johnathan. I thought about how during my bout of cancer almost four years before. I remembered going to Mass at Holy St. Michaels' pleading with God and the Holy Mother to let me see sixty. I knew if I could reach sixty something greater had to be awaiting me.

I thought about how Barbara had taking pictures, how Ruth, whose birthday was the same year, month earlier in March, had advised me to take turning sixty with the same maturity I had forty. I had cried in a bathroom when I turned forty. I giggled remembering. I was five years from that age, still cancer free according to Dr. Ikeda, and yet I feared, now, was sixty would bring. I looked over at the empty portion of my marital bed, relieved it was empty. Reuben would be on the couch when I woke, just where I left him.

Reuben was in front of the television set, the remote in his hand asleep on the couch. I heard the Saturday ballgame as I walked outside. I grinned as the breeze blew my white t-shirt and khaki shorts. I took my Virginia Slims from the top shelf of the broom closet in my kitchen and went out to the backyard. I walked towards the juniper tree, and the white plastic chair under it. I sat in the chair, crossed my legs, determined to enjoy the first cigarette in years. I put the red lighter in my pants pocket. I inhaled, feeling the drag in my toes.

I didn't want to be in the same house with him. I needed space, I couldn't process him in that moment, or the next moment. I started smoking again, doing the same thing that almost killed me to have some control over my life. My husband of my youth and age, now had a noose around his neck. He had early onset Alzheimer's. I even hated how it sounded when I said it--Alzheimer's.

I hated how these medicines looked in my medicine cabinet: Percocet for pain. Xanax to help him sleep. Donepezil hydrochloride for the Alzheimer's. Dr. Miller told me about the side effect of the medications he prescribed. The insomnia. Tremors. Nausea. He recommended, strongly recommended, I get into some type of support group. "You need to get assistance, Mrs. Lewis. Katie, as a doctor, this disease can be a monster. It is worse than you can think of. The first thing is find a support group. Soon." My support group was just me and Ms. Virginia Slims at present.

Under the juniper tree, I started wondering if this is how Elijah in the Bible felt. I wanted to know if this was how he felt trying to outrun what he didn't even see chasing him anymore. I had stopped going to Mass at Holy St. Michael's when Reuben got sick and didn't open the parish mail that came inquiring about my absence. I dug my bare feet in the grass, clasping the lit cigarette in my hands for a moment. Remembering I started smoking after Maeghan started elementary school. Leaving her every morning was so daunting, that I had to smoke to deal with it. I smoked for a decade, till she was in sixth grade. I told myself I would never pick them up again because it was so hard to quit!

Whenever I got stressed or angry, I would *socially smoke*. Just enough to take the edge off, and not want to smoke the whole pack. I remembered having to sneak around just like this in order to smoke, after I told everyone I had quit. I thought I had to get ready to deal with my kids, and everything else! I needed to smoke to cope. And now, in the last two weeks, I stopped at the Schnucks near our house and bought my Virginia Slims 100s like I had fifteen years ago.

I watched the ants go over my feet and began to watch the ashes fall on them. I felt like those ants, small and always working. I closed my eyes, inhaled peace again to my lips and thought of our wedding anniversary celebration. I thought of how my life was before May 15th. I thought about how hard I had worked to keep everything perfect. For so long, I tried to make everything perfect. Just like my Mom taught me. I kept house, I took care of my kids and made love to my husband without complaint. I did what I had to do as a woman. I did it! I saw water on my foot and thought it was raining. I hoped it was raining, I was tired of crying.

This specter, like this cigarette smoke, was over me now, this disease...siphoning my years with my husband. Grabbing at the air in my house that allowed me to breathe easy. It sucked up everything and everyone. I hadn't spoken to Carolyn since she called to ask why I had stood up Babs for our lunch date the week of Reuben's appointment. I avoided her call yesterday and let the answering machine keep better company and memory. I didn't want to talk to her, I didn't want to see anyone. I didn't want to go to this stupid dementia, Alzheimer's support group. It seems like an oxymoron—*support* and *Alzheimer's* in the same sentence.

I didn't know if Carolyn would talk to the other kids about their Dad's condition. She was always such an old soul, the good girl—always would take care of everything. I wanted her to be that now. There was a low place in my soul I couldn't place or seem to fill. I got up from my chair, smoothed my shirt, and stared at the leaves of the juniper tree. Reuben planted it for me, right after we had bought this house. Our house, when we started our life together. I flexed my toes in the grass, flicked the butt under the tree. I watched it smolder, as I felt my cheeks grow slick. I knew I would have to talk to my kids, but I couldn't. I didn't. It would make it all too real. The phantom would have feet.

I paced my yard, hands in my pockets. I concentrated on the grass, how soft and cool it was. I thought of my grandkids. I thought of my kids; how I can could even begin to explain that one day their grandfather, their father, won't even know who they are. That's what Miller said. *One day, his mind, will be a blank slate. Nothing would stick, nothing would stay, and not everything would come out.* He, my Reuben, their father, would be locked away. As far as I was concerned, our life together ended two months ago.

I kept my hands in my pockets, and walked back to my house, our house. I went through the storm door, as I hear the storm behind me approaching. I stood and watched the clouds darken my yard. I blinked hard, exhaled. I began to pray. I prayed like I had when I was a little girl, and my mother had gotten sick, and thought in my little girl mind she would die. I prayed. When my daughters had colic and I thought I might go mad from not sleeping, I prayed. I was steadied when I prayed. It would have to be the divine that sustained me. It would have to be.

The house felt too small to be in with Reuben. I had to get out. I had to not be where he was. I grabbed my car keys from the hook from the back door.

"Reuben?" I heard more ballgame than his voice. "Reuben, I'm getting ready to leave! I'm going to get some air." I walked over to the brown couch where he still lay there asleep. I stood there, watching him. I watched his chest rise and fall. I remembered him being in the oversized Lazy Boy this couch replaced. I remembered him being in that dark blue chair holding Brian and rocking back and forth. Motion would be the only thing that got Brian to sleep. Reuben was laying there, all serene—just sleeping and breathing. I felt disgust then, contempt. I hadn't slept well since he lost his keys last November.

I threw my set of keys at him. Hard. I felt my cheeks redden, as they sat on his red Washington University shirt. I wanted to hurt him. I wanted to disturb his peace. Nothing I wanted more then was to hurt him. He stirred, those oceans in his eyes opened, he grunted and closed them again. I studied his face, the cut of his jaw. The shape of his lip. The graying of his hair. I grabbed my keys and left, putting on my white Keds sneakers I had left by the door.

I went to my red Mazda and threw my cigarettes on the gray interior passenger seat. I started the car, cursing as I pulled out of the driveway from behind Reuben's black Chevy pickup truck. I left our neighborhood with a tire screech, crying as I drove—with no music playing. I wanted silence, to hear my own heartbeat. I needed to hear my own thoughts, I gripped the steering will, willing it to anchor the thoughts which threatened to overwhelm me. I wanted to go back to where the story began... where *we* began. I drove to Washington University, from our home in Ladue it only took twenty minutes. From my door on Mayfair Avenue to the Danforth Campus, I knew would I would find quiet. I could concentrate, and I could remember.

I wanted to see the evidence of the beginning of the love affair with the love of my life. My true first. My love, my Reuben. I parked along Forest Park, sneaking in the Student Parking, glad I my alumni plaque in the rear Mazda windshield. I sat with keys in my hand. I looked in the rearview mirror, saw my eyes sullen and dark. I got out of my car, slammed the door. I walked through the parking lot and towards the sign and the quad toward the middle of campus. I smiled looking at the sepia brick and the cream-colored mortar. I looked at the blend of the new sod. I kept walking until I saw the quad, I grinned as I brushed past the low shrubs and trees.

I walked under the brick cleaned quad and sat on the new wrought iron bench. I saw the bustle of the students, snug and safe in their shirts and backpacks, unaware of anything else but themselves. I looked back at the administration building. I studied the windows, looking at the still brown door, with the cream-colored archway, with people going in and out of it. I remembered Reuben then, how he bumped into me. I remembered how he touched me, brushed past me. I remembered how his smile was crooked, and I blushed when he me what time it was. I remembered how blue his eyes were, still were. I told him at our recent wedding anniversary that he would always hold the ocean, as he held me while we swayed to As Time Goes By.

    I pulled my face in my hands, listened to the voices around me. I heard hushed conversations, love, defeat, joy. I looked at the door again, blinked hard and saw us. Healthy and happy. I saw me, nineteen, looking at my yellow slip of paper, all shiny with new type. I was so pretty, so so pretty. Tall ponytail, bright yellow shirt, capped sleeve and a blue knee length shirt. I remembered Reuben. I always remembered Reuben. 6'1", twenty-one, shoulders solid and hair dark brown. I knew I loved him when he looked at me--and my heart stopped. His eyes, those oceans he held, stopped time had always stopped time. He asked me what time it was, white button up shirt, hands in his denim jeans pockets, face a little ruddy from running. He smiled at me. I was his. "10:43." I had whispered. I cried. Time was stopping again for us, and only one of us could remember that.

Chapter 5- August 1996

It was Sunday afternoon and I was cleaning up, mindful the grandkids were coming to visit. I was relieved the medication Reuben was on seemed to be helping. We had a few good weeks, we talked again. We talked more. He remembered me, he touched me more. Kissed me in the morning and cupped my face when he did so. He remembered more of our life. He didn't mention whoever or whatever Ruby was. I was thankful to God he didn't or wouldn't get to the point where he forgot the names of our children. I was certain by the end of the summer we would all be so much better. I had spoken to the kids about their father. Maeghan had blamed me.

Brian stormed out and Carolyn just sat. I expected all of it. My early August was not pleasant. But tonight? I was determined everything had to be perfect. Everything shiny and neat, just like my mother taught me. "If it's perfect, no one will ever notice what's cracked." This was my mother's favorite saying. Every time my father came home drunk or would break something or lose all his money. Zelda Brigby was determined to make everything 'perfect.'

Everything would be in order. It was going to be the first celebration with Maeghan's new baby, Johnathan. I hoped Anthony wouldn't come. I was in no mood for them together. I pushed that thought away because I was determined to be happy. I was so happy to have Reuben him back and happy there would be a baby in the house for a few hours. Everything would be like it was, as it should be.

I was making a little of all the kids favorite, and Reuben's. I picked up a cheesecake from Schnucks for Carolyn. I was making potatoes au gratin for Brian, and fresh green beans with garlic and mushrooms for Maegan. I peeked in the oven and saw Reuben's roast. It was glistening and golden. The carrots, pearl onions were accented around it. The heat caused me to blink hard and shut the oven door. I checked my pots again, stirred and covered the beans. I went to the dining room and looked in the cherry oak China cabinet. I wanted my wedding dishes for this meal, it was going to be special. I was getting all my family back. Everything would be so amazing tonight. I looked around at the table, smoothed the linen tablecloth and fluffed the lily-fern centerpiece. I loved how the gold and cream dishes looked against the cherry oak chairs. All seven chairs, reupholstered, with Reuben's chair always at the head and me at the right. That's how all the special dinners at the Lewis house are and remain as long as I here and breathing.

The doorbell rang, and I checked the hall mirror. I smoothed my bobbed hair, reapplied my YSL 61 lipstick from my pocket. I smiled, pinched my cheeks for more color. The doorbell rang again, and I answered the door. I heard voices, hushing and grandkids. I opened the door, and Brianna and Logan ran to me. "Nana!" they screamed, all fresh-smelling like grass. I rubbed their backs, and looked into their faces, seeing Reuben's eyes on Brice, deep and blue, and wide. "Nana, Nana, did you make the green beans?" Brianna said, looking past me. I leaned to kiss her, mussed her hair. "If you wash your hands, you'll find out! Go out your things away in Grandpa's study." They dashed off, with a clattering of sneakers and jeans. "Mom!" I looked at Maegan, Johnathan in the pumpkin seat, and Brian and Carolyn behind her up the front stairs. I assumed Jason must've had to do the books for *Zelda's.*

Maeghan's hair was still brunette, even though she was born a toe-head, hair so blonde like my mother. I hugged them all tight, the afternoon wind blowing in behind them. "So good to see you all! I have missed you so much!" We piled into the house, Brian slamming the door as he was so keen to when he was the Brianna's age. I shot him a look over my shoulder and he grimaced. "Brian, you are going to make some woman very mad someday slamming doors!" I smirked as I headed to the kitchen, "Brian, take the baby with you to the dining room. Carolyn, your Aunt Babs is coming over. Keep an ear out, will you?" I heard Carolyn shout her agreement as I began to transfer the food to the serving dishes left out for her on the kitchen table.

"Oh, wedding dishes!" Maegan said. "Don't drop my wedding china, please, Maeghan Kristen Lewis!" I saw her stroking the serving platter. "Where's Anthony?" I handed her the potatoes to transfer into the bowl I set in front of her on the corner of the counter. "He's on his way, Mom. He went to Target to grab some baby things." She swooshed away, potatoes in hand, and red shirt billowing, headed to the dining room. I followed her with rolls and green beans. "Where are Logan and Brice?" I heard the storm door clap against the backdoor frame. "Nevermind."

Brian was dining room, with Johnathan in a chair off in the corner. He put a finger to his lips, mouthing Johnathan was asleep. I saw him moving toward the bowl of green beans. "Where's Dad?" I looked at him, shaking my head. I didn't want him to trade the baby for the bowls I carried. I turned to face the table, back to the tight-shut China cabinet and adjusted the bowls on the table. "He was taking a walk. It was nice out earlier. Can you wait for everyone else to eat, Brian Nathaniel?" He smirked, his finger inside his cheek, my eyes looking back at me, Reuben's crooked smile. "Sure, Mom." I laughed, fanning him off before I went to the kitchen to go get the roast from the oven. "Brian be of some use will you and get wine out of the freezer." Barbara loved a good port, and I had a bottle chilled all day. This meal would be perfect. Everything would be as neat as a pin, tight as a drum—no one would see the cracks.

Anthony came by just before we started eating, simply dressed in jeans and a tee shirt, Target bags in hand. I greeted him warmly as I was able, I didn't want to fight with Maeghan with her being so sensitive about black people. I wished he would have kept his hair short, instead of those dark, dreadlocks. Maeghan we so much like my sister, Rose. Wild sprit, hard-headed. She and Rose always had a close relationship, despite her being career US Navy as a nurse. He had picked up Reuben at a bus stop at Ladue Crossing, far from our house. Anthony said he as sitting on a bench, head in his hand, talking about some jewel, a ruby, and crying. He took pity on him and brought him home. Maeghan clearly had told him about her Dad. I was embarrassed and swallowed my rage with a smile and thanked him. "Welp, don't worry. He's home. There are no rubies here!" I tapped his shoulder to reassure him and smiled.

Barbara had come right as we settled to eat. It was a relief to see her and hear her voice. She hugged me at the front door. Maeghan was sitting on the couch feeding Johnathan before she ate. I hadn't said anything else to her since Anthony had come over. I was on eggshells enough already—I didn't need a minefield to go off. She saw Maeghan, kissed her cheek and the top of Johnathan's head. As we made our way to the kitchen, she could put down the extra dessert she bought, Gooey Butter Cake. I hugged her again. "I didn't know you liked me this much today!" I laughed, hugged her tighter. It was good to laugh with her, to laugh at all, again.

We talked about her husband, Steven, seeing that the second anniversary of his passing had come and gone. "Mr. Redding was the love of my life. The absolute love of my life! And now," she sighed, sitting at the kitchen table to steady herself. She took off her glasses, fist propped under her right cheek. She looked so elf-like with her short blonde hair. "Now, I have to remember I have to go forward without him." Her eyes closed with her mouth in a small, smile. I touched her left hand, squeezed it. "I know you miss, him, Babs. You'll see him again." Barbara didn't open her eyes, didn't move. I left her to her thoughts and went to rejoin everyone in the dining room. I looked at the calendar on the kitchen wall by the door. I had forgotten was Steven's birthday was September 7th, their twenty-fifth wedding anniversary would be September twenty-first. I had to remember Reuben and I were married ten years before she and Steven got married.

Barbara had worked hard to get to a professional height. Honors high school student. College graduate. She helped her brothers make their construction hobby into a thriving business, which allowed Reuben to do more administration things. He was able to retire because Barbara knew her way around a dollar. She had met Steven because he was a client for Lewis Construction, he wanted his house rehabbed. From that day until two years ago, Steven Redding adored her.

I went back to her, wiping my hands on the towel on the oven handle, hugged her tight. "Babs." I choked on the rest of the words. We walked into the dining room, Reuben sitting at the head of the table, in his familiar spot, looking at the lily centerpiece. I smiled as I escorted Babs to the chair across from me, nearest Reuben, on his left. The chatter of the full room calmed me. I asked everyone to join hands to the blessing could be said over the meal. I squeezed Reuben's hand to remind him to pray, wondered if he took the medicine I left out on the bathroom sink.

I saw Reuben look off for a moment, taking his hand from me to check his pockets. Sometimes he did that lately, especially after taking his medication, so I didn't worry. This was one of the side effects of the medicine he was taking that it made him fidgety. I reached over, squeezed his hand and patted it. I whispered his name, his eyes met me. Looked through me. "I have to pay for the room. I have to pay for Ruby's room." I felt the hair on back of my neck stand up. "Look at me, Reuben. Look at me!" I hissed and squeezed his hand.

Babs looked over at us, her gaze went over the family present, everyone was staring at Reuben. He cast his gaze on his sister, empathic and nervous. "I have to get this money to Levi. I owe it to him. I don't want him harassing her about it!" He was looking around then. Carolyn sat next to me, looking desperate at me and her aunt, her eyes were wide like there were when she was a child. I was grateful Jason wasn't here. I needed his to count his pills. Did he take them when I gave him with lunch earlier? I didn't see him take them and he had been doing so well. I didn't check. Why didn't I check? I was so busy getting dinner together. I was so busy.

Brian, seated at the end of the table, started circulating plates and bowls, muttering a quick blessing as he did so. He smoothed his beard as he looked back towards me, his sister and his aunt. I heard silverware clanging, and lips smacking. I saw Maeghan from the doorway, burping Johnathan on her left shoulder head. She left the room again, after taking the pumpkin seat she brought with her. Anthony got up and followed her. I squeezed Reuben's hand again. "Rube, no one is here but us, and the kids. Look," I gestured to Babs. "Mae bought the baby. Don't you want to see Johnathan?" Babs heaped food onto Reuben's plate, the roast and potatoes and green beans, Brain offered the bowl of rolls. He muttered the name twice. "Reuben, we got cheesecake for dessert. We can eat and get some." Babs smiled at him, he looked at her, smirking.

I ran through memories of the day, tried to think if he had taken what I had given him: one white one pink. I called his name again. He turned to Babs. "Babs, Babs! Get Deborah. Let her know that I'll pay Ruby's room tomorrow. Don't put the evict notice on the door, ya dig? That's my girl. I don't care what the alderman said!" He stood up, snatching his hand from me. "I gotta go. I gotta go, dig it? She's my girl." He was pacing around the back of his chair, gripping the back of it and releasing it. He looked at the serving dish, full of roast beef, and smashed it to the floor. "What the fuck is going on!" Maeghan was back in the door again, as Babs and I stood to grab Reuben. "I'm supposed to go pay her room! Let me leave, goddammit!" The kids looked at each other, back at me and the gravy, meat mess on the floor. Reuben left, hands in his pockets, pushing past Maeghan. "Dad!" Brian said, running after him. Brianna and Logan stared at their mother from across the table.

I stared at the China cabinet. I didn't have heart to look at the floor, and the mess left. I straightened by back, ignored my daughters. Maegan spoke first. "What the hell, Mom?" Her tone was accusing and insistent. "How long has he been like this!" I heard the chair next to me grow with warmth. I thought it was Barbara, wanted to be Barbara. My eyes left the cabinet and looked at my daughter. "Mae, please just clear the table. Just clear the damn table!" I slammed my chair up to the table and walked to the kitchen. I heard Carolyn and

Maeghan quarrelling. Maegan swore and said she would clean up, with prodding from Carolyn. I went to my broom closet, saw Anthony pack up Johnathan and quickened by steps as my mouth watered almost for Virginia Slims to smoke. That is all I had time to do. All I wanted to do.

    I found my seat under the tree, the only light to guide was the bright red grill right before the seat. I lit my cigarette before I sat down. I saw Barbara walking towards me. "So, you're smoking again?" I exhaled as she came closer, the back porch's light bathed her form in gold light as she walked towards me. "I don't need this right now, Barbara. My mother is dead, please don't lecture me about what I'm doing wrong or how I'm handling everything!"

    I rolled my eyes and she stood in front of me, arms akimbo. "Katie, this is ridiculous! You're behaving like a child. A spoiled child!" I took another drag off my cigarette, hand through my hair. "No, your brother is! After almost forty years, *he's* a toddler!" I saw Babs get on the ground in front of me, kneeling. "There's a chair behind the tree. Rube keeps it there when we watch the stars come out." She rose slow and moved behind the juniper tree. "You are going to have to tell the kids about this. He's getting worse." I flicked my ashes near her. "And tell them what? Their father is ill? That I can handle. Telling them that one day he won't remember them, me or anything else?" I shook my head. I held my cigarette to my mouth, didn't smoke it. "Who is Ruby?" I stared at Babs, she didn't look back at me, her gaze on the back door and the faces of my grandchildren whom could only stare back at us.

I sat up straighter, leaned towards her. "Who is Ruby?" Babs looked at me, almost like Reuben did when he was upset at me: this look of knowing and aggravation. I looked at her, studied her. My eyes insistent, unwavering. Barbara left her chair and back to me and left me under the moon and the stars, and the juniper tree.

Chapter 6- October 1996

I tried to start attending the support meetings after the family dinner in August. I called Dr. Miller's office and asked for the first four support groups he thought I could go to. I think it was the same black girl I who worked at his office in May answered the phone—I thought her tone was abrasive when I called—and happy when she transferred me to his extension. Dr. Miller said his wife's friend ran one called *Life Connections.* It met every Thursday at this counseling center of the same name. It was down from Barnes-Jewish Hospital and around the corner from the Cathedral Basilica. I went there before Labor Day. This week, I missed my turn before I could park on the street to attend this Thursdays session.

I drove around the *Life Connection* parking spot and remembered additional calls I placed to Dr. Miller a week later after Reuben's dinner outburst. I told him the medicine wasn't working. I told him that he broke my serving dish of our wedding China set. Told him I asked his sister about whom Ruby was, *what* Ruby was! "Sometimes people get trapped in a memory loop", he said. He told me to do orientation exercises—remind of whom I am, where he was, et cetera. "Katherine, he may be deteriorating more quickly than you think." I held the kitchen phone in one hand and my lit cigarette in the left. *More quickly than you think.*

I inhaled, held the smoke as he rambled on. I picked out words like dosage, therapy, respite, support groups. "He's my husband, Dr. Miller. Not a stray dog! I'm asking what is it I can do? How can I fix this! How can I fix him? This is getting insufferable!" I heard Dr. Miller sigh deep on the other end of the receiver. "There is no cure for this, Katie. There is no cure. I cannot stress that enough to you. Reuben is only going to get worse! The medicine he's taking is to control the symptoms and to stop the erasing of this memory, body function. I suggest you come to grips with this, Mrs. Lewis!" I slammed the kitchen phone and heard it shake. *You need to come to grips with this, Mrs. Lewis.* His clinical tone slapped me in my face for the second time.

I was still indignant when I pulled into a parking space, the yellow lines angering more. There was a black truck sitting next to my little red Mazda. The meetings started at six-thirty, and there was always this time of snacks and cold coffee—the time where everyone pretended to be alright. I looked at the pale blue numbers on my Mazda's dashboard clock, glad it was two minutes until the start of this week's meeting. By the time I pulled my plaid cape around my shoulder and grabbed my black tote from the front seat, I would be fashionably late walking around towards the front of the building.

I had been coming to these meetings for the better part for the month after knowing about these meetings for two months and more. That first Tuesday morning I called Dr. Miller, I couldn't bring myself to go that night. The next week I promised myself, threatened myself to go. I made arrangements with Brian to be home with Reuben for a few hours.

I left my house with the intention to go to *Life Connections*. But when I decided to get a Diet Pepsi from the Ladue Crossing Schnucks, I cried in the parking lot. When I pulled myself together, I could only drive around-and did so for an hour before I found myself back at that Schnucks parking lot listening to NPR, National Public Radio. I became a big fan of *All Things Considered*. Those few hours I was sequestered away from my house on Mayfair were my respite. This was my *Life Connections*. I spent at least two Thursdays in September in a car, a Diet Pepsi and NPR.

That next week, after being cornered by Carolyn and her own support group comparison notes, she went to *Life Connections* with me the first Thursday after Labor Day. We sat, got the purple brochures from what *Life Connections* called the Resource Table. We even introduced ourselves. I was greeted with hugs and tears, being told I was on a *journey.* One day my husband won't know me or be able to not piss on himself—what *journey* was I on? I wanted my life back! I wanted my version of perfect back. I wanted my life with my husband back. Carolyn had held my hand the whole time; you would have thought she was the one with the husband that was forgetting and slowly dying inside.

After that strength-infused session the week of the fifteenth, I started going by myself. I started to endure the coffee, the empty eyes and the *'Hi's'* which never got above a whisper or eye level as they stirred coffee and going back to the Indian Rain Dance circle of folding chairs. This time, this week, after weeks of coming, I was going to listen. I told myself I was going to talk this week. I was going to be pleasant. If people asked how Reuben was, I was going to do as the leader for this group, Ms. Frances Green, encouraged us to say: *We had a good day.* I closed my eyes and kept my head on the headrest, hands moved from the steering wheel.

I replayed the family dinner almost two months ago, tried to put it back in the compartment. Something else I learned in group: don't dwell on the bad. Remember what happened and remember how it can be used to make tomorrow better. "Forgive, quick. It's the disease. It's the disease." I thought about the lunch I had with my children the day before. All I did was think, plan and try to hold my sanity together. I sat in the dining room after they left, ready with cigarettes and red lighter stowed in the China cabinet, after swearing I wouldn't smoke in the house. But it was raining outside, and I kept hearing Dr. Miller in my head, *more quickly than you think.* If I was lucky, maybe I would get cancer again and die first. I was always cleaning up messes--maybe I could be free of this one.

I remembered how Brian had brought Reuben back in, ruddy face and dirty. Brian had had to tackle his father into a neighbor's yard almost three or four houses down. He had hit Brian. I had hit my son, our son, like he meant nothing to him. The kids had confronted me, all smug and indignant. I looked at them over my reading classes. I sat at the same dining room table, in my same chair, and looked over the medications my husband was taking. I was counting them. I kept a pair of reading glasses in my pocket now, always reading or counting. I was going to talk to Dr. Miller about something to stabilize his mood.

Carolyn had managed to get Reuben to settle down in the living room instead of the den. She came back to the dining room and grabbed the small pile of pills on the linen tablecloth: anxiety medication, booster dose of his Alzheimer's medication, his nighttime medicine--which including something to sleep. She took a red blanket from the hall closet to drape over him. He had asked her to play a Billie Holiday CD. He asked her to play *Solitude*. Then play *Gloomy Sunday. Don't Explain.* "Scooter, play her music. Just play it, I have to hear her voice. Lemme hear her voice!"

As Billie Holiday's voice carried through the house, Carolyn came back to where I was, tears filled her eyes, the green dress she wore dotted with tears. Reuben was in the living room, where the stereo Brian got him for Christmas two years ago. I heard the cabinet open, and slam. "Dad, you sure you don't want to hear Ella?" I heard Brian's voice. I heard Reuben cry, sobbing. I fought every reflex to go to him, tend to him, to kiss everything and make it better. I fought against the thirty-five-year nature to be his wife. "It's okay, Dad." I thought Brian was crying as well, trying to be strong for his Dad. One of the things that I loved about Reuben was his ear for music. I didn't like jazz as much as he did. I liked Glenn Miller and Artie Shaw. But he loved Billie Holiday, Nancy Wilson, and Dizzy Gillespie's trumpet. I wasn't in love with it, but I liked it because he liked it.

I stared at my burning cigarette in my left hand, and heard Brian slam his hands on the table. The pills shook. "Mother!" I didn't look up, didn't move. "What the hell is wrong with Dad?" I stared at him. "Keep your damned voice down! You don't get to come in my house and demand anything!" I looked up at him, my eyes in his face looking back at me, wide and furious. He looked like my father after a night out. I found my yellow notebook next to the cache of pills, and fumbled to a blank page, pulled a pen out of the spiral coil. "Alzheimer's. I told you this." I didn't look up at him. I was writing, just like I was taught in group—it would help me to process and keep record of everything. "He's having a bad day." I exhaled from my toes. "Carolyn, your sister has involved herself in every aspect of your father's care." I still heard Reuben crying. "So, what the fuck is going on, Mom?"

I looked over at him. Never had I wanted to slap the blend of my face and Reuben's from my son's. "What's going on?" I took off my glasses, dropping my pen to clasp my hands under my chin. "Your father, my husband, has Alzheimer's Disease. I'm sure you know what that means." He stared at me. "I know what that means, Mom. How long has he been like *this*?" I closed my eyes, heard my chest rattle as exhaled, heard my heart in my ears. "He's hit me, Mom. He was walking and just snapped!" Brian sighed, held my gaze when my eyes reopened. "Brian, please! Not right now! Maegan took the baby home. Your Aunt Barbara is gone, and your father is crying to some black woman on the radio!"

I felt his hot gaze on me. I heard Carolyn's voice. "Brian, this isn't helping. As usual, you aren't helping!" There was rustling of chairs then. "Look, Scooter, I don't have time for this! What is wrong with Dad?" Carolyn crossed her arms over her chest, tears still creeping down her face. "If you bothered to see Dad other than when you needed something you would know!" Brian swore, Carolyn swore. My cheeks were wet, hot and wet. "Will you two stop quibbling please!" I slammed my hands to the table. I crushed my cigarette out in the glass candy dish and left the cigarettes and lighter on the table. I got up, pushed past them both and stomped up the stairs to our bedroom, slamming the door.

More quickly than you think. My years with him would be smoke. The faces of our children, grandchildren, friends and surviving siblings—they would all be strangers, meaningless vapors. I opened my eyes, willed my body to get out and try and force my almost sixty-year-old body to *Life Connections*. I stepped quicker than I thought, and opened the door, sitting in the back like one of my late students those many years ago.

"And my husband recognized me today. He kissed my cheek, before I left tonight. Today was a good day for us." There were cheers for this little blue haired lady in this big red shall. Her name was Natalie. She had been with her husband longer than I had been with Reuben—fifty some years. She had been dealing with her husband's Alzheimer's for almost three years. She said he would have good days, bad days and worse days. She lived alone with her only daughter was dead. Her husband, Henry, was in Delmar Gardens in Chesterfield. She couldn't take care of him anymore, and it was her primary care doctor who helped her get her husband in facility after he hit her. Her doctor had to report elder abuse after Henry sent her to the Barnes-Jewish Hospital ER with a black eye. Natalie said he hit her before then but couldn't or didn't think she could tell anyone that would believe her.

Frances was a sweet woman, overly nosy I thought, but you could see she was helpful. She had a red bob and looked like the wife of Jerry Stiller—Anne Meara. "I'm glad you all had a good day, Natalie. I'm so glad you had a good day." I was relieved when I noticed the time and I mad missed *group share*. In the ninety minutes we were in each other's forced presence, we spent fifteen or twenty minutes where we had talk about what we journaled about the week prior. I had only journaled the week Carolyn came with me, being more mother than daughter. Writing it down didn't seem to be the greatest thing to do with this. I called Dr. Miller Monday and had asked for prescription strength Unison for Reuben. I used them more than anything. If Reuben was having a bad night, I knew I would have a bad night.

If he would be muttering in his sleep, I gave him a half sleeping pill to help him sleep sound. Some nights, most nights, I just needed him to shut up. I didn't want to hear him talking in his sleep. I just needed him quiet. I needed him quiet, so I could think.

"Kate! You came!" I blinked hard, irritated Frances noticed me. She clasped her hands like you would for kindergarteners. She held my gaze, I looked. I wished I had taken a nerve pill like I had last week. All of me wanted to sprint towards the door. In taking control of the silence in the room, Frances cleared her throat for the other six people in the room. "How was your week? How is your husband, Richard?" "Reuben. His name is Reuben." She smiled at me, willing an apology with her eyes. "How is Reuben? Is he still having problems sleeping?" I sighed, turned towards the wall and the comfort of the clock. "Yes, he's still having problems sleeping. I can't sleep. I never sleep well in bed with him. He's always talking. Talking about Ruby. I don't know what or who *Ruby* is!" I closed my eyes. "So help me God, I am losing him. I know I am!"

My heart was loud in my ears, hands clammy. I had said what I swore I would have only written down. "It's normal to feel that way. You and Reuben have been married almost forty years. Is the journaling helping?" I lied when I answered her with a nod, still looking at the clock. "Yes." There was sniffling in the room, my hands were still slick. I wiped them on my cape and pulled it around me. The world was spinning, and I was feeling sick. "Kate, I know it's hard. But keep journaling. It will help. Seeing what is happening may really help you, and even encourage your family to journal. Alzheimer's can destroy families. The best thing you can do sometimes is fight it: reckon memory destruction with creating new ones and preserving old ones." The clock ticking was all I cared about—time was my only comfort.

****

I was never so grateful to be sitting in traffic on the way home. I called Brian and left a message on his machine pleading to keep his father with him at his house overnight, telling him I wasn't feeling well. I started to think about who this, Ruby person was: this phantom fantastic that had creeped into my life. I wanted to know if it was something I missed, something maybe I forgot; a detail, a photograph, something that would give me a clue as to what or who this was.

It had to be a woman, it just had to be!

Who was it? I tried to tell myself it was a *Citizen Kane* thing, a thing of nothing---only relevant to him and to his memories, nothing to do with me.

I was never so naïve to think Reuben's life started with me, but I knew I wanted it to end with me. First, Alzheimer's, now this. Between the doctor visits, medication, special medication schedules, accusations of or from my children here comes...a *Ruby*.

I know that some people with this disease fixate on objects or people, and Dr. Miller had told us not to worry, but be aware. He sounded so frustrated about my concerns, so flippant. I had known these memory loops would come, but I wanted to snap him out of it like some patients Brian told me about did. He said there were people who 'came out of this'. I wanted Reuben to come back to me and every day that seemed harder and harder to do. I was fading along with him. For me to keep the us, he couldn't have Ruby.

Chapter 7-December 1996

      Babs and Ruth had taken me to lunch and Carolyn and the kids came over to make dinner. Reuben had a good day, he was a little confused, a little agitated. I told Brian to bring me a Xanax and snuck it in his vanilla ice cream as we sat eating dessert. When I got up to head to the bathroom to replace the bottle of cough syrup Brian gave me and Carolyn caught me. "Mom?" I turned from the shut medicine cabinet. "How are you doing?" She had cut her hair again, similar to her Aunt Barbara's Mia Farrow haircut. Reuben's eyes in her face twinkling. I smiled, smoothing the bathroom mirror.

Carolyn stared at me, didn't smile or blink. She stood there with her arms folded over her chest. She was wearing her father's red Washington University shirt and jeans. She looked so tacky and out of place. "Really, Mother, I'm trying my best to be here for you!" She turned and walked away. "Carolyn Marie!" I screamed and went into the hall. I caught her back and bare feet. I could at least control her temper with just calling her christened name, unlike her hellcat sister.

She turned to face me, eyes already rolling. "I am still your mother! This is still the house my husband and I built. You are my daughter. Never forget that!" She looked at me as if I spit on her. I moved closer to her face, my words harried through my clenched jaw. "I am handling this as best as I can. If you can God can come up with a better way for me to handle the slow death of your father, I'll be all ears!" I turned my back on her, not wanting to give her the option to respond. I left her in the hallway, before being taken by Brianna and Logan to the dark dining room with my husband looking at the glowing fireball cake on the table and my linen tablecloth. As Maeghan, Brian and the girls all sang Happy Birthday to Brianna. I sat at the opposite end of the table looking at my husband. I smiled when I saw his eyes glazed and looked like he was singing. When he met my eyes, I was happy, he would be sleeping as soon as they went to bed. Then I could rest.

From Brianna's birthday on the fifth, my month was pretty quiet. I was determined for it to be quiet. There were two doctors' appointments right after Christmas, one was my dental appointment. There would be no *Life Connections* meetings the week of Christmas. My dental appointment was only a cleaning, and I wasn't looking forward to seeing Dr. Miller on the twelfth. Maeghan and Brian asked-offered to go with me for support. I told them it wasn't necessary. I would drive there with no issue, enjoying the quiet calm listening to NPR and Reuben looking out of the passenger window of my Mazda.

****

Reuben's afternoon doctor's appointment was a few days after Brianna's birthday on the twelfth. We parked in the Barnes-Jewish Hospital parking garage. I had taken a nerve pill before we left, and had a quiet lunch at home with him, Ruth and Charles. I was happy for the company and distraction of other people's voices and sentient conversation. Charles told Reuben he was still an old man, and if he hadn't married me, he would have. "You old sly dog," he laughed sipping his Pepsi. Reuben laughed and bit his bottom lip like he was holding a secret. Ruth and I laughed, and she answered what I was thinking. "If she had, then life might be a little more dangerous for you, Chas."

Dr. Miller had remarked on how well he thought Reuben was doing.

Weight was fine, he hadn't shrunk, and he asked how his motor skills were. He asked if he was remembering anything new or forgot anything new. I talked to him in cool calm tones while Reuben nodded off in his small office chair in the black pea coat Brian had gotten him as an early Christmas present. Dr. Miller was at his computer putting in notes when I heard National Public Radio on in his office.

He slid me the prescription for the Alzheimer's medication, reminded me of the schedule and side effects. I didn't hear the show title, but heard the announcer begin to talk in an excited voice about The Gaslight District, and I giggled. "My Dad used to go there." Dr. Miller's typing answered me first before his voice, "Pardon?" I looked at him and his brown hair and green eyes with is glasses. He looked so young. I saw no pictures of any wife or girlfriend on his desk and wondered why.

"The Gaslight District." I pointed to the small red radio behind him on the opposite side on his desk. "My Dad spent time there, he had a gambling issue." Dr. Miller smiled, the way people smile at you when you reveal too much in a conversation. "How is the company doing? I know Reuben doesn't do the hands-on stuff anymore, but I know Lewis Construction is doing well, right?" I sat straight in my chair, hands on my lap clasped. "Yes, Barbara keeps all the checks coming and scheduling. We have a second office and another team to do more rehabilitation in North St. Louis. I don't know why anyone would want to live there. It's so depressing!"

Dr. Miller smiled again, went back to his computer. "Does Mr. Lewis sleep like this all the time?" I coughed. "Sometimes he does." Dr. Miller made an approving noise. "Are the sleeping pills helping? The Unisom?" I told them they were. "Do you need more of them?" I looked at Reuben and kept my gaze on him, watching his eyes flutter. "No. More Xanax. Sometimes he takes them in the morning after a bad night." I felt heat on my face, I didn't turn. "Sometimes he takes them in the morning after a bad night." I turned to Dr. Miller and said nothing else. I shook my husband to tell him we were leaving and took the medication without looking at Dr. Miller as I shoved the two white squares in my camel colored pea coat. I shook Reuben to get him out of the chair, frustrated he was moving slow and complaining of his hip again.

For Christmas Eve, I demanded the traditional Lewis family sleep over. Maeghan called that morning to ask if Anthony could sleep over, and I gave her no answer—she told me that she would be over in the morning and slammed the phone in my ear. This was a family event! The kids came over about three, and I decided we would bake cookies, take pictures and watch the VHS cassette of *Merry Christmas,*

Charlie Brown! After everyone was settled and fed, Carolyn and Jason retired Carolyn's old room.

Brianna and Logan took blankets in their grandfather's study. Brian commandeered the couch falling asleep to the holiday specials on ESPN. At last, Reuben had fallen asleep about an hour earlier, thanks to Unisom and Xanax. Jason had helped him to bed. I heard the grandfather clock striking ten-thirty. I took my cigarettes out of the broom closet, and red lighter out of the catch-all drawer and smoked with my back to the stove.

I heard knocking on the front door and went to answer it. Looking through the peephole, I saw Maeghan with bags of presents. Her apartment with the North Pole this year. I opened the door and went back to my post in the kitchen. I heard her arranging boxes, and rattling bags as inhaled my cigarette. I would have gone outside, but my coat was in the hall closet and I didn't want to hear or see Maeghan.

I looked up and saw her come in the kitchen. I smiled, in no mood to be hassled. "I told Anthony where I was. He has Johnathan at his mom's. Can he come over to sleep?' I had answered this before. I exhaled smoke in her direction. "No, just family." She crossed her arms over her chest. "He *is* family! He is the father of my son, and my fiancé'!" I looked at her, seeing the tantrum building behind her eyes. "Until he marries you, or you marry someone else, no man whom was not her husband could sleep in my house!" She huffed. "I don't see why not! You let Carolyn sleep with Jason before they got married!" She threw her hands in the air. "I don't know why I bother coming here! I don't know why I have to keep changing my life because you don't like Anthony!"

I pointed my right hand at her, fingers clasped around my cigarette. "You are only being dramatic because your son has a black man for a father! If he's a father." Maeghan looked at me and turned her back, running her hair through her hair. "You know what?" she held my eyes after she looked up from the floor. "I don't know why I keep trying to make this relationship work! She let out a bitter chuckle. "You don't like anything that I do! Anything that I want to do! You hate I'm a station manager!" She pointed her finger at me and screamed. "You can't stand *I'm not like fucking Carolyn!*"

"Keep your goddamned voice down!" I hissed, through clenched teeth and red robe. "It's Christmas! I just want one night with my family here. Just family!" I focused back to the back window and held my cigarette. "Fuck this! Fuck this Christmas!" She left the room, and I exhaled. I listened to doors closing and slamming, unsure if Maeghan left or was just upstairs. With a hand on my forehead, ashes on my sleeve, there was warmth over me, next to me. "Mom?" "What, Brian?" I stood straighter, making sure my feet were attached and under me. "Oh, so you're smoking? And in the house? And on Christmas?" I didn't look at him.

"Why, yes. I am smoking. Please leave so I can keep smoking." Silence, then I heard his knuckles crack. "So, cancer almost three years ago wasn't enough?" I searched my pockets for my lighter. "Three years ago, my husband didn't have Alzheimer's disease. And before then, I smoked because of stress." I scooped up my plastic Las Vegas ashtray Carolyn had gotten me on her and Jason's last trip to Vegas. I made my way toward the solitude of the dining room. "Where is Mayday?" I sat in Reuben's seat. "Where is your father?" I lit another cigarette, my nighttime ritual when I was low on sleeping pills or counting out Xanax. Brian sat next to me, scooting his chair loudly. "Are you even sure it's that? I mean, I called the Mayo Clinic and they said there are some—" I put my hand up to stop him. "I don't need to hear about the crazy medical conspiracy theories, Brian Nathaniel! I don't!"

I crushed my cigarette into the green face of the state of Nevada. "The doctor, his doctor of ten years has said it is Alzheimer's! So it's Alzheimer's!" I put my hands under my chin, staring at him. "So, I'm dealing with it. Let me have one night where questions are bombarding me!"

I looked down at the cigarette as the remaining embers were snuffed.

"Cancer made sense. I know what I did. I knew what to do. I know how hard your father worked to keep everything together." I put my head in my hands. "And I remember the money. Out of state trips to get more business so I wouldn't have to go back to work." I heard Brian sigh, moved his chair to put his head on my shoulder. I heard the television in the other room and remembered where everyone's presents rested waiting for morning. I wouldn't let this day just be ruined—I needed my family. My family needed me.

At about eight in the morning, I heard Logan and Brianna, ripping open wrapping paper. I looked at Reuben, still sleeping. I sat up and watched him breathe. I smiled remembering as I had come to bed soon after my talk with Brian and made love to my husband. Dr. Miller said we would still have sex, and I needed to know I could feel—I wanted his body to know I was not Ruby. Whomever she or whatever she was. He was my husband and mine outright. As I went downstairs, my robe smelled of cigarettes. I sprayed the Tresor perfume by Lancôme Maeghan had gotten me for my birthday over it. I didn't want the kids to smell nighttime cigarettes. I heard Carolyn sigh as I saw her set the kitchen with waffles, coffee and syrup. She sighed to the point I thought I heard the windows rattle. "Merry Christmas!" They all yelled. I scanned the faces for Maeghan. I had planned on giving her my mother's gold and diamond bracelet for Christmas. She had always liked it and thought it would be a suitable peace offering.

"Is Dad still sleeping?" Carolyn asked, no hint of worry in her voice. I sat at the nook and watched. "He sleeps late sometimes." Brian walked behind me, his hair uncombed and striped pajama pants and white shirt. "Mom, I saw Dad's medicine on top of the fridge. Does he really get two Xanax in the morning?" I turned around to look at him, and grinned. "Sometimes he takes two in the morning." Brian looked at me, puzzled with my eyes looking back at me. He replaced the blue rectangle pill box back and continued his coffee drinking from his black Washington University mug.

I watched Carolyn watch her daughters at they opened their Barbies and dollhouses she had stowed in the back of the hall closet. I watched Logan and Brianna hang around their mother. I saw Brian look elated at the U2 Concert tickets I had gotten him. He had been working so hard for the business the last few months and missed the last time they were in St. Louis—it was only right I got him a chance to see them in Kansas City in May. He raised his black mug at me and smiled.

I know that Brian wanted to be a music major, and he quit school to do construction. His aunt and I convinced him to enroll in the Spring at the

University of Missouri-St. Louis and study business. Brian and Barbara carried the administrative piece of this company for the two or three years. Brian wasn't cut out to roof, drive hammers and nails, or set windows. He's an artist not a builder. I used to argue with his father about this desire to create. His argument was 'A man needs to know how to build, and I want to leave my son something he can give to his son." I watched Carolyn open her present, diamond earrings that belonged to my mother. "Grandma Zelda's earrings! Thank you, Mom!" She walked over, red box in hand, and kissed my cheek and hugged me tight. Maeghan had left, and I left the bracelet upstairs. I knew she would leave, I was glad she didn't say. It was our dear Savior's birthday, I didn't want to fight a devil.

As we moved closer around the seven-foot tall Christmas tree, covered in gold, green, red and white decoration, I heard Reuben descend the stairs, favoring his right hip slightly. I saw him run a hand through his hair and heard the grandfather clock in the dining room strike ten. I went towards the kitchen, meeting him at the bottom of the stairs as everyone yelled, "Merry Christmas!"

"Morning, babe!" he paused on the last stair, and I moved to kiss him. I noticed he didn't close his eyes. "Let me get your medicine. Are you hungry?" He looked at me, still foggy, allowing me to lead him to the kitchen. He sat at the small green breakfast table, muttering and yawning. "My head is killing me." I went to the refrigerator, got the medicine from the top of it. I looked at the Wednesday box, counted pills. Remembered the extra Xanax in the bathroom and decided to take one and give him the other later if I needed.

My children wanted their mother, and I was determined to be that. I had a plan in place and knew what I would have to do to keep everything perfect. I am supposed to be the anchor to this family and be at the ready like a dutiful sailor. I had no such strength at the ready but determined to get some.

Chapter 8- February 1997

It was the first solid night sleep I had gotten in month without the pills. I rolled over in our bed, feeling his shoulders on mine. I turned over, nestling between his shoulder blades as I did when we were first married. His heart beating would lull me back to sleep when I was pregnant with Brian and Carolyn.

I purred as he snored, wishing his arm would drape around me. I hoped he would pull me into him, pull me to pull us back together. I whispered his name. I pawed his hair, kissed his shoulder. "Reuben. My Reuben." He shifted in his sleep as I moved away from him and sat up. I watched him breathe, counted the breaths. I touched his face where the moonlight fell. The winter was still present outside, and I pulled the heavy down comforter towards me to keep warm. He curled his left hand under my hand. "I want you to have it. I want you to keep it. Take this ring." There was that voice again, solid and strong. No hint of disease. "Take what, Reuben? Take what?" I whispered in his ear. My support group had told me to try and break the loop: ask questions, watch for his safety, pay attention.

"We're going to get married, doll. You'll always be my girl. There's nothing..." he drifted off again, squeezed my hand. Who was he talking to? He had never called *me* doll. I closed my eyes, heard my heart speed up again. "Ruby isn't here, Reuben." I willed my body to not fly into a rage. I could hate Ruby if I knew what she was or where she was. I exhaled and asked again. "Where-where is she?" He didn't answer. I got up and went to the bathroom. I looked in the medicine cabinet and got the small bottle of antidepressants Dr.

Miller had prescribed for me, grateful he had increased the dosage of Xanax.

He told me that the off-label use for it id inducing sleep. I smirked at the dark orange bottle in my hand. I had only used the Xanax this way when my mother died almost a decade ago this May, before her seventy-eighth birthday. I didn't think I would use them like this, not again. Reuben was moaning. "Just take it. Just take it!" He was whispering. I looked in the mirror again, clutching the pill in my right hand. The clock struck four o'clock in the morning.

I swallowed the pill and went back to bed. I faced the bathroom door, shut my eyes and swore. I sat up and wailed. "Ruby is not your wife, Reuben Lewis! For God's sakes, I am!" I called Brian in tears, I had no idea what I told him. The fury, tears and confusion just poured. "Mom, I'll be there in the morning. I'll talk him somewhere in the morning. I can't come there right now." I hung up the phone, relieved and started on the side of the bed. I looked down at my bare feet, the ivory gown Reuben gave me for Christmas, and tried to remember what it is I needed to do in order to 'hang on.'

I laid down again, looking at the ceiling. I felt hot tears rolling over my cheeks and headed towards my ears. I willed my mind to stop. I willed my body to sleep and got up to smoke. When there was knocking at my front door at 8 a.m., I was relieved. I had fallen asleep on the couch, my cigarettes on my coffee table. "How white trash..." I muttered, pulling my robe around me, dusting the ashes to the rug under that table. I opened the door, and hugged Brian as he made his way in the house, to take his father for a while. "I'm gonna take him to work with Mayday." I hugged him and then waved him off as I pocketed my Virginia Slims and to make coffee. "Fine. Just take him, please!"

I heard Brian's heavy footsteps up the stairs. "Laundry is done! Just get him dressed! There is medicine in the bathroom!" I smiled remembering this was a routine they had every Opening Day at Busch Stadium. They would take off work or ditch school and go. Steven grew up with the owners and always managed to get Opening Day seats for everyone. Barbara would go, and she hated baseball. "I go because I love him more than I hate the sport." That made no sense to me. I let them all go, and rarely went with them—it was a Guy's Day. I let Reuben have that.

He looked at me as he looked at me like he did on Christmas as he helped his father down the stairs: this mix of shock, disdain and confusion. He opened the door for this father with his Cardinals baseball cap turned backwards. I watched him walk with his father out, both clad in tee shirts and jeans, Brian in a black shirt and his father in white. I followed the towards the door, my hands in my pockets. I watched as he opened the passenger side of his blue Ford 4x4, looking back at me for a moment before walking between his truck and my red

Mazda. He shut the door and started his car.

I stood in the front door, wrapping my red robe around me, grateful it had warmed up a little, so they wouldn't be so cold. I watched them back out of the driveway before going back upstairs. Reaching the quiet bedroom, I went to the cherry oak dresser. I looked in my dresser drawer for the card Carolyn gave me. She asked me how the counseling sessions at *Life Connections* were going. I hadn't gone since the new year. Carolyn said she had gone to this event at the local Alzheimer's Association, and was given a card by counselor whose husband had the disease and passed away. "Maybe it would be good, Mom. No expectations, no groups." I had taken that card from her and thrown it in the dresser.

I checked my underclothes drawer, nothing. I checked under my mirrored vanity tray, the one my mother had given me. I cradled the card, ran over the words once more and again. *Rev. Marcia Allen. Beauty for Ashes: Care for Caretakers.* I turned the card over, looked at the meeting dates for groups conducted and the number for private counseling. Every third Thursday meetings were held at the address on the front, and private counseling was at the interested party's discretion.

The next meeting would be in two weeks. I would have to make it two more weeks without letting someone else know I was drowning. I had to somehow wait or hold on long enough to get to a group of people whom will tell me somehow, I'm not alone in all that is and was happening to me. The group I practiced truancy with didn't suit me. I always felt out of step going there. I hoped this woman, Marcia Allen, would be different. I needed to be around people whom had battle experience--nothing else would do. Dealing with my family, dealing with Reuben and this disease felt like I was going into a gun battle with silverware.

I took the card and sat on the unmade bed, looking at the phone number and extension. I grabbed the phone and dialed. As it rang I whispered, "So help me God, I have everything to lose." At the fourth ring, the answering machine detailed the name of a church, and Rev. Dr. Allen's office hours. There was a quote she left on the end of greeting that said, 'Remember love hopes all things and endures all things.' I heard the beep, and took a breath in. "Dr. Allen, my name is Katherine Lewis. I am interested in speaking to you about your Beauty for Ashes meeting. Please call me back." I turned to the side of the bed, left my phone number and hung up. I held the receiver to my chest, head towards the floor. I clutched the phone as I laid back to look up at the ceiling.

I remember what my grandmother, Ardelle, had said about how she was able to survive in America, newly married, in a Protestant neighborhood in South

City St. Louis. She said, what kept her grounded, what kept her from going mad, was she remembered her husband was there. My grandmother told me, her husband, my grandfather, Nicholas, steadied her. She knew *they* were together, she converted for him. She knew as long as they were together, the two of them would be able to get through anything. "Joined." She'd say. "Levi, Tia. That's how you make it."

My eyes watered remembering her voice. "You must remember this even when you are alone. You are a we!" She said that while she made her soups when I was a girl, so long ago. I remembered the sound of her ladle on the side of the Dutch oven, the deliberate scraping. The ring of the tools she brought from the old world, all coming together as she taught me to cook and gave me wisdom. I cried remembering that she had converted from Judaism when she married my grandfather. "For protection." He had said. *For protection.*

As I had hung the phone up and looked at the empty place where the wedding photo once sat. I listened to the grandfather clock tick. I tried to remember that day, the minutia of the day. I had to remember. No one was left to remember. I closed my eyes, pulling at the threads of memory. I pulled that twenty-one-year-old, broad shouldered blue-eyed love. I called to him. I pulled at the nineteen-year-old girl in that skirt who saw him at Washington University. I was pulling at them, rooting for them to get back together! I wanted them together. I wanted the nineteen-year-old girl to remember she loved him as much as I did.

I heard knocking on my door. I couldn't remember when I had closed it. I opened my eyes, focusing on the floor. "Ma!" I didn't avert my eyes from the cherry hardwood. I lay down again, I closed my eyes, listened at footsteps. There was a creak one of the planks in the part floor our bed. There was a nudging warmth next to me, encouraging me to move over. "Where is your father?" He nestled under my chin, his hair flicking under my nose. "You need a haircut."

"You always think I need a haircut."

"Haircuts are good grooming." He paused, took a deep breath. "I took Dad to get a haircut." I sighed. "Thank you, Brian." He lay still. "He's going to be okay, Mom. We're going to be okay." I wanted to tell him this wasn't a cold or strep throat. There would be a day where Reuben wouldn't know him--or me. "Brian, your dad doesn't have a cold. You know that." He coughed, exhaled. "You're coughing because you're smoking again." I stroked his head. "So are you." I sighed. "How ya holdin up with all this?" I kept my eyes to the top of his head. "I'm more worried about you." He coughed again. "Carolyn told me about what Dad was asking for," he paused like he would hurt me. "Ruby." He whispered.

I was silent, heard my heart in my ears. "I know you're doing the support groups, and I want to go with you. I want to make sure that you're okay, Ma. I know you're not okay." I was silent. "I don't know who she is, or what it is. I know sometimes Alzheimer's patients get stuck in loops, but—I don't know."

Brian sat up. "Dad is outside." He searched my face. Reuben's eyes again, intent and focused. "Did you give him his anxiety medicine? Sometimes if you give him the anxiety medicine with his food and Alzheimer's medicine, he has a good day." He smiled at me. "He had a good day today, Mom. He had a good day." He patted my right hand and stood up. "I didn't give him anything but his regular medicine. He's on the back porch now, where I left him." He clasped my right hand, stared at me. "He's going to be okay, Mom." The phone rang, and I looked at Brian. He answered it on the second ring.

He covered the receiver, looked at me. "Mom, it's a Dr. Allen's answering service." I felt my eyes widen. "Rev. Dr. Allen's said she can see you tomorrow morning." I swallowed hard. "Tell her I can be there next week at nine." Brian relayed the message before hanging up the phone to look at me. I held his gaze, willing him not to ask me any more questions. "Bring ginger for your father's tea if you come by tomorrow." I sat up on the bed, looked at my bare feet on the floor. Brian draped his arm around my shoulder, squeezed me. "I'm hungry." I stood up and headed downstairs, leaving his arm and whole self on our bed.

I knew it was the afternoon and knew I didn't want anything. I felt my stomach drop as I headed down the stairs, not embarrassed I was still in a robe and gown after 11:00 A.M. I wanted to feed Brian, so he would leave. It would have to be something filling, like pasta, maybe spaghetti and wondered if I had everything to make it. As I descended the stairs, I heard Brian in tow, just like he did when he was a boy. I saw Reuben at the kitchen table. "Hey, Katie." He said. I shivered. I was so happy he knew me, so happy he didn't mention *her* name. "I'm going to make spaghetti, babe." He smiled, looked up at me, his eyes bright and clear. "And garlic bread, I'd love some bread." I giggled. "You would." I walked over to him, kissed him cupping his face. He was coming back to me. He cupped my face, his warmth going over my face, neck and through my back. I wouldn't let *her* have him--*she* couldn't have him. This disease wouldn't have him, or us. I went to the kitchen and went to make food for my son and husband.

I talked to Reuben while I boiled water, and pasta. Laughed with Reuben and Brian as they relayed the day they had. I warmed marinara sauce, added fresh garlic. "I'm so glad you were home, babe. I am so glad, I could see you today." I ignored the tone Reuben was speaking in. I swore on the inside for

Brian not medicating him. My night was going to be harder than it had to be. "You see me all the time, babe, remember? I've been here for thirty-five years!" I heard him laugh. "I know. I know." I sighed, shook my head as I found my colander under in the cabinet near the stove. As I drained my noodles, I heard Brian and his Dad talk about the upcoming season, business projects and his favorite aunt, Barbara. "She's always been like that, feisty, don't careish, and stubborn. I don't know how she got married. That's why I like her so much, Nate." I dropped the empty jar on the floor.

He didn't say her name, but I knew Nathaniel had been dead for years, and I had never wished anyone dead harder than I did right then. I wanted her dead. I needed her to be dead. If she were dead, then I could have my husband, I could have my life back. I stooped over to pick the pieces up and cut my hand. "Shit!" I looked at my hand that matched the red smattering on the floor. I went to rinse my hand in the bathroom. As the water ran, I heard footsteps as I watched the water. "Leave me alone, Brian! Just let me be!" I cleaned up my hand and tried to remember to hate the disease and not my husband. I began to think if this is what it was like to live in a haunted house.

Brian and Reuben ate in silence on the couch in front of ESPN. I had no appetite. I took a shower and talked to Ruth before I went to bed. "He asked for Nathan?"

Yes."

"Nathan has been dead six years."

"I know. Drunk driving accident."

"What are you going to do, Katherine!" she was cursing then. "You can't keep going on like this." I bit my lip. "I'm going to therapy, the place that Carolyn told me about." Ruth made and approving noise. "Good. Good. Don't rest with all that in your head." I coughed, and my chest began to hurt. "Go rest, Katie. You sound horrible." I hung up the phone on its base. I laid down, in the favored green gown. I went to bed in hope, in hope for the first time since this diagnosis. Since this phantom had been introduced in the thirty-five years I had been with Reuben Michael Lewis.

I went to bed knowing, when I got up the next day, I was going to be on the radar of someone who understood what I was fighting, what I was up against: I was fighting the living for him, fighting to keep him from the dead--and warring for him to remember that I was whom he chose.

Chapter 9-Late February 1997

We had a good week. I still had to give him the extra medicine to sleep, it cut down on the muttering and talking in his sleep. I hadn't heard of this woman over a week. This woman, Ruby, I was finally brave enough to ask about when she came over for coffee in about an hour. Reuben was in the backyard seeding and getting the lawn ready for spring. The same thing he had done right before what he calls the 'breaking of the seasons'. I told him I wanted to start gardening this spring. I smiled as I drank my coffee in my tee-shirt and lounge pants on the back porch.

As the back door clapped against the door jam, he walked over to me, all ruddy-looking and handsome with dirt on his yard working clothes. He said he didn't water the portion of the ground like he wanted. "I didn't douse it but *watered* it." I went to the kitchen sink to wash his hands. "The key to a good lawn is good ground, Katie." Reuben returned to where I was, kissing me soft on the lips, squeezed my right cheek. I shivered as he smoothed my white shirt clad shoulder. I bit my lip as I watched him walk towards the shed, sun on his shoulders, saw the sweat on his red shirt. I fell in love all over again.

I sighed before I stood, going towards the backdoor and through the kitchen. The shiny oven clock read 8:09 a.m. I looked him, watched him, held my breath with my back to the stove watching the familiar of him doing yard work. The thing I couldn't imagine doing a year ago this November.

I finished my tea, rinsed out the cup and saw Babs from the kitchen window, coming through the back yard. She hugged and kissed her brother. I smiled as they embraced and as he held onto her, all familiar and warm. I heard the backdoor slam and turned to see her shimmering with her copper hair, and slacks and jean jacket, white shirt underneath. "Good day, Mrs. Lewis." I walked to her and hugged her. She didn't squeeze back, but just held me. "How are you, Mrs. Redding?" she stared at me. "So formal on a Tuesday?" I chuckled. "Yes, on a Tuesday."

I sat on my perch at the kitchen table and watched her make tea from the heating red kettle on the stove. "I have an appointment today at three with the Alzheimer's group, *Beauty For Ashes*." Barbara made an approving noise before rummaging through the cabinet above the oven for tea bags. "That's good. It must be a new group." I made a quizzical noise. "I'm not sure. Carolyn gave me the card from an event she went to at the Alzheimer's Association a while ago. She told me the woman who runs it is led by a woman whom lost her husband to this disease. Carolyn thought this would be better than *Life Connections*."

She steeped her tea in the blue cup she kept there. "I thought you liked doing the *Life Connections* thing. Is that not working out?" I didn't answer her. I sighed, and looked at my coffee, stirring and watching the liquid swirl. I thought about that afternoon's appointment. I heard her walk towards the table, sitting across from me, which I was glad of because her back was to the back door. I was comfortable when I could watch Reuben when he was outside. I thought about how Ms. Allen would react. Would she indeed understand what it was I was up against or what I was going through? She had to understand. I looked up from my hazel mixture and watched him water the patch of grass I hadn't turned over in two years. I watched him, determined and lean in his green sweatshirt and jeans. I didn't notice he had taken Brian's green sweatshirt outside. It would be a quick job and then he and I would be helping Carolyn shop for a house.

"I am thinking of selling the house. Steven is gone," she sighed. "I could sure could use the money, and I need less space to have Steven haunt me." I sipped my tea and ignored her. I was thinking, had been thinking, about talking to her about selling the company and taking time to figure out what was next. If she was moving, then she wasn't going to take control of what my husband built with her. She went on about the house she found in South City, a townhouse, and she was going to check it out with Brian.

I knew she was close to Brian and gotten closer to him since Reuben's diagnosis. But he was still my son. This was still my family. She wasn't going to do what I thought she was going to do. "If not, there are these row houses off Hawthorne I like, that I could have the guys help me flip in the Spring." I exhaled as I saw that he remembered to wrap the hose up and put it away. I let the heat from the cup seep into me. I had determined I was going to ask Babs about this woman. I was determined to be as armed as I could be when I spoke to Marcia Allen. I wanted to know all I could, all I could know. I had to know. I had to know how many ghosts I was fighting--or if it was even a ghost to fight.

Babs looked at me, she looked at me like she was waiting. She held my eyes, I looked through her, glanced over her left shoulder, saw Reuben there, under my juniper tree, asleep. I closed my eyes, dug in to the anchor I was trying to keep in my soul, and swallowed. "Who is she?" I kept my eyes closed. Silence. I looked up at Babs looking into her cup. "Who is she?" I asked. Babs kept stirring. "Barbara, who is she!" She looked up at me, all doe-eyed and somber, replied quite chilled and said, "Who?" I moved my cup from in front of me. "You heard me. Who the hell is Ruby? *What* the hell is Ruby?" Barbara relaxed in her seat, pulling tea from her cup. "What about her?" Barbara looked past me. "It's not my business. I don't know who she is. I only know of her."

I got up and went to the sink. "Babs, this is not the time for you to dance around this, like you are so famous for! I need to know," I stood up, feeling the anchor in my soul lift as I left myself feel the rage. But, I needed to know why my husband is calling for her. "Why is my husband calling for a woman who doesn't exist!" I kept my hands gripped the table, mouth bitter after I said it.

"Who said she didn't exist?" It was a whisper. "What?" my mouth was dry. My eyes itched. My feet and legs where rubber and jelly. I looked out at the wind-moved trees and compelled myself to keep on my feet. *Who said she didn't exist?* It rang like church bells, loud and unavoidable. "Did she, does she exist?" I choked. Barbara went through the back door, leaving her tea, and I heard the door slam. I thought. I reached back to our days at Washington University. I tried my damnedest to remember any portion of any life that he had beyond or before me almost forty years ago. Had I missed something? Had, had he just not told me? I met Reuben in the Spring of 1959. We had dated two years before we got married. I was determined to finish college, and still wound up having to go back after Carolyn was born to finish. I was sophisticating myself trying to remember. I screamed and knocked over my cup.

My house, my life had been infiltrated. The clattering of dishes did nothing to ease the pressure mounting in my head. It did nothing. I walked towards the staircase, swore I went to the base of the staircase my right foot stubbed. I looked back towards the outside. Babs was in front of her bother, my husband, stooped down, looking like she was talking to him. She knew. Moreover, I knew. This person, this woman was not a figment of my imagination, it wasn't an imp the disease had brought to taint him. It was a person. Someone of flesh, someone who knew, knows and had known my husband before he was my husband.

This person had a name and had left footprints in my marriage. She had become the living invisible: a phantasm, a ghost, the thing that lived under the bed. I told my children when they were young to not fear what they could not see. I would open closets, look under beds with flashlights, and leave hall lights on. I went upstairs, smoothed my slacks and cursed that I smacked my right foot of the bottom stair, thought she could see me then. Wondered if she had been in my house, been with my husband. This is what it must be like to be haunted.

Babs stayed with her brother while I went to my meeting. I gripped the steering wheel loose, thinking that if I had gripped it as I wanted, I would have ripped it from the shaft. I was still remembering, trying to remember the conversations I had with Reuben when we were dating. I kept coming back to the night he proposed to me. I remembered how cold it was, it was November before my birthday, it was before the Thanksgiving holiday that year. It was cold, November 17, 1960. It was in the quad at Washington University. He had a gotten me a hot chocolate from the cafeteria before it closed. He sat next to me, while we were sitting on the new wrought iron bench. I remembered it was overcast, I said to him I had wanted something warm to drink. He told me to find a warm, covered place and let him get me something. I wore cigarette pants because the sun was bright that morning, the weather had fooled me.

I wore a black trench coat my sister had gotten me from New York. My hair so long, still brown. I warmed my hands by blowing on them. When I had looked up, he was there, sitting next to me. He was nestled close, kissed my forehead. "Hey, babe. I got you a chocolate. Here, Katie." I took it, clasping my hands and round about his. That is when he slipped a ring on my finger. My left hand locked with this, and he pulled me into him. "There is no one I would want to do this forever thing with than you. Stay mine, and I will always keep you warm." I looked down at the odd silver ring. I had looked up at him as he pulled me close, telling me what each symbol meant.

"It's a Claddaugh ring. It was the ring my grandpa gave to my grandmother. She gave it to me, when I told her I found me." He kissed my forehead. "The hands mean friendship, the crown loyalty, and the heart love." I didn't remember saying yes, I kissed him as he cradled my hands against the cup.

I kept that ring on until our wedding day, when Reuben replaced it with a gold and diamond set. I still had the ring, and planning to give it to my granddaughter Logan.

I was on I-270 heading towards Hazelwood, needing traffic to ease. Ms. Allen's office was right off Lindbergh. As I looked for the Taylor exit, I steadied my breathing even though I gripped the steering wheel tighter. I tried to focus on my radio, furrowed my brows when I heard music. My ears were pricked because I left the radio on NPR—and there was never music on NPR. Some young girl was singing a cover of a Billie Holiday song, *I Cover The Waterfront*. Reuben played that song often off the CD Brian got him.

It was some music festival the University of Missouri-St. Louis was advertising. Her voice was so sad, I tried to focus a glance on my directions that sat on top of my purse in the passenger seat. I went through the light and I adjusted my glasses as I took Taylor exit right and examined the driver's side for letting my vision scan business and houses, and the imposing LaQuinta Inns & Suites. "160 Taylor Road. I just need 160 Taylor Road!"

The young woman on the radio pulled me in with the longing in her voice, and I was headed deeper towards the direction of the airport. I had been looking at the odd-side of the street. I managed a U-Turn in a church parking lot and crept back towards my destination. I looked in my review mirror and saw a police officer following me, I rolled my eyes and kept going at my geriatric speed. I slowed to the point I thought I could run faster than the car I drove and found 170 Taylor Road. I parked behind a parked behind a black Audi and next to a white house. "It's a house. A house." I put my head on the middle of the steering wheel, closed my eyes. "It's a two-story house."

The disc jockey came on, cheery to all listening, convincing us all whom where listening not to be as sad or as lost as her voice would dictate. "That was Maya Rainier singing her version of *Good Morning Heartache* by Billie Holiday. Sad, sweet and worthy of her voice. I look forward to hearing more of her voice during UMSL's *Notes On St. Louis* March 9-12 at the Jazz Fest on West Campus sponsored by the University of St. Louis-Missouri's Music Department."

I turned off the car and reached for my purse, shoving the black ink directions into my Liz Claiborne tote. I looked in the rearview mirror. I dabbed my eyes, sucked in a breath and opened the car door. I walked around the front of my car and up the bricked walkway towards the beige dual-doored porch, framed with sparkling white door frames. I went up the short set of stairs, knocked on the door marked *Pastoral Assistance, M. Allen, MSW, LCSW*. Not to look as rumpled as I felt, I smoothed my hair, jeans and green blouse.

I knocked once, held my breath for a silent count of five before I knocked a second time. I wished Barbara had come with me, I wish I hadn't come. I started to turn and go back to my car. As I fished for my keys as I made my way down the stairs, missed a stair and my purse spilled. "Dammit!" I stooped to picked everything and saw a card. "Mrs. Lewis?" A slender, black woman answered the door. "Yes, yes." I stammered, giving her a panicked smile as I shoved the contents on the ground back into my purse.

Ms. Allen held the door open for me, wearing a sweatshirt and jeans and sneakers. Her hair was red, long and she wore flattering gold eyeglasses. Looking around the room, it had hardwood floors, clean and comfy looking chairs everywhere. There was a kitchen behind that area, and I smelled coffee. "Mrs. Lewis?" She asked again, I turned to face her, startled that she was startled. I focused on her smooth features, her dark eyes with warmth coming from them. She was dressed quite casual: denim jeans, a sweatshirt and sneakers. Her hair was red, like fall leaves where red. She had a look to her face that betrayed her age. She looked to be in her forties, but I wasn't sure. She didn't look like a person associated with pastoral care or ministry.

"I'm sorry, Ms. Allen. I just—" She gestured towards a taupe overstuffed couch under a painting of colorful flowers. I looked at the lush gladiolus, all different colors. Vibrant and intense, I picked out the red ones, and smiled.

I settled on the couch, staring around the room, feeling like a frightened child. Ms. Allen sat in the chair juxtaposed to my seat. She looked at me, could feel her watching me. "Are you alright, Mrs. Lewis?" I heard the coffee pot sizzle. I lifted my eyes to follow the sound, kept my glasses on, didn't answer her. I heard Ms. Allen tear pages, the ripping soothed me. "I'm—I'm not okay. I am not okay." I couldn't face her, so I looked at her white Reebok she wore. "I love my husband, Ms. Allen. I have loved him from the moment I saw him. I knew--." I took a deep breath. "I knew, he was what I wanted. I was nineteen when he proposed. I was almost twenty-one when we married. It's now thirty-five years later."

I heard her clear her throat and heard scribbling. There was a phone ringing in a back room. I heard my heart in my ears, warm in my cheek. "How long has he been diagnosed?" I closed my eyes. "A year." My voice its own whisper. My head lulled to my lap, propped up on my interlaced hands. I heard my life end as I listened to the seconds tick on the clock on her kitchen wall. "It's something altogether monstrous. It has taken my husband!" I was still looking for spaces in the floor slats, I heard her feet on the floor, tapping. "It is a disease of no friends, Mrs. Lewis. My husband died within five years of his diagnosis. He went down swinging." She scoffed. "He was a boxer, Golden Gloves, Navy. As he slipped— "she paused, I didn't look up, kept hearing the coffee. I saw the light in the kitchen and how the curtain ebbed around it. "How do you—deal with the slipping away?" I heard her stand with a slight grunt. "You deal with it, by staying put. Would you like coffee, Mrs. Lewis?"

I looked up, following her footfalls. I watched her come into my field of vision, reaching for cups from a near cabinet, a white one and a green one. "How do you take it?" She asked. "I would prefer tea if you have it." I saw her rummaging through the same cabinet the cups where in. "I'm out of tea." I sighed. "Coffee is fine." She brought the two mugs, mindful of each step she took, stopping to give me the white cup and taking the green back to her seat. I turned to see her adjusting in the matching black overstuffed chair across from me and the black coffee table. "You deal by remembering whom they are to you, even when they do the opposite."

I stared down at the molasses colored liquid, willed not to cry or pry too deeply as was polite. "For almost forty years, I have given him my..." I took the spoon she had given, stirred my drink like a witch's caldron. "I gave him everything he could have ever wanted. I made him a home, gave him my body, my youth, my love. "I looked up at her face. "My strength. I feel like I'm being replaced! After all I have done for him, I'm being replaced!" I put the cup on the table with a thud. "Replaced!" I stood up, paced. I looked toward the light in the kitchen, how warm it looked and how quiet. "I'm being replaced. I don't know how this happened, but I'm fighting for my husband! I've never had to do that. I want him back! I want him back!"

There was ticking against my screams. "How are you, have you lost him?" Ms. Allen was so calm, so knowing. She had no husband. She had been through this before, this thing I called the double-grieving. I was grieving the loss of what is and what was or never will be. "How have you lost him?" I felt myself melt to the floor. "I know I have, I-I know I have." I balled up in the direction of the kitchen, knees in my chest. She repeated her question, and I answered like an insolent child. "I have, dammit! I have! I don't even know who she is!"

I heard nothing but my own heaving and warmth of tears. "Do you really believe that?" I fought back the ball of rage that lay in wait in my throat. I swallowed it down to the bitter in my stomach. "I don't know who she is. I can't even have the satisfaction of her being alive to try and slap her!" I tried to control my breathing to think, make the words make sense. "He is my husband." I heard her stir in the chair behind me. "He has a disease, Mrs. Lewis. He's not having an affair." She slurped from her cup. "Your life didn't start with me, and his certainly didn't start with you. Do you and your husband—well, did you have full disclosure when you were dating?"

I spun around on the floor to look at her, looked at her all perched and perfect on her chair. "I told him all he needed to know about me, and he told me all I needed to know about him." I sniffled and shook, wrapped my arms around myself. I was spinning, reeling. "That's what you did in those days." I put my knees on my chest, trying to will my heart to remain in my chest. "All I know is, her name is Ruby. I don't know what it is, whom it is, and he—he asks for her. Most often in his sleep. The other night, he called her name."

She looked up at me, parroted my phrase. "Called her name?" I looked at her pretty white, clean Reebok sneakers. "He called her name, barely a whisper while— "sighed, looking up at her face from the floor. "While making love to me. He's done it more than once. I swear, Ms. Allen, he called her name!" She looked at me, not stunned, not understanding, but searching my eyes. "Mrs. Lewis, your husband is in neural loop. This is common with those with this disease. He's in a loop. All you can do is ride out the loop."

I stood, went back to the sofa. "A loop? You--." My head in my hands, I heard the clap against my forehead. "You sound like those idiots at Life Connections." I faced the window, back to her and watched my red Mazda do nothing and traffic go by behind it. "My husband called another woman's name, while inside of me, and you're telling me I just have to hang on!" She sipped again. "I'm not telling you anything. I'm telling you that you have a unique set of circumstances and you cannot do it on your own. The best thing you can do, is to arm yourself with information." I swallowed and heard her voice continue. "You have to get as much information about this woman as possible. You have to find out whom she is."

Ms. Allen was quiet again, sighing before I heard her cup be placed on her desk. "If you want your husband, you need to find out whom Ruby, or even what, Ruby is." I turned to face her, heat radiating from me. Her face softened for a moment. "Alzheimer's disease is a puzzle. For my husband, I had to brush up on US Navy history, and knots." She chuckled and took off her eyeglasses. "You are going to have to fight for him and you. If you are not willing to do that, you will not only have lost him to her but the disease." I crossed my arms over my chest.

"You are going to have to remember, even when he doesn't. The disease takes so much, don't let it take everything or anything else." I sighed, moving back to the couch, letting my head roll back to the cushion. "How?" I asked, more like a yell. I didn't mean to yell. "Mrs. Lewis, I was married for almost forty years. I fought for my husband. I fought as I lost him to the disease. At the end," she sighed. "I was the last person Edward, my husband, forgot." She looked at me, I could see the piteous understanding in them. She sat there looking all-knowing, just stirring her cup and sipping.

"I gave up my career, gave him children," I let my mind trail off, words rambling. "I gave to him, and our children and relationship." She was silent, kept looking out the window.

"I know what it's like to live and feel dead." I looked at her, studied her face, still not seeing the age she spoke of. "How old are you, Marcia?" She grinned turning her focus back to me and said, "Sixty-five." I cried. I felt that same bitterness I had tried to swallow roll around and stir in my stomach. "I know this is hard, but I won't make you talk, Mrs. Lewis." I squeezed the couch cushion, looking for cracks in the floor. "My daughter said she met you at an Alzheimer's event, and said you were a great therapist." I closed my eyes, swallowed again. "What made you want to do this?" I felt tears on my face again. "I mean you lost Edward, why not just say 'the hell with this?'" She giggled, putting the cup in her hands. "I didn't say it was easy. I've been a counselor for twenty years, doing pastoral care for about a decade." She sniffled, rolling the cup in her hands. "I know what it looked like to help—and I also know what it looks like too not have any."

I heard the cup thump against the coffee table. Her green cup like the green light Fitzgerald talked about. "I know what it's like to not be alright and have to keep going." I sighed, tears slick over my cheeks. "I decided to help families in transition with this disease because I know what it's like to need insider information and have no one to give it to you."

I listened to another phone ring, rolled over her words before I spoke. "I need insider information." I looked at her face, watched the light from the window in this space we occupied make her shimmer almost ethereal. "If you do, then you are going to have to make time to get it. The first session is always free, the next ones are at your convenience and at an hourly rate." She smiled at me. "Carolyn told me how your attendance is with therapy sessions."

Ms. Allen giggled and sipped her coffee. I swallowed the ball of bitter which had escaped my belly. I had been weak more than I wanted to be with a woman I didn't know. I felt like I had been shot out of a cannon and could finally see the net.

Chapter 10- April 1997

Reuben and I drove in silence back from lunch at Denny's. I was feeling better, I made and effort to see Mrs. Allen almost every two weeks since the initial meeting in February. As we left the parking lot, I thought about how awkward lunch had been. Reuben had drunk his coffee out of a beige stone colored cup, looking around the chosen beige table. I felt like he didn't see me, I was there, but he didn't see me. He looked around me, his back was to the door watching other people and past me.

I remembered my last appointment with Mrs. Allen. She had talked to me as if I were readying for a championship bout. "This disease is the enemy, using memories as it's weapon." I stopped at the night before getting back on I-64 West, thinking my husband was turning into my roommate. I had squeezed his hand, shaking it while he looked out on the parking lot and midday traffic.

We ate in relative silence—save for the customers coming and going out, it was as if the world had ended. I ate my chicken salad, he had a burger and it was as if we were college roommates. We were tolerant of each other, for the sake of being civil. I had got on I-64 West, sniffling when I thought about how he chose not to come to bed last night. Reuben slept on the couch rather than make love in our bed. I wanted my husband. He was there, and yet he was never there. I had worn my red cardigan, a white blouse with these jeans Carolyn had gotten me. Reuben wore his favorite Washington University sweatshirt, and jeans. If we were acting like college roommates, we might as well have looked like it.

I was happy we had taken my car, rather than his truck, much easier to handle. "Reuben?" I looked over at him, he was dozing off. I was glad I had extra Xanax at home, thought of giving him an extra one when we got home. I turned the volume on the radio up, I felt my eyebrows furrow as I heard music again when NPR didn't play music. My radio didn't leave NPR anymore. "Welcome to *Notes On St. Louis.*" The intro music played and a young sounding man I hadn't heard before spoke, introducing himself as Johnathan Foster, sounding like a young Frank Sinatra. He started to talk about the Gaslight Square from forty years ago: *The Plum Bottom. The Upper Room. The Gypsy Hand.*

"As a student of local history, Whitney and I have decided to try and find the woman whom sang this next song. It is credited to a local composer, Samuel "Jack" Robinson, and was sung by a local singer, Ethylene Gibeaux. We have no idea if Ms. Carter is living in the area, or still living." There was shuffling papers, and soft tapping with a pen. "But, we aim to find her. If anyone has information about Ethylene Gibeaux please contact *Notes On St. Louis* with the call letters KWMU here on campus of University of Missouri-St. Louis." There was radio silence as there was adjusting of microphones in the background. The hum of the road in tune with it. I turned my blinker on to head to the exit to the Brentwood Exit to go home. The traffic went past, I heard her lips part as the young woman, Maia, began to sing.

Her voice was deep, filled with this almost melancholy hope. I felt my eyes itch, heard other sniffling. Then that sniffling turning into crying. "His love is like nothing I have ever known." "Sing, cher! Sing." I didn't want to look at him. I didn't want to see light in his eyes I didn't put there. "I didn't know you liked jazz." Silence. "Did you know her?" I asked. I sped up, searching for the exit. I heard his head smack off the passenger window. "Dammit." He pushed me.

"Really, Ruby?" He called me her name. I screamed and let go of the wheel. There was a white tractor-trailer that pulled alongside of us and honked. I swore at him, as I cut over two right-hand lanes of traffic, and took the Skinker exit.

Through the green light, I pulled in to the AAMACO gas station. I parked at the end of the lot, slammed the car in park and pushed him back. I unclicked my seat belt, as Reuben looked out of the windshield. I wanted to throw him threw it, be a widow and start over. "Look at me, dammit! Look at me!" I grabbed his jacket, pulled him towards me. "Who am I Reuben! Who am I?" I shook him, trying to free her grip from him. I pushed him against the window again. "Say my damn name! Say my damn, name!" He looked at me, I moved my head to look at him, chase his gaze. "Who am I, Reuben Michael? Who am I to you?!"

All that I had learned in group had left me: be patient, don't overreact, be aware of the environment. All Mrs. Allen was trying to teach me, the inside information I was paying by the hours for was leaving me. Every tool I had garnered was slipping my mind and flung from my wife toolbox. I was losing my husband, while fighting for him, for us. Hell, for any portion of the us! I heard my voice become shrill as Maia continued in what I could only deem a siren song. I screamed his name inside that tight car. I started to cry. I wept while I beat against with my tight rage-balled fists, hearing how my hands connected to the warmth in his chest. The warmth he said was mine, that he would always give to me. This bitch couldn't have my life, have my husband! I would die before that happened!

"Say my name, Reuben!" I slapped him. I saw the startled look on his face, the shift come over his blue eyes, and I stopped before I could slap him again. I saw the shift come over him, I thought he could see me at last. He was present in the same space I was again. "Just say my name." Stopped my hands, wrapped his hands around my wrists, searched his eyes. I slid my wrists from his and folded into his chest. I wrapped his arms around me, unbuckling his seat beat. He held me as I cried. "What's wrong, Kate? It's going to be okay, babe. I'll be alright. I'm---I'm here." He held me and felt my breathing stop. I heard my heart in my ears. "I did it again, didn't I?" I heard my chest heave, tears running down my toes and cheeks. "I—I forgot you. I-- help me, babe. I'm slipping. I'm slipping, and I can't help it." Before he could start speaking again, I kissed him.

I kept kissing him, kissed him until I heard his breath ragged with hands in my hair. He pulled me to his face, nose to nose. He kissed me soft, like he did so many years ago when he proposed. When he kissed me like this, it made my heart stop, and my heart jump. This was our kiss, only I could have him this way. Ruby wouldn't get him, couldn't have him—she would stay a memory or become a demon. I couldn't let her have him. He cupped my face, his hands slipped to the back of my neck, caressed them there and I moaned. I bared my hands against his chest and looked at him, "Reuben. Who am I?" I wiped his face. He caught my right hand, kissed my palm. "You're my wife. You're – "he paused. I nestled against his chest. I put my ear to his heart. I sat there with him, like we young again.

The radio was on, Mazda engine working harder than it should be, while Johnathan told all listeners the time of the next show. I had fought of the ghost for the moment. I fought so hard, still fighting, to keep him with me. The rain started plopping against the windshield and we sat on the gas station's parking lot. I left my head on his chest, and willing time to stop—I needed the grace of God to just have one whole moment with my husband. Mrs. Allen told me in my latest session last month to treasure the good days. "Embrace them and remember there may be more than one day." She made habit of telling this phrase after every session, "The good days tell you to have hope."

Before we left the parking lot, Reuben had wanted to drive. He had kissed me and looked over at me after we changed seats. I smiled at him, felt warm knowing all that clear blue ocean he held was for me. We went home, taking the street, avoiding the highway. St. Louis drivers are notorious for being incapable of driving on non-dry streets. Mrs. Allen had told me driving would get perilous as the disease advanced. But I watched him drive, letting him have the good day was all I could do. I watched the rain as it fell and watched him glide my Mazda into Brentwood and past the Saint Louis Galleria.

Upon passing the Saint Louis Galleria he turned towards Eager Road and feeling safe I had closed my eyes as he drove. We were almost home; the rain had ebbed, and he was fine. There was only so far, we could go. My eyes opened as I felt a bump as we went over what felt like a curb. "It should be around here somewhere." I looked around, frantic, not knowing where we were. I thought we hit something or someone. "What are we looking for?" He gripped the wheel, hawk vision present, squinting. He didn't look at me. My chest felt tight, I couldn't breathe, and I was gasping for air. I pressed him, I asked again where we were going, more panicked. "Where are we going, Reuben?!" I adjusted in my seat, I looked at street signs, anger focused my vision. My throat was dry, and I scanned for anything familiar. I saw street signed for Lindell Boulevard, the Fox Theatre and my sister's alma mater, Saint Louis University. I was from home and I thought about how I could get him to pull over and stop this from getting worse.

My friend Ruth was the only person that lived nearby, and she was on Indiana Avenue in a modest brownstone townhouse. That was still South St. Louis, and we were a good twenty minutes from where we were. We turned toward the university, passed school buildings, he was slowing down. I held my breath, bit my lip and looked. He was at the traffic light before the overpass that would have taken us towards Ruth, but he made a left at the light and we were on i-64 again headed towards, Soulard Market.

Reuben had begun muttering as he drove. I resigned to wait until the car stopped. I saw the quarter tank on the Mazda's gas gage. I knew if I could get him off the highway, I could reorient him. In my group, and with Mrs. Allen, I was reminded not to try and disrupt the loop, especially if found to be in a car. "Reuben, if you pull over, and off the highway maybe we can find what you're looking for." Reuben took the next exit and leading us to downtown St. Louis, and near Busch Stadium. There was no game this afternoon, and he just drove around. We pulled over near Kiener Plaza. I thanked God he did so before the light changed else we would have been hit by the black Audi coming from the opposite direction on Olive Boulevard. We parked behind a white Buick, and I touched his shoulder, reminding myself to breathe before I spoke.

He looked straight ahead. "She was singing tonight. She—she was supposed to be singing tonight. She sings her long set on Thursday. What day is today, Doc?" I closed my eyes "Who's singing tonight?" I exhaled and thought about Mrs. Allen. *Breathe. It will help you think. Break the loop. Break the loop is all you need to do in the moment. Ask questions. Be calm. Keep your voice controlled. Be deliberate.* "Reuben, you're in St. Louis. No one is singing tonight.

We are headed home. Home is on Mayfair Avenue in Ladue." He shook his head, grabbed the wheel again, he muttered, before closing his eyes again. "Ruby is. Ruby is singing tonight. I—I told her I was coming. I had a drop to make, and I would be there." He exhaled, opened his eyes and grinned. "Then I can talk to her. I'll talk to her and make her listen to me."

Reuben looked at me, looking passed me as he gripped the wheel. I swallowed, felt heat cascade down my neck and through my shoulders as I reached to get out of the car. With my hands into fists as I went to the driver's side door. I dug my nails in my right palm as I opened the door with my left. I studied the paint on them, a pale pink I thought was perfect and unnoticeable. I snatched the door open, moved his hands off the wheel. I let go of the breath I was still holding. I got close to his face, gritted my teeth, held his face in my left hand. He sat there silent for a moment, eyes still far from me. I willed them back to this time, this place. "Get out, Reuben. I want to go home." I gritted my teeth, willing my heart to stop racing. I inhaled, felt my eyes close and open again. I put my nose to his, my voice became a hissing noise, "Now!"

I drove home in silence-- no radio, no voices. I looked over at him, sleeping sweet while facing towards me. I looked at him, as I waited for the light at Clayton Road to change. I studied his face, remembered the blue eyes under those eyelids. The honking car behind me startled me, and I skidded forward through the light going home. I heard him moan and bump his head against the window. As we turned left onto Mayfair Avenue, I hit a pothole, and heard his head smack against the passenger window. I bit my lip and looked for our house. I spotted Brian's blue truck in front of our home, and I whipped the Mazda around, tearing up and upset. My front wheel hit a wet patch. I pressed the gas to get through the puddle, and the small hole I was stuck in. I just had time to scream as I crashed into the back of Reuben's truck.

"Dammit! Oh!" I opened the door, making sure the car was in park. I was shaken and looking at the front end of my car, and Reuben's truck with the late spring sun gleaming off its cab. "Oh my God!" I looked at Reuben, with his body slumped against the dashboard. "Reuben!" I shook him, looked at the gash on his forehead, the blood which trickled down his face. I shook him again, screaming. I slapped his face, screamed his name. I leaned into the car, with my knees on the grey interior seat, grabbed the lapels of his jacket. With the ease he came towards me from the dashboard, I realized he never put his seat belt back on. I had given him a half a Xanax I had kept for me, with a bottle of water I had in the car. I could hear him breathing. "Reuben, babe, wake up!"

I ran to my front door to get Brian, and there was a note: Mom, I met Whitney here and will be back soon. Brian. I crumpled the note and ran to my neighbor next door. I screamed and beat down her door. I beat and screamed on the beige yellow door before I slid down the front of it. I didn't know I had passed out until an officer tapped my shoulder.

Chapter 10-Accident Aftermath

It was all a blur: sirens, and people and dogs barking. There was an officer who looked like Brian, asking if I was okay. I don't remember answering him. There was a shapely woman on the porch, with red hair and purple cat-eye glasses, in a big yellow bathrobe. She had been in the bathtub when I was knocking. She was smoking on her front porch, talking to an officer with blond hair. There were a small crowd old people gathering across the street, looking and walking other distressed-looking dogs.

Everyone was asking if I was okay. I just wanted to know where Reuben was! All I could think about was how he was slumped over and bleeding from his head on the passenger side of my car. "Where is my husband? Where is Reuben Lewis!?" The doppelgänger of my told me to remain calm, "Mrs. Lewis, calm down. I'll talk to you in a minute." He gestured to the lawn below, I sat on her gray painted stairs, shaking and crying.

It was Mrs. Rogers across the street who had called the police. She didn't know what was going on and had reported a woman screaming on this her neighbor's front porch. The neighbor, I found out was an artist who called herself Mae West, with her real name being Margaret. She blew smoke away from the officer's face and spoke. "I didn't know what the hell was going on! It was just yelling and screaming, and I didn't recognize the voice. No way in Hell when I was coming to the door!"

I looked at her from where I sat like a naughty child, the blond officer with the baby face still taking notes on what was happening, stood next to Margaret. I noticed he was shorter and heavier than Brian's doppelgänger. I grabbed the banister next to the stairs, felt my legs shake as I focused on Brian's blue truck. "Reuben, where is Reuben? Where is my husband?" I looked at my car, door still ajar, broken front end --and empty. "He's been taken to the hospital." I turned to look at him, seeing he could have been no more than thirty. "I have to get to him. I have to get to him! Where is he?"

"Are you okay, ma'am?" The doppelgänger held my eyes a moment and I wanted to shrink. Margaret looked at me. "You okay?" I looked her and tried to move to my car, and he grabbed my arm. Not enough to startle, but to settle me. "I have been married almost forty years. Where is my husband?" I looked at his name plate and badge, he startled me how much he looked like Brian. Tall, soothing, green eyes and dark hair. "Officer Mayhen, please let me go! I need to— I turned in the direction of my Mazda. "I have to get to him."

I snatched away, with my red cardigan sleeve flapping against my jeans. "Am I being arrested?" He put his pen and pad away in the pocket across from his badge and name plate. "Mrs. Lewis, I think you need to calm down." I glared at him, walking down the final three stairs and the lawn beneath. "I don't need the patronizing! I need to get to my husband! Where is he?"

I heard my voice cracking, broken sounding. I looked from him, Margaret still smoking in her bathroom, and the blond officer watching and judging. "Where is my husband? He has..." I took a breath in, looked at the ground, and his black patent shoes. "He has Alzheimer's disease and he wanders sometimes." I was tearing up and talking with my hands. He hasn't had his afternoon medication." I sighed, looking up to find God, and kept crying. "I need to find him!"

I put my arms with a thrust in the prone position at my sides. This was the position I gave as a last resort to my first-grade kids so many years ago, up onto my last taught almost a decade before. It was my sign of exasperation, my point of no return, of giving up. I opened my eyes and looked at these strange people, looking and judging and staring. I let my gaze travel to all three of them, as the yellow bathrobe spoke in a loud voice, "Get some help, lady!" Before I could offer a retort, Officer Mayhen turned his body from me and spoke, "Mae, just go in your house, okay? We can handle it from here. Thank you!"

In turning back towards me, motioned me to come towards him. I refused to move. He walked towards me in that cadence all police officers have. His eyes softened as he touched my shoulder, "Mrs. Lewis, your husband had a heart attack, and he has some cuts, so he's pretty banged up."

I began to shake again, and Officer Mayhen kept talking. "He was taken to St. Louis University Hospital. I can take you if you want. I don't think you should drive." I focused my eyes on him, trying to bore into him; his green eyes didn't flinch. "I can drive myself. I know where the hospital is and am quite capable of getting there without a police escort!" I clapped hands at my sides again and turned to my car. I didn't care about the damage, I knew it would start when I got in. When I shut the driver door, I turned the key to start it, but the car refused to cooperate. I got out, opened the door to the back seat to grab my purse to go to Brian's truck—I knew he kept his truck unlocked when he visited and keys in the glove box.

I pulled open the driver's side door, feeling eyes on me as I got in and shut the truck door. "God, let this go quick." I reached in the glove box and there were no keys. "Dammit, Brian!" I got out, purse in hand to shut the door, running towards the Ladue Police Department squad car. I heard the car start and saw the blond officer in the driver seat. "Officer Mayhen, my son's truck won't start!" I hung on the window frame, looking at the street beneath my shoes. "Could you please take me to the hospital?" Bewildered, they stared at each other and then back towards me.

****

I rode in the back seat of a Ladue squad car to Saint Louis University Hospital with the siren on. I felt my eyes itch, mouthed Reuben's name over and as we sped down I-44 East. As we took the Grand Boulevard exit, I saw an ambulance drive into the Emergency Department. I pounded at plexiglass divider, "Take me through the emergency room! Take me to the emergency room!" Officer Mayhen looked as his partner again, making the block so they could take me through the Emergency Department. As we went up the hospital's ramp to Emergency Department, I wiped my face with a handkerchief from my purse, and began shaking, waiting for Officer Mayhen to open the door. I walked in front of an ambulance, and walked through the Emergency Department, saying a small prayer for whomever was on the other side of the ambulance doors and kept going.

I went from the older black woman in her blue security uniform at the Emergency Room security desk, who routed me, to the Information Desk on the main floor. I went through the Emergency Room door that a gracious young man with red hair and freckles in blue surgical scrubs let me through a side door which lead to the escalator. When I all but dashed by the stunned black woman at the Admissions Desk and headed down the escalator, I was greeted by a long-haired blonde, with her hair in a ponytail, wearing a red shirt. She smiled at me as I tried to compose myself. "I need to find my husband. He was brought here and hour or so ago. His name is Reuben Michael Lewis."

As she turned to tap on her computer after, a guard with a badge tapped my shoulder and asked if I had arrived in a squad car about ten minutes ago through the Emergency Department. I didn't answer him, the only way I knew it was a security guard was because of the patch on his shirt beneath his walkie-talkie. "Ma'am, if you came here by squad car you—" I spun to look at him, taking him in quick glances. He was clean shaved, haircut military close, and his jacked emblazed with the hospital insignia. His eyes were green, and he had these large hands he rubbed his face with and wore a wedding band.

He was tall walnut brown black man and I refused to be intimidated by him. I put my hand in his face, before poking his badge into his chest. "I got in an accident with my husband in the car! My car is fucking broken, and can get another car, keys and whatever else! I need to find Reuben Michael Lewis, my husband who was born August 18, 1935!" His walkie-talkie crackled, as he spoke hushed into it. "Ma'am, please refrain from touching me to talk to me. What is your name?" I huffed and kept my eyes to the floor, my voice loud. "I am Mrs. Reuben Lewis! I am Katherine Anne Lewis!" I was trying to catch my breath, trying to help it outpace my fury.

More static and hushed voices. He turned from me and I from him, keeping my attention to the blonde at the desk and her pretty red shirt. Her glossy plastic name badge read Tori. Her ponytail was high and tight minimal makeup, but her lips were as red as her shirt. "Don't worry about, Paul, Mrs. Lewis. He's just doing his job." I cupped my right hand to my forehead. "Just tell me where he is please. Please!" My voice was louder then, frantic sounding as it echoed in the lobby. "I see Mrs. Lewis, he's on the ninth floor. Room 908." I heard Paul, the security guard, gave me a glare as he walked away, speaking into his walkie-talkie.

"How do I get there?" I had laid hold to the information desk, anxious and sweaty. Tori gestured her acrylic nailed hand behind me. "Take those elevators up to the ninth floor and then go to the Division 9 South." I went towards the elevator, only to be stopped by Paul trying to catch my attention I reached into my purse to find my mirror to touch up my makeup. I didn't want Reuben to see me so unkempt. He seemed to always like me in a red lipstick. I smiled the reflection, face placid, eyes sad. I pushed the UP button for the elevator, deciding who to call first. I would call Brian first because he could go and get Mae. He would be able to pick his truck up from in front of my house soon. He would then call Carol because she lived nearby.

The middle elevator opened, spilling its crowded contents; frantic, anxious-looking people getting to their loved ones. I boarded the elevator, and as the doors were closing, there was a crowd of maybe six or seven people, crying and holding one another. I was nestled on the left side of the elevator, overhearing tears and sighs of a family whose mother was dying. I swallowed hard, rung my hands together, pulling my purse closer.

The doors shut, and I pushed the ninth floor again, and the eighth-floor button glowed without my touch. The world for those moments was contained in that elevator car. "Mama! Mama!". I looked over, seeing his overcome black family, continuing to talk about how bad off their mother was. I closed my eyes and exhaled, looked at their faces, these black people, crying and unkempt, on the right side and center of this small silver box, with eyes reddening and swollen.

They were falling all over themselves. "She's not even remembering us, she's calling for people who ain't even here! Why the fuck did we come back here?" There was more crying as the door opened to eighth floor, allowing them to all trickle out and go towards this dying woman's room in this flood of rainbow-colored shirts, scarves on their heads and jeans and pajama pants. When the elevator stopped at the ninth floor, there was a tall, skinny brunet doctor on a pager, muttering about his shift. I waited until he looked up at me before I exited. His glasses looked foggy, and he was unshaven. I smiled at him remembering, Reuben's thoughts of going to medical school.

I walked past him, remembering Tori's direction and the sterile dark blue signs. I found 9 South division and tried to find 908. I looked at the signs down the first hall, right down from the elevator. I looked at the hallway which looked to be L-shaped, directly across from the elevators, and I was drawn to the room with the white piece of paper affixed, figuring that had to be the room. I walked towards the paper, which read all visitors needed to go to the nursing station before entering. I went down the third long hall, seeing life and busyness at the nurse's station.

I found a brunette at the desk in dark blue scrubs and black framed glasses. I tapped the desk to get her attention, and a phone rang. She picked it up and looked at me or she was looking through me. She answered the person's questions on the other end of the receiver with one of her own, and ended with a quick "Okay", to end the call. "May I help you?" She tried to smile. I took a deep breath. "I—my husband is in 908. I wanted to see him, but there is a sign on his door."

She spun around on her wheeled chair towards a rack which housed blue binders, in the middle of the nurses' station. She came rolling back to me in almost the same speed with a binder in her hand. "Oh, Mr. Lewis!" He looked through the binder, thumbing through divided sections. "Yes, he's in there. He came in by himself and was disoriented." She looked up at me, as if the words she just uttered didn't make sense. "He asked for his wife." She wasn't looking at me again. "I am his wife," I searched for her name badge. "Carrie." She looked up at me. "According to the Social Worker that saw him in the ED, he said his wife's name is Ethylene Rose Lewis."

My heart dropped, and jaw tightened. "I'm his wife. I'm Katherine Lewis. I rooted through my purse, found my wallet and showed her my identification. She took the card and stared at it and me." Carrie looked around, card in hand. "I am his wife, and I have been since June of 1961! Let me see my husband! "Carrie stood, leaning on the small table below the counterspace I occupied. "Mrs. Lewis, I cannot let you into a room with someone you have no relationship to." Carrie adjusted her glasses and continued. "He is under observation right now, and the doctors have asked to minimize stress, and outside visitors. That is Saint Louis University Hospital policy!"

I reared back at her and squinted at her "The hell with this hospital and its policy!" I was hissing at her, and saw she had to be no older than Maeghan, and just as bitchy as she could be. "That is my husband of almost forty years in that room! No paper is going to take him from me! You can tell that to the President, God or the Devil himself!" I stormed down the hall amid the screams telling me to stop. I pushed open the door and saw him laying there with his eyes shut—looking small and hooked to wires and tubes.

I moved towards the bed, and whispered his name, kept my hands to my face. "Reuben." I went to him and held his hand, squeezed it, willing his eyes to open. "Reuben!" I squeezed his hand. He moaned. I tried to get in bed with him, so he would know I was there, I heard footsteps through on the door, "Ma'am, you have to leave this room! Ma'am!" I held on to Reuben's hand as these mean brown hands pulled me from him. The more I swatted at them, the more the hands came towards me, pulling me to them. "Reuben!" I had maneuvered from one security officer, managing to get back to Reuben's bedside to shake him, called his name again. "Ma'am if you don't come out of this room, we will have to call the police!"

It was that horrible bitch, Carrie. She must have called these people to subdue and take me away. I wouldn't leave. Let them call the police. Let the call the big scary black man, Paul come stop me. If they hurt me I was going to call the Bright Law Firm—Ruth loved a good fight and wanted a new building for the practice she and Charles built. I heard the PA system, and alarms then with Carrie's voice shrill and irritable, "Security to 9 South, Security to 9 South." I managed to pry one of his eyes open, seeing the blue of his eyes rolled up in the top of his head.

I whispered hushes in his ear when he stirred. I heard more footsteps behind me, I willed time to stop again, "Rube! Baby, it's Katie! Katie, I'm here!

Tell them whom I am, babe. Goddammit, wake up!" He moaned again.

The door thundered with noise as and men came in, and I turned to see Paul and another black man with darker skin and a security cap, along with a woman and brown hair, short like Mia Farrow once had it cut in a white jacket. "Mrs. Lewis, you have to come with us!" I hung on to Reuben's bed, concentrated on the beeping machines, his heart beat, his warmth. There were hands on me, pulling me from him, pulling me from his warmth. I cursed, I kicked, and I demanded to see Carrie, her boss and whomever else was listening. "Dammit! God in Heaven put me down, dammit! This is my husband! What are you doing, let me go!"

They handled me out of a room, walking me around to the 9 North Division, with staring people in dark blue and maroon colored scrubs. They kept my hands behind my back, tight like I was a feral cat. I was looking for the woman with the white lab coat and dark hair. She could help me, I know she could. She was sweet looking like my Carolyn. "I just want to see my husband!" I screamed as they lead me to the end of Division 9 North, to the left where there were more white walls and brown office doors. There was one door open and they took me towards it. I was grateful it was empty.

Once the door was shut, I sat there looking at the wall, tears streaming down my face. I felt like a wounded animal was bleeding out. My black purse was on the small beige loveseat. I moved to get it, to pull myself together. The door opened as I searched for a mirror. "Mrs. Lewis," I looked up from the scavenger hunt of my purse. "I'm Madison Harper. I'm a Social Worker here at Saint Louis University Hospital. Can I speak to you?" I looked at her again. She was the nameless white coat in the room moments ago. She had short dark hair, and blue eyes. She reminded me of Babs as she stood there standing there. "Why?"

She walked towards the desk juxtaposed from me and sat. She tuned on the red lamp on the desk, casting a golden glow over her chin and her lab coat. I saw the glint on her left hand, a wedding ring. Her black and white striped shirt peeked from under her jacket. She wore jeans which I thought was totally unprofessional and Nikes. She looked like no social worker I wanted to talk to. "It's not every day that we have a woman your age removed from a room kicking and screaming like a child." She reached for pen and paper at the desk, beginning to write.

"Mrs. Lewis, who is your husband?" She was scribbling, not looking at me. "My husband is in the room that I was removed from!" I rummaged through my purse looking for my compact. I touched up my powder and dried my brimming tears. "What's his name?" I looked at her earrings. They look like they may have been diamond ones and I wondered if she had bought them herself. I studied my reflection. "His name is Reuben Michael Lewis. I have been his only wife for almost forty years. I married him when I was twenty. I am almost sixty now." I folded my purse onto my lap, looking at Madison, wondering what wisdom she could possess. "More than half my life I have been with him." Put my mirror back in my purse, returned it to the beige loveseat. I crossed my arms over my chest. I glared at the top of her head as she wrote her notes. "Just him."

She kept scribbling. "He came in by himself with only his wallet and called another woman his wife. I can't tell you much more than that." She finished writing her notes before looking up at me. "By law and policy, I can't tell you more than that. The name he gave as is wife, is the name that is in his chart." She looked over at me, swatted her bangs at and she leaned back in her chair. "You would need to produce proof you are whom you say you are for us to discuss things further." No emotion, no warmth.

"I'm going to have to bring proof I am whom I say I am to a man I have shared a bed with for near forty years?" She glared back. "Yes, Mrs. Lewis, you need to do that. Otherwise, we would have to change his status in our system to a special code and no one can see him unless they bring something beyond identification." I stared at her badge. Her hair was short on it, her olive skin was so clean-looking. She propped her head on her left fist on the arm of the chair she rocked in. "Mrs. Lewis, I think that you should either leave the premises or talk to someone one."

I exhaled. I pressed my hands to my sinuses and tried to breathe. I thought about whom Ethylene was. It had to be this Ruby. I hated her. She didn't know what I had endured to still say I was Mrs. Lewis. She was not Mrs. Lewis, I don't care what Reuben said or whom he said it to. I was his wife, I was going to stay his wife. "Why should I leave?" I didn't look at her, didn't open my eyes. "I am staying here. I am looking to see my husband as soon as possible!" There was a tapping on the hardwood floor, I was irritated until I realized it was my own foot. Madison swiveled in her chair, looked at her watch. "Do you drink coffee?"

"No." She raised her eyebrows. "Soda?" I shrugged. "I could go for one." I sniffled. "Preference?" I licked my lips. "Cold." She stood with a small smile and turned towards the door. Her shoes didn't even squeak as she left. I searched the room. I found a telephone above my right shoulder in the chair where I sat. I stood, taking a deep breath—it seemed to unlock my chest. I held the beige receiver to my left ear and listened to the steady beep of the dial tone. "Mae. I'll call Maeghan."

I picked up the phone and called Maeghan. It rang, and I counted. Her cheery voice picked up and I started to leave a message, before there was a break in the recording. "Hello?" I heard rustling in the background and Johnathan. "Hello?" She was more impatient then. "Your father is at Saint Louis University Hospital." More rustling. "What?! What happened? Mom?" I took a deep breath and started again. "He's in room 908 on the ninth floor. I need, I need you to go to my house and get the red clutch in my closet and bring it here." I heard slamming and crying. I didn't know if it was her or Johnathan the tears came from as the I tried not to cry in the receiver. "Just wait at the nurse's station if you get here before Brian." I wiped my eyes. "Please hurry, Mae." I hung up, leaned against the wall, yet holding the receiver. I needed to call Carolyn. I needed to call Brian. I needed to see Reuben.

I took another deep breath and called Carolyn. It was Tuesday, she would be at work at her catering company. I would call her at home and leave a message and call her at *Zelda's*. I looked around the room for a clock. I found a red rimmed one behind the desk and looked at my gold watch to make sure it was almost six in the evening. I was sure I could call her at home and get her. There were already too many people whom only had an idea as to what was really going on. I needed to keep the lid, control what was going on and who would all know what. I knew she would be on her way home anyway, so the message would be there when she got in. I rushed to dial her home number as the door opened again.

Ms. Hayden came back in with a Pepsi and a tea. She handed me the Pepsi. I opened it as Carolyn's answering machine clicked for a message. There was another voice that chimed the message service was full. I took a swig of the Pepsi to force the dryness away that crept up the back of my throat. I slammed down the receiver and retook my perch on the beige loveseat beneath it. I cradled the phone receiver as I dialed Brian's pager number and left a message for his answering service and called my home number and left a message in case he came back to get his truck. "Brian, it's Mom. Dad's at SLUH hospital. Room 908. Please get the red clutch from my closet, the one behind the albums.

She sat there just looking at me, looking sorry at me. I wanted to see my husband. I wanted my children. I needed my red clutch that had all the important papers in it, so I could set this situation as right should be. As I always, I had make it right. This feeling reminded me of when I was a girl and my father came in from gambling and drunk. I had to make sure my mother didn't hear him, or that he wouldn't hit her if he lost too much money. I always had to make it better, smooth everything out, shape what people heard and knew. Madison spoke first. "Is your husband well?" I drank my Pepsi. "He's in the hospital. I'm going to guess no." She smiled at me, smug and knowing. "Would you say he's competent?"

"Yes."

"And how long have you been married?"

"We just celebrated our thirty-fifth wedding anniversary."

She took another sip. "Unless this is greatest con, and you are indeed psychotic, my professional opinion is your husband has severe dementia, I am not sure if it is Alzheimer's." She caught my glance. "And I think you're scared." We stared at each other, I heard my soda bubble in my hand. "Your concern is appreciated, but unneeded." I adjusted my shoulders, making my back straight. "My children are coming. They are bringing paperwork to show just how badly you all have mishandled this." I sipped my flattening soda. "I don't want to call my husband, but I will." Madison wasn't looking at me, she was making notes, her jean covered legs crossed. "I am not afraid to call my lawyer! I am his wife. I know him better than anyone. If you want papers, I'll get papers. I'm going to the lobby and wait for them."

I smoothed my slacks and red cardigan when I stood. "I will see my husband tonight, Ms. Hayden." I turned and got my purse and put it on my left shoulder. "Whom must I show this paperwork to in order to see him and have his information updated?" She stood, more comfortable in her lab coat and badge. "You would have to show me. I'm the social worker on-call." She smoothed her collar on her lab jacket. I pulled my purse close, adjusting the strap on my left shoulder. "Fine. Will I need your card to contact you, or would it be better for you, Ms. Hayden?"

She stood, walking towards the shut door, opening the door to free us from mutual presence. "I'll come back to the floor if I'm paged." She produced a pager from her pocket, shifting it in her left hand before putting it back in her pocket. "Carrie is actually his nurse for the rest of shift. I am not sure whom his night nurse will be. I will make sure I leave a note, so they can contact me." I went through the door back towards the elevator.

****

I waited in the at lobby for two hours. I made Tori let me use her phone at least six times. I didn't want the snacks she offered. I didn't want anything else to drink. I wanted my documents, so I could see my husband. As I went to the desk again, Tori averted her eyes but looked up when she heard someone scream. "Mom!" I heard Brian yelling through the lobby and I ran from the Information desk to hug him. I told him what was going on, told him what the hospital did to me. He wiped my eyes again. "I just wanted to see your Dad! I just want all this bullshit to end! By God, I just want it to end!" He held me to shush me more than comfort me. "Mom, it's okay. It's okay. I came with Mae." I looked up at him, saw he was worried and scared. "It was Mayday that went to get this clutch. That's why Dad calls her Mayday, right? She always does the hard stuff easy."

He kept his arm around me and we made our way to the main elevator. He pushed the UP button and we waited for the doors to open, I saw the wave of other distressed looking people as they emptied the elevator car. Brian held my hand as we went in, kept it as the doors shut. "She called Carolyn. She's coming. I have the red clutch." It felt like his first day of school at Reed Elementary School again. I remembered how scared and mad he was. I smiled remembering how brave he tried to be. I remembered I tried not to cry when I had to leave him. "I'll be like a lion, Mommy. I'll be like a lion." His dad had taught him that phrase whenever he was scared. "Lions may be scared, but they never show it. Be a lion."

Be a lion. His left hand gathered let my hand go for a second to hand me the red clutch from his right hand. "So, they wouldn't let you see him at all?" I rummaged through the clutch. "No. I have to show my marriage license to the on-call Social Worker, Madison Hayden. She's a hateful twit." Brian giggled as the doors opened. My heart jumped, and I looked at the glowing floor number on the elevator board. "Nine." I closed my eyes and exhaled to steady myself again. I found the sepia colored certificate with his name at the top of it. "Got it!" Brian looked over at me, his baseball cap backwards, jeans and a white tee shirt and kissed my cheek. "Good. Mae and Carolyn should be here shortly. What's the nurse's name?"

I took out the license and dropped the clutch as the elevator came to a stop. "*That* harpy's name is Carrie, I'm not sure who it is now." Brian guffawed as the doors opened. I walked towards the waiting area, grateful for the blissful darkening room with its windows and city lights everywhere, among the quiet setting of the white cubed furniture. "I handle this, Mom. You go ahead and sit." I frowned and looked at Brian. Reuben's eyes icy and strong peering back into my face.

I had my purse tight and the clutch tighter in my right hand. "No!" I shook the clutch at Brian. "No! I am. I want that little twig to see what she had allowed to happen on her watch!" I walked towards the same side of the nurse's station, watched the buzz of the hive of blue and maroon scrubs. "Hey!" I screamed, slamming the large envelope clutch the white counter. "Where is Carrie?!" A black nurse looked up at me from the central table among the other activity, walking over to me with raised her eyebrows, she answered me with snark and attitude. "Carrie is at gone for the day. Is there something I can do for you?" I narrowed my eyes at her. "I need to speak to Madison Hayden. I was told to see my husband she needed documentation to have his chart updated."

I took the license out of her clutch and shook the license near her face. "Now, I have it. Page her, goddammit!" The other nurses, new faces, who hadn't been there when I was so rudely treated hours ago, turned to look. "Okay, ma'am." Her badge read Toshia. "You need to calm down. I see you're upset, but I'm going to ask you to be patient. There's a waiting area by the elevator. "She picked up the black receiver to dial a number, after looking away from me. I saw she had a little graying at her temples in the upswept bun she wore. "Page on-call Social Worker to 9 South, please." She hung up the phone and looked back at me. The navy scrubs she wore seemed to darken as her voice became sterner. "I will tell her where you are. Your name?"

I leaned over desk. "I am Mrs. Reuben Michael Lewis!" I dropped the license on the desk below the upper counter to table below, taking the clutch with me. After I hissed the words, I turned to see Brian at the end of the hall, his eyes were ghost wide. I walked past him gesturing to the waiting area. "I'll be waiting on Social Work." Brian said nothing. He quickened his pace to grab my hand again. He guided me to a seat in the far corner of the room where there were green sofa chairs. He fumbled with the red clutch as he took a seat in the windowsill. "Mom?" He looked at the ground. "You may want to get a drink before you look in this thing." I scoffed and snatched it from him. "Brian, I have had this bag for almost thirty years. I know everything in it."

I put my hand out for him to give it back. He looked at the floor as he handed it to me. On top was a yellowed newspaper article. I licked my lips and read aloud under the caption of black woman with a flower in her hair, white dress. "Ethylene Gibeaux shines in her Gypsy Hand set." I looked at Brian, and back again at the article. "Ethylene Gibeaux, also known as Ruby, is known for her local vocal talent to make any song her own. Especially the song, *My Man Made Me* by a local composer, Samuel 'Jack' Robinson." I looked at Brian, whom had begun to cry. The moment was broken when he got up to great his sisters. They all cried together when Carolyn and Maeghan stepped off the elevator.

Chapter 11-Early May 1997

Reuben lay in the hospital for an entire week. From the end of April until the beginning of May. I visited him every day, Wednesday April 30th to Wednesday May 6th. I made sure his face was washed, he had been bathed. I asked about medicines and medication dosages. I talked to doctors. I yelled at nurses. I helped him go to the bathroom. I spoke to him in hushed tones. I reminded him of who I was at least once a day for seven days. I told him how long we had been married. On nights he couldn't sleep, I smuggled in some sleeping pills, or his Alzheimer's medication from home to put in the ice cream I would request for him.

One doctor, a young doctor, Dr. Joseph Wheeler, came in with a nurse one night while rounded, unsure if I was sleeping. I had covered my head in one of the blankets Maeghan I gotten me from home. I had seen him several times on night shifts, meandering in in and out of Reuben's room during this unfortunate hospital stay. He was young, wore dark glasses, and reminded me of Peter Parker out of the Spider-Man comics Brian and Carolyn read as children.

This Tuesday night, with his discharge in sight, I slept upright in the chair. As he spoke, I turned myself towards the window in his room, staring into the nighttime city lights and listening to everything. I overheard Dr. Wheeler talking to one of the nurses the bruises he had on his chest when he came in. Dr. Wheeler remarked he was happy he was improving but was wary that it had taken him so long to improve. "He should have been home days ago. I'm glad he's going home tomorrow." He spoke to a nurse whom answered his questions in a soft voice, and I didn't turn in my chair to recognize the voice. "Did his wife say he was like this? Him being this lethargic his normal?" I didn't hear the nurse answer. "Glad those bruises are healing. I guess he hit that dashboard harder than his wife thought. I'll make a point of checking on him before he'd discharged today."

I was glad he was leaving in the morning also. It was the kids' idea we all take shifts staying overnight after the first night fiasco of trying to see him. I had decided I would stay with him the last night. I drifted off to sleep again, I don't know how long, but I woke up to strange voices. When I turned over, I saw black girl whom I thought had to be Maeghan's age. When she started singing, I knew who she was. It was Tamera, she worked the overnight shift, and had been assigned to Reuben every night he was admitted. I saw how her looked at her, it was the look of lust, peace and comfort. Every time she came in, she sang, or she hummed. She did runs of gospel songs. Tamera sounded like a bird. His eyes would always open when he heard her voice.

This night, Reuben's last night at Saint Louis University Hospital, she came in. I watched her, listened to her hum as she took his vitals. It had to be after midnight. I watched her with him from my chair, wrapped in a blue blanket. I watched him stir as his heart monitor beeped faster as she touched his right arm to take his blood pressure. "Hi, Mr. Lewis. It's Tamera. I'm going to take your vitals real quick." I saw his eyes flutter and he reached over and touched her hand. He touched her hand! I bit my lip and kept watching, feeling rage course through me as fast as my blood did. Her singing settled him better than me being just feet away.

Brian alerted me to this little relationship his first night with his father, Thursday, it was May 1st. He told me and Maeghan when we came to relieve him Friday morning. Maeghan thought it was harmless, and suggested she do that night and Saturday. I remember glaring at Tamera as she smiled at me as Brian wrapped his arm around me as we left. I mouthed 'black bitch' as she turned her head back to a chart she was writing in. I watched them interact this last night. Tamera turned on the light over his bed, I saw that her hair was this dark auburn tint, long and hung about her shoulders with headband. She was humming. As she put on the blood pressure cuff, and Reuben stared at her, smiled. Even his eyes looked to be shinning. His head lulled, but said nothing, just looked at her.

I heard the monitor she wheeled with her inflate the cuff he wore, and she had smiled back at him. "Keep singing." He whispered. Tamera smiled again. "I'll sing something soft and low Mr. Lewis." She started singing, tying a knot in the sheet at the end of the bed.

"Don't explain...

You know that I love you
And what love endures
All my thoughts of you
For I'm so completely yours

Cry to hear folks chatter
And I know you cheat
Right or wrong, don't matter
When you're with me, sweet".

There was thunder then, it was overcast when I came in and God finally let it rain. I told my granddaughters there was no need to fear storms, God and the angels were protecting them. I had no idea who would protect me in this situation with their grandfather. He wasn't on the oxygen anymore and his color was returning. She pulled back from him when he tried to touch her cheek. I watched as she finished her work, removing the blood pressure cuff, writing down her numbers.

Tamera continued to hum while she tucked him in. "You sang so good tonight, doll. You sang so good." Tamera smiled and said. "Thank you, Mr. Lewis." Tamera looked at him, set his hand back down on his belly when he reached for her again. She turned and left, turning out his light. I got up and went after her. I saw her walking down the hall with the same machine she had used with Reuben. "Tamera!" I choked out. She turned and looked at me, shroud in a green blanket and walked over to me. "Are you okay, Mrs. Lewis?" She looked concerned as she moved towards me. "Don't sing to my husband anymore, do you hear? Do not sing to him anymore!" She furrowed her brow and then relented. "It calms him down when he's restless. I did--"

"I don't care what it does! Don't sing to him anymore! I am his wife, not you or anyone else in this godforsaken place! Me!" I heard footsteps closing in on where we stood. It was Natalie, a short blonde with a high ponytail, and red-rimmed glasses. I had seen her on my second night there. "Is there something wrong, Tamera?" Tamera held my eyes, her sight now a stare at me from head to toe. "No, Natalie. I'm okay. Just doing my vitals." She turned and went into the next room, 909. Natalie stood looking at me, adjusted her stethoscope draped over her neck. "Is there a problem, Mrs. Lewis? It's about two in the morning." I swallowed hard. I pointed to the door Tamera had just entered. "I don't want her to come back in my husband's room! I don't want her in here!"

Natalie looked at the closed door Tamera had gone through and back at me. "What did she do?" "She sang to my damn husband! he sang to him! Can't you keep the negro harlots you employ under control around white men? We are to be leaving in the morning! I don't want her back in his room!" I yelled. Natalie looked at the floor and then back at me. "I'll pass that on to the other nurses and our supervisor." I wiped my face, feeling the weary tears coming over my cheeks. "Do that! Don't let that black bitch back in here!" I turned and went back to Reuben's room and I shut the door to find him sleeping sound as I turned the overhead light on.

I took a deep breath and thought how easy it would be to smother him. I saw how the staff had turned on the machines, turned off the machines. I saw how the IV pumps worked. I could simply just put me out of my misery. I heard my voice in a hiss. "Traitor." I reached for the extra pillow at the foot of the bed, squeezed it in my right hand, thought about how quick it would be to snuff his life out. "You're a goddammed traitor!" I screamed.

While I watched his chest rise and fall, I pulled the pillow to my chest. I watched him breathe, angry he was still breathing. "Fucking traitor." I said, tossing the pillow at his face. I left the room, still shrouded in my blanket and bare feet. I headed to the sitting room by the elevators. I looked at the storm that was raging and decided to call Brian and ask if he could please pick up his father from the hospital.

****

The Friday following Reuben's discharge from the hospital, I called Barbara still in my red robe. Her machine picked up. "Barbara Lewis Redding, you need to come and see me as soon as you are well and goddammed able! I know who she is!" I closed my eyes, breathed again. "I know your there, and you know I'm here. Bye!" I went to the broom closet and got my cigarettes and took the red ashtray from the window sill and made my way to the kitchen table. I would be ready when she came. I knew she would come.

I smoked, enjoying the cigarettes as they burned in my hand. I watched the smoke swirl, and the ashes drop into the ashtray. I smoked and watched and listened to the grandfather clock. It was 10 a.m. when I called Barbara. Cigarette in hand, taking my ashtray with me, ascended the stairs to go to the bedroom for the red envelope from the dresser. I went to my perch at the kitchen table again, lit another cigarette. I looked at the ends placed in the ashtray. I was at number three. I didn't care. I carefully looked over the articles in the clutch. All yellowed, all either with her name or face. There had to be ten or more photos of her. Article clippings, folded notes, a matchbook.

I smoked the third cigarette, inhaling deep like I used to. The clock chimed again. It was about 11:30 a.m. I remember Barbara's voice on the answering machine, how flat and unaffected it sounded. The phone rang, I moved to answer it. "Hello?" there was as an exasperated noise at the end of the receiver. "I'll be there about one." It was Barbara. "Fine. I'll be here." She hung up the phone before I could. Walking back towards the kitchen table, I examined the scraps of paper, the phrases he had underlined. "Gypsy Hand Night Club." I tapped my ashes, I ran over in my mind where that club would have been.

I paced around the table, smoking and in thought. I wanted to know what Barbara knew. I needed to know what she knew, how long she has known it. I went upstairs to shower, putting the cigarette out on the first article Brian had shown me, and I glowered as I watched her face and body be consumed by the light of my cigarette. As I went up the staircase, there was a knock at the door. I went down the stairs again, careful with my steps. I looked in the mirror on the landing of the stair before the last six stairs. I pinched my cheeks and smoothed my bobbed hair. I went to the door, looking through the peephole. It was Maeghan. I opened the door to her beaming. "Morning, Mom." She hugged me and kissed my cheeks.

"I came from seeing Dad at Brian's house." She sat at the dining room table, where all my evidence laid. Her hair was down in her face and clad in jeans and sneakers. "Where is Johnathan?" She didn't look up at me. "With his Dad." She walked toward the pile of clippings on the green kitchen table. I locked the door and went to sit next to her. I went to my cigarettes again, secure in my left pocket. I closed my left hand around them, exhaled. "Is this her?" Maeghan whispered. I looked away, I held my unlit cigarette in my right hand. "She's pretty." I glared at her, walking towards her and my empty seat. "No, she's black." Maeghan looked at me like I was dirty. "Really, Mother!" I slammed my cigaretted hand on the table. "Really nothing! This woman is ruining my life, and I don't know if she's dead or not!" I leaned against the wall, eyes to the back door. "I really hope she is."

Maeghan looked at me before she gathered all the clippings in front of her. "We've decided to find her." She clasped her hands on top of the clippings. I snuffed out my cigarette. I glared at her, roasting her with my gaze. "You will do no such thing!" She glared back at me. "It makes no difference. We have decided to find her." We sat there, stalemated. "You will not find her. You don't even know where to start!" She smirked at me. "We are going to find her, Mom. You want everything so perfect, looking just right. Now," she snorted. "you don't know what to do. Everything isn't perfect. Can't be perfect. You tried to make

Dad perfect."

She stood up, bared up against the table. I swear to God she was grinning when she spoke again. "You can't stand that you weren't the one!" I walked over to her and slapped her and slapped her again. "Shut up! Shut up!" I put my finger in her face. "If you do this Maeghan, I will never forgive you! I will never forgive you for ruining my marriage!"

She didn't even clutch her cheek as it reddened, she blinked hard. I saw that Lewis hardness come over her face. She was so much like her father. "I'm doing this for my father. He deserves some happiness before he leaves the world. Lord knows he's entitled to it!" She returned to her seat. I pointed to the pictures and clippings on the table, "She is not your mother! No matter how many black children you have with the boy you're with, this woman is not your mother!" I took another cigarette from my pocket, to lit. I put it out on an article that talked about the Gypsy Hand.

"What the fuck, Mom!" Maeghan got up and went to the door and took the cigarette burned article before she turned to leave. "Where are you going?" I followed her to the door, snatched her arm. "I am your mother. How can you do this to me? Our family? Your father!" She snatched away from me to unlock the door. "The same way you slept with Mr. Stevenson, the fifth-grade teacher at

Reed. Remember that?" My stomach began to roll and churn. I hadn't thought about Gordon in years. "And he called the house, and I answered, and he said, what was it?" she tapped her chin, and I fought the urge to beat her with my fists. 'I can't wait to taste you again, when is Reuben leaving for the weekend?' Yeah. Because he thought your thirteen-year-old daughter was his mistress."

"Get out! Get out!" I snatched the front door open, pushed her out of it. "I am doing this for my father. That's the least I can do." She went through the door and to her black Jetta. "I'm doing it the same way you cheated on him! Easily!" I watched her walked to her a Green Mazda, probably Johnathan's, a beeline from my front door. As Barbara parked behind the Reuben's truck, she almost ran into her aunt. I heard Maeghan's tires squeal as she veered down the street. I slammed the door and went back to the table. I saw tears on the cigarette box. I was wiping it on my robe as Barbara walked in carrying a small black box.

She sat across from me, black collared blouse and khakis and a red flat shoe. I saw her run a hand through her fresh cut copper hair. I took out a cigarette and held in my left hand on my thigh. Barbara cleared her throat and kept her head down. "Can you make tea?" She whispered. I looked at her before I obliged and prepared the tea kettle. As I turned on the water, I filled the kettle and turned the stove on. I took out two sunny yellow mugs and my Lipton tea to accompany on the counter. I walked away after adjusting the fire under my red kettle. I sat on my chair again. I watched her as she produced a black box from the floor where her purse sat. She decided to occupy the seat Maeghan had. It was probably the best thing for her to do—be a far away from me as possible. I was in a war and needed to know where and who my enemies where.

"Robert died in Boston, after Korea, he was our older brother. He wanted to be a doctor. Reuben was the youngest boy and idolized him. When he died, he wanted to be a doctor. Y'know, for legacy." She set some pictures face down next to her right hand. "He wanted to go to Washington University, because Robert wanted to go." She had letters, other clippings and photos. I looked down at my unlit cigarette, thirsty for it. "But..." she slid the pictures over. I turned them over in my hand, still not yielding my cigarette. The kettle whistled, and she moved to stop the noise. "Leave it!" I shouted.

I saw a small stack of pictures. There were pictures of a black girl playing the piano, a photo labeled *New Year's Eve* 1956, it had water marks all over it. It was the third picture which got my attention. I took the picture into the kitchen, it was a picture of a young man, a much younger Reuben with this woman on his lap. The black and white photo didn't tell the color of her hair. She had full lips, and a black dress, and heels. They were smiling, and his arms were wrapped around her, her feet in the air. On the back of it was written *Keys and Ruby.*

Gypsy Hand, 1957.

I took the picture and laid it the flame after I moved the kettle. I watched it melt and lit my cigarette with it before I put smoldering picture in the sink. I opened the backdoor, feeling confided and stuffy. I heard the water pour into a cup. I heard scoffing behind me "You really think you can control this too, don't you?" I exhaled into the direction of the backdoor. I refused to look behind me. "You can burn this picture, but you haven't burned her from his memory. Brian told me today he was asking for her, that he had seen her in the hospital." She pushed past me and got honey and a spoon from corresponding cabinet and drawer.

I turned to her, inhaled my cigarette, next to the open back door. "Did he love her?" She walked away from me and I stomped after her. "Answer my question, Barbara!" She sat in her seat again, as calm as if this were English High Tea. "If you have any respect for me, *ever had* any respect for me, answer my question! Did he love her, ever love her?" She slipped her tea, looking at the black box. "What do you think, Katherine? I was fourteen, fifteen when he met her. He took me to the club one night to have me watch her sing." She stirred her tea, scraping the sides of the cup.

"She was amazing, I have not heard anyone else like her sing." She looked up at me. "He loved her, like I had never seen." I sat down, looking at the face down item. "He loved her. Ha! They couldn't even be together then! What did your—" Barbara put her hand up. "My mother didn't approve but didn't discourage it. My father had a black sister-in-law in California whom we saw from time to time. It was on a trip there where Reuben first heard jazz. A Billie Holliday Deca album." She sipped her tea again.

"I don't know what Reuben did for money in high school but when my father had a stroke, but he was able to fend for himself and help me get through school." I sat there and flipped over a scrap of manila paper, ink faded. I "Where did you find this, hide this?" I looked at the handwriting. Barbara sipped her tea loud. "I kept them because I was asked." I took in the letter and the words they made on the manila paper. I made out *love you, Shug* and the letter **E** signed at the bottom.

I sat there numb. I ran over everything in my mind. Every moment I thought my own, and my belonging to him. "I don't know what you're pulling, Barbara, but I don't believe you." I slid the letter back towards the piles of other items. I felt my eyes burning, my ears were hot, thought the room was spinning. "I don't believe you!" I pushed the papers and pictures away and ran up the stairs. I hung on the bathroom sink and watched my eyes water, with that same water escaping. I hung on the side of the sink.

I thought my heart was in my mouth it was beating so hard. I heard footsteps up the stairs. "My brother getting Alzheimer's disease was the best thing that happened to him! The absolute, best thing! "her footsteps determined as she came to where I was. "He's tried to be everything you wanted for so long, and it seemed not enough!" I glared at her reflection. She stood behind me, arm folded across her chest in the same bathroom, on the same floor she gave me an emotional anchor for a year ago. "How can you say that? How can you say that?" I heard fury in my voice, it echoed in the bathroom. "You have made everything about you! Holidays. Birthdays. Everything orchestrated by the Grand High Bitch Katherine Lewis!" I bit my lip and shook my head, looking at the sink's silver drain. "And when you cheated on him after Brian was born? You begged him to take you back, begged him, Katherine!" I wiped my eyes, snorted loudly, feeling slickness leave my nose. "I was stressed, I was overwhelmed. I was lonely he was always working!"

Barbara moved into my space in the bathroom. "He was working because you didn't want to!" She turned me to look at her. "You cheated on him again with that teacher at Reed Elementary! You planned to leave him for Gordon!" She sighed, still screaming. "He grew up with him!" I tried to move past her to the bedroom, the house felt like it was spinning so fast it may go to Oz. "He has done everything you have asked him to almost forty years! Now the moment he needs you, all you can think about is yourself!" Barbara grabbed my right shoulder, and I snatched myself from her claw grasp. I made my way towards the window on the other side of the room, Reuben's side of the bed. Barbara blocked the doorway to the bedroom, arms across her chest.

"And I gave up teaching for him because of Gordon! I gave up catering to please him! I helped with this god forsaken business! It's more mine than yours! What about me!" I pointed to my chest. Barbara smirked. "He built. That my brothers and his son built." I looked at her, wanted to spit on her. "I'm buying your goddammed share, and I'm done with you! I don't have to take this from you, Barbara!" She rolled her shoulders like boxers do during difficult matches. "I'd like to see your try! The company is in trust while my brother is ill. You're not the only one that knows lawyers." She grinned, "I'm interim CEO." I turned from her, to her, grabbed a suitcase from my closet.

I started to throw clothes and shoes on the bed, along with underwear. I needed to leave, I had to get out of the house, the city, the state. I couldn't be there anymore. I couldn't think. I couldn't hear my own thoughts. She watched me from the door, look of pity, rage and contempt on her face. "She's alive, Katherine." I glowered at her, and she laughed. I saw that same hardness in Barbara's face I had just seen on Maeghan's earlier. I heard my own heart in my ears. "She's alive." She repeated it slower, made sure I heard every word.

"Everything I did, I did for my family! How dare you judge me!" I looked at Barbara's face and only saw her brother in it—no sympathy, no understanding, nothing. "Just like when you told your children you wanted white grandchildren?" I looked at the pile of clothes on the bed. "How you *wrestled* with Maeghan even being pregnant by a black man?" She looked at me, we caught eyes again. "Just like when you told me you hated that Brian got a black girl pregnant, and told me you wanted no Lewis mutts?" "Don't turn this around on me Barbara Redding! Your brother betrayed me!"

Barbara moved from the door, towards the bed, her green eyes never left my face. "Brian came to me devastated you gave the girl he got pregnant, what was her name?" She rolled her eyes and head around the thought. "Hope. That was her name, Hope. You gave that girl money to get an abortion, and she did!" I I started throwing the pile of clothes and shoes from the bed at her. She moved further back to the door. "Brian came to me with fury because you had given the girl he had gotten pregnant money for an abortion! Remember that?" Her voice was cool and definite. I looked at her, wanted to slap her, hurt her, claw her eyes out. "I wanted their lives smoothed, and they wouldn't have to go through anything they didn't have to! I'm their mother!"

Barbara shook her head at me, sighed, and spoke in a dry tone. "This isn't about you. This is about Reuben. Brian and I know you have been giving him extra medication, and I think you tried to kill my brother in that car accident!" She walked over to me, and my mouth was dry, hands turned into fists. "You were their mother when you cheated on my brother. You were their mother when you slept with your childhood sweetheart too after Brian was born, and Reuben found out." She down to my left hand, looked at my ring. "You wanted everything that came with being a Lewis. You wanted the influence, the stature, and you saw what my brother was going to be!"

She backed me into the wall near the headboard on Reuben's side of the bed. She moved closer to me, and I tried to steel myself. "You wanted to be a doctor's wife. You wanted this life to be easy!" Barbara poked my chest, and I slapped her hand away. She backed away from me, putting her manicured hand at the bed's cherry oak footboard. "You are afraid, because now you wonder were you ever really the one he wanted." I refused to cry. "You know nothing, Barbara! You have been trying to take my children since you found out you were like a desert! Barren and dry!"

She let her hand drop She turned and left me in the bedroom. "I bet it kills you, too—keeps you up at night." She chuckled. "Stay away from my brother, Katherine. This is your only warning. I'll be serving you with paperwork on behalf of the company next week." She turned, looking back at me, with that look her mother used to give me. I stood there, planted and irritated. "He's my husband, Barbara. He is my husband! You can't keep him from me."

She smirked at me. "That's true, but I can keep his money from you and that grave you dug for him closed!" She started down the stairs, let me with my heart breaking in my chest. "I hope you never find her! You'll never find her! The hell with you, Mae, Brian and Reuben! The hell with all of you!" I heard Barbara's footsteps stop and then the front door slam. I looked at the pile of clothes sitting as dirty laundry on my bed. I walked around to my side of our bed, called Ruth, fuming. It was Friday, she was at work. I dialed her extension. Her secretary, Laura answered. "Good Afternoon, Bright Law Firm." "Mrs. Bright, please." There was a slight pause, then Ruth's voice. "Ruth Bright." I sat on the bed, energy wiped from me. "I need your help, quickly." I could hear her eyebrows furrow. "What's wrong?" I exhaled. "Why?" I bit my lip, closed my eyes, "I'm going to need an attorney. I'm suing my sister-in-law for custody of my husband." Ruth laughed. "I'm serious, Ruth. Barbara is freezing me out, and turns out this woman, this Ruby is real!"

"I'll be over after work." I walked around to the window, needing to know Barbara had gone. "I may want to go shooting." Ruth laughed again. "I thought you didn't want to do that anymore—your Dad and all." I saw Barbara get into her black Jetta, looking up at the sky, with that black box under her arm. "I know, but I'm out of practice."

Ruth prattled on about schedules and what I needed and what was actually going on with the company, but all I could think about was getting Reuben's brother's .38 Special found in the attic and cleaned. Barbara declared war on me. If I couldn't get the black girl in my husband's head, I was going to figure out how else to get her out.

Intermission

St. Louis, Missouri

(1956-1957)

March 1956

St. Louis, Missouri

"I wanna get married." She said, rolled on her side, clutching the pillow blue neon light spilling along her back. She nestled in the cover, turned to looked over at him, shirtless and smoking his Lucky Strikes. "Keys, you hear me?" He looked over at her, grinned shirtless and smirking. He touched her naked thigh. "I heard you, doll. I heard you." She rolled over, happily unclad and before him, red hair freshly pressed fell about her shoulders. He touched her brown face, the neon hotel lights spilling into room. "I gotta pay Levi for another week." She purred under his hand. "I know." He countered. "Go get cleaned up, doll. You gotta sing tonight don't cha?" She nodded, smiled. "Keys, you are the end." She leaned forward, kissed him bold and slow, his hands fisted in her hair. He looked at her, cupped her face, nose to nose, kissed her again.

"You know Sam Robinson, y'know, Jack? He has this song for me to sing tonight." She kissed him again, moving from her resting position to the side of the bed where he sat. She stood to retrieve the pink robe left on the back of the chair by the open window. She sauntered to the chair, grinning, knowing he was watching her. "Ethylene Lewis." She whispered as she put on her robe, leaving the sash undone. She went to the bathroom, smoothed her face in the mirror. Looked at him from the bathroom, cigarette behind his ear. Keys moved towards her, watching and grinning. He slipped in behind her, kissed the back of her neck, licked her ear right ear. He grinned, growled low as he smoothed over her covered hip. She moaned. "Keys." She whispered, putting her hands over his. He nuzzled the robe from her left shoulder, planted slow kisses. "Reuben." She giggled. "You gotta let me go some time, flyboy." He chuckled in her neck. "Nah. Never. You will always be mine, doll! Ain't ever a way around that." She smirked down at the floor. "I know. You'll die lovin on me." She looked at their reflection in the mirror of them together, relaxed against his bare chest and smiled. Ruby squeezed his hand as it lay on her left hip. "Do you love me?" she asked, barely a whisper, looking at his blue eyes as he blinked slow in the mirror. There were kisses along her shoulder blades, soft and lingering.

"Ruby, there is nobody I love like you. Look up at me, babydoll." He made her meet his eyes in the mirror, seeing the water in them. "I love you. Since I saw you, I think. You think a color would stop me, and make you and me some closet case?" He spun her around to face him, cupped her face. "Ethylene Gibeaux, you are what I look forward to every stinkin day! Hearing you sing is like," he looked off, voice quiet. "Is like hearing the sky open and angels talking just to me, you dig it?"

She leaned back against the small white sink, smiled as the tears fell. "You know what I mean, Keys. I still ain't met your Mama, and your sister can't keep a lid on all these things she sees downstairs when you bring her." Reuben smirked at her, eyed her up and down. "Barbara will tell her, what I want her to tell her." She smirked, looking up, watching him speak. "Babs. She likes to be called Babs now." Reuben giggled, his eyes searching hers and her body again. "You're good for her, she digs you." She turned from him, and went back to the mirror, and picked up the black brush and started to do her hair. "Baby, what time is it?" He stared at her, hearing her and not moving sitting on the side of the bathtub. "Babydoll, it's about time for me to go, so you know what time it is. About nine. I've been here all day with you." Ruby laughed. "You ain't complained. You loved every bit of everything I gave you." She gave him a pouty look over her shoulder before walking to her closet. She walked the length of the room; the size was more like an apartment.

Mr. Levi Williams owned the two-story building outright and rented the upper floors to some performers of the Gypsy Hand— 'constants' he called them. The Gypsy Hand had started as a night club in 1948, and an institution at 3624 Boyle Avenue. Ruby was becoming a popular local act, and Mr. Levi, as the constants called him gave her the small loft space right above the Gypsy Hand's front main floor. "Did that delivery make it to you today?" Reuben's voice echoed from the bathroom. She looked inside the maple doored closet and produced a cream and gold box. "Yeah, they came. Where did you find them?" She sat in the white upholstered other chair by the window, still robed and unclad underneath.

Ruby opened the box left on the chair for her, set it on her lap and pulled out a pair of red baby doll pumps. She turned them over in her hand, leaning over to turn on the lap on the small table covered by a blue tablecloth. He stood in the door way of the bathroom, black slacks and bare feet, smiling as she sat toying with her shoes. She looked up at him, unlit cigarette in his right hand which braced the door frame. "Try 'em on." Ruby stared at him, warmth in her cheeks. She leaned over the box, dropping it from her lap. She tried to slip on the shoe and it rubbed her heel. "Keys, you got the wrong size baby."

As she struggled with the left shoe, he saw his hand gaze over her ankle as he knelt at her feet. "What'chu doin, Keys?" He put his right hand under her foot and rubbed her heel. "If the story holds up, the princess needs help to put on her shoes." Ruby relaxed in her chair, pulling the robe closed, sighed softly as he rubbed her feet. "I saw the movie *Cinderella*, because Babs wanted to see when she was a younger kiddo." He grabbed the left shoe in his hand, motioning for her to relax in her chair. As she relaxed, she flexed her left foot in his left hand. Keys put delicate kisses along her toes and top her foot. He held her foot, kept kneeling and keeping her gaze. "The story says that this Prince Charming found the one that ran off with his heart with a shoe." He licked her ankle and got the left shoe. "Point your toes to me." Obeying, she pointed her painted pink toes as he slipped on the shoe. Ruby began modeling it on the carpet as he slipped the other on. "Looks like I found my girl." Ruby smirked, cupping her face on hands as elbows rested on her thighs. "And what will you do with her, now that you caught her, Prince Charming?" Reuben sat back on his haunches. "Well, the rules say we gotta get hitched, Cinderella."

She stood from her chair and walked past him, robe sweeping past his shoulder as she modeled in the mirror. Ruby looked at the shoes and grinned pointing the toes up and down. "A buddy of mine saw that actress Dorothy Dandridge in movie a while ago," he said. "He said he saw a picture of her with a pair of these on while he was in New York. I made him get me pair. Send 'em to you special. "Ruby spun in the brown cheval mirror and smiled, piling her hair on her head and posing. She strutted around her small space, making him grin in return. "Keys, as red as these are, I'm not Cinderella. I'm Dorothy." He stood and smiled coming behind her in the mirror. Reuben turned her with a flourish, catching her face to kiss her. "I love how you taste. The night I took you home, I knew—old myself---I don't want to die not knowing how you taste."

Ruby melded into him just as she had hours before. In those same hours where nothing existed but them and future stretched out wide and bright before them. She moaned into his neck as his hands found the small of her back. In clumsy step they fell back into the same warmth the linens on the daybed he bought her provided. He whispered in her ear, "Then Dorothy, let me come home." She echoed his name from the walls that housed this symphony of their together and opened her thighs to greet him. He put his nose to hers and kissed her bold and slow again. Ruby caught her breath, and said "Jack can wait, he's never on time anyway."

Reuben sat in the back, on his favorite red leather stool, swirling his Scotch and soda. He grinned as he watched her walk on stage, licked his lips as she found her place under the lights. The Gypsy Hand patrons erupted at as she shimmered under the stage light in her black gown. Her red hair, pinned up with a big magnolia flower in her hair, matched her lips. "Sang it, Ruby!" someone in the front shouted. "Sang it, Cher!" She smiled, nodded to the Carolyn, the young lady at the piano. It was her brother, Jack, who introduced them when Ruby had to drop a package at her house from her aunt, Linda, who was a seamstress.

Her brown skin, luminous under the light. "Ruby." He whispered, smiled up at the stage, watched her sway as she sang, legs peaking from under her dress. She had worn the shoes he had gotten her. He sipped his drink, watching those closest to the stage move tables and chairs to opposite sides of the room to begin to Lindy hop. She started to sing a song Carolyn wrote, *Get My Hands On You*. Carolyn played the upbeat melody on Levi's piano, her dark brown face alight as Ruby sang her scale before she started. "Ooh, if you don't love me now, you never will. But I bet if I get my hands on you, you will." She sang.

"Is she doing the whole set?" He asked the bartender. Mr. Levi laughed. He stood a little over six feet tall, with the white tee shirt damp from water. "You know she is." He chuckled, drying off glasses with a red rag, turning every so often to replace them on the top of the mirrored bar back. Reuben looked at cuckoo clock at the end of the bar. It was already 10. Her whole set would take her to 11:30 or midnight. "Okay." He downed the rest of his drink, sliding the tip under the coaster. "Levi, tell her I'll be back." Levi chuckled. "Aight, Keys. I'll tell her." Reuben put on his hat, and left, amidst Ruby's voice filling the Gypsy Hand club, out onto Boyle. Reuben crossed the street, to find phone booth two doors down with the light on and vacant. Putting in his dime, he dialed his brother, Nathan. "Hiya."

"It's me."

"You ready?" he asked.

"Yeah."

"Meet you by the farmers market in a 20."

Reuben phone hung up. Soulard Farmer's market was about 10 minutes from where he was. He could have this meeting and get back to Ruby in time for her last song. Reuben smiled at that. She was supposed to sing the new song tonight, this new creation by Carolyn's brother Jack, "My Man Made Me." Reuben walked back to his father's 1939 Plymouth, still secure in front of The Gypsy Hand. He started off towards I-44, his headlights bright as he drove. He turned the dial on the radio to a station he picked up every now and then that played Sarah Vaughn songs, he couldn't pinpoint it enough to memorize the dial number. He laughed when he heard *Whatever Lola Wants.*

Reuben exited the highway, parking a street over from the seventh street exit in front of a lamp post. He sat He knew the police where making rounds at this hour and wanted no issue. He wasn't there to buy a woman or hide with a woman or get rid of anything. He was here for access. He leaned against the brick wall that juxtaposed to his car, this way he could watch the car, the police and the street. As he waited, the light flickered, and he thought of Ruby. Ethylene Gibeaux. He knew she disliked her first name, and when she moved to St. Louis at age seventeen from New Iberia, she changed it. Reuben looked at his pocket watch. 10:30 p.m. Nathan should be there any second. He chuckled to himself remembering how he met her.

It was about six months ago, just after the fall. He and his two brothers were counting lottery numbers in the back room of the Sailor Den on Olive. A new waitress with red hair, and brown eyes busted in the room. "The coppers are here! Get cha asses in the safe room!" She slammed the door with the same force she had stormed through it. Dumping everything in pillowcases, they scrambled toward the back door, and one by one in a straight line through the narrow hallway to the blue door towards what the owner, John Lee, called The Count Room.

When they were through the door, they all listened for the evidence the all was still quiet. His older brother, Robert, turned on the overhead light bulb with a string, and dusted off the table. "C'mon Keys, we gotta divide this up." He looked over at his oldest brother, the dust in the air floating in front of his glasses. "Yeah, that's right you have kids to teach in the morning." Nathan laughed. "Some teacher. He's an educated number runner!" Reuben and his brother found chairs in the dim room, dumping out the pillowcases to count again. "Who was that broad?" Reuben asked.

"Oh, the colored girl?" Nathan asked while organizing the tally sheets, his blond hair glowing white under the light. "Ethylene. But no body calls her that." Robert laughed. "That's Ruby." Reuben slid Robert that week's lottery numbers picked out by Robert's wife, Alice "How long, she been here?" "A little while-- couple months. She just turned eighteen in May." Nathan still hadn't looked up from tallying numbers. Reuben grinned. "Cute." Nathan and Robert chuckled, "Easy Keys, her cousin, John, owns this joint. We got an agreement here." Robert said, pointing his pencil in his direction. He watched his brother with is glasses and messy brown hair. "Okay, Nate. I got 7, 4, 1, 87, and 9. Alice, sure can pick these numbers."

As Reuben counted, his mind went back to the red head whom had cursed them out minutes before. "What else does she do?" Robert looked over his glasses at his brother, his balding head and brown eyes firm. "She sings." Robert looked over at Nathan. "How many got close?" "Mary." Nathan answered. "The lush?" Robert answered, his suspenders and collared shirt glowing under the light which had begun to flicker brighter.

"No, the other one. The one whose brother got pinched for the boiler gin in January. Mary Umpstead." Robert smoothed his face. "Okay. $40 pay out. Anyone get 'em all?" Nathan scanned the list. "Nope." "Keys?" Reuben was still counting tens. "Reuben!" He looked at his brother, Nathan startled. "Yeah?" "We got one $40 pay out. What all we bring in?" "$440." Robert made motion for the money he hand in his hand. "Alright. $40 for Mary. $150 for John. $250 for us. That's about eighty bucks each." Reuben watched has his older brother divided the money among them, sliding each their portion. "I'll be back, I need to go to the bathroom." Nathan stood, pocketing his money and left, slamming the door. "Leave Ruby alone, Keys." Said is bother, taking an envelope from the pillowcase. "Let her be. You're like this money in my hand." Reuben looked up at him. "A fresh twenty." He slammed the money on the table. "Leave her alone, brother. Colored girl, or not."

Reuben smiled at the memory. He drove Ruby home that night to her house on 3612 Arsenal, a two-family flat. His brothers said the bus she would catch sometimes wouldn't stop because she was a colored girl, and they would have to take her home in the back seat if her no one else would. She stayed with her mother's sister, Linda. "Why they call you, Keys?" She said, her hand on the door, and he noticed how brown her eyes were. "Because I get what I want, in where I want." He had shrugged his shoulders like he had seen James Dean do. "Just like a set of keys." He had brushed her shoulder, just to touch her. Ruby laughed and rolled her eyes, as she let herself out the car. "Mm hmm. Bye, Reuben." He watched her saunter inside the duplex, going towards the right side, waited till she got in. Reuben swore she smiled at him when she before going inside.

There was a car slam then, quick footsteps. "Over here, Nate." His brother said emerging from the shadows on the opposite side of the street with a brown paper bag. "I got it." Reuben shook his head loose from thoughts of Ruby, made out Nathan's figure from the shadow and lamppost. "Got what?" Nathan materialized in front of him then. "The key money." He shook the bag at him. "What key money?" Nathan looked around. "Look, know how we've been talking about leaving and going West. Well, I got the money to start something up out there now."

"How?" Reuben furrowed his brow at his younger brother. "I've been doing some side work for a family in Ladue. You know, nothing fancy. Some number running, some errands, look out stuff." He took out his hands for the brown paper bag, looked at the money inside. "What family?" "I'd rather not say." Reuben's eyes got wider, looked back up at his brother who was grinning. "It's ten, ten grand. It's t That's enough that me, you and Robbie can get outta here and stop all this shit to keep current with stuff." Reuben sighed, closing the bag up, and heading to his car. It was enough he could attend college, maybe buy a house and start a real life. "I'll be at Robbie's house in an hour or so." Nathan disappeared into the darkness towards his car, yelling "Come there quick, Keys, okay! Ruby can wait. Don't catch any nails!"

Reuben checked his watch, it was just then 11 p.m. Ruby's set was almost over. Nothing about Ruby could wait, he thought. Nothing. He would go to his brother's house, but after he saw Ruby. It there was enough money to do some of the things he wanted to do, but not nearly enough money to do what he wanted to do. Reuben wanted to leave St. Louis, and two grand wouldn't be enough. He had been thinking of going West with his father's brother, Uncle Warren and Aunt Charlotte, whom loved it more when you called her, Charlie. Ruby wanted to leave, she wanted to go to New York, but he was determined to change her mind.

Ruby was his girl. He always made sure someone took her home if he couldn't, made sure no one came in her dressing room when she finished her set. Made sure Mr. Levi indeed paid her for all the set, and the $25 per week was paid to him for her room. Driving back to the club, he saw the neighborhood drunks, fighting under the lampposts, screaming and fist fighting. He took off his hat and smoothed his brown hair. He was almost back to her. Parking in the back of a police car, he walked toward the red door of the Gypsy Hand. He heard her voice before the door opened. As we went through, he nodded to Levi whom pointed him towards the direction of her dressing room. He took off his hat, sat on the green sofa chair and listened to her sing her version of Billie Holiday's *Don't Explain*. "My life's yours love, don't explain."

    Her set would be over soon. Reuben went to her closet and picked out her champagne colored robe and laid on blue upholstered chair he bought. He slipped his shoes off and jacket, placing them behind the bronze hooks of dark oak door. He smiled, remembering and confident she would be in his arms again, slick from the lights and sweat. Her ritual would begin when she opened the door: she would unpin her shoulder length hair, shake it out, kiss him. Ruby would get her soda water, prop her feet up on the ottoman, sigh deep in the chair. She would grin at him, ask him how long he had been there. He'd lie about either where he was or how long he had been waiting. He would kiss her, cup her face, and pull her into him from the chair. Ruby would giggle, say she loved him only to remind him how she couldn't wait to leave St. Louis.

June 1956

St. Louis, Missouri

Ruby sat at her aunt's table as she did her cards for the day. She turned nineteen the night before on the third. Her cousin threw birthday party for her the night before, at the Sailor's Den. With it being a Sunday, the Sailor's Den was closed for the day. She celebrated with a cake baked by John's wife, Lallie, Reuben with his brothers, and her friend from the Sailor's Den, Deborah. Reuben slow danced with her, humming and holding her close. He told her how much she meant to him, how happy she made him. John gave her a shot of boiler gin, saying now her 'liquor cherry' was popped. It was a ritual for all the employers or customers who were under twenty.

"Liquor cherry?" Reuben snickered, as Ruby leaned against the damp bar, holding her head. Her stomach swam, and her nose burnt but willed herself not to get sick. Reuben had laughed at her as she held her head all the way home. Ruby watched her aunt lay the gold-specked backed cards in systematic order, according to what the spirits told her. Ruby had known her own mother, Mae-Reavis, knew how to do the same thing, 'talk to the cards' they called it. But out of respect for her father, Oliver, her mother she never did it in his presence. "Conjurer don't ever get old, cher. The spirits got a lot to say." Ruby looked towards the window, watched the breeze tickle the red kitchen curtains. "Really, Auntie?" She heard the cards shuffle again. "Yes, really, cher. Really."

Ruby looked over to her aunt, studied her brown face, her dark hair with its patch of gray at the temple as she turned to lean against the farm sink. She looked at her dark blue housedress and was relieved she didn't look up at her. "I know it's in dese cards I see you and that white boy, Keys, gon be together forever." She flipped over the top four cards, studying their placement. "You in his heart cher, you in dere like a tree root!" Her aunt laughed, ignoring her niece's stare. Ruby stood from the sink and went to the Frigidaire. "You want some of this sweet tea, auntie?" She gave no answer save for the shuffling of the cards. Ruby set the glass pitcher on the table where her aunt worked, turned to get a mason jar from the talk white cabinet. "Watch that pitcher, girl! Hurry up and get that damn thing off where I'm working! I'm listening for spirits! I can't be mad and listen!"

Ruby poured her tea and replaced the pitcher in the Frigidaire. "Yep, y'all gon always be together." Ruby snorted. "Ethylene!" She turned to face her aunt, face hidden in her jar. Her Aunt Linda pointed a bony finger at her, breeze catching her sleeve. "Don't chu scoff at dese cards! The spirits come from God and God know everything! Keys gon be your husband in this life. Or he gon be your heart husband. Ain't no woman gon love him like you do! And he gon look and never find! Believe what I say, cher!"

Ruby sat at the table and watched with the cards. She licked the sugar from her lips and squeezed her Mason jar. "He don't love me like that, Aunt Linda." Her aunt snickered and shuffled the cards again. "Cher, look at dis table." Ruby turned to leave her drink on the farm sink counter, turning her body and attention back to her. "Shuffle dese cards, girl." Ruby swallowed. "Auntie, I don't want no reading! I don't need no reading. I ain't marrying Reuben!" Her aunt looked past her, through window to the shut red back door. "Shuffle the cards!" Ruby reached for the cards and shuffled the deck. "Three times, cher." Ruby shuffled and gave them back to her aunt. "Your grandmother taught me how to do my conjure. Your mama too. Those white women in New Iberia would come and see her and get truth from the spirits. You gon sit here and hear what they got to say, cher."

Ruby rolled her eyes, patted the scarf that covered hair. "Aunt Lin, I don't—" her aunt held her hand up, shushed her. "No. Hush up. The spirits is talking 'bout you." Ruby watched her deal face cards and numbers and she began to speak. "Reuben is your heart husband. He is what you want." She paused and looked intent at Ruby's face. "He love you, Ethylene. He always will." Ruby pushed away from the table and walked to the sink, mouth dry. "Lin, I ain't doubtin that. But what we gon do? He can't—marry me, we can't have nothing together unless we leave." She was swallowing hard, she stared out the window. "I ain't ready to be nobody's nothing."

Her aunt shuffled the cards. "Ask a question. Settle ya heart, cher." Ruby sighed and braced against the sink. "I—I don't know, auntie. I know I love him. I know that." She turned around, hands on her thighs. "He's good to me, he takes care of me. But...it's too many things up in the air. Too many things." Linda made a noise. "That ain't stop nobody. Colored or white. If he be in your heart, cher, God the only person that can pull him out." Ruby walked out of the kitchen, leaving her drink in the sink. Hot tears pushing their way out of her eyes. "I got a reading in a hour, make sure you don't come down here." There was card shuffling Ruby heard as she went to her room on the second floor. She was suddenly grateful her aunt owned the duplex. "Miss Charlotte scary about people hearing what the spirits tell her."

Ruby made it to the staircase, the air too thick to breathe in. "You sanging tonight, baby?" Ruby took a deep breath. "Yes ma'am. I'm sanging tonight." She bounded up the stairs, she went to the bathroom at the top of the stairs. She looked at the mirror. "A wife? Who wife?" She snorted and looked at the reflection. She remembered Reuben then. Remembered how it was now almost nine months since they had started courting. Ruby remembered telling him how she wanted to be married. She didn't need conjure for that. They needed a plan. She was saving money in the wall of her aunt's linen closet to leave St. Louis. She wanted to know if Reuben would go with her. She was unsure of how her mother think about her husband being a white man, and a white man from the north no less. "Will he go if I go?" she asked the empty room. The clock the living room chimed 3 o'clock. It was time to go.

****

"These men are fresh as crawdads up here! I can't believe Alderman Parker! He needs to agitate the gravel!" Ruby's friend, Deborah, applied the new Clairol color to her hair. "Dee, this isn't the first time that he left me gift! He left me money inside some flowers." Deborah massaged the color in her hair. "Mm. How much money?" Deborah craned her neck around Ruby's hair to look her in the eye. Ruby sighed and shifted on her stool and peach colored bathrobe. "A hundred dollars." Deborah massaged the rest color into her hair. "Mm. So he feel that he can hire whores and make Mr. Levi club a flophouse!" They cackled in laughter as she massaged the color into the sides and back of her hair.

Ruby's laughed rattled through her chest and through her toes as she flexed them back and forth, head back as the laugh continued. "Chile, ain't no body thinkin about Finnus Parker!" Deborah took off the gloves and threw them in the waste can by the sink. She patted her blonde pin curls in her pink satin scarf. "Doll, that red is going to be the end!" she smoothed her blue polka dot dress. "Ooh, I was so worried I got some of Miss Clairol on this dress!" Ruby stood up from the stool and adjusted her color cap. "Dee, ain't nothing on be on the dress but your Howard!" Deborah giggled and sashayed away towards the bathroom leaving her to sit on the stool for the color to set. "That's the only reason you so dolled up tonight. You know he comin."

Ruby made her way to the bed, tracing the edges of the box with gold ribbon. Deborah came from the bathroom looking the box as she at opposite it. She arched her eyebrows at Ruby. "Did you give that creep his money back? You know he gon think he own you now." Ruby stared at her, thought about Keys. "Let him thank what he wanna thank. I ain't for sale, and I ain't giving nothing back." Deborah looked at the box. "Gon head and open it."

Ruby was happy that Deborah had left the Sailor's Den and started to work for Mr. Levi. She was her only real friend she had in St. Louis, and she trusted her. She helped Mr. Levi balance the books and did bartending for him every now and then. Ruby adjusted the peach robe Keys gave her and pulled the lid off the box and onto the floor. "Oh," Ruby pulled out the red gown from its enclosure. She stood to see the length and sheen of the dress. She twirled with the dress in front of her. "Ethylene, Red indeed suits you, ravishing and hot. It is only fitting, a woman of your notice be indeed noticed. –F."

Deborah held the letter tight in her right hand. "F?!" She screamed. "Ruby, what the world is happ'n here! Don't he got a wife! You just gon take all the colored-loving white men, huh?" Ruby turned at her, dress still pressed against her and her reflection. The tag showed it cost, and Famous-Barr the department store that delivered it on Friday when she was out. "I ain't stuttin him! And yes, he does have a wife. I think her name is Jean." Ruby walked back to the bed, throwing the dress in the box. "I don't want shit from another woman's husband!" she smashed the box lid on top to close it. "I ain't free and I ain't' bought! He can keep this bullshit dishrag!" Ruby walked in the bathroom, and took off her color cap. "Girl, come wash this red out!"

There was paper rustling inside the box, and Deborah appeared in the doorway, box on her hip. She sat on the toilet while Ruby fussed about looking for a towel to let wash her hair. "Ethylene." Ruby gave her a desperate look. "I don't do nothing to encourage this man. I really don't! He want a Sophie, and I ain't no body's whore!" She looked in the cabinet behind the toilet. "Baby, nobody said that. Who would think that? I know he's been sniffin round you like a stray cat for a while now." She paused and looked her up and down. "Look, Dee, I don't like attention I don't want from a man I don't need." Deborah found an old red towel on back of the white door to the bathroom, handing it to Ruby whom was kneeling over the tub.

Ruby looked at Deborah from the floor. "Keys is enough. I don't need anyone else trying to come through here trying to wig out because the honky too close with the colored girl that sangs!" Deborah shook her head and sighed. "Girl, as long as Levi like you, your boarder rent stay paid, don't no body care what you do." Ruby turned towards the tub and Deborah turned on the water. "I just don't, I don't want to be just the colored girl that sings, Dee." She leaned over the lip of the tub, Deborah's voice softened, like her mother's did when she was trying to make something better. "Lean over, cher. Lean over."

The water ran over her hair, changing it from clear to sin-colored red. Ruby watched the water change, and then she held her breath and closed her eyes.

*****

Ruby went on stage, in Keys' shoes, and wore his black gown, complete with elbow-length white gloves he had gotten her for her birthday. She had Deborah to her hair like a picture of Rita Heyworth she found. Carolyn looked at Ruby and winked. As Carolyn began to tickle the keys, Ruby started into her rendition of *What A Fine Romance.* As she started into the second song of her set, she saw Alderman Parker walk in with roses, and he had left his glasses. He sat at the bar, in Keys' seat, and stared at her. She finished her note, took a deep breath and closed her eyes for a moment. With her heart thumping in her ears, she opened her eyes again looked over at Carolyn who smiled, taking a sip of water.

Amidst applause, she addressed the crowd, arms outstretched. "Okay, dolls and gents! I'm gon do this song one more time, for y'all that didn't hear it until a while ago." The packed Monday night crowd cheered. "Carolyn's brother Jack, wrote this for another dame, but I sing it better!" The crowd laughed. Carolyn through giggles, turned to the crowd saying, "That's cause you do sang it better! Jack knew what he was doing!" Carolyn knocked her knuckles and started the slow melody of *My Man Made Me.* Reuben had told her there were newspapers like the St. Louis American which were spotted in The Gypsy Hand, and a few had taken her picture. Reuben had told her, "I always want you to look gorgeous, doll. Make these other dames rags. Cream 'em."

"He made me love him, when I thought I was through with love." She looked out, saw Alderman Parker looking lovestruck and parched. Ruby caressed the microphone and its stand. "He keeps calling me closer and tells me I am divine." There were cheers and whistles as the male crowd saw how form fitting the dress was to her frame. "When he touched me, all I felt was fire, my man made me—made me love him like I do." She closed her eyes, sang the first verse again. She opened her eyes, saw Reuben sitting by the door, blow ing her a kiss. When she winked back at him, she saw Alderman Parker turn blow her two.

September 1956

St. Louis, Missouri

"Keys and Ruby. Ruby and Keys." Reuben sat on his back porch of his parents' two story three-bedroom row house playing with a gold-tinted Zippo lighter Ruby had gotten him as a birthday present. Reuben watched the sun come up. He held the Lucky Strike in his hand, twiddled it between his fingers. He thought of Ruby and smiled. It was Sunday, and his mother would be up and bustling around soon. She would be going to 9 a.m. mass at Holy St. Michael's Church and ask if he was going. He would smile and lie while she would fuss at Babs to get ready. The church was nowhere from their house on 4021 Indiana Street. Living there, made getting Ruby a matter of minutes.

He sat there, soaking up the fresh light. He marveled at the reds, and golds, and thought of Ruby's sleeked hair on his chest. He thought of how she felt, she smelled and how warm she was. She was always warm. Without a doubt, she kept a 'spread' on her bed. He asked her one day what a 'spread' was. She had turned over and looked at him, those eyebrows all knotted at him, eyes smoldering and sexy, she answered him, and said. "It's a blanket, Reuben. It's a blanket, now han' it to me, baby." She gestured to the foot of the bed he bought her. Hair spilled over her cheek and shoulder, the lamp so golden over her skin. He forgot to breathe that night. Reuben had fought the urge touch her, and only drank her in, as she turned to sleep again facing him.

He studied the pout of her bottom lip, how round her cheeks were and how her skin all but shimmered beneath the sleeping gown she had bought. "Ruby," he whispered. She had squirmed in her sleep. She looked like something out of a movie, he thought. He thought about her again and felt shivers in his back and belly. He stared at his unlit cigarette and thought about how she looked back at him. Her eyes were deeper than brown, they were deep enough to have him not want to every come out. She had blinked slow at him, woke up for an instant, and grinned at her. "Yes?" She had a lift in her voice when she didn't know what he wanted. She was staring at him, and he shook his head. "Nothing, doll. Nothing."

He adjusted the blanket and pulled the covers back on them both. He looked at the alarm clock on the small nightstand. "2:08 a.m." He whispered. Ruby nestled her head under his right arm, and he breathed her in. She was wearing something new, a new perfume. He closed his eyes and inhaled. "You smell so good, baby." He heard her giggle. "It's something my Mama sent me from home. She said lavender and jasmine are for luck and love." Reuben pulled her closer to him, she sounded like she was purring. He loved that contented sound she made. "Did you find it yet?" She nestled in his chest and was silent. He had rubbed her back, tracing her back to the nape of her neck. "I wanna leave here, Keys." He held her then. "We will." He answered. "We will."

The screen door shutting made Reuben drop his cigarette. His sister had come and sit next to him on the back porch. Her feet were still bare, and she had a long ponytail. "What's the haps, Daddy-o?" she said. He looked at her and giggled, pulled her close to him and nuzzled her new-brushed hair. "You going to see her later?" Her big green eyes searching his. "Her who?" Babs looked around, "the colored girl—Ruby?" she choked on her name it seemed. "What's it to you, squirt?" he looked off, patted his pockets for matches. "I was just askin, Rube." They sat for a moment watching the sun.

"I like her." Barbara said. "She's nice." Reuben chuckled. "Glad you dig her, Babs." He found his matches in his back pocket as he stood. "Are you gonna jacket her?" She was shielding her eyes from the morning sun. Reuben felt is face get hot. He lit his cigarette and walked away from his little sister. She ran up behind him, he heard her feet slap the stones beneath them. "Squirt, go in the house. Get ready to split." He exhaled in her opposite direction. "Mom says she doesn't know why you like that colored girl, but she said she doesn't care."

"I wouldn't care what her or Pop said." Babs studied his face as he continued to smoke. "I love Ruby. I always will love her. She's my girl, Babs." He stared at her hard. Barbara nodded in response, smoothing her black skirt and white sweater. "You takin me when you go see her again?" Reuben held his cigarette and looked up at the sky, saw the trees shimmering. "Yeah, I'll take you Babs. But you gotta be cool, dig it? Mr. Levi and some other people are coming by this week about boycotting and getting people to vote." He put the cigarette in his mouth, looking around, wishing he hadn't left Ruby's bed only an hour or so earlier. "You gonna let me cut back with you and Rob and to count the take?" Reuben chuckled. "Nah."

He walked her back to the backdoor of the house and walked through the back door. "Ma!" he yelled. His mother sat at the table, sipping her tea as she always did before church. She looked at him over her cup, watching him come in from the sun porch. As her eyes were finding his, she shook her head. Her brown hair up in a bun and her dark blue dress pressed. Reuben snuffed his cigarette on the oak stained window sill and hid the butt in one of the hanging ferns in the kitchen. Her feet were bare as well. "Barbara Ann, please go get your shoes and jacket on so we can leave?"

Barbara looked at her brother and looked over at her mother again before going up the stairs to her room. As Reuben sat, his mother, Mary, lowered her voice to speak to him, whispering. His mother only whispered when people where sick or she was trying not to gossip. "How are you, son?" Reuben shrugged his shoulders. "I'm doin'. Mom. Rob and I are still lookin to get our feet wet with construction. Who knows? We might start a business." His mother nodded. "Your father isn't feeling well lately. I think he's getting pneumonia again. He was trying to clean the gutters the other day. Getting a head start, he said." Reuben shook his head. "He's always been like that, Ma." She smiled at him. "I know. He's a lot like some other man I know." She looked over her cup at Reuben. He saw the gray at her temples then, it made her look wizened he thought.

Reuben sat there, listening to his mother talk about how his father was doing, what he wasn't doing, and what she wanted Babs to do. "I'm gonna have to start taking in wash again. If your Dad gets sick this time," she dropped her head. Reuben's ears pricked. "Whatcha short on, Ma?" Mae let out a bitter giggle. "Everything." Reuben reached for the cigarettes in his pocket. Thought about the take he and his brother had taken in the night before. There was three hundred he had on hand in his room. He could give his mother some of that. He would leave it in the white cookie jar his grandmother gave his mother as a wedding present. All the extra money always went there. The treasure chest, his father called it. "Okay." He whispered. "I still want Dad to show me how to make those chests, Mom. Y'know, when he's better?" His mother nodded. "Of course. He's resting this morning, but he should be up by the time we come back from church. I made the pot roast you like, dear."

Reuben smiled at her and rose to hug her. "I will, Ma. I will." She hugged him back. "You smell like jasmine." He grinned against her cheek. "Is that what she's wearing now?" Reuben had forgotten he hadn't washed that shirt. He had seen Ruby a week ago, and again last night. There was no use sleeping after he left her, he could never sleep. He slipped on the dirty shirt he had last seen her in with hopes sleep would come quicker. "Do you love her, Reuben?" the concern was in her voice, as velvet as its comfort. Reuben looked at his mother's hand. The wrinkles in it, the small callouses on her fingers from the side work she did as a seamstress. He looked at her ring and thought how much it meant to her, and the story she told about how his father had given it to her. "I do, Ma."

He got up from the table, huffing. "I don't want to hear anything guff about her being a colored girl, Ma! He faced the wall, away from his mother, his eyes stinging. "I don't wanna hear it!" He sighed heavy. His mother sighed as he heard the chair she sat in creak and groan. "Reuben Michael Lewis." Her voice still and definite. "I have not seen you act this way about any woman or doll, whatever it is you call a pretty girl these days." Mary moved towards him, her petite frame hugging his six-foot frame. Her hands brushed his shoulders. "But I know that you are in a dangerous and different position. This is not California. Ruby is a colored girl, and you are not a colored man. With that your aunt called your Dad about in Alabama and the people at that club—"

"What difference does that make, Ma!" he still didn't turn to face her. "That didn't stop Uncle Warren and Aunt Charlie! He loved her and married her!" Mae tapped her son's shoulders to have him face her. "Charlotte, Charlie is a lighter skinned colored girl. Emma said that the reason they were able to get married was because she wasn't dark, and her eyes were green. The justice of the peace didn't know what she was. "Reuben's eyes darkened. "She ain't a stray dog or the flu, Ma! She's a damn person! What does it matter what color she is?!" Mae stared at her son. "Did we teach you that people are people? Yes. What you forget is not everyone will believe that!"

Mary's sigh filled the room. "You love a woman you may not ever be able to have as your wife, Reuben! You can't marry her! Not now maybe ever!" Reuben sat in his chair, dejected. "I love her, Mom." He stared at the floor. Mae smoothed his hair, tried to massage his scalp. "I know you do. I see you do. I want— "she sighed. "I don't want your life to be harder than what it has to be. But I know you are gonna do what you feel you have to do." Reuben raised his eyes to his mother, his blue eyes looking back at him from her face, soft and glassy. "You can't marry her Reuben. What about your life together?" she sighed and grabbed both sides of his face. "What about my grandchildren?" he stared at her, held her gaze as he stood. "She ain't a animal, Ma. She ain't. I'm not fuckin a horse!" He turned and walked towards the front of the house to front porch. He wanted to talk to Nathan, he was more level headed, like their Dad.

He walked around to the back of the house where the big white garage was, tucking his cigarette behind his ear. He didn't want to see his mother again or risk her asking him about his life decision. Reuben heard metal clanging and called his brother's name. "Nate!" "Yeah!" a voice screamed back at him. "Fuckin grease monkey." He said and slapped his oil slicked shirt. "Bastard." He said. He was tinkering with their father's old Ford pickup truck. "What's the haps?" He still didn't look up at him, his arm like a crank around the engine. Reuben fiddled with the cigarette behind his ear. "Ma knows about Ruby."

Nathan's grunting filled up that quiet space. "She doesn't want me to marry her." "You ain't 'posed to marry no body ya only known not even a whole year, Rube. I didn't even think you wanted to get hitched." He turned to his brother and grinned, "Only thing I pegged you to love is money." Reuben scoffed and wiped his brow, watched his brother tinker with this father's 1945 black Ford Business Coupe. "Wait a sec. Ain't she the colored girl at the bar you run games at?" Reuben made a confirming noise. "Does Ma know 'bout dat?" He grunted as he tightened bolts, gripping the side of the chassis. "She doesn't need to know what I'm up to. Pop is sick, bills still need to be paid. Bob's is teaching school and helping me—and trying to get his GI money from fightin chinks and you're still fixing cars. We gotta still eat, Nate."

Nathan made an approving noise. "Mm. So Ruby, that's her real name." Reuben chuckled. "What about going to Wash U? The doc thing?" "That's still gonna happen!" Reuben snapped. "Look, Ma needs help right now. It's just for right now. Any leads on this construction thing? That money you showed me months ago can't keep getting nipped off to help Ma and Pop. I need to split with my babydoll." Nathan looked towards his brother with wide eyes. "Ya seriously leaving? Leaving with a colored girl?" Reuben stared away from Nathan. "Yeah. I'm leaving with a colored girl." He mocked. "I'm fuckin a colored girl." he squared his jaw, pointed at his brother with his Lucky Strike, "I'm gonna make a fuckin colored girl a fuckin Lewis! I don't need any of you sonsabitches crackin wise on where I put my cock!" Nathan stared at his younger brother, shaking his head and giggled. "I didn't think you were looking for a Sophie anyway."

He turned away from Reuben and rose to shut the hood of the car. "Rube," he started while wiping his wrench off "Look, you're fuckin nineteen. I can't tell you the do with ya life." He shrugged his shoulders before he continued. "You wanna leave here? Do that. But don't do something doofy to make ya life harder than what it really gotta be." He moved towards Reuben, his tone lowered as he put a hand on his oily right hand on his left shoulder. "Look. If you love the girl, colored or not, you gotta be ready fah what that means." Reuben put the unlit cigarette in his mouth, studied his face and nodded. He looked at the direction of the open door and the light that spilled from it. "Ma, said that Pop knew she was gonna be his wife as soon as he saw her. He knew,

Nate." He stared at his brother again as he turned to put his tools away in the metal red tool box in the garage. "Does Ruby know what you want with her? Talk to her about leaving?"

Reuben started towards the door, dragging his feet and thinking. "She knows enough." He said. Nathan followed Reuben started back to the house as to check on their sleeping father, Johnathan. Nathan stopped in the kitchen for water, and to wash his hands as Reuben went upstairs. "Pop would understand. He gotta understand." Reuben went up the flight of stairs and he reached the closed white door which was his parents room. "Pop?" he asked as he knocked. He heard a noise and opened the door. "Pop, I need to ask you somethin." His father was sitting a rocking chair, looking out the window, his pipe still in hand. He didn't discourage his youngest son coming towards him. Reuben leaned against the chest of drawers near the window and his father. He took a deep breath and looked at the floor. "Pop? How did you know, Ma was it?"

Johnathan looked at the floor and coughed. Reuben waited for him to finish to speak or answer him. "I just knew." He said. He smiled at the floor and then over at his pipe. "A man knows who he wants with him, Rube. That will never change, no matter how the world may." He looked up at his son, smiled again. Looking over his glasses, he asked, "Who is she?"

"A singer." His father grinned. "Pretty?" Reuben exhaled. "As Hell, Pop. As hell." He ran his right hand through is cut hair and chuckled. "Mm." His father coughed again. "That's always good." Reuben turned to leave the room when his father called him again. "Why do you need to know why I chose your mother? You gettin hitched, Rube? You should at least let us meet this, umm, doll as you say now." Reuben felt his face flush. "I'm working on it, Pop."

October 1956

St. Louis, Missouri

"No, I'm not going anywhere with you, Alderman." Ruby stirred her lemon water after her set. She turned to look at the clock behind her. It was 11:30 at night. Keys would be there in a few minutes. He had to pay for her room the next week and ask her something. "Real important" he had said. "Hurry up, Keys!" she hissed to the clock. She wore her hair down that night. Nighttime fall breezes found their way into the Gypsy Hand every time the big red door swung open. She took out her magnolia and set it next to her drink. "Ruby, please. Just one dinner."

Ruby looked back at him. Every time he came in he reminded her of Benny Goodman. She smirked. "No, Fin." His eyes grew wide behind his wire rimmed glasses. "I love it when your call me that." Ruby rolled her eyes. She let her gaze drift to find Levi. She tapped the bottom of her glass three times the queue someone was bothering her. A twice tap would denote her drink was empty. She moved his hand from her knee, and he seemed hurt. "I don't cotton to married men, Fin. No matter what color they are." She stood, smoothing her navy dress. "Ethylene," he began, grabbing her hand. "Please. Please, one dinner, one drink, one conversation. A voice like that will make you famous. Let me connect you."

Ruby heard a door open and she looked at the clock. It was a little after midnight. He kissed her hand. "You smell so good, skin so soft." She snatched her hand away, and pulled her towards, his hands on her hips. "Finn, get the hell out of here! Get out! Levi! Nate!" She knew Nathan was in the count room near the boiler and prayed he hadn't been drinking. She closed her eyes and struggled away from Alderman Parker. Ruby then felt hands around her, pulling her towards the lower part of the bar, and smelled Royal Crown shave powder. As Ruby turned to go to her room upstairs, she heard Finnus screaming at Mr. Levi. pleading behind her. "Ruby! I'm sorry, I" "Goddammit, Parker! Get the hell outta here!" she heard Levi's voice as she held her back to the hallway way before the staircase.

She held her chest, willed her heart stop beating so quick. She wondered where Keys was, and what would have happened if Mr. Levi wasn't there. The alderman had a reputation for being a womanizer, and there was a rumor he had his way with waitresses and a few other singers in Gaslight Square. But because most of the girls were colored they weren't believed or laughed at when they tried to make a report. There was even talk a white girl had accused him of rape and was laughed out of the downtown precinct. If Reuben saw that, would he think that Alderman Parker was trying to move on her and she cheating on him? Or thinking of quitting him?

"Ugh." Sundays she stopped her set about 10:30 or 11. Alderman Parker came in right in the middle of her final set, in the middle of *What A Fine Romance*. He brought white roses and a big, lusty grin. Keeping in mind of he had a wife at home with a little boy and was pregnant again. Mrs. Parker whom didn't want the colored girls that worked for her using her bathroom and had a cabinet of glasses and plates they could use because being from Louisiana she was taught 'that's just what you do for the coloreds'.

As she opened her eyes, she saw Richard. He was always around in late hours or early mornings. He sold papers and shined shoes and was smart as a whip. Ruby would often make sure he went to bed at a decent hour and sometimes made sure he ate dinner. His mother had died the year before and his father was a longshoreman and was a cab driver for Laclede Cab. Richard was smart and seemed to know almost everything about everyone that everyone at the Gypsy Hand started calling him "Doc." "What's wrong, Miss Ruby?" he asked, rubbing his eyes, his stripped pajamas a little too big on him. "Nothing, shug. C'mere, Doc." He grinned and ran to her from the third step from the bottom.

She made a noise as she squeezed him. "All this warm and love you gave me, Doc, I think that I can make it a little while longer." She kissed his cheek. "Take that with you, Doc." He looked at her, wide eyed, and listening. "Why is Mr. Levi yellin'?" he asked, looking past Ruby. As the yelling and swearing continued, she guided his face back to hers. "Look here, Doc. Go to bed. You got school in the morning." He looked at the floor. "I ain't goin!" he pouted and looked at the floor. "How come?" She stood to her full height, arms akimbo. Richard was still looking at the floor. "That dumb teacher is mean to me and don't never put my smile faces on the board with them white kids!"

Ruby squatted again, not caring about the new navy dress she wore. "Look at me, Doc. Look at me." She insisted, her hands on his shoulders, and he still didn't look up at her. "What do you wanna be when you go up?" She cupped his face, and saw the tears in his eyes, seeing those young eyes look so dark and aged. He blinked slow and looked at her. "I wanna be a doctor." He whispered. "What cha say?" he swallowed hard. "I wanna be a doctor, Miss Ethylene." She pulled him to her, covered him with her torso as he hugged her tight. "Richard, you are a smart boy. You almost too smart for that ole Scullin school, and smartest boy in that whole second grade." He smiled as he looked up at her. "You can be a doctor!" She pointed at his nose, and he stuck his chest out. "Don't let nobody ever say different, hear me? Miss Ruby finished high school before I came north cause my mama made me." She hugged him again as he sniffled, and she felt him nod in the crook of her neck. "Like she believed in me, Imma believe in you, hear?" With one last squeeze, she told him to go to bed and watched as he bounded up the stairs to the apartment his father rented from Levi.

She crept back around the corner, to see Levi wiping the bar back off and humming. "Hey, cher." He said not looking up. She grimaced and walked back over to her seat. "Levi, why won't he let me alone?" Levi laughed, sounded like it was from his toes. "He won't let you alone like most men that come through here don't let you alone: want what they can't have." She put her head on the bar and sighed. The clock chimed midnight. "Keys come through here, yet?" Levi made a disapproving noise, and Ruby in turn made a corresponding one. "He said he had something he needed to ask me." Levi was silent. She put her head in her hands and heard him move before sweeping of the wooden floor began. "Most likely." She followed footsteps, and looked up turning on her leather stool, feet bare against its legs, placing her bare arms in the bar.

She studied Levi swiping his bar. He watched how his shoulders rolled on his frame as he swept. He was a tall man, ebony dark and was a sweet as honey or mean as a junkyard dog. She watched his white undershirt strain against his back as he moved chairs to replace them. "Levi?" "Yeah, cher?" She loved it when he called her cher. It felt like she was home in New Iberia again. "You think," she sighed. "You think Keys loves me?" Levi laughed again. "I can't answer that, cher. I just go on what I see."

"Well, what you see?"

"The future." He answered. Ruby stood and grabbing a rag behind the bar. As she started wiping off tables, sweeping past him in her gown. With her back to him, hair falling her face she asked, "What? C'mon, Mr. Levi, you better explain yourself!" Levi leaned on his broom and chuckled. "Ethylene, when I was in the navy, I dreamt about this place. A place for me and for me to help other folk." He chuckled, and Ruby sat in a chair two tables from where he stood. "I see the future when I look at you and Keys. I see how he looks at you, and how these other wolf-howling men look at you." Ruby sat on a low chair in front of him, hand on her face and listened. "But when Keys, when Reuben looks at you," he whistled. "That's how I look at my wife. How I knew couldn't nobody ever be, Naomi Mae. Not no body."

He turned his back to her and made his way towards the stage to sweep. "Yeah, cher, he loves you, more than you thank." Ruby looked at the damp ashtray on the table. She rolled over his words and stood to go upstairs. "Levi, I'll see you Tuesday." Levi made an approving noise as she went upstairs. Ruby pushed open her room, with the window cracked. She saw Reuben there in a chair a letter on his chest, asleep. "Fire escape." She smirked before kneeling in front of him and kissed him slow. "Keys?" he stirred, and his eyes opened. His eyes were swollen. "What's wrong?" she asked. "Bob is dead." She exhaled and stood as he balled up the letter. "My brother is dead! Somebody hit him in Boston while he was with his wife, Anne Marie!" Ruby sat on her bed, their bed, and looked at him as he paced the room. "I came over here, the back way, and saw that alderman staring at you like you where steak! If I see that sonofabitch," Ruby watched as he stood in front of her. "I'm gonna fuck him up. He cupped her face. You are my girl. Ain't no body gon disrespect you." Ruby stood and hugged him.

"It's almost Thanksgiving," she started. "I was gonna go home for a few days, see my mama, and come back." He held her tighter. "I don't, I don't want you to go." She backed away from him, feeling cold after their hug was broken. "You don't own me, Keys. I can go where I want." She walked away from him, and when to the bathroom to change, closing the door behind her. She shimmied out of her gown, and turned on the bath, grabbing the peach robe he had gotten her. "Thanksgiving is in a whole month! I ain't seen my mama in a year. My sister is gotta baby. I wanna see my family, Keys!" She sat on the side of the ivory tub and looked at the tub fill. The knob turned, and door opened as she concentrated on the water.

"Dollface, I don't wanna own you. I wanna," she looked over at him, sitting and looking at the floor on the toilet. "I want you," he was wringing his hands. "Baby, I never," she turned and looked at him, and held her robe closed.

"Reuben, what is it? Spit it out, or swallow it, because ya choking on it right in front of me."

Reuben looked up at her, sullen and weepy. "I want you," he reached of her left hand. "I want you to be my girl, more than that. I want you to be my wife." Ruby stared at him, couldn't breathe. "I got family in California, we can go there, be together." He looked at the floor. "We can do what we want, babe. We can— "he started crying again. Ruby held his hand, squeezed it. He was speaking quick then. "I got a uncle in San Francisco, he's married, and we can start over. We can be together. No more clubs, no more number running, gambling no more hundred-dollar hand poker. I can," he stared at her, his tears slicked his cheeks. "I ain't gonna love no woman, like I love you." He paused. "like I wanna love you." Ruby stared at the blend of their hands together on his lap. They sat in that quiet, the steam from the bath filling up another space they were sharing. "I don't wanna go home, Ethylene. I—I wanna stay where life is tonight. Ma is a mess, Babs is outta her head and Pop is getting worse. I wanna stay where life is. Let me stayover." He still didn't look up at her. "Let me take my bath first."

She stood with her back to him, and he helped her out of her robe. Reuben washed her back, brushed her hair, and helped her dry off. Kissed her shoulders as he gave her the gown to sleep in while she was wrapped in a towel. He had cried on her, with her as she just let him ramble on. As he spoke, they agreed she would go home for Thanksgiving, but see his family for Christmas. They developed a plan that they knew would bloom in another year. They would go to California, stay with his uncle and his wife and never come back to St. Louis. In June, by June 1958, she would be Mrs. Reuben Michael Lewis. Reuben swore by God he would and loved her to sleep.

November 1956

New Iberia, Louisiana

The sun woke her up on the train as she sat in the Colored passenger car. The sleeping car porter's voice woke her. "Ma'am, we made it safe." he said. She stood on shaky legs as she exited the car. "Thank you, Uriah." She whispered. He put out his hand to help her from her window seat. "Where do I get my bags from, Uriah?" "At the green wall office, ma'am." She smiled at him, nodded and exited is the car. She had heard this man that was almost old enough to be her father, called a 'boy' on and off during the day trip to New Iberia from St. Louis. She couldn't stand it. At one instance, she screamed that his name is Uriah. "He ain't a boy, your boy, or nobody else boy! He is a damn man, and his name is Uriah!" She met the eyes of the green-eyed man who said it, not even thirty feet from where the car divided. He was wide-eyed and looked, she looked at him, unwavered. Before she left St. Louis, she has a pregnancy scare, telling only Mr. Levi's wife, Ms. Naomi and Deborah.

She hadn't slept with Reuben in weeks, though he begged. When she told him why in the early part of the month, he didn't come to the club for a week.

He only called to check on her or left messages. Alderman Parker started to come by more and when she would refuse his advances, but he'd leave money under her glass in a napkin with some tawdry note. Babs had sneaked by before she went home from Roosevelt High School to check on her and give Ruby a message. She had caught her at a table talking to Deborah about what was happening in Montgomery, Alabama, cleaning out the count room for a meeting, and a man named Martin Luther King, Jr. Ruby was in no mood to deal with anything else. St. Louis was making her tougher than she thought.

Walking towards the green walled office, Ruby held on to her cream-colored hat, and smoothed her emerald green dress, grateful for the sun and light. She remembered the message Babs gave to her. "My brother said to tell you," she looked around and leaned in even though no one was there, to listen before she continued. "You're still his girl. He loves you. And don't get lost down south." She smiled as the wind blew.

Ruby was happy she wasn't pregnant. Deborah said Ms. Naomi knew a colored doctor in The Ville that could help if she didn't want Reuben's baby. But she was home now, and whatever problems she was having in St. Louis, would have to stay there. Her father was coming to get her from the station in that old Ford he bought from his old neighbor, Mr. Gillespie, knew he was going to be so happy to see her. She remembered the telegram that was in her room above the

Gypsy Hand. As she remembered the cypress trees, Lake Fausse, and the warmth of her mama's kitchen as she read the words her father sent, she knew once she got home, she would be alright again. After the baby scare, she needed space from Reuben.

As she made it to the office, she took her ticket and handed it to the clerk at the counter. She was rummaging through her purse looking for her dime, that she didn't notice the porter bringing her bags around and called her name. "Ethylene?" she looked up from her cream-colored bag and looked up. "Why, you look like that white girl from that Bogie movie in that hat." It was Moses. "Thank ya kindly, shug." She grabbed her bag and went to the Colored platform to wait for her father. She found the phone outside the office door and called home. Her sister answered on the fifth ring, and she told her Daddy was already on his way. She went to the platform bench, past a white couple that was crying.

The man was going to Chicago and wouldn't marry the woman before he left. She wasn't sure that the tears were happy or sad. Ethylene thought of Keys then. He had called her before he left, but she had told him not to drop her off at the train station, to go home and be with him family because it was the holiday. "Be careful. I love you." She remembered the warmth of his hands on his face, how soft his lips were that last time he kissed he. She remembered how confused he looked when she talked about the baby.

She adjusted her hat and looked out into the November sun. She pulled it down over her eyes a little more as she heard the footstep approach, and the warmth that nestled beside her. "You still pretty, Ethie." She rolled her eyes and scoffed. "What'chu want, Mo?" He chuckled as she stared out, looking for her father's red Ford. He touched her hair, and she bristled. "You went up North, and got you a white girl hair color, huh?" She moved away from him. "You need not never touch me not never again." She still didn't look at him. "Oh, you pinned now? Got you somebody waitin in Saint Louis? One of them white soundin nigras?" she rolled her eyes, prayed for her father to come. "I don't need to be pinned, I ain't no prize pig, Mo. I got things I'm doing, and I owe you the same thing them pigs yo people raise." She looked at him from under her hat, "shit."

Ruby heard the bench creak, and Moses stand. She looked down at his shoes, scuffed and brown, and his dark slacks, she moved her vision up, looking at his Hamilton Railway shirt, wrinkled, with sweat pockets on it. She made it to this face, hard, high-yellow and unfeeling, his hair was cut but it did nothing to soften his face. He adjusted his hat. "I work for my family. I work to take care of myself, I ain't run like you did." She stood up, her gloved hands on her hips. "I ain't run, I rode. I ain't got nobody to run from. I got a life to run to. These rails, this soil, and these waters can't and ain't gon hold me." She heard a car horn, looked around his right arm to see her father park, just over the track.

She walked down the platform, looking at the brown baby doll pumps she wore. She steadied her breathing. The last thing she wanted was Oliver Gibeaux upset. She thanked God, as she came close to the car, and she got in putting her bag suitcase in the truck bed. Her father looked at her and laughed from the lowered passenger window. "You ain't been home an hour, and here this nigga come trying to sniff ya like you his wolf cub, see if you belong to him." She put her hand on the car handle and heard, "I'll see you later, Ethie! You still my girl!" She turned her head to watch Moses as he watched her. Her throat got dry as she held fast to her hat as she watched Moses saunter away with this hands in his pockets. Ruby felt her father's hand on her shoulder, pulling her body and vision from Moses. He opened her door, tucked her in the car and drove away.

As they headed to her childhood home on 528 Fulton Street, her father asked her how St. Louis was treating her. Ruby laughed before she answered him. "Daddy, I like St. Louis, but I ain't droppin no anchors there." She looked over at her father, studied his blue dress shirt and slacks. He chuckled at they stopped at the stoplight on Joule. "They put that Woolworth's up after you left, Ethylene." He motioned toward the shiny sign on the driver's side of the car. She looked out at her father as he drove, her heart sinking in her chest. She closed her eyes and shifted in her seat. Her eyes began to water as she bumped along in her father's car beginning to hum the last song she had sung before the Gypsy

Hand closed for the holiday, *Good Morning Holiday*.

She woke just as they pulled up to the house behind her Uncle Chad's red pickup truck. She dabbed her eyes with the back of her hand and smoothed the wide brim of her hat. She had taken off her shoes before she fell asleep during the remainder of trip. As she swung open the door, she sighed as she opened the door and felt the clay under her feet. Ruby grabbed her shoes as we sauntered to the dark wood oak porch with white siding. The wind blew over her skin and she almost sobbed. She missed Reuben. She had tried not to, tried to forget him as she rode from Union Station in Missouri now a world away to Hamilton Railway in New Iberia. Here she could breathe deep, but as she did, she could feel her soul weep. As she passed her grandmother on the front with her tobacco, sister shucking corn to fry for dinner, too, in bare feet, she though, just maybe, home would never be where Reuben was not.

She called her mother's name as the screen door clapped the door frame behind her. Ruby didn't bother to wipe her feet; a bath was what she wanted soon after. "Mama!" she called, letting her drawl be full as she called for Mae-Reavis. "Here me!" Ruby heard her voice from the dining room, right through the front room and its dark brown furniture, and taupe drapes. She made her way toward the kitchen, tossing her hat on her father's favorite white chair, where her mother's quit lay over the headrest.

Mae-Reavis sat in her kitchen chair in her yellow housedress, back to the open rear door. She was still snapping green beans, with her red lined apron. Her French braided hair always made Ruby think it was a crown. She sat in the chair across from her and watch the deft of her hands shuck the beans. The kitchen smelled of vanilla and butter, and game birds. "Don't sat there girl! Gon get them pies together from the icebox." Her mother said with a giggle in her voice. "Stella been in here with me all morning and most of the night. She and the baby in the backroom sleep. 'Least you could do it put these pies together." Ruby stood and went to the icebox and saw the big red bowl with sweet potato pie filling. She looked in the freezer compartment for the tin pans with homemade rolled dough.

"Make sure you pinch my dough, shug!" Ruby moved towards the counter near the white farm sink to wash her hands and looked out the window looking at her neighbor, Mr. Earl, wave. He would always brag he knew A. Phillip Randolph, 'Mr. Phillip' as he called him, and was a part of first class of The Brotherhood Of Sleeping Car Porters. *Ain't nothing here changed.* She found a spoon that was hanging on the rack by the yellow sheer curtains.

As she ladled the filling in the pan and smoothed it, her mother spoke. "Cher, how is St. Louis treating you?" She grinned down at the bowl. "It's okay, Mama. I like it so far. It ain't snowed yet." Mae-Reavis was silent. "Good. Is that ole Levi treating you right, givin' you all you 'posed to have?" Ruby tapped the pan to settle the pie. "Yes ma'am. Mr. Levi is a good man, mama." Mae-Reavis made an approving noise. Ruby felt her face flush, wanted to know what Reuben was doing or if he was thinking of her.

Mae-Reavis's chair scooted back from the mint green table, and she moved towards Ruby. "Let me see these pies, girl. You taking till the Lord's return to get these pies together." She giggled and shoved Ruby out the way. Mae-Reavis looked over her shoulder, and Ruby smelled her magnolia perfume. The moved quick to the robin-egg blue stove, opening the oven door. She pulled out the black roasting pan with her red pot holders, sitting the pan which held the large turkey, on the sink. "Gimme those pies, Ethie." Ruby handed her mother the pies, sat as she watched her replace the door and wipe her hands on her apron. "Your Nan, shole glad you came back for dinner, shug." Ruby grinned. She regained her perch and watched her daughter.

"Baby, I am so glad you home!" She slapped her hands off her legs. "I'm glad I came home, Mama." She listened to the red clock above the door tick away before sounding 3 p.m. It had taken her all night to get home, but she was determined to be home by the time dinner started. She was grateful to the porter, Uriah, who had let her clean up and change in the washroom on the Whites Only part of the car—she was able to get in because the white couple traveling in the last seats, one of them being the white man she had yelled at, not paying attention because they were asleep.

"Baby, gon brang that corn from Mother Oscella brang, so we can fry it and finish this dinner." Ruby blinked and stood. "Yes, ma'am. And Imma go to the lake and think for a minute." She turned her back to her mother and started towards the front door. "Think? Think about what?" she scoffed. "Don't think too hard, cher." Ruby smoothed her face as she went through the door, listening to her mother mutter about time and dinner. As she walked down the wood stairs, she tapped her grandmother on her shoulder, and asked for the bowl of corn and turned back into the house to give it to her mother. "Instead of going to thank you should be thanking about what you need to be thankin about."

When Ruby went back through the door, her grandmother asked, "Where you finna go?" Ruby didn't turn around to answer her. "Immabe back!" she yelled as she went through the gate. "Don't get lost, know you new round here, cher! You know your brother Frank gon be here later!" her Uncle Chad bellowed. Ruby turned and waved to her family, grinned at her dark skinned smoking uncle in his shirt and overalls on the porch with his straw hat, as she continued down the clay road. How she missed and hated this clay! The ground under her yielding nothing but worn paths to old places. She passed the Gulf gas station, and past Widow Howard who was fussing with her window box, her white hair pin curled with a pink hairnet over it. Ruby smiled at her as she pulled her window down.

She passed the Colonial Theatre saw *The King And I, Babydoll* and *Forbidden Planet* playing. It was deserted because of the holiday. She frowned at the *Colored* sign above the right-side entrance. Ruby mused that maybe the Fox theatre in St. Louis would be also. She walked she noticed the road was will brick and dust, her body tensed. She knew she was near the old sugar plantations, and the lecherous white man, Curtis Morton, who had tried to have her sister. He followed her home to the point her father and his brother had to deal with him. Ruby just wanted her space by her piece of Lake Fausse, her favorite Spanish Moss and cypress trees. She hugged herself as she saw sugar cane off to her right, the wind blew the stalks and she shivered.

She smiled as she reached Lake Fausse, seeing the johnboats and straw-hatted fishermen sitting along its banks. Ruby found a notch around the root of a cypress tree to sit, bringing her knees to her chin. From her perch in the hollow of the tree, she closed her eyes. Ruby listened to the wind that rustled the moss. She listened to the plopping of lures in to the water and the far off swearing of fisherman wrangling catfish. Exhaling, and still sitting crouched down, she thought of Reuben. He had asked her to marry him, be with him always. He had asked her that the night his brother died. *I want to be where life is,* he had said.

She never gave him a real answer, or a real denial. The question was hovering over them like smoke. All she wanted was more and better. She remembered what her mother had told her about wanting more, and it being okay to want more.

Mae-Reavis Gibeaux told her that with glassy tears in her eyes as she watched Ruby leave to go to St. Louis, "You need more than what a sugar plantation or this dust and water can give you." She had reached in a white cookie car on the counter behind her flour jar. She called it her Mammie Jar. "Mammie always keepin secrets." She had given Ruby the two hundred dollars she had saved to get her to St. Louis. Ruby remembered she had pressed the money in her hand, and just let the tears fall over her reddening face. Before Ruby could protest, she shushed her. "You been helping them white women with they dresses and keeping books for Mr. Morton's mama. I know he gon try and either not pay you the rest of yo money or try and have you." She hugged her, pressed her warmth into her daughter. "I want more for your, Shug. Take this lil bit and make yo more." Her mother hated that sometimes her Creole ancestry would betray how she felt. Ruby thought more than likely she would have the same tears when she left again. Coming home wasn't a bad idea, it just wasn't the best idea.

Ruby stretched from her perch before headed home, walking towards the water's edge and flexing her feet in the grasses, remembering the words of her grandmother, Mother Oscella:

Home ain't never been about folk, cher. Home is where you take folk you love and care for. Home is what you make it and where you make it, and who you brang when you make it. She had been telling her this since she was a girl learning how to make hoe cakes. *You take home with you. You don't never have to be where love never will be, cher. 'Member that. The folk in ya heart, stays in ya heart. The deeper the love, the harder they is to come outta dere.* Ruby smiled, knowing that home was where Reuben was. She stretched again towards the sun and started home again, face towards the sun.

****

"This duck and these greens know they was good, Mae!" Her aunt Bette said as she pushed her plate away. Ruby watched her family as her mother grinned and propped her hand under her chin. She looked around the table and living room and grinned at her father's brother siblings as they began to talk about aunt Bette's husband and how Oliver had stopped her from marrying him a second time, thanks to Bessie Coleman, the rifle kept in the living room behind the white linen curtains by the door. She looked at her older brother, Franklin, looking like new money in his new red dress shirt his wife, Nola, made him. She watched how he fawned over their new baby daughter, Beatrice. Ruby smiled at Nola as she gave kisses to Beatrice. Mother Oscella kept telling Franklin to 'stop kissin that baby in her face'. She sat next to her sister Esther who had her son, Thomas on the lap of Mother Oscella, whom had a blue blanket draped about his year-old shoulders as he slept in her arms in the car whose back was to the hallway, so she could watch the door. Mother Oscella was dozing as she rocked Thomas.

Her aunt Bette cleared the table, as she Ruby sat and talked to her brother. "Oliver, get out here with that liquor so we can finish this poker game, man!" Chad yelled from the kitchen table. Ruby laughed as she heard her father curse from the back room. Franklin got up and kissed Nola whom was on the couch sleeping. Ruby blushed as she watched her brother go to door. "Ethie, come out here with me." Ruby looked at Esther and her mother, Esther rolled her eyes and smiled." As the dishes clattered in the sink, Mae-Reavis said, "Gon out there with your brother. We gon be in here. I gotta get this cobbler together for tomorrow. I want you to have something good to take back Saturday."

Ruby pushed back from the table, smoothing her dress as she stood. She followed her brother through the front door, watching him pull his Camels from his pocket. He had started smoking after coming back from the War and told Ruby when he got back he wasn't leaving the military. He told her how much he loved the navy, and for the most part it had been good to him. He admired President Truman for seeing 'men as men' and 'stop letting color stop service.' They made it to the chain link gate, and Franklin had lit his cigarette and began to smoke.

They stood there, watching the stars and lingering traffic. "There that boy is again. Thankin he slick as oil." He gestured across the street to the slow moving red pickup truck. "That's Moses daddy truck. He fount out you was home and don't know how to act." He chuckled, and Ruby looked at the ground at her newly dirty feet. "I saw him at the station and he been on me like flies on shit." Franklin scoffed. "Mo don't want no wife. He just don't want you to have no husband that ain't him. Men love to see what they wont but can't stand when someone else get what they think is theirs." She shifted her weight as she stood next to her brother, watched the truck slink by. Franklin looked up at the red truck and took a drag off his cigarette.

She went closer to the chain link fence and leaning against the post, played in her hair. "So, you went North and try to be a white girl?" Franklin laughed. Ruby shook her hair out. "Nall. I just went North cause ain't nothin here. Hair color ain't got shit to do with it, Frankie." He nodded, taking another drag off his cigarette. "That's why I'm staying in the navy. I ain't coming back here. They tryin to send me to, um." He exhaled. "California, I think it is. That's plenty fine with me. I can't wait to take Nola from here for good. Her and my boy. Iberia ain't home no mo. Just Mama and Pop is here." Ruby nodded. "That's only reason I'm here." She sighed, listening to the owls and crickets. "I ain't trying to be Mo's wife. I got my own life to live. That ain't got nothing to do with messin wit Mo."

The screen door slammed, and their mother stared at them for a moment. "Don't make your Daddy come out here with Bessie, hear? Ya'll finish up so we can get the house closed up." The door clapped against the frame again. Ruby moved closer to her brother, head on his upper arm. "You should see St. Louis at night, Frank. All lit up like Christmas. Folk going, coming and hustling." They laughed. Franklin flicked his cigarette over the fence. "You gotta fella in St. Louis?" he whispered. Ruby felt her throat get dry. "I ain't a stable horse, Frank. I get out." Franklin looked at her and shrugged. "Just know that you can always come home, don't think that you gotta stay anywhere." Ruby rolled her eyes, stared off into the screen of sugar pines across the street. "I think you got a fella and don't wanna spill. But, it's okay. Ya grown. You'll tell everybody or nobody when you wont to." Ruby sighed, and turned to go back in. "C'mon, Frank. I don't want mama to come back and bring Bessie with her."

*****

Mother Oscella rebraided her hair before she took her bath. Tomorrow would come and go, there would be more people to see, cobbler to make with Mama, and to see her family once more before headed back to the train. Mother Oscella saw her come in with Franklin and she called her name, just as if she had been six again, running in her vegetable garden. "Chile, all that hair on yo head! Get over here so I can braid it, so you can look right." Franklin laughed at her as he woke Nola with a forehead kiss to go home, they only lived three houses down. "I'll see you in the morning, Ethie." He sniggled and helped his wife from the couch, before going left down the back hall to get their son whom, too, was asleep.

"Gone getchu a scarf out Esther room and come back her with the comb and grease." Ruby nodded, mouthing, "Yes ma'am." She went down the hall and same to the second bedroom on the left, seeing her sleeping sister and nephew in his crib. She watched them both, their chests rising and falling. She looked in the heavy beige dresser, in the middle drawer, rifling until she found a scarf that matched her hair. Ruby decided once her hair color changed, red would be her signature color: *Wherever there was red, is where I'll be,* she mused. She turned to the twin sized bed under the window that held her brown suitcase. Opening it, she was happier still she had brought her peach robe Keys bought her. She placed it tenderly on the pillow, before rearranging the clothes inside to shut the suitcase again.

As she moved the suitcase to the floor, looking at her sister once more. Grinning she whispered, "Don't worry, Sis. I ain't stayin here, Esther I can't. This ain't livin here. I need more." She through her sister's top chest of drawers and felt for a jar of Royal Crown in the small glass jar, her robe, wrapped the grease and comb in the scarf, heading back to her grandmother.

Ruby hung the robe on a nail on the back of the bathroom door, then tiptoeing back to Mother Oscella. She was sitting in her chair, watching *Playhouse 90* on the floor model television. She gripped the items in her red scarf as she sat between the knees of Mother Oscella. She giggled as Ruby put her head on her thigh. "My sugarbaby got all this hair! Mmph!" She closed her eyes as her grandmother hummed and oiled her scalp. "This yo crown sugarbaby, don't let folk cut in it and be all silly wit yo hair. Don't let nobody else get holt to your hair either. They bin din made a doll from it." Ruby kept her eyes closed, enjoyed her hair being combed. "This red hair you got, girl." She giggled. "Make me thank about them johnny girls on Bourbon. You ain't onna dem, is you?" Ruby stifled a chuckle as her grandmother started to plat her hair in one braid. She nestled her head on her left thigh, closing her eyes as she braided. "No Nan. I ain't a johnny girl, and I ain't wenchin nowhere either."

Mother Oscella made another low approval noise. "Good, sugarbaby, good. Turn ya head." Ruby obeyed, moved her head from the left thigh to the right, listening to her grandmother hum again. She told her how loved she was, and how pretty she was and to never stop singing. "You gots a gift, baby. Don't let nobody steal what God give you, hear me?" Ruby closed her eyes as Mother Oscella finished the second braid. "You can always come home, sugarbaby. You can always come home to me or yo Daddy. Don't be so high up you can't have nobody reach up and getchu." Ruby sat straight again, groping for the red scarf she left at her grandmother's bare feet. As Ruby handed it to her, she began to hum, closing her eyes tighter as the scarf was positioned.

Tucking her braids in, she heard her grandmother chuckle. "Hair red like them rubies them white womens in the Garden District wear." Ruby stood and smiled at her grandmother. "Thank you, Nan." She smiled at her from her recliner. "I love you, sugarbaby. Gon back and do great thangs, you gon do great big thangs too." She smiled at her grandmother, as she sat in her recliner she slept in sometimes when her heart bothered her; it was easier for her to sleep in. Ruby studied her sepia colored face and violet gown she wore with her matching violet scarf. Esther had braided it before she went to bed. "I love you too, Mama Oscella."

Mother Oscella reached out to her youngest grandchild, and Ruby felt warmth infuse, strengthening her. She kissed her cheek and Ruby pulled away. "Hand me that spread on the sofa 'for you go get in the tub. Make sure you get in the tub, now." Ruby smiled as she moved to the brown sofa and grabbed her heavy dark quilt, on back of the sofa. "G'night Nan." Mother Oscella squeezed her hand and closed her eyes. "Night baby." Ruby smiled and walked down the hall and to the bathroom. She took a deep breath as she closed the door behind her.

The house clock chimed ten o'clock. She would be leaving tomorrow evening, bound again for St. Louis and Keys. She turned to the clawfoot but and turned on the water. She slipped out of her day-worn yellow dress and slipped in her peach colored robe. She wiped the quick steam off the mirror and looked at her reflection. As the thunder of the water flowed in the background, she untied her hair, leaving the scarf on the sink. She looked at the two braids her grandmother made. The hairstyle denied her almost twenty years of life. Ruby looked at the braids, feeling her eyes water and began to undo her braids.

Feeling her pressed hair hit her shoulders after the dismantling of the second braid, she watched the bathroom fill with steam. "Pin curls, I want pin curls." She reached for the medicine cabinet and took the shot glass full of Bobby pins and closed the cabinet. Taking the comb and setting lotion on back of the toilet, she began to pin curl her hair. Ruby turned to shut off the water and curled her hair and thought of Keys. She thought of the last time she has seen him before she left. Ruby remembered how he smelled, how he felt next to her. She remembered how mad he was that he had to drop her off at the Colored Entrance of Union Station. But most importantly, she remembered how he told her he wanted to be where life was, when Robert died. Ruby remembered how sure he looked even with tears in his eyes, how he held her hand and told her he wanted just her.

As she finished pin curling, she retied her hair. She washed her face in the sink with cool water like her mother taught her and followed with Nadiola cream to keep her face smooth. Ruby studied her face again and smiled. She let the robe fall to the floor, stepping past it, she got in the tub, letting the heat of the water and the cool of the tub soothe her. She closed her eyes and heard Keys' voice as if he was sitting next to her. Ruby's mind drifted to that same Wednesday. How they watched Levi do is daily night count as they sat on the stage. He had kissed her over and over. Keys had snuck in the back of the club as he was known to do, when he didn't want everyone to know where he was.

They had argued, spoke in hushed tones about the baby, and he took her towards the stage, just out of earshot of Levi. He told her that he was going to leave, he was going to take her with him. They were going to go to California and start over. "See that, doll?" He had pointed to the large brown envelope on the bar. Ruby had shifted in the blue dress she wore and craned her neck to see it. "See that breadbox? There's 1500 bucks in that envelope, doll. The take tonight was twice that."

He looked at Ruby, kissed her again. "Doll, we are going to leave. This place is too small for you. You sing just as good as Billie, or any other girl I heard on the radio!" Ruby had blushed as he tipped her chin to his face. "You are my girl, Ethelyene. You are gonna be Ruby Lewis." He hugged her tight, while she had cried from belief and relief.

Ruby had asked Keys how he had made his money, and why he kept a blue cookie jar in the closet in her room. He called it the *Treasure jar.* He had smirked at her and said, "real estate." Ruby had only smiled at him and knew better. She had seen him at the still in back corner of The Gypsy Hand. She knew he was making boiler maker gin and Moonshine.

Ruby knew he had a lottery going and high stakes gambling. Levi was a godly man she knew, and knew Levi knew what he did. But Levi took a piece of the kitty every week. Ruby had seen the young men Keys hired to throw some of the player out when the game got too hot. Ruby knew what happened when some of the players demanded more for their tab or couldn't pay the one they had. She, and Babs on occasion, had seen the black box—The Keeps box, Nathan and Keys called it. In that box men and some women, put possessions in: from wedding rings to pinks to their cars to keep playing Blackjack, Keno and Poker. She knew. She had said nothing because she knew the reason why: his father having a stroke, his mother trying to care of his sister and his desire to leave St. Louis.

Ruby began to bathe, and she smiled. "Ruby Lewis." She giggled, clutching the towel and soap to her chest. She knew that when she went home, she would count the money in her savings box. She would add it to the money in the Treasure jar and tell Keys how much they had. Smiling, she thought of how and when would get in his car and leave and start life together.

****

Thomas put her hand in her face to wake her up. His steady patting and the fresh sunlight stirred her. His babbling happy and insistent. "Thomas!" his mother yelled. "Thomas!" The footsteps startled him in his shirtless state as he turned to the door to see his mother burst through it. "Boy!" she yelled, he arms akimbo and hair in her now signature polka dot scarf. She wore a yellow shirt and a blue duster skirt. "You heard me, Tommy!" He cooed at her. "Wake up Ethie! Mama lookin for you, and she made grits." Esther went through the door, sounding more like a gallop than walking. Ruby smiled listening as Thomas cooed in the hallway.

Ruby lay on the twin bed, looking at the dust floating in the new sunlight. "Ethie!" She rolled her eyes at the shrill in her brother's voice. Putting her hand into the light, she turned it over and over, watching the shadows on the floor. "Here I come!" She managed while she sat up, deliberate and slow. Her bare feet to the floor she looked outside the window, watched the clouds in the sky. She smiled, remembering how she, Esther and Frank and gotten spanked so often for trying to climb a flour mill it trying to reach Heaven. She remembered the horror on their mother's face when she had made it to the top the windmill as a nine-year-old child. Mae-Reavis had said after then nine-year-old Ethie once she had drug her off the scaffolding of the windmill, "If you want to leave the world, get grown and leave Iberia first!"

As she stood, stretching in the sun, she thought of the train ride home. She thought about how she hated to go to the Colored car on the way to a place where she was still a colored girl, and not a woman. Ruby sighed as she smoothed the green housedress she had worn to bed. Opening the door, she was welcomed by sizzling ham and laughter. Franklin greeted her with a red bowl of grits with butter, as he hugged her to him. "Here, girl. Eat so you can get out my mama house." Ruby laughed as he kissed the top of her head before as she sat. "Hush, Frank!" their mother said, sitting in her perched chair by the back door, cutting ripened peaches. "Girl eat these vittles, so you can get ready, I gotta get your cobbler together." Ruby stirred her bowl, watching the butter melt. Franklin sat next to her, drinking his coffee. Nola was home with the baby and was entertaining some of her friends from Chicago. "Mama, Ethie got a fella!"

Ruby forced herself to swallow the butter-sweet mixture, letting the spoon linger in her mouth. "Mm." Mae-Reavis chuckled. "I figured. So did Daddy." Mae-Reavis began to giggle, the juices coated her hands while cutting the fruit over the bowl on the table. "I wasn't gon press it." Mother Oscella sat next to Mae-Reavis, in a red housedress, watched Thomas tap at the back door, and coo. Ruby thought her plum colored scarf tied high in front looked like a crown. "Where is Daddy?" Ruby managed once her mouth was empty. "He went fishing with Moses. He came by this morning tellin my son the bluegill and trout where jumping. You know Moses' family got them some mo land for their farm." Mother Oscella said, smiling as she watched Ruby's reaction.

Esther emerged from the stove, gracious and caramel skinned as she was, wearing a red housedress. Mae-Reavis had made her when she married Big Thomas. She gave Ruby a piece of the fresh cooked ham, in the red bowl her grits sat in. Esther gave her sister a wink before she replaced the pan of ham in the robin egg blue stove. "Yeah, what's his name, Ethie?" Esther asked. There was a giggle in the room which was wrapping around her. "Reuben." She whispered looking at the bowl. "Speak up, Ethie! You said his name is what, Billy the Kid?" her brother asked. Ruby laughed, feeling her face flush as she began stabbing at her ham and grits with her spoon. "No!" Shooting her brother, a look, she rolled her eyes and remembered to breathe. "His name s Reuben!" she said, shaking her head at her brother. "Mm. That's a good name." Franklin looked at his younger sister, cutting his eyes. He sipped his coffee in his white undershirt. "That sounds like the name of a man that know what he want."

Franklin shoved her shoulder as she ate. "Wait till I tell Mo you got another colored boy up north sniffin round you!" Ruby swallowed hard. Esther turned around from fussing in the sink, eyebrows arched, "He is colored, Ethie, ain't he?" Ruby inhaled. She began to what her grandmother said about having to 'drop an anchor in your soul.' Looking up, she exhaled, before speaking. She opened her eyes in the direction of her mother and sister. "No."

Mother Oscella sniffled, eyes widening. Her eyes were so wide Ruby thought she was crying. She kept eating. "Hol on nah. He could be one of them Italian boys come from the gulf! Is he one of dem?" Ruby shook her head, still eating. "Does your Daddy know?" Ruby heard the voices and remained silent. Mae-Reavis stood, slapping her hands and bowl on the table. "I got wash to do, and you got a train to get to." She went through the door, grabbing her brown woven wicker basket by the door as she went, her blue housedress as a cape flowing behind her. "Ooh, whee! Who made mama mad?" her father said as he came in the front door thereafter his wife. "She was calling for the Lord and her dead Mama!" Oliver moved dishes around in sink. "Mo you was right! Them fish all but jumped in the johnboat." Ruby heard Moses's voice and advancing heat towards her back. "Hey, Ethelyene." She heard her brother's voice after a moment. "Mo, get out my Mama house! We ain't invite yo hantin ass in and you ain't ask! Take all your bullshit with you!"

There was rustling near the sink, rushed voices and slapping of the fishing pole against the back door frame. "Franklin Delano!" Esther screamed. "Yo grandmama is right there!" Mother Oscella spoke, voice like thunder in Ruby's ear. "Oliver, sugarbaby got a fella." Oliver began to laugh, arranging the fish in the sink. "Mama told me. Moses, look like you crossed the Red Sea too late!" The room stayed silent, heat still at Ruby's back. "When you gon brang this health colored boy home? I know you was gon meet somebody son up there with your Great Auntie Linda." Ruby looked up from her half-eaten bowl to see him pouring out the crabbing bucket. Ruby watched his shoulders flex and roll in the white shirt and overalls he wore, sweat sheen gleaming off his balding head. "What's his name?" "Reuben." She answered. Esther cleared her throat before speaking, "He ain't colored, Daddy."

Oliver laughed. "What is he then, a white boy?" Silence answered him. Oliver turned to look at her, Ruby stared ahead. "He's white? You courtin a white boy!" he yelled. Mother Oscella hummed, Thomas cried as she did. He leaned on the table, hands baring him up. Mother Oscella quieted him on her lap. "I told you when you started sangin in that juke joint to watch them white boys that come in there!" Oliver's jaw squared as he continued, his face reddened. "I told you the boy me and Bessie Coleman had to chase of the front porch that was after ya sister!" He shook his head, his stare boring into her. "I told you these white men like to take any colored girl they can get and use 'em like outhouses. I— "

"He ain't like that, Daddy! He's good to me! He don't— "Her father clapped his hands together and pointed at her. "I told you, Ethelyene that you could leave here and do better! I ain't send you to the north to wench with some cracker!" Ruby looked down at her bowl of cold grits. "Moses, get out my house, you about a sunbeam from away from meeting Miss Bessie." He pointed towards the door and the room echoed as the door once more. "Ethylene," her father sighed, there was a new warmth behind her then, Franklin's and Esther's hands on her shoulders. "You can always come home." Mother Oscella spoke over him. "Always, nothing gon keep us from lovin on you, sugarbaby." She looked at her, searched her eyes. Ruby looked at her, then her father. He closed his eyes and sighed, rubbing his temples before opening them. "Till that boy come to my door and ask for you. I don't wanna hear shit else about him, hear?"

Ruby opened her mouth, and he repeated himself, same thunder Mother Oscella had. "I meant what the hell I said! Till that boy can come to my door, at this house, in New Iberia, L'sana, and ask for you?" he paused again, his voice louder. "I don't wanna hear shit else about him!" Ruby looked at him, eyes watering. "Frank, take yo sister to the station. Her train gon be here this afternoon for long, and I gotta help Mama get these damn fish clean!" Ruby watched him leave the kitchen cursing as he went and called "Jesus!" as he door slapped and clapped behind him. Ruby stared at the yellow curtains as Mother Oscella began to sing than hum, low and sweet. Franklin and Esther sat next her on either side, unwilling to move. Ruby felt slick tears over her face as she stared at the cold food.

"You love this boy?" Franklin said. Ruby couldn't catch her breath. She heard her grandmother moan. "Yeah she does! Why else she stand up fuh 'im? She ain't the only colored girl been tricked by a white man?" Ruby looked at her grandmother, tears leaving her eyes despite her strength to will the water in. "I ain't been tricked, grandmama. I do love him. Even Daddy and Miss Bessie can't change that!" She wiped her face and shifted in her seat. "My train come this afternoon, and I can't wait to get out from down here wit'chall!" Ruby stood from her seat and Franklin grabbed her hand. "I'm wit Daddy on this. See and mess wit who you wont to. You ain't been taught to be no body keep ho."

"Franklin!" Mother Oscella screamed. "She ain't, Nan! My baby sister ain't a ho or be nobody johnny girl!" he looked at his grandmother, eyebrows furrowed. "Now, if Reuben want my sister, he gon have to come to my Daddy do'r and ask for her." Franklin searched her face, his eyes, too glassy. "I gotta get ready to go, Frank." He released his sister, and she returned to the room she was sharing with Esther to finish packing.

****

The steam whistle woke her from her sleep. "Chattanooga. Next stop Memphis." Ruby looked out of the window, saw the separation of people funneling in and off the train. She saw tears and hugs on the platform. People scurrying like field mice, and the porters that looked like satchel trees with bags and trunks. Ruby shifted in her seat, watched the traffic below her window seat. The fading light washing her red seat in gold. She remembered her grandmother's words as she sat, how she had packed her peach cobbler in a linen handkerchief. "Sugarbaby, you got so much world in you, so much you wanna do. Always have." She mused from her kitchen chair. "I want you to remember you as you go back up North. You might care for this boy oh-so, but you got to have you a life too!"

She told Mother Oscella she had planned on going to the colored nursing school she had found, the St. Louis City Hospital Number 2 School of Nursing. Ruby assured her grandmother as she started to cry she would be alright. She wouldn't let Reuben hurt her or make a fool out of her. Mother Oscella clasped her face, pin curls spilled on her hands and kissed her forehead. "Bless ya, sugarbaby. You don't got tah leave, you can stay here." Ruby had pulled away, kissed her left palm and told her she would write and call when she got to her Great Aunt Linda's house. "Immabe alright, Mother Oscella. I promise you I am."

Ruby watched the traffic on the train slow and she nibbled at the lunch her mother packed. She opened her red lunch pail and rested it on her lap. She didn't want to leave the train to sit in a Colored Only café only to get back on a train that had the same name slapped on the side of it. She nibbled at her cobbler, remembered how determined her mother looked when she made the filling and the crust it was spooned into. "In this life," she said, "you make decisions with the best sense you got at the time. You have to make some decisions and deal with some things that you don't 'speck sometime too." She handed her the pail with the turkey and dressing and cobbler like it was a set of army rations. Her mother had tears in her eyes and hugged her. "Be careful, with everything, Ethylene, hear me?"

She dabbed the back of her hand against her eyes and put the food away. The train was almost to Memphis, about four hours from home. Ruby shifted in her seat and let her stomach rumble as the older colored man next to her snored soft. As a porter came down the train's aisle, she asked the time. "3:30 in the afternoon, ma'am." She smiled, remembering she would be with Keys tomorrow. As she looked out the window, watching the sun chase the trees, she thought of what her mother said when she met her father. She had asked Ruby to stir in the sugar as she spoke, now calm after the revelation about Reuben.

Mae-Reavis told her youngest daughter how she knew her father, her husband, Oliver Gibeaux was the one. She told Ruby she knew he was it when he touched her for the first time. Mae-Reavis said she met her Oliver at a party. He was working for family that owned another sugar plantation, and a farm. "Good white folk." She had told Ruby. They paid him right, and even helped them buy their house. Mae-Reavis was working on a farm and working as a washer woman. They had gone outside of a party that a friend of her was hosting, because he said he wanted to 'show her the moon.'

"It was in June, and," her mother looked through the window, smiling. "We just sat on Orpah's back and he held my hand." She sighed, Ruby had watched her face and the flush that came. "I remember I felt fire when he me. This warmth that 'rapped 'round me so and pulled me into him." Mae-Reavis had taken the bowl back to add the peaches. "I knew he was it, Ethie. I knew. Couldn't nobody tell me different." She went on to tell her whenever they were together, she felt safe, and like they were the only two in the whole world. "That feeling of safe, Ethie, couldn't nobody give you unless they were the one you was made for."

Ruby smiled as she closed her eyes, listened to the clatter of wheel and track as the train ran towards Missouri. "The one I was made for." She whispered and drifted off to sleep again. She smiled knowing the one she was made for would leave a note for her at the Colored Only platform.

December 1956

St. Louis, Missouri

Ruby shook as Reuben gave her a quick kiss on the cheek as he knocked on the door. They stood huddled and close on the front porch, as it started to snow. Nathan answered the door. He stared at Ruby, and his brother, looking as if something was dirty on the porch. "Nate let her in. It's cold." His brother closed the door and relocked it. Ruby looked at Reuben, eyes wide. She watched him reach into his left coat and grab his keys. As he fiddled with them under the amber dim porch light, they dropped as the door swung open. "Ruby!" She looked up at the in the direction of the voice, Babs grabbed her. "Hi shug!" They laughed as the snow fell on Barbara's hair. "Rube said that you never seen snow, how is that?" she pulled back from her, watching the snow fall on her black peacoat, too a gift from Reuben. "Well, it ain't rain, and I'm sugar, so I ain't about to melt."

Babs grinned at her. "C'mon, Barbara, let Ruby in." Babs gave her brother a funny face and opened the front door to allow them both to pass. The warmth of the house wrapped itself around them both, as Reuben helped her out of her coat. "Nathan!" Barbara yelled. He came out of the kitchen like a phantom, wiping his hands on a dishtowel as he went. "Hiya." He whispered. "You need to apologize, now!" Reuben hissed. Nathan walked over to the three of them standing by the door. Reuben hung her coat on the dark oak coat rack. Nathan looked over his shoulder, before looking at Reuben. "Look, Mom is nervous, okay? The only colored girl that has come to the house, ain't ever come to or through the front door!" Ruby looked at the floor, fighting back hot tears. Barbara squeezed Ruby's hand, and before walking towards the kitchen. Reuben slipped his right hand around her right hip pulling her towards him.

The red dress she wore made by Deborah. "It looks like something that Pearl Bailey would wear." She had told her. Ruby had suggested she change her hair to black. She remembered how Reuben had looked at her when he had come up after her set last week. Mr. Levi had been sick, but Reuben was running Sunday night Poker games. He had come to her room, looking at her and the towel wrapped around her which looked to be covered in ink. "Babe, that you?"

he had said. She had grinned at him, enjoying the stunned look on his face. "Babe, you said I was seeing your family for the holiday, so I didn't want to scare them with all this fire-color hair! So, Dee dyed it dark for me." Reuben walked over to her, dropping his hat on her bed. He kissed her before smiling at Deborah and her red satin scarf and matching robe.

Reuben leaned against the door jam, his crooked smile making his eyes bright. "Babe, I hate to be bad news, but it ain't all the way red." Ruby had stood up, clutching the peach robe she wore. She laughed in the mirror. Her hair was the color of a cherry cola. It was dark, yes, but the untrained eye could see that it had been red before. Deborah brought her hands to her face, eyes wide. "Ruby I ain't mean to! The box said— "Ruby held her hand up and shooed her out the bathroom. "It's dark enough, Dee. It'll work."

Ruby stood in the living room of Keys' parents remembering what he told her about his father, Johnathan. His father thought Reuben was in construction, so not to mention money or work. He told her his dad had been a druggist but had gotten sick, and from the illness had a stroke. She stood still, Keys squeezing her left hand and Babs holding her right, and they looked up when they heard their mother's voice. "Nathan, the door, did you- "she paused looking at the three of them near the closed front door. She had a tea towel in her hand drying a glass. Mae Lewis stammered as her eyes roamed between her two children. Reuben pulled Ruby towards him, Babs spoke first. "Mommy, this is Ruby." She looked at her mother, steeling herself for Ruby. "She's Rube's Sophie."

Mae looked at her son, puzzled. Her brown hair in a tight knot and blue dress crisply ironed. "Her name is Ethylene, but we all call her Ruby." He kissed her cheek, and she felt more of that fire her mother mentioned course through her. "You said she's a Sophie." She pointed at Ruby. "No, Ma, a Sophie is a steady." Mae shook her head. "You kids." She shooed them away, before turning on her heels towards the dining room. "We're about to eat dinner, bring Ruby."

Reuben moved in front of her, tipped her chin to his eyes. He kissed her. "Babe, the moment you ain't comfy, they get fresh, we agitate the gravel! You got my word." Ruby nodded and hugged him, kissed him again, forgetting Babs was in their vicinity. "C'mon, Ruby. You get to meet Daddy before he goes to bed." Hand in hand the three of them walked toward the dining room. Their footfalls echoed from the foyer, through the kitchen alcove, and left towards the dining room just off the kitchen. Ruby saw a sleeping man with glasses in a chair at the head of the table. He looked so fragile and needy. Mary's voice filled the room, sterile and knowing "Johnathan," he was wearing a blue striped pajama shirt under the blanket about his shoulders. "John, Reuben brought, um, his Sophie to dinner."

Johnathan stirred, shifted in his seat, attempting to focus. Mary rubbed his back, adjusted his blanket. Focusing his gaze, he looked at Mary whom was straightening plates, said, "Who does the colored girl work for? Our girl didn't come today, did she? Or did you fire her?" he said pointing to Mary. "John, Lizzie comes on Tuesdays, its Friday. The colored girl doesn't work for us."

Reuben pulled out a chair near him, one chair from the head of the table. Mary and Johnathan seated at the table's head, Reuben on the left of his father, and Nathan on the right. Babs insisted on sitting next to Ruby. Reuben left his right hand on her left thigh and squeezed. Ruby surveyed the food on the table, the crystal and china to be served on. There was ham, a green bean dish she didn't recognize, rolls and mashed potatoes. Ruby thought she recognized what she thought to be dressing, but it wasn't baked. There was even a roast, with pearl onions like her mother used to make for the white family she worked for on occasion. "Everything is so perfect." she whispered. Reuben left his hand on her thigh, starting to massage her left and hand wrist. "Nathaniel, can you say grace?"

Nathan was drinking water from the crystal glass and shot Reuben a look of desperation. He swallowed, setting his glass down with a bump. "Bow your heads." Ruby held on to Reuben's hand, let his warmth calm her again. Ruby opened her right eye to see Babs smiling with hands clasped under her chin.

"Gracious God, Our Father, thank you for your love and many blessings. Bless this food for our body and the love we all share. Amen." There was a chorus of 'Amen' with the Lewis's performing the sign of the cross.

Mrs. Lewis began eying Ruby as she passed dishes and platters around the table. "So, umm," "Ethylene, Ma." Reuben corrected. Mary gave her son a disproving look. "I'm sure she can answer for herself, Reuben." Ruby met her eyes and felt her back straighten. "My given name is Ethylene, but everyone calls me Ruby, Ms. Mary." His mother made a surprised noise as she took the bowl of rolls from Nathan. "umm, Ruby," she started. "Where are you from?" Johnathan stared at Ruby her and she felt that he was looking through her clothes. "I'm from New Iberia, L'sana. About a day drive from New Orleans." Reuben nudged her for potatoes and roast. "Roast is Reuben's favorite, and I make it with pearl onions." Ruby began to make her plate, taking polite portions and making notes about Reuben's favorite foods. The green beans, the rolls and roast. "Well, umm, Ruby, this is Sunday dinner for us. Tonight, I made Reuben's favorites. Next week," she paused, her bottom lip quivered and spoke swiftly, "but, more talk about you all."

Johnathan cleared his throat as Ruby memorized the meal to her palette. "Umm, Reuben, when would you tell us you where courting a colored girl?" Babs dishes clattered to the plate. Nathan snorted. Ruby's cheeks got hot. "Really,

Daddy?" she said. "Yes, really!" he answered. "It is a polite question! Where you going to tell us, you were courting a colored girl?" he kept his voice even. Ruby chewed and stared at his father. "I didn't think it mattered. You didn't care when Uncle Patrick courted Emma!"

"Joe is not my son."

Reuben lifted his hand from her thigh and wrapped his right arm about her shoulders. "Pop, I brought Ruby here, so you can know the woman I was talking to you about a couple months ago. Remember how you asked me to bring her by?" Reuben looked at her, willing her eyes to meet his. "Here she is." Johnathan looked at his son, Reuben squeezed Ruby's shoulder. Nathan continued to eat as the grandfather clock struck seven o'clock. "I don't like it, Mary. I don't like it at all." Ruby's left leg shook with fury. "There's nothing to like, John. He's an adult." She leaned over to whisper something in his ear and he began to eat. "Just don't get hurt."

Ruby felt her shoulders relax as dinner continued. His parents asked about her school, her plans and how she meet their son. "Where do you work?" Nathan asked from across the table. "The Gypsy Hand. It's a lounge in the District. I'm a waitress and I sing." Ruby concentrated on cutting her roast, tasting her potatoes. "Mm. Dinner is the end, Mom!" Babs answered with no one asking a question. "Thank you, dear." She said. Ruby chewed politely, eating to study not for hunger. "Oh, so you sing?" Ruby swallowed, took a tip of her water. "Yes ma'am, I do. I think I'm pretty good at it." She looked over at Reuben. There was plate and cutlery clanging. "Oh, so you're a paramour of Miss, umm, what's your last name, Ruby?" She took a sip of her tea. "Gibeaux. Gib. Bo." Mary gave a polite smile. "So, Reuben you have been paying her visits at this lounge?" Reuben shook his head.

Mary and Johnathan remained silent, concentrating on the meal. "The Gyspy Hand." Johnathan repeated. "Yes, sir. The Gypsy Hand. Ruby sings there." Johnathan watched his wife as his roast, finishing the last bites before continuing. "You sure she's not one of those feather boa girls? Or a shake dancer? There's shake dancer lounges around there too." Ruby looked at Reuben and dropped her fork to her plate. "I am a singer, Mr. Lewis. I don't dance or shake for the people I sing for."

Johnathan set his fork to the side of his plate, staring at Reuben, taking off his glasses. "I know a lot of colored girls are shake dancers, and boa girls—I don't want my son around loose colored women." Reuben stood and looked at Ruby. "Doll get up. Let's split!" Nathan looked at Babs and their parents. Ruby stood and took his hand as he pulled her into him again. "Ruby wants to be a nurse, Pop. She found a school and is gonna go when she saves up enough money."

He whispered in Ruby's ear, brushed it with this lip. "If she were that Rachel girl, whose friends with that Katherine girl you wouldn't be like this!" Reuben turned towards his mother, who was dabbing her eyes with a handkerchief. "Like what, Mom? Like what?" Mary Lewis stared at her son, watching him help Ruby from her chair. "You sit your ass down Reuben Michael!" Johnathan slammed his hand on table, rattling. Ruby shivered as she was lead her from the dining room. "That colored gal can't be anything to you but clean your house! We're you're family! Reuben! Reuben!"

Reuben helped her with her coat when they made it to the front door with Mary and Johnathan still arguing, still calling for him to come back to where they were. Reuben grabbed his coat, checked for his keys and left through the front door. He kissed her once they were on the front porch, the amber porch light making her face sepia. "Are you okay?" Ruby squared her shoulders, wiped her eyes. "I ain't a whore, Keys. I don't know what your Pop's fix is, but I ain't no body's whore!" Ruby walked towards Reuben's Plymouth, the wind whipping her face as she pulled the front door. Keys moved to open the driver's side door, to reach over to open hers.

They sat there, quiet. Reuben turned on the radio for heat. "I'm not riding in the back either." She hissed. Ruby put her arms across her chest, pouting and angry. "I love you." He whispered. Ruby furrowed her brow and turned towards the window. "Hmph." The radio turned on, Billie Holiday's Solitude began to play on the radio. There was more warmth on her back then. "I love you. You know that I do." Ruby sighed, still facing away from him.

    The front door opened and Babs walked down the front stairs. With quick steps, she was at the passenger window. Ruby rolled down the window. Ruby kept staring at her as she began to speak. "My Pop ain't always the smoothest, Ruby. But he means well." Ruby watched the same determined anger that motivated Reuben fall over Babs's face. Ruby sucked her teeth and sighed, fixing her gaze ahead and looking at the snow on the car in front of her. "Babs, when a man calls you a whore, and you ain't one, you tend to take offense." She looked back at Babs. "Damn who it is." Babs shook her head. "Babs, we're gonna split, I'll be back later. Tell Ma not to wait up." Babs stood with her arms akimbo, smoothed her ponytail. "Where are you going? It's the day after Christmas!" Ruby didn't turn from Babs to see his reaction but heard the Plymouth's engine answer Babs.

    As they pulled away from the curb, heading towards Gravois Avenue, Reuben spoke. "I ain't letting nobody muck this up. Nobody! There's some heat in there now, but," he stopped at a stoplight. He looked at her, cupping her face.

"you are special, doll. And…" he moved closer to her, meeting his forehead with his own. "you're my girl. You will always be mine." Ruby kissed him, hands running through his hair, tasting his mouth as Gloomy Sunday played on the car's radio. *"it was all a dream, just a dream,"* Billie Holiday sang. "Keys?" she said finishing the kiss. "Yes?" "Can we get a shake?" Reuben giggled. "Sure, babe. Sure. And don't you dare get in the backseat. If they can't take you in my front seat, they can't have the money in my hand."

His lips were still warm from her, hands ached because she wasn't in them. He sat in his bedroom window as smoked, thinking about how her body had just felt. Thought about what she had told him about her visit home, and how he would get there and speak to her father, Miss Bessie Coleman be damned. He tucked his snubbed cigarette behind his ear, cursed the ember that fell on his right ear. *My Daddy said until you come down home and ask for me, he said he didn't want to hear shit else about me being with you.* He it and went to the top drawer of his dresser. As he rummaged for the box in the top of the dresser, there was knock. "Yeah!" he hissed. He turned around and cursed when he saw Babs. "Jesuschrist, Barbara! Get a damn bell, will you! You're sixteen not a cat!"

Barbara looked at his face puzzled then the box he held in his hand. "What's the haps?" she asked him, smoothing her purple gown. "Nothing." He said, turning around again, returning to his perch on the window. "Is Ruby okay?" he nodded, back still facing her. "Babs, promise me one thing?" she walked over to him, staring out into the December night. "If anything happens to me," he looked down at the black box on his lap. "Make sure your keep, y'know, sight of Ruby. There's a pouch in my drawer with her pictures, clippings and all that jazz." He took his cigarette from his ear to gestured towards the chest. "Keep it everything in that drawer." He smirked, looking at the window. "And she has a Treasure jar in her closet, make sure she keeps it."

Barbara looked at her brother, pulling her shoulder towards her face. "What is going on, Rube?" Reuben looked at his sister, heart heavy. "I'm gonna marry her. She's..." looking over his sister, he inhaled before he opened his eyes again. "life makes sense when she's in it. Don't lose her, Babs. Don't lose her." Barbara walked towards her brother with the box on his lap. There was a smaller box inside, burgundy colored. Reuben didn't stop her, kept looking out of the window. Once she opened box, saw the glint of a ring. "She's gonna go over the moon, Rube!" Babs squealed. He began laughing and reached to put the ring back in the box. "That's the plan. I'll pop the question after her set on the 12th. It's already after Christmas and that's not my style."

Barbara and her blonde hair danced around the room. "Ruby's gonna be a Lewis!" Reuben shushed his sister, half giggling. "Pipe down, Babs, okay? Now, I gotta plan it. And you gotta be there." He pointed at her. "Consider me dead, Rube. And dead men tell no tales. No one's gonna no nothing from me." Reuben nodded towards her, flicked the cigarette butt out of the window. Shutting the door, he turned towards the left side of the room and his bed. He wished he had just stayed with Ruby. Nathan was at it making boiler gin again to get around Alderman Finch, and sometimes he would forget that still Levi had kicked. He shrugged it off. There would be a game tomorrow and his head had to be clear. Reuben knew the timeline was about to be in concrete once he asked her to marry him. He didn't need extra heat or hitches. With Robert gone, he had to do the books, run the numbers and make sure the games were played straight. He didn't know if he could watch Nathan too.

He laid back on his bed, still smelled her on his skin. Looking up at the ceiling, he shut his eyes. He felt Babs sit at the foot of his bed, happy she was silent. "Yeah, Ruby's gonna be a Lewis."

January 1957

St. Louis, Missouri

Ruby looked at the fresh cut white gardenias in her room. She sat at her vanity, her hair still cherry cola red as it had been when she saw Key's family in December. Shifting at her vanity, she smiled as she applied her mascara again. She wet the long handled spooled brush to dip into her black cake Maybelline mascara, concentrating as she darkened her eyelashes once more. She groped for her Revlon lipstick she had worn earlier in the evening. Ruby swore, muttering the name of the shade. "Fifth Avenue Red, dammit! Where is it!"

Ruby looked on the floor, finding the black and gold tube against the far leg of the gold painted vanity. Grabbing the tube, she reapplied her lipstick before she went downstairs to start her encore set. From her mirrored reflection, she saw Richard in the door. "You so pretty Miss Ruby!" he said as he ran by her room as his father, Albert, called him. She rolled her eyes and giggled. Jack told her there would be reporters from the St. Louis Post Dispatch, St Louis American and The Black Star Pages at this show, everything had to be perfect. Ruby gave encore shows on seldom occasions. She has only done four of them since she began singing at the Gypsy Hand. She stood from her vanity and in looked in her cheval mirror, looking at her black dress she bought from Famous-Barr and the red shoes Keys gave her. She grinned thinking she indeed looked like Dorothy Dandridge in a black Rita Heyworth dress.

Ruby secured her bobby pins in her hair, keeping her length off her shoulders. She smiled in the mirror and headed down the back stairs, being careful to not tumble down. Getting to the bottom of the stairs, she heard a wolf whistle from Levi and heard a chorus of them as she went towards the stage. She waved at Babs who sat at the bar with a Pepsi-Cola. Reuben was in the back with the count, she knew it would longer if Nathan was helping. It always took longer when Nathan helped.

Ruby heard the clatter of camera flashes and applause as she Carolyn helped her up the three wooden stairs to the microphone. She squeezed Carolyn's shoulder, too clad in black, stepped back to look at her. "I know you wrote this song, Carolyn." Carolyn looked at her, smiling, eyes still shining. She put her arms across her chest, sighed and answered Ruby's akimbo stance, saying, "Tonight is your night, Ethylene. We will talk about Jack and mine old partnership later. Gon over there and sing that song girl! Carolyn gave her a shove as she made her way to the microphone.

She blew kisses to the crowd, waved at cameramen and reporters as well. "Thank y'all so much for staying for a red headed, clay foot L'sana girl." She grinned as the crowd laughed. "I'll do a couple more songs and," she trailed off seeing Alderman Parker come in and go in the back room and looked harried carrying some sort of box under his brown overcoat. "and I'll get out ch'alls way, okay? Come on with these notes, cher!" she gestured towards Carolyn, who smiled at her.

They started with a cover of *What a Little Moonlight Can Do*. She followed that cover with their own rendition of *Satin Doll*. On the final note, Ruby introduced Carolyn to the thirsty room amidst the cheers and whistles. "This is Carolyn Robinson. She has been the piano player at The Gyspy Hand for, what, cher, two years?" Carolyn looked over her shoulder at her, thought and answered, "Four." There was more cheers and applause. "Four years! I couldn't do this without her, and her brother Samuel, whom y'all all know as Jack." She gestured behind her to the fair skinned man with the Sammy Davis, Jr. processed hairstyle and pressed blue suit, with the alto saxophone. Jack waved doing a quick scale on his saxophone.

She watched Barbara push through the throng of people to give her a glass of what she prayed was lemon water. Barbara handed the water to her as the camera flashed, continued flashing as she took a drink. Setting the glass on the short stool next to her, she saw Keys come from the back room. Keeping her eyes on him she started her signature song, *My Man Made Me*. He sat next to his sister at the bar, and even Levi stopped to hear her. With the piano soft, she kept eyes to him. "My man made me love him, love him like I do. Can't no other compare, to ever love him as I do." There were tables moving as those that came as couples began to dance cheek to cheek.

Keys smiled as he watched her sway, felt fever all over as she had sung this song for months, but never the same why twice, just like Billie Holiday was known to do. "And when he's gone, home is exactly where he is." As she closed her eyes and sang the chorus:

> *My Man made me love him,*
> *Love him like I do...*

If I ever lost him,

I'd never know what to do.

My heart is in his chest,

In his arms I find my rest...

In no other love I have

Will ever be his best.

As she finished, she saw Reuben gesture for something under the bar. Levi smiled as he retrieved a box in a cloth. He nudged Babs to get the flower box. Ruby was washed in photos flashes along with questions. She answered them being gracious, taking all bouquets and business cards. She arranged the stacks of flowers, and cards on her stool handing the water to Jack behind her. As the crowd arranged, pushing towards the stage, even putting more money in the tip jar that was at her feet, Levi whistled, and the throng of people and cameras turned to look at the direction of the bar.

On shaky legs, Reuben put the box in his pocket, keeping eyes on Ruby. "I know you all think that she's just a pretty face with a voice that could make angels cry." There was laughter that filled the small room, pushing him toward the stage. "But there's something else you need to know." Reuben sighed, willing his body not to fall. He wrapped his hand around the box in his left pocket, transforming it from jewelry to anchor in his suit jacket, using his left hand to adjust his Fedora. "But this girl here, is off the market." Their eyes met, and she mouthed something to him he didn't quite understand.

When he reached her standing on stage, he took the flowers from the table and motioned for Babs. She stood on the side of her brother as he knelt, taking off his hat. "Ethylene 'Ruby' Gibeaux, I want just you." There were whistles and screams, his heart in his ears. "No one else. I don't never wanna love another woman that ain't you." He looked at the floor before looking up at her once more. He shook his hand in his pocket, retrieving the box. Levi whistled in the back again, saying, "Make her honest, Keys! Make her honest!"

Reuben's hand shook taking her left hand in his right as she bent over towards him, the light she stood in revealing his hiding place. "Marry me, baby? Please?" Ruby looked at him, shook her head, screaming "Reuben, this is—this is the end! Yes!" She hopped off stage into his arms. Reuben found a nearby chair someone has been considerate enough to move closer towards the stage. She wrapped her arms around his neck as she kicked her legs up, and there were camera flashes. "Did she say yes?" someone shouted in from the back. Reuben shimmied the ring on her left hand and she kissed him as the clatter or cameras. "Yes, the hell I did!" Ruby yelled. The laughter and applause where broken up with a crash to the floor.

"You bastard! You and that rotten sonofabitch Brigby can go to Hell! We ain't for sale! Go home and tell your wife your tried to hock her car to get in on another four hundred clams for a poker game!" Alderman Parker got up and looked around like a trapped cat. He saw Ruby on Reuben's lap and scowled. He got up and slowly walked out, slamming the door behind him. Ruby watched him go and a shiver rolled down her body from ears to ankles. Reuben kissed her bare shoulder to bring her attention back to him. "Baby, you are gonna look so good in white?" Ruby smiled and admired her ring, the diamond glinted in the camera flashes. "You think you're pretty slick, don't you?" He kissed her again, more of that fire she was now sure she couldn't live without. "As a canna oil." She smiled, more camera flashes. "I'd have it no other way." They kissed again as the cameras flashed. "Tell my brother I'm going to help count, Levi." Levi looked at her, puzzled but nodded. "You know where it is right? Cause if I go back there…" Barbara nodded and went towards the back room.

Reuben sat on her red sofa chair in her room, the blue Treasure jar in his hands, and his shirt gone, comfortable in his shorts. Ruby lay covered in her sheets and hair in a scarf not yet pin curled. "The way I see it," he started. "We can get married in California!" He rolled the jar between his hands. "We got about 3000 clams in here." Ruby smiled. "I ain't never seen the ocean. Can we get hitched on a beach?" Keys laughed. "Anything you want babe." She sat up a little, moving the sheet to cover her form. "I think we can leave in May. That will give us enough time to tie up loose ends and let Levi know I won't be back." Reuben nodded. "Yeah, that would be plenty of time. In about 3 months we're splitsville."

Ruby lay back on the bed, grinning at the ceiling. "I cannot wait. I cannot wait!" The floor creaked. "My uncle and aunt are gonna love you!" Reuben had moved over her, kissed her mouth again, motioning for her to move over in bed. "Let me in, Ruby." He whispered. "I can't stand not being where you ain't." His lips where in her throat. He had pinned her under him again, kissed her ears and over the tops of her breasts. As she moaned, she opened to him again. "Reuben..." she trailed off as he entered her again. "I don't ever want to love another woman like I love you." He said, nipping her left ear. He quickened his pace releasing her hands to push her legs part, she tightened around him in kind. "I love you." He said. Repeated it. Ruby grinned as she crested with her nails in his back.

Approaching the edge together, he locked his hands on her hips, holding back his own release to fulfill hers. "Ain't no other woman gonna get all of me, 'cept you." As she found anchor in the metal of the headboard, she blessed his name aloud to the rafters, and all that would hear on Olive Boulevard below. "I love you." She said as he lowered himself on her. "What can keep us apart?" he said, nuzzling her neck. "Nothing." She said, pawing through his hair. "Not a damn thing."

March 1957

St. Louis, Missouri

Friday nights were always late. Reuben sat at the bar and counted the kitty making small talk with Levi. Reuben had Ruby before she got in the shower.

He glanced at the clock at the back of the bar. 1:30 a.m. He and Ruby had been engaged almost two months, and they had only been apart for only two days at a time. Reuben had begun to get copies of his birth certificate, and his high school diploma. Once he had given it to Ruby to put in the Treasure jar, she "Reuben Michael Lewis, you ain't a gangster. You're businessman." Reuben had kissed the top of her head and put the jar back in her closet. They had agreed it would be after Mother's Day, May 12, is when they would leave. They had come to the date in the last week of February decision with a calendar, cigarettes and driving schedules versus trains schedules.

He sat at the barstool with Levi and smirked. "Mm hmm! How that girl doing?" Levi had asked him, slapping the bar as they counted money. "She's aces, Levi! We're leaving next month to visit my aunt and uncle out west," he smirked, and kept money in their separate piles before looking up at Levi. "So, she can see the ocean." Levi laughed as he did his tallying on his scratch paper. "Take care of my girl, hear, Keys?" Reuben smiled, sealing the manila envelope, sliding it across the counter. "She's not a girl anymore, Levi. She's my girl, remember?" Levi smirked at him. "Oh, I know! And so, does all St. Louis."

Reuben hopped off the stool, left his suit jacket on the barstool next to him. "I gotta run home for a spell. Ruby went to read to Doc, and he fell asleep in her room." Levi took the money and put it in a safe deposit box under the bar.

"You know Richard thank that Ruby is his woman when he don't see you!"

Reuben laughed as he headed out the door. "Well, I'll tell him that she's about to be a married woman and we don't no take strays!" Levi laughed. As he headed through the door. On his way to the car, he saw Alderman Parker from across the street. "Hey, Parker! What the hell are you doing?" Alderman Parker crossed the street and made his way towards Reuben's car. "Hey, um Reuben." He was stammering, stuttering as he pulled his coat together. "Did you get your fix yet? You look like ya got a monkey on ya back." Alderman Parker looked around, silent. "Look, I want you to know that I have it on pretty good authority, that it's more than just the press that knows about you and the colored singer." He adjusted his glasses, smoothed his hair. "What of it? I also have it on good authority that you been an unwanted presence here for months, a junkie itch, always red faced and staring after my girl for longer."

He stared at Reuben, a sly smile coming over his lips. "She is a such sweet flower." Reuben grinned. "You wish you had an idea." Alderman Parker leaned against his car. Reuben saw his shoes hadn't been shined, which means he hadn't been home. His face was unshaven. "For a man that prides himself on being concerned with family, you sure are hellbent on tearing yours up." Alderman Parker stood to his full height again, just a little shorter than Reuben's six-foot-one-inch frame. "Don't give me your shit, Lewis!" He hissed through clenched teeth. "I'm sure the police would have a field day with the info I have on you and that nigra in there and the gambling you all do." Reuben's laugh echoed into the alley. "And I'm sure that wife of yours," he snapped his fingers trying to remember her name, "Annie, right?"

Alderman Parker's hands went to his sides as he continued. "I'm sure she will want to know that her husband that helps with the organization of the VP Fair, and at St. Peter and Paul Church board, has a taste for colored girls that sing." Alderman Parker. "You will do no such thing!" Reuben stared at him, watched the alderman's eyes go glassy. "I'm sure Annie may wanna know exactly why she can't open any mail or come the Square." Alderman Parker swung wildly at him, Reuben moved out of the way keeping his hands in his pocket. "You shouldn't try to punch a guy when you're sauced, Finn." The puddle splashed against his glasses and face.

Reuben stooped down to him, cut his eyes at him. "Annie doesn't really know you, and it kills you that Ruby does." Reuben adjusted his glasses on his face. "Go home, Finn. This ain't no place for your type." Reuben walked around to the driver door and started towards the riverfront. He thought about the liquor to be delivered next week, and the money he had put in their Treasure jar. "Eight weeks." He said, relaxing in the driver's seat. "then we split this scene." He parked up the street from The Gypsy Hand, watching Alderman Parker leave in his white Cadillac. Nathan had told him after the engagement the only reason Alderman Parker had and took this job was because his brother was a cop. "He's sniffin around her because we got a rat somewhere. My bet is that Brigby!" Nathan had told him over a count that same week.

Reuben remembered counting money, making notes of Alderman Parker's behavior since Ruby had been there. "Brigby wants more credit, right?" Nathan made an agreeing noise. "No dice, Nate. He burns money and friends. He needs to pay the three hundred he owes us." He exhaled and closed his eyes, confident the alderman had driven away. Reuben thought about the last time he had seen his Uncle Patrick, he got him more than his father did. Always had. There was still a couple thousand in key money he and Nathan hid in their mother's floorboards in the pantry. The day before, he followed the funny feeling to split the money in the floorboard. He left Nathan's there, and moved his to the linen closet on the second floor of the house on Indiana. He knew it was more than enough to put down on a house.

Reuben closed his eyes and thought, smiling as he thought about the rosary Ruby had gotten for him to replace the one he always carried when he was setting up deliveries of boiler gin. "God'll keep you safe." She had told him as she gave him the white rosary in his hand in early February. Reuben took the rosary with him when he made deliveries, before he had Levi's sons to help.

"Almost, baby, Almost." He reached into the glovebox, looking at the white rosary and putting it in his pocket, before closing his eyes to rest. His nap was interrupted by sirens and engines backfiring. "It's on fire! Who all in there!" someone shouted.

Reuben jumped out the car startled watching the rush of people go back to their cars from hotels and fleeing nearby clubs. Reuben yelled for a young man that was running back to his car what was going on. "Mack, The Gypsy Hand is on fire! It just came over the late night KMOX radio!" Reuben felt his throat tighten as he smelled smoke and flame as he approached. The place was engulfed, with people screaming and crying and flames. He found Doc safe barefoot, crying with a blanket around his shoulders. "Doc!" he yelled, "Where his Miss Ruby?" he turned front the direction of the building, tears down his face. "She went back in Mister Keys! She thought you was in there, because she saw your jacket! Miss Ruby in the fire! Miss Ruby in the fire!"

Reuben hugged him, rocked him, as he surveyed the Gypsy Hand. The first floor was gone. Carolyn's piano. The still. The back room. The upper floor where the storage was. And the second floor was engulfed. Reuben placed Doc on the ground again. "Doc, you sure she went back in the fire?" Doc had begun to cry and scream louder as he looked and pointed. "Miss Ruby! Miss Ruby!" The fire department yelled at people to get back as they started the attach hoses across the street to the new black and red fire hydrant. "Doc? Where is Mr. Levi?" Through tears Doc managed to tell him that he went home, he wasn't there. Reuben took Doc by the hand motioned for another colored woman whom had come out of the apartments across the street to hold him. As he willed his eyes to focus, he recognized her as Elenore. She was a nurse, who Doc sometimes carried groceries for. "Elenore!" he yelled at her across the street. "C'mon, Doc! Get your wings and run with me!"

They trotted across the street to the older woman in the red scarf and curlers and red housedress. "Elenore! Could you watch him for a sec? I gotta to get my girl." she obliged, nodding and keeping Doc behind her with a hand on his back. "Mr. Keys! Don't go in the fire! Don't go in the fire!" Reuben made l across the street, and found the battalion chief, tried to push through. "Chief, my girl is in there! I gotta go get her!" The battalion chief turned and put both hands on his shoulders and pulled him off to the side. "Hold on, son. Who's your Sophie?" Reuben took a deep breath, the night air cold in his chest. "Her name is," the battalion chief told him to go on. "Her name is Ethylene, but we call her Ruby. She lives on the second floor." He pointed, tears in his eyes. "Son, we haven't seen anybody in there? She a white girl?" Reuben shook his head no. "She's," he swallowed the bile that came up. "She's a colored girl." The battalion chief looked wide-eyed at him. "There is no one in there, son. We checked." Reuben sunk to the damp sidewalk and screamed. His tears answered by the water shed from the fire hydrant.

It was almost the end of March before Reuben was able to go the ruins of the Gypsy Hand. He had only heard from Levi and Carolyn, but no one said they heard from Ruby. Babs had said she hadn't heard anything either. After mass on the last Sunday of the month, he and Babs had driven to the burn ruins of The Gypsy Hand. He heard Babs sniffling as they got closer, to the ruin and parked. Reuben had bristled against the breeze, shifted in his white dress shirt and slacks. He had even worn loafers to church with his sister and mother. He all but had to start screaming for his mother to let him leave the house after they gotten home from mass. Walking to the charcoal colored door and bright colored tape, he pulled down boards that were meant to keep everyone else out.

He heard his footsteps echo in the ash and broken glass. His thoughts went to the life that was once there with Ruby singing, people laughing and Levi soaking it all in. Levi's wife had called Reuben last week to tell him Levi was at Homer G. Phillips Hospital, the same Elenore worked for. "Don't you worry, Keys. He's just here for observations." She sighed before she mentioned the heart attack. He looked under the ashes that was the bar, found the safety deposit box missing. He prayed that Levi took it home or he told his wife, where it was. He looked in the back room, found the blue door. Opening the door, he found the still as a soot and melted metal. "They set it. They fuckin set it on fire!"

He surveyed the still room, and all the char in it. Reuben was thankful he left the lion's share of money made from the liquor and poker games at his mother's house. "This is," he kicked the still with is dress oxfords before he found the back staircase that lead upstairs.

Babs cursed as she looked around. "What is Levi gonna do now?" she asked her brother. His mind went back to Doc and Elenore. Talking to Doc's father, they agreed Eleanor would watch Doc when Albert went out. Reuben had given Eleanor some money to help her take care of him, as she had a daughter that was already grown. He decided he would send her fifty dollars a month to help. Even though Eleanor was a nurse, Doc was still a kid that needed things. The back stairs creaked and moaned as she ascended the stairs. "Be careful Squirt, this ain't the sturdiest."

Tears left his eyes as has stepped onto the landing, seeing char everywhere. Reuben heard his sister's footsteps behind him, her hands on his shoulders as she squealed and cursed. Opening the second door from the stairs, seeing the soot and char around the door. The bed he gave her was almost untouched. The linen was gone, but frame looked to be intact. Reuben and Babs scoured the room, looking for any trace of her. There were shoes in the closet, but the Treasure jar was gone. He sat on the bed and thought of Ruby. No way to call her, had tried to call her Great Aunt Linda. In tears he had called hospitals and the morgue for the better part of a month. He called Deborah it felt like on the hour at least once a day. No one knew where she was.

He lay back on the bed, indifferent to the soot and ruin round about him, remembering his last words to her. *What can keep us apart?* He had asked her. *Not a damn thing.* Babs rustled in the soot covered bathroom, knocking things over, and sounding as if she had found nothing. "She's gone, Rube. There's nothing in here." Reuben looked up at the charred ceiling, the splintered beams. "She ain't just vanish!" He sat up and looked towards the still opened window. Babs crossed her hands over her chest, "Reuben, we gotta get outta here. Mom told me to keep an eye on you, let's not catch any nails, okay?" Reuben looked up at his sister, sweet and demure in her pink shirt and poodle skirt. He nodded and looked out, gripped the sill and tore a piece off and tossed it from the window.

As they drove home, he cried. He pulled over by Saint Louis University. Babs walked around the front of his Plymouth and drove the rest of the way home. As they parked in front of the house, their father sat on the front porch. He eyed the soot on their clothes from his chair. He had gone to mass with his family hours prior, in matching slacks and a dress shirt. He was smoking, the same thing which caused his stroke two years earlier. "You got a message, Reuben." He said, still smoking and watching the street. Reuben unlocked the door, letting his sister in first and headed towards the kitchen where all the messages were by the rotary phone. In his father's scrawl, he read: *Eads Bridge. I got the goods. Wednesday night. Eight o'clock.* The name of the person: Deborah.

Reuben took the message and went to shower. He ran past his mother on the stairs, who muttered about him running in the house. "I'm making dinner soon, are you staying?" she yelled as he went towards his room. "Yeah, Ma! I'm staying." He headed to the shower and made sure Wednesday would stay free.

****

Reuben waited like the note said, he leaned against the hood of the car. It was past eight. When he checked his pocket watch, it was eight-thirty. He turned to get in his car to go home, as a police car drove past him. He heard the hoot of the barges and tugboats below. He shivered in the night air, fought the urge to get his jacket in the front seat. "She better hurry up." He heard the low toot of the barges, watched them pull through the mid-March night. Watching the boat push, he didn't see Deborah behind him. "Keys?" she said, voice wavered. He turned and hugged her, and she began to cry. They sobbed together a moment, before Reuben pulled away to give her his handkerchief. "Thank you." She dabbed her noise and round face. She had dyed her hair blonde again, the color and the big curls suited her. It made him think she had light everywhere she went, a halo as it were.

"So, what's the word?" He asked her. "Any sign of her?" Deborah teared up and shook her head. "The only thing I'm hearing is that she ain't dead, but everybody is mum." Deborah pulled her coat tighter around her ample frame. "She ain't dead, Reuben. We just ain't found her. I think that Alderman Parker set that fire because he couldn't have her." Reuben nodded. "I can see that soft sonofabitch doing it. Fire is for sissies!" Deborah giggled. "Look, I'll keep listening and looking, but you gotta get outta here, Keys." She put her hands on his shoulders, pulled him closer. "The heat is coming. Even you being white won't stop that." Reuben looked away. "I ain't leaving St. Louis, Dee." She scoffed. "I'm saying don't get foxy now. You need to make the money you have work for you." She kissed his cheek. "You got a way out, Keys. You can make this money legal with nobody getting wise, see?" Reuben kept his gaze on the water and the barge, his shirt collar slapping his cheek. "You ain't a gangster, Reuben. You're a business man. So be one."

"You sound like her." Reuben looked at the ground, gave her a note, slid in her pocket. "When you find my girl, let her know where I am. Okay? And give her this." Deborah nodded, as he moved to kiss her left cheek. "I will, Reuben. I will." They stood there, looking at the barges. "Nate and I got enough money to do this construction thing we been kickin' around. I might as well start it." Deborah put her head on his shoulder, the night air colder. "You can do it, Keys. Just don't forget us, hear?" He patted her arm as they walked. "Lewis Construction Company." Deborah laughed, throwing her head back. "Ooh, that's real square, Keys?" "I know, Dee. I know." They reached the car, and they looked around before Deborah got in the front seat.

The car started with KMOX in the back ground as Deborah gave her commentary about what she thought Reuben should do. As he headed towards her house, the duplex with the black doors on Sarah, he asked her what she planned to do with Ruby missing. She flipped her hair and giggled. "I'm gonna own a salon and make more colored girls almost as pretty as me!" They laughed and listened to Sarah Vaughn's voice on the radio.

Easter Sunday, April 1957

St. Louis, Missouri

There would be a peace in Memphis. Ruby cried for a week, her caramel face was swollen and red. She had called her cousin, Bessie, and asked her to get her out of St. Louis. She didn't know where Keys was or even if she could talk to him. The Gypsy Hand was gone, packed her things at her aunt's house under her protest and talk of spirits, and her need to stay in St. Louis.

Ruby had to get out of St. Louis. Alderman Parker thought she knew had set that fire, tried to kill her and Doc. He had threatened her, was following her. She had to leave. "Where you gon go girl, the moon?" Ruby flew around her small room, for a week. "Memphis. I talked to Bessie, and I'm leaving. I just need to get outta here, auntie! Just for a while!" her aunt had looked at her from the hallway, looking like a troll from the story books Doc had read to her. "For a week or so maybe, I'll be back." She told her. Her aunt had left her.

It was after Easter, she would leave next week. She sat on her bed. Head in her hands, remembering the fire, and the police and Alderman Parker's brother, Dennis. They were going to try and pin the fire on her. They had locked her up as a criminal, stole her away and left her in a holding cell that night. Alderman Parker told her 'for a night with him' he would make everything go away. She had refused. "I'd rather be dead than be a wench to a weasel!" He had stood and left her in the cold room. When the door swung open, she saw Avery, one of the white patrons of The Gypsy Hand. He was one of the policemen Reuben had given him money for his sick baby boy, Reuben had told her. She pleaded with him with her eyes was still in the gown she had performed in, feet bare, and tears over her face.

The next morning, she was free, and Avery had driven her home. She had showered and called Deborah. Her aunt had prayed over her for an entire day, giving her tea and telling her to rest. Deborah had come over that Friday just to put eyes on her, making sure she was alive. This time, she had to tell Deborah to make sure she stayed missing. This would be the last Easter in St. Louis. She was leaving Friday.

As she finished her Easter dinner of ham, sweet potatoes and green beans at her aunt's table, the doorbell rang. Her aunt was in the garden, and she dashed to the front door. Deborah ducked in, closing the door behind her. They went to the kitchen, still in their Easter dresses and hats. Deborah smoothed her emerald green dress, and Ruby shifted in her pink frock and they began to speak in hushed tones. "I saw him." Deborah said. Ruby propped her hand on the table. "And?" Deborah sighed. "He misses you, Ethylene! Are you still leaving!"

Ruby looked through the open backdoor to the kitchen, watched her aunt in her straw hat and gardening clothes. "Yes." She watched her aunt break open the earth to pull weeds. "Why? Ya'll are leaving next month anyway! Why not just hang on?" Ruby turned her attention back to her best friend. "For peace." She teared up. "These last few weeks wouldn't give us no peace. Not with a colored girl trying to be his wife." She shook her head. "Keys has his color and his money, and even the money he gave me. I have to leave for him. I want his life better—even without me." Deborah looked at her, cupped her face and watched life leave it, her eyes darkened. "I gotta leave to think. I can't think here. Not with Finn looking for me and Dennis trying to snatch me for him."

Deborah stood up, taking Ruby took her feet as well. "Don't make this a habit, Ethylene. If you start running now, it'll be who you will stay." Ruby sniffled, looked at the floor, and sat down again. Deborah opened her black satchel purse and left her a slip of paper. "I gotta go home, Ruby. You gotta whole lot to think about." Deborah's footfalls clicked towards the door and ceased. Ruby looked at the paper, opening it and began crying while she read.

Ethylene-

I know you're still in St. Louis. Know that I love you, like nobody else. I ain't running and I ain't scared. I meant what I said. You are home. Come home to me. I'll drop the whole world to see you again, doll.

Ethylene left her cleaned plate on the table, going towards her room with letter in hand. "What life would we have? I love you, Keys, but I gotta go. I gotta split."

In her room, she double checked her bag to make sure the Treasure jar was nestled in her slips and her pillowcases. Ruby went to her aunt's linen closet by the bathroom and felt for the small hole she cut out of the wall. She removed the stained Clairol box, grinned at the money it contained. If she was leaving, it wasn't going to be empty handed.

Going back to her room, Ruby sat on her bed and began to count the money she had saved. Alderman Parker's money was added to the pot. Her mother told her to give whatever a white man gave her back, especially if it was money. "They'll thank they own ya, cher. Don't do 'courage up don't take nothin from 'em!" Ruby started humming the melody for My Man Made Me. "When he touched me," she closed her eyes and exhaled. "all I felt was fire—made me love him like I do."

There was eighteen hundred dollars between the jar, and her Clairol box. Ruby walked to the window, pulled the blue curtains and watched the traffic on Arsenal, the children hunting Easter eggs in Tower Grove Park. Keys made one last attempt to find her. She would try and do the same.

Still in her Easter dress, she ran down the stairs to the kitchen, looking in the drawer her aunt kept her cards in. "Paper, a piece of paper." Ruby saw the scraps of manila paper in the back of the drawer that her Aunt Linda wrote her numbers on to give her to take to The Gypsy Hand or for groceries. Her aunt was still outside, talking to a neighbor, Ms. Alice over the fence. Ruby scribbled on the paper.

Reuben-

If you read this, see this, I'll be gone. I'm headed to a cousin in Memphis. I don't want to make this harder than what it is, but I know what started the fire. Know Fin wants to pin me for it because I won't be his woman. I love you, shug. -E

There were envelopes in the back of the drawer. Tomorrow she would leave the letter for her Aunt Linda. Richard delivered her groceries once a week. It would get to him. It had to get to him. "I gotta go, I gotta go." She kissed the letter before sealing it in the envelope. She placed her hands on atop of it, and felt cool waves go up her back. The tears came, and she let all hope of being strong go.

Part II-

Ethylene Gibeaux Carter

Memphis, Tennessee-1998

Chapter 13- February 1998

I looked for my keys in my workbag as I walked towards my red front door. I cursed as I fumbled in my camel-colored workbag. There was always too much stuff in it. I found the keys at the bottom of my bag, as I went up the five steps, relieved to see the front door. Under my sepia tinged porchlight, I pulled my keys turned to chirp the alarm on my blue Nissan Altima. I unlocked the front door to be greeted by my alarm chirping the front door was open. My last gift from James. *I'm tired of you coming home, late. I don't want nobody coming in on my girl!* After thirty years, I was still his girl.

As I pushed through the front door, and locked it behind me, I saw my answering machine flicker on the cherry oak end table. I smiled at the blinking red four while looking through the day's mail. Junk mail. Bills. I smiled at the reminder for a charitable donation to the American Red Cross. Even in all my years of nursing, I couldn't forget the how I gotten into it. It's true how fire changes people.

I smiled down at the stark white envelope, with its comforting logo on the left side. I held it in my hand, setting down my workbag and purse. I thought of him, it happened from every now and then. I didn't fight the thoughts when they came anymore. Especially, after James died. I found myself this very

Wednesday morning over coffee in the Cardiology Team Meeting, wondering how he was. I smoothed the back of the envelope, whispered his name. "Reuben." I smacked the envelope on the back of my palm and moved to the answering machine.

After pressing play, I went through the lower level of my house leaving my beige flats by the front door. "Hi Mrs. Carter! This is Julia on the fourth floor of Methodist University Hospital. Your Avon order is in. I'll see you Tuesday." I smiled at Julia's cheery voice.

There was beeping for the next message. "Hi Mama. This letter came for your today. I'll bring it with me when I come see you this weekend." Beeping. "What letter?" Beeping. "Ms. Carter, this is station KWMU, we would like to talk to you about your singing career in St. Louis. We got your information from a Mrs. Barbara Lewis Redding. Please call us back at 314-820-6310 and ask for Madison." Beeping. I leaned against the wall. "Babs?" I whispered to the empty house. "Babs?"

Beeping. "Hi Shug, it's me. I'm still stuck up here in New York. I miss you like crazy, babe. I'll be home as soon as I can. I love you." I closed my eyes, ran through the name again. There was only Barbara Lewis Redding. And I hadn't spoken to her in at least three or four years.

I went upstairs, erasing the day from the answering machine, making my determined march to my shower. Charles would be home from New York in a few days. It would be good to see him, smell him, have his arms around me. It's always good to have him near to chase ghosts away. He reminds me of the right now, and where to go next. I walked through my master bedroom, bed neat and made towards the warmth of my red and cream-colored bathroom. As I undressed and stepped in the shower, pulled the red shower curtain behind me.

I thought about Babs. I thought about the two years I had to go before I had full retirement. My coming birthday assured me that when I stopped working, everything world still keep spinning. I couldn't wait to travel with Charles. I had James's life insurance money I had saved and invested. I knew how much my pension would be. I leaned against my forearms the shower wall, careful not to get my hair wet. I thought about my kids, my grandbabies, and Babs. "Call me for what? There's nothing for me in St. Louis." I washed the day off, the blood, rubbing alcohol and sweat. I thought, as soap rolled off me. I thought hard, and wondered about the radio station, about Babs and why it was the station called me, or even got the number. "The hell..."

I replayed the message over in my head, rolled the possibilities over. I thought about this as Case Coordinators are taught. I thought about the problem, the options and resolutions. Thought about Babs: how she might have been doing, how she was, and how Reuben was. I turned off the water and thought. I wrapped myself in my favorite cream colored Egyptian cotton towel Charles had gotten me as a set from Macy's and bit my lip, habit since I was a girl in New Iberia. It helped me think, settled my mind. I looked in the bathroom mirror, wrapped in the towel. I looked at my reflection, smoothed my dark shoulder length hair. I looked at the patched graying at my temples. I smirked. "Nothin a bout with Miss Clairol won't fix!"

I walked to my room and got ready for bed. I sat on the King sized empty bed, alone for the first time in years. I looked to the left at the mirror above my vanity, and watched the water fall from my face. I didn't stop the tears like I used to. I missed James. I had almost thirty years with him. "I miss you, babe." I whispered to the empty room and dim light. I put my face in my hands and cried. I howled. I curled up on my bed, our bed, the last bed I bought with my husband and sobbed. I wanted my husband. I started my life over here, I was able to move on beyond New Iberia and St. Louis. I could be someone else again. That's what I needed.

I had called James my anchor in a hurricane. He was sweet natured and could be hellish if you crossed him. In those pretty new sheets, white sheets and dark green comforter and wished for him. I don't remember how I got to sleep, but I was grateful for that metered level of peace—God smiled on me.

I rose from my bed, looking at my nightstand that the clock that stared back at me. I had gotten home around five, and it was almost eight in the evening. I went to my dresser, happy I still had the towel and pulled out this green gown, my last present from James. I grinned thinking the last thing that I could have of him, would be something he could hold me in. I dressed for bed, thought of James. I thought of his steady heartbeat, his arms, even how he smelled coming back from work as a construction foreman. I loved how comforting his sweat was. "Boy, go shower for you try and lay up under me!" I would tease him. He would furrow his brow and tell me, "Girl, in this great big ol' house I built, you mine and so is everything else." I would laugh, and he would think he was so funny. He'd kiss me that his scratchy beard and hold me close.

I missed him. I miss him so much. I loved him like no one else. The only person I had hurt this badly over was-- I couldn't even say his name right then and shook my head free of the thought. I burrowed under the covers, and sat up stock straight, hadn't wrapped my hair up. I got out of my bed and walked downstairs in my bare feet. I went to my backdoor and slid it open. The night air brushed my face and strewn hair. I stepped out on the deck, the same deck I had asked James to build me when we got this house. This oak, and he stained so it would remain as red as long as possible. I looked over the deck and watched the stars. *I wanna be where life is. Don't send me home.*

The tears came again, hot and quick. I didn't know how it was possible to mourn two men and be one woman. I thought of the silly younger male nurses at work that didn't think I was old enough to have grown children. I smirked. "Black don't crack." I'd smirk and say. I thought of the life that I had planned in St. Louis, in California, with Reuben. We would lay in each other's arms and dream. He always looked at me that I was the only woman in the room or the world. He always made me feel like I was all he wanted—even back then. I felt safe. I would think that maybe that was the reason why I loved James like I did and like I do.

I stood, listening to the night, smelled rain coming. It had stormed when I went into work, and I hated it. My tires slipped a reminder I needed to have them rotated. I welcomed it the distraction of what I need to do, comforted by the maintenance of things needed to be done. I wanted to feel the soft patter of the water of my skin again. It had rained the day of James's funeral, it had rained on an off that whole week five almost six years ago. I felt like he was nearby whenever it rained. "James." I whispered. "Babe, I love you." There was thunder off in the distance. I remembered the trick my father's mother told me about how to 'catch a storm foe it get over you' she'd say. He would always tell me to count and sing Miss Mary Mack between thunderclaps. At clap number four, there was more rain, louder a thunderclap.

I went inside, shutting the door as the sky opened. I watched the storm from the living room on the other side of the sliding door. I didn't need to talk to Babs. I didn't need to call any radio station. I sighed. It took me years to get over Reuben, to move my life past him. I had found James, made a life with him. Stayed in that life with him, having children and in love until he died. But just like this storm, he was ever present again.

Chapter 14- Early March 1998

I was off today. I called Michelle and Samuel over, because Michelle had called me so early. "Mama!" she had said, "Mama! I gotta show you something! Imma come over soon as I leave work. Then the answering machine had beeped. "7:25 am." She had to have been leaving the floor, and whatever she had to show me was with her. "Girl." I rolled my eyes and poured my coffee. I smiled remembering James knew how I liked my coffee and wished I didn't have to get up to make any. After she called me, I had gotten up and made a pot of coffee. If she was working as hard as I knew she was, she would need it.

I stirred my coffee, sitting in my red bathrobe, waiting for my oldest to barge through the front door. What would this thing be that she just couldn't wait to show me? She's been like this her whole life, bounding in the world with energy. I smiled and sipped. I thought about Babs again. I hadn't thought about her since the message from the radio station two weeks ago. What could she really want? Why is this radio station calling me? I laughed to myself, hair still in my roller set and scarf. I looked at my yellow curtains, when my lock turned. "Mama!" Michelle screamed. "Mama!" I chuckled at her, in her blue and white scrubs, hair pinned up and black. She had her glasses on. "Good Morning, shug!"

I chuckled at her as she made her way to the table where I sat. She didn't get any coffee and knew then she must have been tired. Michelle looked like me when I first started my nursing career on a cardiac floor, with her, her brother and James at home.

She came to the kitchen table waving this yellow envelope. Her brown face flushed. She slammed it down on the table and went to the cupboard and got her favorite red mug. "Mama, I don't know what is happening in San'Louis, but it din spilled churre!" I looked at her, thought it too early for her to be that loud and bubbly. "Baby girl, what are you talking about?" I giggled in my cup. "Mama, my phone has been exploding the last couple days! Why would a station in St. Louis be looking for you?" I sipped my coffee again. "Chile, I'm your mother. You don't run me, and I don't answer to you."

Michelle sat at the table, looking at the yellow letter between us. I sat across from her, sitting my mug down and looking at Michelle at my kitchen table. I saw my eyes in her face looking down at this envelope, this thing now encroaching on our space. I saw the KWMU station stamp in the upper left corner, and the pretty ink with mine and Michelle's names. She stood to get the coffee I made. I stared at the letter, heard the cabinets opening and shut. "Where did this come from?"

I heard her sipping coffee from behind me, heard her words catch in her throat. I heard the chair move and saw the blue cup settle next to left arm. She began unfolding the letter from the yellow prison, I saw her adjust her glasses and then read. "Ms. Gibeaux, we would like to interview you for a historical music portion of our radio show, Notes On St. Louis. Please contact us at the following number."

She looked over her glasses at me, my eyes looking at my face again. "Mama." I didn't meet her gaze. "Charles will be home today. I have three vacation days this week. I plan on being 'fast.'" I arched my eyebrows at her. Michelle made a face. "What time did Charles say he would be in?" I smiled. "This afternoon, about four." Michelle smiled. "I'm glad you and Mr. Charles get along, Mama. I'm glad that, y'know, you seein people." I looked back at her, sipped long and thought. "Babygirl," I sighed. "thank you." Michelle smiled. "One day, you gon tell me everything, old woman."

I set my cup down and got up from the table. "All you need to know about ya Mama is that I wasn't always a mama." I could almost hear her roll her eyes. "What about this letter, Mama?" "What about it?" I had my back to her as I stretched. "Mama, I know you still sing, and I know you sang before." I heard the letter and envelope rattle. "What's the harm in talkin to some folk on the radio?" I turned and looked at her. "Little black girl, you can't pull my ho card, hear me?"

Michelle stood up, resigned and tired. "Imma leave this here, Mama." She tapped the letter, leaving it on the table. I rolled my eyes and went back to my seat. "That still don't explain how they knew I was in Memphis." I stared at her, as she stared at the letter. "Mama, you should at least call them. Tell'em it was some mix up or something." She stood, stretching and handing the letter to me. "You have been Ethylene Carter for how long?" I moved the letter, I reread it, trying to memorize the phone number. "Gon head and sleep in the guest room, Chelle." Michelle obliged turning on her heels, throwing me a peace sign behind her head before heading the guest room off the front hall. "I'll see you a few hours, Mama." She yawned. "Girl, put that baby lion I heard to bed!" I heard her laughing. "I am! Mama call the radio people!"

I smirked as the phone rang again, I couldn't be bothered to answer. I stared at the yellow envelope and white letter. "Notes On St. Louis, huh?" I walked towards my sliding glass door, coffee in my right hand, with the letter in my left, and I sipped and thought. I thought about James before my thoughts went to Reuben. I had to thank Reuben, really. If it wasn't for him, I would never have found James. I opened the sliding glass door and went to the deck. The warmth of the red wood under my feet relaxed me more than the coffee I held.

Charles would be back in the late afternoon, and I was off tomorrow. I could really take the week if I wanted to, I had the time. After James passed, I threw myself into my MSN course work to apply for one of the three open positions in the Case Management Department. I remember I had to take time off before what I can only determine would be my mind breaking at the pace I was going. James died in 1993, I wanted to have a lack of time to mourn. I had done twenty years as a floor nurse, needed a change. I knew the Case Management Department had an opening. It was Michelle that told me to go ahead and finish it, just as she was finishing her nursing courses while working at Methodist University Hospital. I knew that floor nursing was getting the best of my body. I knew I could do it and encouraged Deborah to come finish with me.

I hated to think about how empty my house was and my husband in a metal vault under the earth in Southwoods Memorial Park, it was more than what I could do. I could understand symptoms, care plans, advanced pathology and new drugs. I could handle insurance quarrelling, letters to be sent along with e-mail and phone tags. I had buried my husband of thirty-one years. He was gone by July of 1993. I had buried him, left him in a place I couldn't get to, and I had to keep going. After Deborah and I had finished the MSN program at University of Tennessee, I felt even more ready for the position I applied for.

I even looked forward to the fights with Social Work or attending physicians; those people whom may have they thought they knew more; or better, than I did. I was ready to fight, not grieve. When I let myself grieve, it meant that James was really gone. When I allowed myself to remember he was never coming back to me, I would sob like he died all over again. The most outrageous thing I thought God made me do was to keep living, to move past grief--like I had to with Reuben Lewis.

I looked at the birds nesting in my elm tree, happy about the birdhouse James had left there. He always loved nature, loved life around him. We bought this house because we loved the trees which grew around it. James had added the room in the back and the deck, so we could enjoy it together. He said it leaving a piece of himself on this world. I watched the robins, wrens and cardinals. "They are using the house, Jay." I smiled watching the birds flutter. I leaned forward on the rail and watched some chipmunks and concentrated on them scurrying. This one day, after being someone else's something else for so long, today I purposed not to think about anything or anyone. I wasn't going to call the radio station. I wasn't going to go to any show. I wasn't going to be anything to anyone today, but me. For one day, just me.

*****

I fell asleep in James's big overstuffed red armchair in the living room. I didn't know how long I had been asleep. Some of my rollers had fallen out of my hair, and I put them in my robe pocket. I sat on the edge of the chair, looking out the window. I had no desire to see Charles, but I had told him I would be picking him up from the airport. I was trying to be a woman of my word; my grief group pushed the idea of intention versus being non-committal. If I said I was going to do something, do it. If I didn't think that I would be able to, then be wise enough not to say yes. If I didn't feel I was able to do something, even after I had committed. I had to be wise enough to know if I really could. Some days were a push, even five years later.

I went upstairs, happy I was alone again, sure that Michelle had dashed home to her quiet life with her husband. I was confident I would be able to shower, and not cry. I would get dressed and function. I would wear the perfume he got for me for Mother's Day. This Lancôme scent, Tresor. The funny thing was it smelled like something my Mother got me years ago. As nice as it was, I seldom wore it. I wore the Chanel No. 5 James had gotten me most days. I made it to my room, to on my bed, looking at the mocking red 2:00 pm on the clock. Charles plane would be landing in two hours. I sighed with my face in my hands. Took a deep breath and got up to shower. *I said I would go, so I will go.*

As I ran the water before turning on the diverter in my claw foot tub, I went to my mirror. In the left sink drawer placed the rollers that were in my hair and pocket in that drawer. I looked at myself, smiling at the young woman that never really went anywhere—she just grew up. I loose-pin curled my hair and put the red satin scarf around it. "I see you." I winked at myself and got in the shower.

The water poured over me and I hummed, then the notes came just as they had before. *"When I get my hands on you I will."* I closed my eyes and rinsed off, still singing. "My man made me, made me love him like I do." I wrapped my towel around me, and let the notes sink into my chest, and slowed my own alto, let the pain be present in it. I looked at my steamed reflection and continued. 'And if I ever lost him, I don't know what I'd do.'

I smiled remembered that was always the part Reuben loved. That was his favorite song; he called that song Carolyn wrote and her brother stole *his song*. I could time him by the song. Whatever he was going to do, about to do, stopped when I sang that one. I remember how blue his eyes were, how he would sit in the back and watch me, almost like he was hunting. It was always a turn on, always made me feel like I was all he wanted. I knew he watched every movement I made on stage, not being possessive, never possessive. But, fascinated.

I had caught him staring at me on so many occasions when I wouldn't be doing anything worth watching, let alone remembering. I remember one night we were together after a show, and I had asked him to hand me the spread at the end of the bed he bought me. I could feel his gaze on my face, like he was trying to put me in his pocket to never forget me. James didn't even look at me like Keys looked at me.

I hummed as I went to the closet and picked out pink blouse and khaki slacks. I turned my nose up at the pink and reached for the red shirtdress instead. Red for me always had presence that's why I made it my signature color. Pink had a grace to it, unassuming and beautiful. I tossed a pair of gray heels with it. Michelle had got them for me on her last shopping trip to Las Vegas, and I hadn't worn them enough to lie and say I liked or didn't like them. I looked in the mirror and smoothed my hair. I had thought about going red again, but it was the Spring, and I wasn't ready yet. I smiled, remembering when the red-headed *Ruby* would have been looking back at me.

I grabbed my red Coach purse from the back of the door and put my diamond studs in I got for myself for my birthday last year. I put my hands on the top of the dresser, and exhaled. "You can do this, Ethylene. You can do it. Just go to the car." Deep breath in, I went from my bedroom, down the stairs towards my front door. I took my black Nine West bag from the end table, I unlocked the door and walked towards the car in my driveway. I chirped the car to unlock, opened the door and sat. "Hard parts done." I turned the car on, slowly moved the car out, watching for my neighbors' kids that darted out of nowhere—either on bikes, running or chasing balls. Last summer, I almost hit the three of them as they dashed behind my car.

I turned on the radio, relieved when there wasn't music playing, yet I had no idea what was on it. I fiddled with the dial, thinking it was in-between stations. When I turned the dial as before I left my driveway, I came to a University of Tennessee station. They always interesting conversations on WUTK. As I took off towards Memphis International, my ears perked at the mention of Reuben on the radio.

It was the confessional show I sometimes caught on Saturdays. Those Saturdays in the that stuffy, homey office on the 6th floor of Methodist University Hospital, surrounded by pictures of my husband, kids and degrees. I would listen to the wails and tales of the children old enough to be my own. I turned the volume up as I sat in traffic on Deale, looking at the couples walking, young girls looking in the boutiques at the prom dresses, and shoes. I smiled at the girl in the red sweatshirt with the cream-colored bags in her hands, jeans and sneakers. I studied her face, as I sat at the light. She caught my eyes and grinned. I smiled, but my eyes back to the road and went forward.

It was a blur of traffic as I went towards the airport. The young lady on the radio told all those that were listening about how she was dealing with her grandfather that had Alzheimer's Disease, how her grandmother was a writer and kept journals about his disease. Heart wrenching, really. The girl went on to say the journals her grandmother kept detailed just how he managed to forget almost everything but her. But he was slowly doing that now. I got to the light before the airport on Winchester and tuned my ears to her voice. "My Grandma said that my grandpa Reuben doesn't remember when they got married, not always. He remembers when they were dating, but not their four children." I shook my head as I went towards the airport, I wanted underground parking. Charles's plane would be landing in forty-five minutes.

"Grandma said, it was like light was going out in him. Day by day, she said it was like his light was going out. She was scared to leave him, because she thought that one day he would forget about her. Even after all their time together." I found a spot along the wall on the second level of the parking garage, made my way towards it. The male disc jockey spoke. "That had to be hard for her. How long had they been married?" I furrowed my brows, felt them knit together as I tried to park. I cursed and wished I had put my glasses on. The girl spoke then. "She and Papa had been married almost fifty years." I smiled as I put the car safely in its space. "That's why I thought it was important to publish these journals she had. Maybe it'll help someone else."

I cut the car off, looked at the dashboard clock for the time I had remaining. I listened to the young girl on the radio, decided I would pray for her. She sounded so broken. I thought myself so blessed then that James had been taken from me suddenly. There was only a need to miss him once, not over a series of months or God help me, years. "The book is going to be called *Hear Comes the Water.* I have a mentor for the book, Professor Claudette Harris in the English Department right here at U of Tennessee. She is amazing and is really helping this book come to life. I couldn't—it would be impossible to do without her. It's a labor of love for my Nana." I grabbed my purse from the floor. The DJ's voice was back again, "Shannon, where are your Grandpa and Grandma now?" There as a sigh, mine and hers as I put my purse on my lap. "Well, Allen, my Grandma has passed away, 'bout a year ago. My Grandpa is at Graceland Rehab Center. On good days, there aren't a whole lot sometimes—but he still asks for her." Her voice drifted off, and I took the keys out of the ignition.

I sat for a second, squeezing my keys in my right hand. The clock read 3:32. "He still asks for her?" The DJ, Allen, spoke again. "What do y'all do when he does?" Shannon sighed, more pained. "We tell him, that she's at home. She is waiting on him." She cried a little then, real soft. "That's the only thing we can, otherwise, he tried to be combative and get up and find her." I wiped my eyes, felt so bad for her. I put my hand on the door, opened it and all the lights went off.

I walked towards the green sign that led towards the upper level and terminals. I thought about Shannon, her family and even her parents. She didn't say if this person was her father's father or mother's father. Either way, that indeed had to be a tough for anyone, I wouldn't wish that on an enemy. I shook my head clear and looked at the security guard and he smiled at me. I watched the busyness of the terminals before finding Gate 9 where Charles was going to be coming.

I watched as the hive of people with their suitcases, and their chatter and thought about Shannon with no last name on the radio. I bit my lip and thought about her grandfather. I sat by Gate 9 and watched the planes land and take off and thought about Keys. I thought about this life we were supposed to have in California all those years ago. I smiled watching throngs of people go through the gate. *I got family in San Francisco. Water is so blue, Ruby. We can go and be together. Nothing to stop us. I love you, Ruby—like no other woman.*

My vision blurred, and I searched my purse for my handkerchief. I thought about him, how he looked when I last saw him, and when I had seen him again when he was in Memphis on business about four years ago. He had brought Babs with him--still tall, still so handsome. I smiled remembering, he spotted me coming out of The Gypsy Salon. I felt these eyes on me and ignored the heat that came over me. I looked from across the street and froze. It was still

March, hands in my jacket pockets and we stared at each other. I kept walking to my blue Nissan, brand spankin' new then. I thought if I didn't walk away from him, I would have run screaming over where he was! I told myself that it wasn't him, couldn't be him, and how did he get to Memphis and why would he even want to be in Memphis?

I thought about that day, as I watched and listened for Charles. I thought about his eyes, his crooked smile, even so many years later. He looked confident that it was me, like no time had passed! I snorted. "Keys." I snickered. I kept people watching at Gate 9. I waved at soldiers in their desert fatigues on their way to or back from wherever they had come from. One whom happened to smile at me, and thought of my brother, and all the years he had given to the United States Navy. I needed to call him soon, I'm sure he called me in my haze of sleep. I watched for the Delta Flight 498 from New York, anxious for it to land. I thought of all the excuses I could have given to leave, to not have come in the first damn place.

I rang my hands, still sitting in thought. His flight should be landing soon. I prayed that his flight wouldn't be late, but I could stand for it to be late. I had this sense of dread in my belly, I couldn't shake. I knew something was wrong, so wrong. I pulled at my purse strap as the overhead went off saying that the United Flight 498 from New York was landing. I still sat, watched the plane, big and blue and white, land without error or complication. I forced myself to think of Charles. I couldn't waste time thinking of a man that was married. Keys was married the last time, I had seen him.

Babs had told me the story of how she couldn't stand his wife, but I couldn't waste time thinking about her just now either. I remember she had given me the heads up they were thinking about coming to Memphis for business before I saw them on the street. I tried to focus on the people leaving the plane and its steady, streaming people. The normal looking people who weren't Reuben Michael Lewis. The people I could see, touch and remember just as they were, and forget just as easily.

Charles came into view maybe about five or six people from the front of the gate. I saw his smile before he saw me. I stood, opening to shake Keys' ghost. I heard his voice in my head as if he were standing next to me. *Let me stay with you, Ruby. Let me stay were life is tonight.* I thought of the visit to my people's homestead in 'Iberia that same year Reuben's brother died. Thought of what my father had said. *Until he can come to this door, and ask for you, I don't wanna hear shit else about it.*

I felt water come from my eyes, tried to dab it away before Charles could see it. I sat again, fumbled through my bag and found a handkerchief and mirror. I dabbed my makeup, just as I felt warmth in my space. I looked up to see Charles, in his purple collared Lacoste shirt, and khakis. He hadn't shaved his face yet, but his hair had been cut low with a razor. I liked his bald head, and think he kept it cut low for me.

"Hi beautiful." He whispered, kissed my cheek. I dabbed right eye too quick and poked it. I blinked fast, looked at him to keep him from asking me anything else. "Hi handsome," I answered, putting a smile behind it. He moved in close to kiss me, the Amani cologne he wore attempting to soothe my fraying nerves. When our lips met, there was nothing. Nothing. I looked up at him, he smiled at me. I wondered if it was because I was just tired. But how can I be imagining it? I had been seeing Charles for six months, a year really, and this was—odd. "Are you hungry, beautiful?" his eyes were searching mine, trying to see if all of me was still with all of him. "A lil bit, I think." I put my hand on my stomach before I stood up again. I looked that the floor, took a deep breath and stood. I looked at him, smile was still just as warm.

I stared at him again, almost as if I had never seen him before. His mouth moved before I could protest. "I din had New York food for a week! Let's gon get us some Uncle Lou's and I can tell you all about these crazy folk up North!" We walked through the terminal, quiet and arm and arm. I still had belly dread when we made it to the car. I got in the car, Charles had offered to drive, and I had refused. "I got it, babe." I had managed to tell him. He put his suitcase in the trunk, carryon bags in the backseat.

When we made it Uncle Lou's, he ordered for the both of us. He put his arm around my waist a little bit, and I wanted to scream. I wanted to sprint back to my car. I couldn't shake this feeling! I felt like the dread had made it up to my throat and It taking my voice. Charles ordered a chicken plate with his extra helping of greens, and his cornbread. I made some sound like I had wanted red beans and rice, no cornbread please, and a sweet tea. Charles took me by the waist and led me to the side wall to wait on our orders. I held myself, willing the funny feeling away. Wishing the dread out of my throat and wanting everything in my body that was on high alert to rest.

Charles stood next to me, nuzzled my cheek. I pulled from him, looked over at the young girl behind the counter cooking and prepping our lunch I knew I wasn't going to eat. "Ethylene?" I didn't look at him. "Babe?" I still looked at the girl, and name tag on her shirt that said Donna. He tipped my chin back to him. "Cher, you in there?" I blinked tears back. Concern took the warmth out of his face. "You okay, babe?" I nodded. "You look like someone about to die, baby." I froze. I wanted to bury my face in his chest, I wanted to leave the little dining area we were in. I wanted—I wanted Reuben.

"I'm, I'm okay. I'm just, I'm tired, Chas. I just wanna get home." I looked at the floor, then up at him. "But I'm alright, Charles. I'm alright." I let him hold me, and think he was really doing something to soothe the ghosts that had just shone up. I hadn't seen Reuben in four years. Before then, I hadn't seen him in decades! I thought about him from time to time, but—I hadn't missed him. At least, I hadn't missed him like this since I was in my twenties. It didn't scare me, but I knew that something was wrong. Something was not right about how I was feeling. I sniffled against Charles's shirt, inhaled him again as our number was called for our food. It was a shrill and impatient noise, and I was elated. I watched Chas walk over to the counter, he put a few loose bills in the plastic tip jar, and then smile at the cook before returning to me to head towards the car.

Charles decided to drive me back home, we had agreed that he would stay over we would talk, and then we 'would just let the rest of the evening happen to us'. He held my hand as he drove from Uncle Lou's and towards my house on Foxhall. I let him hold it, no warmth in his hand. I willed there to be some, there had to be something that would make this feeling, this feeling of feeling nothing, go away. He gripped my hand, as he steered my car. I willed my eyes to close and the cool air from the A/C to soothe me.

I was cold, I hated when he drove, and he always put the damn air on! I exhaled, tried to let my mind wander, didn't want to think. I really didn't want to think about the past. I didn't want to think about Reuben. I didn't want to think about the last time I saw him, the last time I heard his voice, how it was still fire when he touched me. Oh, the last time he touched me! I shuddered, and Chas squeezed my hand harder believing his was infusing heat.

I felt a bump and thumped my head off the window, I kept my eyes closed and took my left hand from Charles, covering my face. I steadied my breathing. I went back to my early days of nursing, thinking how you calm someone down who is under a lot of stress, and may not be thinking clearly. First thing was to make sure they were still breathing, tell them to calm down. Orient them. Ask what their name is. Ask them where they are. Ask them their birthday. Ethylene Gibeaux Carter. Memphis, in a car going home. May 30, 1937. I felt my pulse slow a little, it wasn't in my ears so loud. But, as I kept my eyes closed? I saw him. I saw him as the young man he was. The last time and next to last time I saw him. He had said the same thing he had said to me so many years ago. He told me to hold on to him, trust him, let him stay with me. Let him stay with me.

We made it my house, I was steadied by 4936 on my mailbox, the garage door going up smooth. I heard it, eyes still closed. The car became still, and we sat. I heard Charles breathing, almost exasperated. Like something had got on his nerves or he had lost some money. "Ethylene?" I didn't even like how he called my name. "Yes?" I opened my eyes away from him, facing the water hoses on my garage wall. I caught my eyes in the side mirror, glassy and faraway looking. "Cher?" I turned and looked at him, smoothing my face with the tissues I snuck in the door the last time I visited Kroger. "Hm?" He studied my face, looking and not seeing. "Is there something you wanna tell me?" I smiled, shaking my head, "No." He looked at the steering wheel and then out at the messy garage wall that still had some of James's tools. I reminded myself to call Maurice to come and get them.

The driver's door opened, and I opened my own. I pushed the garage door opener on the passenger visor to signal its close. I took a deep breath and left the car, closing the door. Baring against the old garden hose, I went to the door up the two concrete stairs, opened the door, remembering Charles was behind me. I went to the kitchen, thirsty and dizzy.

I went to the cupboard, got a glass and filled it with water. I took my glass and purse heading to the living room and the safety of James's chair. I dropped my bag on the floor next to me, I kicked off my shoes near those, and sipped my water. I forgot I wasn't in the house alone when Charles put the bag of food on the table on the kitchen table "Babe, could you hand me a Coke? I know you got some in that Frigidaire!" He giggled as I heard the box open. I didn't move. I closed my eyes. I heard the Frigidaire open and close, I was glad he got his own Coke.

I stayed with the refuge of my husband's chair, eyes closed, willing myself not to start screaming. I rolled the glass in my left hand, thought and bit my lip. I was happy he stayed him right where he was in the kitchen. At least he was teaching me enough to not ask me anything when I wasn't able to stay saved in regular conversation—I used to tell James, "For everybody's safety it's good I just hush up sometimes." "I think Imma dye my hair again. I'm gonna go red again." Silence. "Oh?" I heard him rustling bags and containers, I heard my drawers open and shut. I felt my ears get hot. "Yeah. Red." I heard footsteps towards the living room, heard him eating. I opened my eyes to see him eating across from me on my cream couch. Michelle and Maurice had picked that couch out for me, but I couldn't part with their father's chair.

I watched this country Negro eat from a clamshell container, in the plastic bag with my silverware. His open Coke was on the floor, I was hoping it didn't spill on my new carpet. I rolled my eyes, seeing his feet were bare, wondered where his shoes were. He made a remark about the Coke in my Frigidaire, "They ain't that cold." I ignored him, sipped from my glass, reaching to let it on the coaster on my honey oak colored coffee table. "I ain't been red in a while, and this dark hair is getting on my nerves." I watched his eyes, he didn't flinch, immersed in his Uncle Lou's. "I don't think that I would like that red hair on you, babe." He was smacking. "You gon eat, girl?" I looked at him, arms just, watched his mouth move. "Nall. I ain't that hungry."

I reached for my glass again, walked to the window, happy it was getting dark. I rolled the glass in my hands, needed the chilled glass to will the ghosts away. I prayed silently, willing the thoughts of Reuben and Babs from my mind. Pleaded with God to help me, to save me from almost forty years ago, to forget what happened four years before then. I willed it back, wished it back like I had done with storms when I was little girl in L'sana. Every time I got scared, Mother Oscella told me to just be like the Lord and will the storm away— *"Tell it 'Be still.'*

There was warmth behind me, Charles squeezed me, kissed my cheek. "Let me stay with you tonight, Ethylene. Don't make me leave again. I want to just—be here with you." I touched my right hand to the left one that was on my shoulder. The tears came, steady and hot. I got my legs to stand, let him move from behind the chair to hug me. I know it soothed him more than it did me. I moved from his warmth, putting my glass back on its coaster, and returned to his arms, put my arms around his neck. I looked in his eyes, for a moment, maybe only a half a second, they were blue.

I kissed him, bold and slow, and looked for the warmth. Something that would anchor me to where I was now, who I was now. I wanted that, needed that. "Stay with me, babe." I whispered. I didn't know where the need had welled up from, but I couldn't deal with the ghosts tonight. I didn't have the strength to fight, not right now. I refused. He held me, all his warm with all my warm and I hugged him tight. I thought I heard the mailbox but thought nothing of it. I wanted the ghosts to be real, so I can be rid of them. I wanted the ache in my heart to ease. I didn't want to admit that I still loved Reuben Lewis, and that I had never stopped. I had never stopped. I was still haunted.

Chapter 15-May 1998

Charles had tried to make love to me a week ago, two weeks before my birthday. He had tried to make love to me and I had given in. I gave in with a man who I just needed to chase the world away, chase thoughts away. I did the things women do with men who don't know the bodies of the women they lay with and will never admit they don't. I forced my body to respond to touches that weren't in the right spot, thrusting at the wrong speed, and I moon-howled like he had indeed climbed the holy mountain.

He held me afterwards, kissing my bare shoulder. "Cher, you are so beautiful." He clasped my bare right thigh, "Red hair at this time in life ain't gon do nothing but make folk thank you tryin to be young." He kissed under my right ear, below my diamond earrings. I stared at the ceiling, I sighed when I heard his breathing slow, happy he was asleep. When he left that Tuesday morning, and we both got ready for work, he left beaming like a young man. It was a beaming like he had indeed popped my cherry, the first to lay claim to my womanhood all over again. My husband couldn't even claim that right.

We drank coffee in the sun streaked kitchen. Through the light of my yellow curtains and I sat there, watching him, talking with him about the remainder of his trip two months ago. The World Trade Center Meetings. The Staten Island Ferry. The Statute of Liberty he almost missed because he was looking the other way. He left me a small envelope on the table, he knew I loved pictures. I thumbed through the envelope he gave me, smiled at the postcards, the keychains and random photographs he left on the table. As he sipped his coffee, my eyebrow raised at the photo of a woman he left in the envelope. He had his purple Lacoste shirt on, the same one I had picked him up from the airport in. She was white, young-looking, with long dark hair. She was kissing his cheek.

As he made move to kiss my mouth, I moved so he would only get right cheek. He handed me the mail as he left, kissed me on the cheek once more. I told him to call me later. Later was almost two weeks ago. I kept the manila envelope on my dresser. I would smirk at it every so often. I had been looking for a way to leave Charles alone, and it looked like God had given me a tent peg just like he did Jael.

****

It was now a week before my birthday. I hadn't called Charles. I did tell Deborah what happened. I told her I found the picture, told her about even him being in my presence was getting on my nerves. I was proud of myself, I exercised that morning, showered and wearing one of James's old shirts and Methodist University Hospital sweats. I looked at the week-old mail on my night stand, the letter from WGMU on top. They were looking for Ruby Gibeaux or Ethylene Gibeaux, the singer from The Gypsy Hand night club. They knew whom I was really, but the letter asked specifically for her. I sat on the chaise in my room, listened to the quiet that was encamping me.

I smiled, remembered The Gypsy Hand. I remembered Mr. Levi, and Deborah and Doc. I remembered and began to cry. I remembered my dresses, I remembered Reuben and all we planned. I remembered our engagement party, how spur of the moment it was. So, Reuben to do it that way, and have been so classy. I remembered Babs and how she would let me do her makeup and she would watch me do my hair. I looked out of my window, on the second floor, and I remembered the fire. I remember how I almost didn't make it out. I remembered the firemen that thought I was a high-priced whore, before I could tell them who I was.

The letter asked Ruby Gibeaux to contact *Notes On St. Louis*, to ask for Madison or Maeghan. I got up, still in my red robe, and went to my closet. I had pleaded with James for a walk-in closet, and now half of it was empty. It took me a year and more to give away James's clothes. On the top in the very back was the Treasure jar. One of the few things I had of the life of the time, the life we had together. This jar was the thing which made me remember that it wasn't all a dream. This jar held the money he and I were supposed to go to California with. I reached up on tiptoe and grabbed it. I looked inside it, looked at the clippings I squirrelled from Lewis Construction Company that Babs had given me when she was last here. I looked on the back of the card. This red card with white writing that had Reuben's last name in bold, and his title as founder underneath.

Babs had given me a white envelope on their last day in Memphis. The same visit when they had seen me on the street. I turned the card over, saw Babs's number. I put everything back, taking the jar with me to my bed. I had no idea if her number even worked or if she would believe that it was me that was calling her. I sat the jar on my nightstand, next to my phone, the sun pouring over everything there. I sat on the bed and got up again, pacing around the room. I was still pacing when I screamed when the phone rang. On the third ring, I answered it. "Hello?" I said, voice too sharp. "Hey, Mama, Imma swing by the house if you still there and grab them tools right quick." I sighed at Maurice's voice, closed my eyes. "That's fine, baby. I'm over here."

"You off today, Mama?" I swallowed hard. "Yeah, I'm doing some paperwork today. You can come by, Morrie." He coughed. "I'll be by about two, Mama. Did you need something, you sound like sumthin wrong?" I sat on the bed. "No, Morrie, I'm alright." I held the receiver with both hands. "I'll be here." Maurice told me he loved me, and then hung up. I sat after I hung up the phone and stared at the Treasure jar. I wouldn't, couldn't hurt anything to call Babs. I knew Reuben was married, at least he was still married when I has seen him. His wife was sick, he had told me. It wouldn't hurt to talk to her—it wouldn't be like I needed her to find out about Keys for me. It would just be one stupid quick call.

I looked at the clock on the opposite side of the bed, James' side. The green digital clock read 11:30 a.m. I had been up since about six. I had made some calls, did paperwork, called the social worker on 8 East, and set up conferences for Hospice care next week. I thought about Reuben. I thought about the night of the fire. I thought about the last time I saw him. Oh, dear Lord. The last time I saw him. I lay back in bed, and just exhaled. I reached back to him, to us, and that week he was here.

I was Friday, it was May 1993. I was a fresh widow. James had been gone almost 3 months. His headstone had just been put up. This gorgeous smoke colored granite. I had cried when I picked it out, I fainted when I went out there with the kids. Maurice and Chelle helped me from falling in the dirt. James and I had raised them to be strong, and then, right then over his resting place, I witnessed how strong they were.

I had made my breathing steady, feet sure and kept going. That's all I could do, keep going. In that space of keep going, I threw myself into work. I picked up shifts. I rearranged my office. I volunteered to be on-call. I started my MSN program, finished it powered by grief and anger at the Almighty in a year! I did everything I could to not be at home, our home. The home my husband made for us. The home with the changes made for me because I asked. I wanted my head to be filled with something else. I wanted—I wanted something I could understand. Medicine, facts, germs and Methodist University Hospital I understood. I didn't know why my husband of thirty years was hit by someone young enough to be his youngest son would run a stoplight and hit him!

Michelle had told me that I looked tired. She told me I looked like I needed something to 'shake the dust off' me. "Mama change your hair. That's what you told me when I was younger. You told me the quickest thing a woman a can to change her life is dye her hair." She called her hairdresser, Deidre, and made an appointment for me to see her. "Mama, Daddy ain't gon come back because you are choosing not to live." I had looked over at her, with my hair in a red scarf, and unwashed in the third week, in frumpy clothes at my kitchen table and nodded.

She had taken me to The Gypsy Salon on Abel Street that next Thursday after work, right before Memorial Day. "I don't want to go to a salon all your lil fast girlfriends go to! I need somebody in my head that know what they doin', cher!" Michelle had laughed at me. "Mama, I'm your child and you still ain't got no faith in me!" I smiled remembering how Chelle had laughed. "Gypsy is my salon, Mama. Its clean, it's lit, and Deidre does my hair." She pulled in front of the storefront windowed building. The sign was red, and the windows bright. People everywhere, even for a Thursday.

There were women with different colored hair, and cute outfits and music playing from the speakers. I smiled when I recognized *I Can't Let My Heaven Walk Away*. We walked in the front door, Chelle somehow got behind me. We checked in, and this cinnamon brown girl with honey blonde hair and a pretty purple dress with black smock with stickers and scissors on it. "Hi Chelle!" She had her arms open, hugged her tight. She had her arms akimbo, voice was husky and warm. "Hi, Mrs. Carter." Her voice was just warm and inviting, waving at me. I smiled at her, and she just hugged me almost as tight as she did Chelle, who then joined in on the hug. When we all pulled back into this small circle, Deidre looked at me with all this hope and said, with her hands back on her hips and said. "Red. We gon take you a ruby red, Mama!"

With that, I was in her chair whisked away thirty years when Deborah dyed my hair the first time. She was the first person I met in St. Louis who ain't try to see my slip and drawls right off. We dyed my hair in the bathroom at the Sailor Den where she was a bartender sometimes. It was this color called Shimmer Scarlet by Clairol. I smiled as Deidre hummed and walked around me applying color. "Ms. Ethylene, when is the last time you had a good cut and color." I giggled, "Baby, it had to be before when my husband died." Deidre still applied color, watching my reaction to the red mop forming on my head.

"Well, we gon make and keep you beautiful today Ms. Ethylene, trust me." I closed my eyes; my nerves were soothed by the vanilla she wore. I closed my eyes after she applied the color and processing cap, leading me to the dryers. When I closed my eyes, I was transported to that second-floor building on Boyle in St. Louis. I heard Deborah's voice. "Girl, if you gon be in St. Louis, you need something that's gon catch!" She had washed the dye out in a sop sink in the back room where my cousin John did count for The Sailor Den every night.

I remembered my face when I looked in the mirror and saw my brown face with this long red hair in this dirty mirror and about cried saying, "My hair bout as red as that girl's shoes in the Wizard of Oz!" Before the tears could fall she crossed her arms across her chest, saying "Ruby!" She clapped like she had done something clever. "That's gon be yo moniker at the Sailor Den and erre'where else! Ain't no body gon remember Ethylene. That's too country!"

Deidre worked her magic on my hair. From color, to washing to the new haircut. "Lookahere! Ms. Ethylene looking like a you twenty!" She spun me around in the chair and my eyes were closed. I opened them and saw me again. Not the mother, not the nurse, not even the woman that married James Carter all those years ago. I saw me again. I bit my lip, and my eyes watered. "I love it!" I whispered. I played with dark red strands, pulling a few behind my ears. I loved the swing bob she had cut. "What does a young girl know about a bob?" I snickered as I played with my hair in the mirror. "Ms. Ethylene, bobs is back in style!" She motioned to someone to the right of her, the wall of mirrors blocking my view. "What I owe you for this, Deidre?" She caught my reflection in the mirror, hands still in her apron pockets, her long blonde hair shimmering, curls all healthy and perfect. "Nothing, Ms. Ethylene! Chelle took care everything." I turned to her, slow so I could take all her in again.

For second, just a second, I saw Deborah in Deidre's face. All her light, all her love for me, and then I missed her. I made a note to call her. I reached in my purse and gave her a twenty and hugged her again, "Thank you, Deidre!" "Mama, you welcome! Come back and see me so we can keep you ruby red." I froze, swallowed. "Oh, so this is my color?" I said, playing with my hair in the mirror. Deidre nodded. "Yes'm. I whipped it up 'special for you." I spun in the mirror and began to hum. "Miss Ethylene, you sing?" I looked at her, she tucked her side bang behind her left ear. "I did. Long time ago. I ain't had a reason to in a while." Deidre looked at me, motioned to her next client. She looked back at me and said. "Shug, it's always a reason to sing! Life, no matter how bad it is, there is always reason to sing! That's what my Nana say."

Michelle said that she would meet me at Hubbard's, this local dinner owned by her husband's family. I smiled remembering that birthday, and how amazing I felt. I went out of the salon, back straight, new lipstick on and smoothed my white collared shirt and jeans. It was windy, so I tossed my Methodist University Hospital jacket on again, the collar tried to bounce off my lip. I walked to the left Gypsy's and let the May wind blow my hair. I smoothed by slacks at the crosswalk where my car was, happy that Michelle had driven it. No sooner did I look up, I saw him.

My heart had stopped in my chest, I didn't think he had seen me, not right off. I thought it was a ghost. I watched him, or what I thought was him. His hair was short, I saw the blonde next to him, thought it was his wife until I saw her face. As I heard the crosswalk go off, I don't know if I willed him over to me or I willed myself still—but I saw blue eyes looking at me over the bed of black pickup truck. The blonde with him, she too was frozen. I blinked, watched him come closer, hesitated. I walked backwards to the brick wall, kept upright by the brick-made Post Office behind me. I put my hands in my pockets, kept my purse on my shoulder, and just watched them.

I saw his eyes register me, see me, turning back to the blonde with short hair. He pointed at me, then she pointed. She looked down and pulled out a pair of glasses, adjusted them on her face. I saw her eyes light up before she ran towards my side of the street. "Ruby!" the blonde screamed, her jeans, blouse and jacket flapping. "Babs!" My arms opened, and she ran into them. We laughed, cried and hugged again.

He watched us from across the street, his brown hair still thick and full and he had had pockets in his gray slacks and collared, button up shirt, untucked. Lord, he was still handsome. My heart felt like it wasn't beating, it hadn't beat in months. He walked over to me, Babs squeezed me once more. "Reuben." I whispered. He walked till he was right in front of me. It was the night he took me home all over again. His eyes? They still held the ocean. "Hi, Ethylene."

I heard his voice ring in my ears again as I sat in my bedroom alone. I kept my eyes closed, made him come back to me. I willed time back, to bend for me, just as I had done when James had died at first. I willed time back just, so I could hear his voice and sleep. On bad nights, I would will time and memory back to August 18, 1961—my wedding day. The warmth I felt when James held my hand, as we left the Greater Mount Moriah Baptist Church, and didn't let my hand go until we got to his grandmother's house to pick up our car to drive to Chicago for our Honeymoon.

But right now, I focused on that day, that corner when the world was set again. We just stood there. He reached for me, like slow motion, and wrapped me up in him. He nuzzled my neck, and breathed me in. I wrapped my arms around his neck. His hands dropped to my hips still over my jacket and pulled me to him. I hung onto him, so I wouldn't melt.

I took him in, breathed him deep like I used to do Mother Oscella's flowers. I took him in deep so that he would stay with me. "Ahem." I broke away from him, looked at Babs. "What are y'all doing here?" She grinned, walked over to her brother, grabbing his arm. "We're on a turnaround trip! We're on business. What are you doing here?" I looked at her, arched my eyebrows.

"Think real hard, Barbara Ann." I chuckled. I didn't look at him, but I knew he was looking at me. "I'm meeting my daughter for lunch at Hubbard's." I gestured down the block. "They have good coffee and chili." I sighed, moved towards Reuben, grazed his wrist and smiled when I felt fire there. "We'll catch up."

When our eyes found each other again, he smirked. After so long, it hadn't changed. It reached his eyes, that smile a little bit crooked. "It's about three now. Would two hours work?" He reached for my hands, pulled me towards him slightly until I was standing in front of him. He leaned in, kissed my cheek. I could tell he hadn't shaved yet. "That'll work." He squeezed my hands and brought the left one up to his lips, more fire. He caressed my palm and just looked at me. My face was hot, and as I started to move towards him, Babs cleared her throat. "We will see you in two hours. Come on, Rube." She leads him away like a small child, still grinning. "Two hours! That's four o'clock, Lewis! Hubbard's! 708 Poplar Avenue!" He waved at me as they disappeared in the other side of the sidewalk.

I walked to car on the neighboring block, happy The Gypsy Salon was on Jefferson, and Hubbard's was a three-minute drive on Poplar Avenue. I got to my car and tried to keep my heart in my chest. I was breathing and floating. In what had to be the matter of eight heartbeats I was there. I parked ace deuce in the back of the building. I didn't speak to my Pastor's daughter, Monica, whom was a manager there during the early evening hours. I saw Chelle waving and sat with her. "Mama." She looked up from her sweet tea like I had called her a name. She didn't have her glasses on. "Mama, your hair so—red!" She sat back and looked at me. I tossed my hair a little at her. "I know. I like it, I really like it!" Chelle propped her hand under her face and looked at me. "So, them fast-tail girls in the salon actually could do something right?" I rolled my eyes and giggled. "I guess. Every now and then."

As we sat there, I thought about him. I thought about him as we ordered coffee, and I stirred it. I thought about him as Michelle told me about her day, and what thing her husband did. "...and the doctors say that the baby is--"I sputtered on my coffee. "Baby?" She smiled and drank her sweet tea. "Yea, Mama! Imma be a mama!" I got up and hugged her, and she just giggled, that same giggle stayed with her since she was a girl. "What you gon name the baby? I know y'all want a girl!"

Michelle grinned. "Ruby." My eyes got wide as I stood tall again. "What?" Michelle put her glasses down and her eyes got quarter-big around. "That's the baby's nickname, if it's a girl." She sipped her sweet tea. "Robert and I got Colin, so if it's a girl, we wanna name her Scarlet. So, her nickname would be Ruby." My eyes got glassy. "Mama, what's wrong?" I sighed, moving from my seat to kiss her cheek. "I'm so glad for you, babygirl. Now, if your brother would get married, I could know he would be alright." I tapped her left hand, I went back to my seat. "Baby, number two? Mm!" I went back to my coffee, the warmth soothing me. "Yep, two babies, Mama!" I shifted in my chair and looked at her, just glowing. Just glowing! I saw so much of me and James in her. His humor and charm and my finesse. No wonder she got Robert their Senior year of college at U of Tennessee. I remember he called her 'Honeybee' because she just drew people to her.

I looked at the clock after, watching Chelle eat: salad, chilli and a chicken, rice and gravy dish. "Watch that salt, babygirl!" Michelle laughed and rolled her eyes. I looked at my watch, it was a little after four. This left Reuben about thirty minutes before he decided if he was going to come. Rob came by to get Michelle and brought Colin. He was my little ball of sun. "Hi, Grandma!" he had bounced on my lap, all heavy and happy. He hugged me, with this black Nike jacket brushing my chin. He Looked up at me with James's eyes and said, "Oh, Nan! Yo hair a crayon!" He touched it like it was hot. Michelle and Robert sat in the booth, cuddled and quiet.

"And how are you, Mr. Sawyer?" I asked him. "Daddy two times!" Robert was tall, dark and handsome and owned his own barbershop and did some investment banking. "Yeah, Mama. I'm happy." He looked over at Michelle, he kissed her nose. I smiled at Colin, "You about to be a big brother!" He looked up at me, eyes wide. "But I'm little Grandma!" Our table laughed. I was so happy for Michelle. I looked at the clock on the far wall once more, before bringing my attention back to my company; chiming in to not have them think I wasn't paying attention.

About 4:30 p.m., they packed up and left. John told me I looked like I could be singing with Ella Fitzgerald. "That's a Etta James red, Mama!" he sniggled, and so did I while I slapped his shoulder. He stood to his full six-foot ebony dark height, grinning. "But the color looks good on you, Mama. I'm glad you're getting better." He leaned over to kiss my left cheek. He zipped his jacket and Colin jumped in his arms and he blew me kisses as he left. Michelle hugged me, told me she would call Maurice and she would call me before she went to sleep. I looked at my coffee and thought about the baby. Thought about how the baby would have my name of my eighteen-year old alter-ego.

I looked at the clock again to steel myself to Hubbard's. He wasn't coming. Why would he? I went to the counter with my purse and cold coffee to ask Marjorie about the cobbler. "We got peach and apple, Mrs. Carter." Her brown skin sheened in sweat, and her hair short with her blue Hubbard's shirt had grease stains on it. "I want some peach cobbler, and some hot coffee." I sat at the counter with my cold coffee. "I am way too cute to go home." Marjorie giggled as she took the fresh coffee from the pot, pouring me a fresh cup.

I planned on eating my cobbler and calling Deborah when I got home. She would flip when she saw my hair! As I sat in thought, I felt someone sit next to me. I didn't look at over, I kept my eyes on Marjorie's shirt and short dark hair as she darted behind the counter talking to her husband, Kyle, whom was cooking as she tended the counter. "After all this time you still drink it the same way?" I scoffed. "Why change what works," I turned to my right. "Babs." She giggled, ran her hand through her hair. She nudged me. "My brother is parking the car." She smiled.

I laughed and shook my head. "I'm just going to go, Babs. I don't have time for this. I really don't." Babs looked up at me, put her hand on my left wrist. "Ethylene. Please." I looked at her, shook my head, I felt hot tears stinging. I shook my head and she patted my hand. "Here. Take our card. My number is on back of it. We will be in Memphis one, maybe two more nights. We do construction and looking for houses down here to flip. After then, we have to go back to St. Louis. Please," she blinked hard, tapped my hand for me to look at her. "Don't let him leave and not see you." I saw how insistent she looked, how serious and sad. "Please, Ruby. Please. Don't do that to him. Not again."

I had my purse on the red stool next to me, giving her two cards that had my work numbers on it. I found a pen by the glass cake dish to write my home number down on back of them. I took a deep breath and turned back to her.

"Tell him," I exhaled so deep I thought she would hear my chest rattle. "Tell him the numbers work, and he can call me."

My front door slammed. "Mama!" It was Maurice. "Mama, I got the mail! You got something from St. Louis! Where you at, Mama?" I opened my eyes, staring at the ceiling, wondering aloud exactly where I was. I closed my eyes, remembering why it was he was there. "Here me!" I screamed louder than I thought. I heard him make quick work up the stairs. I saw I in my doorway, looking so much like James, in his work clothes. "Mama, why you in here with no lights on?" He cut a light on and sat in the chair next to the window. I looked at his Ford Plant overalls. "Are those duds clean, boy?" Maurice threw his head back and laughed. "Mama, I'm finna go in. My clothes are clean." He slapped his hand off the arms of the red chair. "I was just checking." I sat up, and he handed me the mail. "Thank you, Morrie." He leaned forward.

Water bill. Missing and Exploited Children Card. Letter from that NPR St. Louis station again, in the sunny yellow envelope. I could feel Maurice's eyes on me before he ever got up. I keep looking at the envelope, I knew what it said. I had thrown the other one away I had gotten before that Michelle had brought in. "Mama, Imma go get these tools right quick. I need Pop's ratchet set." I was remembering to breathe. "That's fine, Maurice. Gon get em." I sat in the chair he had left empty. I opened the yellow envelope, read it again. Put it on the same stand. I heard him rustling downstairs, thought about how he didn't wash his hands when he went in my refrigerator.

I thought about Deborah. I thought about her work schedule since we shared an office. I wanted to talk to her. I reached for the phone and dialed her work extension. "Case Coordination. Deborah speaking." I swallowed. "Dee, when are you going to lunch?" I heard her chuckle. "Chile, as soon I'm able. In about thirty minutes! I have a meeting with the Social Work department, then I'm free." It was almost noon. "Dee, I'll make something here. I need you to come by. Please say you can." I heard her tap her nails on the phone receiver. She did that when she was thinking or nervous. "I'll be there. I'll grab a sandwich from somewhere." I sighed and smiled. "Okay, Dee. See you in what, thirty minutes?" Deborah laughed. "Chile, I got keys in my hands right now!" With that she hung up.

"I'm finna go, Mama, I gotta be at the plant at 1, 1:30 today, and today is the day I start the foreman position!" I smiled, happy he didn't come back upstairs. "I'll see you Sunday, Mama! Love you!" he slammed the door, and all I could do was laugh. James always screamed where he was going, and so did Maurice. James did that when he was trying to just leave without being hindered with hearing my voice—so I wouldn't ask him to do anything before he left to wherever he was going. I wanted him to cut that grass, and he knew it. I sat and looked out the window and decided that I was going to need Deborah to go to St. Louis. I couldn't go back there without her.

Deborah blew in with all her bobbed blonde hair, white scrub bottoms and lab jacket with a yellow shirt under. She smiled as she made her way in the door with and hips, big sunglasses, and work bag. She was sipping something out of Subway cup. "Chile, I was glad that you called! If you hadn't, I would have had to go to boss-man Mark and tell him I'm about to take my Friday on this Thursday!" I laughed as she swept past me towards the kitchen. "Whoo, girl!" Deborah smiled at me and we sat at the kitchen table. She reached in her workbag and got her Subway sandwich. "I got sweet tea."

She made an approving noise, as I went in the fridge and got the pitcher with the yellow top and poured myself glass. I left the pitcher on the sink in case I needed a quick refill. I sat in the chair next to her keeping my glass towards me. I watched her eat and watched the sun over the trees from my seat. I reached in my left pocket for the letter from the radio station, slid it towards her, and said nothing. I sipped my tea and waited. "Charles had a something in

New York." She didn't turn around from the Frigidaire. "Mm. He one of them Negroes 'less some woman is on him or he on some woman."

I made an approving noise. "He sat on my couch and ate out of an Uncle Lou's clamshell." I heard Deborah cackle as she came back to the kitchen table. "Quit him. I know it ain't that good." I stared at her and laughed. I propped my right hand under my cheek, rolled my eyes, remembering our last escapade. "It ain't." She took a bite of her sandwich, "Knew it." I laughed. I took the yellow envelope out of my pocket, setting it on the table between us. Deborah looked at it, turned it over twice before leaving it face down. As I got up to fill my cup, I heard her clear her throat. "So yo gon go?" I reached the refrigerator. "Go where?"

"St. Louis." I heard Deborah sip her cup, hitting the bottom of her cup. "You gon call these people?" I didn't turn around, I filled my cup with the tea pitcher I left on the side of my sink. "I ain't going." I turned to her, hand on my hip and got sipped my tea. "Look, I can't go back to St. Louis. I don't want to go." I sat back down. "Look," Deborah had her sunglasses on top her hair, and her lipstick was faded. She clasped her hands. "St. Louis ain't Rome! You can make it there in a day and be in our own bed that night." I looked at her, crossed my arms over my chest. "What the hell you talkin about girl?" Deborah sighed. "Jackson saw," I looked at her. "What?"

"Jackson was dating this girl, Eliza, last year. She's from St. Louis." She shifted her weight in her chair. "When I went with him to her graduation last year from Saint Louis University, I saw some friends of this girl at the graduation mingling dinner. This girl knows Maeghan." I looked at her. "What? What Maeghan?" She took a deep breath, looking at the table before looking back at me. "Maeghan Lewis. Reuben's daughter." I almost dropped my glass on the floor. I sat down again. I put my face in my hands. "Her aunt was there." I exhaled. "Babs." She nodded. "Babs was there. I spoke to her, only because Jackson was taking me around with Eliza." She wiped her mouth with a Subway napkin.

"Babs saw me, and we talked, and she asked about you." I looked up at her. "Barbara needs to worry about herself." She went back to her sandwich. "Call the radio station people, Ethylene. It's an interview, what else could it hurt?" I sighed, looked at her, felt my face get hot. "I don't need this type of shit, Dee. They want Ruby, not Ethylene."

"Ain't they the same person?" She sipped her tea, pouted when she realized it was empty. She popped her lips, keeping her eyes on me. "I, I ain't that girl anymore, Dee." She chuckled low, watched her shoulders shake. "Ethylene, you know that Reuben loved you with all his might! You know you love him. You ran from St. Louis after that fire." I couldn't look at her, found the trees outside the window more interesting. "I left so he could," I looked off.

"You left because you didn't want to stay, shug!" She smacked the table. "And you ran to James! You ran to nursing school! You runnin right now!" I looked at the floor. "They weren't ever going to let him have any peace, us any peace, Dee!" I stood to the sink, leaning against it, smoothed my hair. "Not from California! Not from Missouri! What life would we have had?" I heard Deborah sigh. "You won't know now! The world is better now, or at least a little different!"

"You ran too, Dee! You ran to Memphis to start over because of Howard!" I had my hands on my hips, sure I looked like a tired child fighting a nap. Deborah looked at me, eyes soft. "I did. I wanted something new, but this ain't about me. This is something you gotta do! Don't make a whole city off limits because of one man that couldn't handle not being with you!" She had the letter in her hand. "It's a project they're doing." Deborah stayed seated, reading the letter as if it were a patient chart. "Shug, answer the questions. It might even be fun!"

I got up, shrugged my shoulders. "I had to leave. You know why. Alderman Parker was stalking me, and the haven of The Gypsy Hand was gone." I closed my eyes. "I ran because it didn't make sense to stay." I opened my eyes, to see Deborah relaxed and looked at the floor, listening. "I wanted his life to be better. This was almost forty years ago! He probably for—" Deborah laughed. "You better not finish that lie, black girl! You ain't forget him, so you know he ain't forgot you!"

"What if I still love him?" I smiled at little, remembering his voice and his visit. She adjusted her posture in the kitchen chair. "It's okay if you do." I sighed. "How did they get my address?" Deborah chuckled. "Me and Babs." I looked at her, bit my lip. "I filled out a contact card with Saint Louis University and gave it to Eliza. I told her to let all that stuff come to her house." I laughed, couldn't do anything but laugh. "I'll call them tomorrow." Deborah got up to get the tea I left on the kitchen counter. "Call them today, shug. Call them today." I looked at her like she had called me a name. "What would I even say?" Deborah stood up, making her way to the tea picture on the sink counter. "For one, tell them stop mailing shit to your house." I laughed walked back to my empty chair.

Deborah started to gather her things to leave, smiled at me over her sunglasses. "They just want to talk. That's all." She sighed, and I put my head on her shoulder. "It would be nice to see the stomping ground again." We stood there, together again, and I thought about the night of the fire. I thought about the jail, and the belly pain I had, and the baby that should have been. I remembered my Aunt Linda that brought church mothers from Union Missionary

Baptist Church over to her house on Arsenal came over to the house and prayed for me. I would call *Notes On St. Louis.* I wanted to see what all this trouble was about a little colored girl from was 'Iberia.

My birthday the following week was wonderful, my children rented out a Cordova Skating Rink for the entire evening. There were gold balloons, cake and presents. Maurice and Michelle had planned it with Deborah's help. "Mama, we know you met Daddy at this skating rink," Michelle told me in the parking lot, covering my eyes as we walked up to the front door with my airbrushed pink and black *Birthday Girl* shirt, they made for me. "So, we thought what better way to celebrate your birthday than with a skate party!" I heard Maurice's voice before I saw him.

Michelle let go of my eyes, and I saw the rink was decorated with balloons, and streamers! It was amazing to see James's nieces, nephews and sisters there! "Happy Birthday, Shug!" They screamed. I hugged and kissed every last one of them I saw, and Colin with his red and black shorts rolled me a pair of skates, "Vroom!" I laughed, kissed him on his forehead. "Thank you, baby!" Charles was there and brought red roses. I saw Deborah's face, and her rolling her eyes.

I got to enjoy life for a while, remembered that my life was in Memphis,

Tennessee, and St. Louis had just been a pitstop. But I almost burst into tears with Colin told me he couldn't find his skate key. "It's always keys. Always. Keys." I whispered, watching the world roll by while we looked for it.

Chapter 16-July 1998

I chose to work for the Fourth of July. I needed not think, I wanted the distraction of work, the organization of work. It took me a week to pack for a three or four-day trip. I cried, I cursed, and I worked. I talked to people, I was present in meetings, talked to people and helped orchestrate needed patient services. I spent time with my children, I took Colin for haircuts and met, Sandra—the girl Morrie was dating. I did everything but call and leave a message for KWMU.

I had even packed clothes and made sure I time to take off. I looked at the letter on my fridge and held the phone in my hand for the last three days, started at the 30th of June. The only reason I didn't call on the holiday was because it was a holiday. When I called, I knew the number worked and knew there would be was this efficient, mean sounding answering service for the *Notes On St. Louis.* I would hang up, once and called back twice to make sure I had heard all the information right. It was the sixth before I could call and leave a message. It was that Wednesday of the same week when I was contacted by Madison. She seemed astounded of two things—the first was that I was alive and a nurse living in Memphis.

From my quick interview with her, we decided on Saturday, July 18 for the interview. I moved my packed bags from my room to the front door. The morning of sat at the table the morning before I was supposed to leave. I called

Deborah to makes sure she could and would still go with me. We decided to drive, rather than fly—I wasn't that eager to jump on plane to get back to St. Louis. Deborah suggested we leave the 17th, so we would have time to rest and then go to the radio station.

In going home after my shift on the 16th, I sat in my car. I took a deep breath, thought about the steps into the house. I thought about the bags by the door. I thought about the interview, and I bit my lip. I checked the clock on my dash and it wasn't four yet. I decided I was going to call the kids over. I would talk to them before I left. I listened to the garage door close, before I got out. I went inside, leaving my work bag. I made sure all calls were returned, all mail sent, and work emails forwarded to whom needed to see them. I determined to be free of Methodist University Hospital before I went to St. Louis.

I locked the door to the garage, and set my purse down on the kitchen table, before going to cordless phone to call Maurice and Michelle. I called Michelle first, I grinned thinking about the bible scripture because 'the last shall be first.' I thought it was so funny my baby girl would be the person I talk to first. It rang four times before Robert picked up. "Rob, hey! But Chelle on the phone." He laughed and called for her. "Yes ma'am?" I giggled, she sounded like me so many moons ago. I heard Colin in the background. "I need to talk to you, cher. It's important." I heard her breath catch, "Chelle, I'm fine. Just come by."

"Do I need to bring food?" I laughed. "It would be a good thing, I'm not cooking." She laughed before she told me she loved me before hanging up. I leaned against the wall by the end table, looking at the answering machine. I called Maurice's answering service and told the young woman whom answered to have Maurice come by my house to talk, that it was important. I, too, reminded him to bring something to eat. I hung up the phone on the wall and I went upstairs to change out of my work clothes.

When I got to my bedroom, the phone rang. I kept going, thankful for the diligence of the answering machine. I was going to shower, change and get ready to talk to my children. I hoped Chelle would bring Colin. But I knew Robert's mother was in town, so it assumed she wanted time with him. After the shower, I through on a pair of light blue scrubs, old ones I would never wear to work. The softness of the carpet relaxed me, as I wrapped my hair in the red satin scarf. I smiled as I tucked stray hair in it. I went down the stairs again, looking at the blinking light on the machine. I frowned as I pushed the play button. I rolled my eyes at the loud beep. 'Hey, cher. Umm, I know we haven't seen each other in weeks. But I want you to know I'm here if you want to see me." There were two loud beeps. I stared at the machine, couldn't find my breath. I didn't want to talk to Charles. I had broken up with him in my head and didn't think it was necessary to speak to him anymore. Have him call the girl in the picture.

I had to talk to my kids. I had to let them know I would be gone for a few days. I remembered to check the mail and went to the front door. In checking the mail, I saw Morrie's big red Ford truck and parking in the driveway. I smiled at him, and the waving Chelle in the passenger seat. I saw her blue nursing scrubs and glasses. She must have decided to be comfortable too. "Hey!" I screamed, "I hope y'all brought something to eat, because ya Mama did not and isn't going to cook!" Their laughter soothed me, as they came up the walkway to the door.

They hugged me and together we walked inside. Maurice was in his basketball clothes, smelled of Zest soap. He locked the door behind him and put the big white plastic bag on the kitchen table. "I got Uncle Lou's, Mama. You sounded so serious, and serious conversations need serious food." Michelle laughed. "Yeah, this ain't sound like a McDonald's conversation, Ma." We sat at the kitchen table after grabbing paper plates from the pantry by the Frigidaire. Morrie spoke first. "Mama, I know you going out of town, but what's all this for?" I put red beans and rice on my plate. "I'm going to go handle business, some old business, and I wanted y'all to know so you wouldn't have to lie at my funeral."

Chelle laughed, sipping her tea she had brought in. "Okay, Mama. Tell us." I arranged my fried chicken breast on my plate, along with my cornbread.

"Well, this radio station in St. Louis wants to interview your Mama." They kept eating. "They want to ask me about the singing I did before I came to Memphis." Maurice made some type of grunting noise, and I assumed he hadn't eaten all day, with the new position and all. "And I think I may see someone I was courting before your Dad." Maurice looked up at me. "What do you mean, see someone? Mama, you too old to be trying to sow oats and play fields, now!" he laughed as he finished his plate.

I fanned his comment off. "No, there is someone who may or may not be in St. Louis looking for me." I turned to Michelle, already looking over her glasses at me. "Seeing?' I just looked at her. "You heard just want I said. Now, I'm not going to be fast nowhere, I'm just saying, I may see this person." I started to stab at my dinner. "And he just might want to see me. I don't know. I don't know." Michelle looked at her brother, whom then looked at me. "What's his name, Mama? 'Least tell us that." I looked at him, his Daddy looking right back at me. "I'm still your mother, Maurice James Carter." He took his gaze from mine, pushed his empty place from in front of him. "Now, I'm letting y'all know I'll be on this radio show, *Notes On St. Louis,* on KMWU on the 18th on this this NPR station. I'll be gone a few days."

I filled my mouth with food, happy it was there, trying to feed the flow of words that threatened to tell them everything. I chewed with purpose and swallowed slow. "So, I'll make sure I get the mail and make sure the lights are on timers." I patted Michelle's left knee and nodded, "Thank you, Chelle." "I still wanna know who this meet-up person is!" Morrie said, getting more food from the boxes in the middle of the table. "Maurice," I sighed, exasperated. "I'm not telling you nothing else about my life!" I had to laugh. "You may have to just wait like Liz Taylor's fans—wait till I'm dead to find out everything, how about that?" he paused, frowned at me. "That's messed up, Mama!"

We laughed and talked more, finalizing my plans for the next day. Michelle had to do he regular night shift so she and would come by the house in the morning after her shift. Maurice said he would come by Saturday and Monday before I got home. They helped clean up and left me to my thoughts and the empty house. As I locked the door when they left, I went to the blinking light on my answering machine, played the message again. I erased it before heading upstairs to pray for sleep.

I was happy the morning of the 16th came quick. I had coffee, hair in rollers and probably crust in my eyes. I got up with the intent to pray and think. When I had gotten to my knees I paused. I thought about Reuben. Would I see him? I put my head down, wrestled with the part of me that still waited for him.

The part that knew that he and I—I shook the thought away as I stood. I replayed the day only weeks ago when I had given in to call the radio station. I wanted to curse out the machine, I wanted to be left alone, but Madison, the cheery sounding white girl whom I spoke to first, made that impossible.

I replayed that conversation at early in the month. I had spoken to Madison, and then to I was transferred to the show's manager. "Notes On Saint Louis." I coughed, totally prepared to curse out the machine. "Could you spell that?" I asked before I thought it was rude or thought better. She laughed. "I get that all the time. M-a-e-g-h-a-n. Last name Lewis." I reached down and found my professional voice. "Yes, I have received letters from your station, and according to the letter, I was advised to speak to either yourself, Madison or the other young woman was Whitney."

I heard paper rustling, something dropping. "Yes, ma'am. May I ask what this is regarding?" My accent jumped out before I could catch it. "I heard you were looking for me. I'm Ruby. The singer from The Gypsy Hand." I heard her gasp, and then more paper rattling. She asked a list of questions ending with how quick I could get to St. Louis. I remember how harried she became, how excited she was to schedule me, and double checked all my contact information. I thanked her for her time, and now that morning had come.

I said my morning prayer. I knelt for a few minutes, waiting for the anchor to drop in my soul so I would be steadied to get into a car with my best friend to get to St. Louis. Deborah had already called before seven, and it was eight then. I put on a half pot of coffee, happy I wouldn't have to drink it all. I had done so for the first month I was a widow, forgetting James's *Dad* mug would remain empty. I left it by the coffee machine on the little island below the phone. This morning, I was focused. I had gone back upstairs to steady myself in the mirror when the I heard knocking. "Ethylene!" It was Charles voice. I took a deep breath remembering I hadn't decided to give him a key, thanking God for that moment of wisdom. I slipped on the clothes I would be riding in the car with Deborah in, jeans and a tee shirt and headed downstairs.

There was more knocking, and I almost didn't open the door. I made sure the chain was on the door and opened it just wide enough to see his face to talk to him. Charles stood looking at me from the door, he was in a black polo shirt and khakis. He looked so out of place at my front door then. "Yes?" I said as if he were a Jehovah's witness. "So, you're not letting me in, babe?" I shook my head no. "I'm getting ready to leave. What is it that you need?" He leaned against the doorframe. "You are the only sixty-year-old woman I know who got this many secrets!" I stared at him. "Chas, I have something to do today, unless you dropping off money or Jesus, I must let you go!" I started to close the door. He stopped it from closing. "Who is he?" I rolled my neck at him. "What?" His brown eyes narrowed at me. "Who is he, Ethylene?" I crossed my arms over my chest and stared. "Who is who, Charles?" He sighed like he had lost all his money somewhere or on someone. "This man. I know it's a man, Ethie."

I laughed, threw my head back and laughed. "You need to tell me who the white girl is in the pictures you showed me!" He looked at me, like I called his Mama a whore. "I'm going with Deb to St. Louis. I don't have time for this." I kept my hand on the door, remembered that Maurice was at work since it was a Friday, and the police were within ten minutes from my house. "I have been grown along time, Charles Johnson." I saw him back away from the door. "Ain't been no man here full time in almost five years." I straightened by back. "Now, I advise you to take all of this bullshit with you when you leave my front." I twiddled with the doorknob, not letting my eyes leave his, betraying nothing.

"You got you some white girl red hair and now your Negroness can be bothered." He looked me up and down, and I watched the sun glint off his bald head. "Just make sure you go when you leave! I know your car and license plate!" He went to his Jeep, fanning me off, "He can have you!" I laughed closing the door before he went to his black Jeep Cherokee and sped off. I shut the door and leaned against it. I went back upstairs, happy he was gone. I went back to the end table where my large Jackie O glasses that Michelle had gotten me on her last shopping outing lay. I put them in my hair, looking in the mirror reminding myself to breathe and the need to keep breathing. Deborah was going because Jackson was in St. Louis, and she would be driving these four hours from here to there. I adjusted the new red curls that Deidre at the Gypsy Salon gave. I smoothed the back of the tapered cut, smiled at the dramatic look it gave. I heard a car horn then, knew it to be Deborah and her white Lexus to unlock the trunk. Unlocking the door, I peeked out, seeing Deborah in her black Methodist University Hospital shirt and jeans.

I moved my bags to the front step. I took my black Nine West purse form the bottom step where I had left it earlier. I locked the front door and headed towards the welcome sight of her Lexus. I opened the front door, put my purse on the floor and taking off my glasses, I sighed. We pulled out of my driveway with Deborah's radio tuned to KLOT 98.7, the music station Michelle sometimes listened to when I was in her car or she was bold enough to be in my car turning it from my 'old stuff'.

I settled into my seat as the morning sun warmed my legs through my jeans. "You ready for this?" Deborah asked, turning from the driveway heading towards I-64. I kept my eyes forward, took a deep in. "Nope. Let's go."

Chapter 17 -St. Louis, Missouri/July 1998

Deborah and I had gotten to downtown St. Louis at three in the afternoon. We had checked into the Holiday Inn, this gorgeous building that faced the Mississippi River. The muddy water reminded me of home, cypress trees and Lake Fausse. We checked into Room 220 and went to dinner at Calico's on the advice of the desk clerk. At the advice of Deborah, we walked to the restaurant, maybe a ten-minute walk---even for women our age. "I'm glad I came, Dee." I said, answering the question in her head. She smiled at me, as we entered the restaurant.

The scents of sauce, fresh pasta and bread soothed me. The hostess, Emma, in her bright green shirt, had gotten us a table by a window flush with plants. As we sat and looked at the menu, we were welcomed in a surprise engagement. "Yes!" We looked at the small gathering of black people present, and the balloons. We smiled at each other, then the Deborah yelled, "Congratulations, baby!" I smiled, thinking about what I would try and eat.

We made it back to the hotel, showered and sleep came swift. I stirred then, woke up. I was staring at the wall. I couldn't sleep. I sat up in bed in my Holiday Inn room, with clean sheets wrapped around me and a few small rollers in my short hair. I got up, grabbed my comfy red robe from the foot of the bed, making my way towards the bathroom and wash my face again. I thought about the night I had to lie to leave Reuben. I remembered how he smelled, what he said, and how I had believed every word of it. I believed it because I had to. I looked at the mirror, willed that young red head back into my vision. I caught glimpses of her as I turned my face this way and that, and when I saw her—I saw the man who loved her behind her, whispering in her ear. "Let me stay where life is."

I hung on the side of the sink, closed my eyes. I thought about my Aunt Linda. She and my mother, Mae-Reavis, were twins born on Christmas. In our family, that meant they were psychic. They talked to spirits, read cards and palms. Aunt Linda told me when I was silly enough not to believe her that Reuben 'was the husband of my heart'. When I married James, she hadn't come. I was so upset and determined to find out why. When I asked her why on the phone, almost two weeks before the wedding in August of '61, she had told me what haunted me on my wedding night and after James died. "You makin a mistake, cher. He ain't the one. You gon be happy, but he ain't in ya heart and you ain't gon never let him in." Her words stung, and she had been in ground a decade and some. That little house on Arsenal sold and lived in all over again.

I looked at the small bathroom mirror and exhaled, heard Deborah sigh in her sleep. I walked back towards my bed on my side of the room and sat in the too hard brown easy chair under the big single window. I tugged at my robe and remembered something Michelle had told me when she went through this phase of gobbling up everything that was Tennessee Williams. I looked out on the fading night, and insistent day with its far off red and orange light, remembering that he had called St. Louis 'a necessary adversary.' He couldn't have been more right.

Deborah and I got up like school girls! We turned on a local radio station and thrilled when it played real music like Ella, Billie and the Temptations. We talked about old times as we got ready in the bathroom in shifts. Hair curlers, curling irons and lipstick tubes sprawled out. The mystery radio station announced its call letters and the DJ told the time was fifteen before the nine o'clock hour. The radio interview was in an hour.

We got dressed as *Cloud 9* by the Temptations played in the background. I looked at my red hair again, it looked like it shimmered. I smiled at my reflection. I went over my outfit once more: simple black heel, blue pencil skirt and a white blouse. I tucked my hair behind my ear to make sure the diamond earrings were in. "Heifer, will you please get out the damn mirror!" Deborah stood in the bathroom door, curling iron in her blonde hair held tight with her left hand, with the right on her hip. She wore white cigarette pants, and black blouse, her shoes weren't on yet. "Dame, you are not Rizzo from Grease! Who you tryin to catch?" She finished her curl, pumping the curling iron, and shook her chest at me. "Whomever wanna jump in my boat! Ha!" We cackled laughing.

I left the bathroom, heading towards the desk by the television. "You ready for this?" She said, invisible in the bathroom. I sighed, slapping my hands off my thighs. "I mean, I'm here that should 'count for something." Deborah rustled in the bathroom, and I looked at my face in the mirror stationed above the table again. I found my makeup bag on the bed and began to touch up my foundation, inspecting my eyebrows. "All that means is you had sense enough drive safe and follow a map." She came out of the bathroom with her red plastic travel makeup bag, scanning the floor. "I'm saying are you ready for these people to ask you some Ruby-type questions, Ethie?" I watched her adjust her items in her suitcase, found red heels. "Girl, we gon be on the radio. Who are you getting sexy for?" As I looked at her, she rolled her eyes. "I ain't dead, and I have determined to be fine until I can be casket gorgeous!" She flipped her hair, fanning me off and I cackled, holding my head. "I cannot stand you!"

Cherokee by Charlie Parker started playing on the radio, and Deborah put on her heels and sat on the end of her bed. Clasping her hands, she looked at me, and held my eyes. "You ready?" I exhaled. "No. Let's go. The instructions from my letter from *Notes On Saint Louis*, told me to come to the University of Missouri-St. Louis, and go to Lucas Hall." We went out from the hotel room, putting the key in my black Nine West purse. We made the way down to the first floor, and out to the parking lot. I had started to hum a scale. When we got into the car, Deborah started the car and headed towards Interstate I-70 West towards Kansas City and the University of Missouri-St. Louis.

I fiddled with the radio dial, looking for the local NPR station. I got frustrated and just left the radio alone. "Are you okay, shug?" she asked. I looked out of the passenger window. I sighed and fidgeted in my seat. "I'm trying to be okay. I really am." As we went under the overpass, I saw this old cathedral with a cross on the top of this steeple. I smiled and took it as a sign. I groped for my purse on the floor for the letter with my instructions. My letter told me to park on the K lot. After negotiating walking students and other traffic. We found the lot, which was the winding set to parking spaces and parked. We surveyed the lot and assumed we would have to walk to Lucas Hall. Leaving the safety of the car, I had to bear against it to breathe. Deborah looked at me, concern and her nursing assessment eye sharpened with complete focus on me. As I looked up from the ground again, I saw her face soften, a smile warming her face, as she walked around to where I was.

We walked across the street, surely looking alike *Laverne & Shirley*, the show that had gotten us through bad nursing shifts and family stress. As we walked up the small flight of stairs, I smiled looking at the welcoming name plate of Lucas Hall. As we headed towards the front of the building and going up the stairs, we passed a young man coming out of the glass doors. He was tall, brown haired and he looked at me with this look which made me think I knew him. His eyes were blue, and he almost tripped over a parking pole as he walked past us. Deborah looked at me and arched her eyebrows. She adjusted her pocketbook and we went through Lucas Hall's glass door.

We headed to the elevator to the left, only because there was a sign on the far wall indicating to those who I was sure was able to be lost in a building this big, where we could go. As we made our way downstairs, we found our way to KWMU and checked in at the desk. The pretty African-American girl at the desk with long dark hair and reading and *Essence*. "Hi! Good Morning I'm Michelle!" He smiled, clad in a red UMSL tee shirt and shorts. "Let me show y'all where to go. Madison and Whitney let me know you were coming Mrs. Carter." She ushered us towards the heavy brown door to an area, where Deborah and I were greeted with coffee and donuts.

There were frames all around the room, awards and signed tee shirts. There were two yellow gift bags with shirts, a thank you note and keychain. There was another door that opened, I presumed to the actual studio with producers with call letter shirts ushering us in and out of doors. Steven, one of the, producers in a black KWMU shirt, told me to relax and Whitney would be in to talk to me. "Hold tight, she'll be in in a shake." He was short, long brown hair and his green eyes looked more worried than calm. I looked at his reddening face and took the overview that he gave me concerning the show. I smiled at him, which seemed to settle him. "Thank you."

I watched Deborah drink her coffee out of the white Styrofoam cup, looked at the Saturday morning news. I scanned the overview on the starch white paper given to me and found out *Notes On St. Louis* was started in the Music Department at the University of Missouri-St. Louis. It was started by a few professors that had grown up along the Gaslight District and playing in clubs. The show started because there was a longtime professor whom had passed a couple years prior of cancer. "Deborah! This show is dedicated to Carolyn!" Deborah stood, walked over to where I was near the percolating coffee pot. Deborah read the last lines of the paper. "It was at the end of Dr. Carolyn Robinson's life that she could only remember the music she played at a local club. Notes on St. Louis is dedicated to her."

I thought about the clubs they had mentioned. The Plum Bottom. The Red Lounge. The Gypsy Hand. I thought about how the show found me, why they had found me. I thought about how the club looked. How I had accidently on purpose auditioned for his club. I thought about how I loved singing, and how Jack had given me this song, and how his sister really wrote it, but no one believed her because she was so young and black. That same song, My Man Made Me, I wound up singing every night.

I needed coffee then, too many memories flooded the room and made it cramped and hot. While I doctored my coffee, a storm of long curly brown-blonde hair blew into the room. "Ms. Ruby?" She said, shutting the door behind her. "Ethylene. You must be Whitney." She walked over to me, apologizing. She put out her hand, and I shook it. Whitney walked me back to my seat my coffee in hand. She shimmered it seemed, with her smooth brown face, and long eyelashes. "Mrs. Carter, I want to thank you so much for coming to the show today." She wore this olive green dress and wore a scent that reminded me of something my daughter wore. It was sweet and warm and made me feel at ease.

"The show is about thirty minutes, and we tape it live. Just be yourself!" I looked up at her, the youth in her face. I wondered if she really knew what 'being okay' really meant. "Thank you, baby." Her brown eyes looked in mine, trying to tell me what I already knew: this was going to be hard, and there was nothing she could say to make it better. She smiled after that, turned to leave the room. The front door opened again, and there was Michelle's sweet face. "We have about fifteen minutes Ms. Carter. Maeghan will come back and get you."

I nodded at her and sipped my coffee. I fought the urge to fan her off. Deborah looked at me and tapped my shoulder. "I got bras older than her." I looked at Deborah and rolled my eyes. As the end of the Ford truck commercial, I closed my eyes. I thought about Carolyn, and how I wasn't even able to see her on this homecoming. I tried to remember what she even looked like and could only remember the chocolate complexion girl who could play the piano. I remembered how her eyes always shone. She was so sweet, and so talented. I hated that this good-bye was at the reporting of this paper.

My eyes opened at the opening of the door. It was Steven, harried and in jeans and sneakers, ushering us back to the recording space for the show. Our heels clicked through the dim hall as Steven walked ahead speaking to a woman with long dark hair, glasses and a clipboard. They were speaking in hushed tones. When he stopped talking to her, she saw us right behind him. She adjusted her dark framed glasses, leading us to a recording booth. "I'm Maeghan, I'm a station manager for KWMU. Are both of you going to do the interview?" She asked, a bossy tone to her voice. I looked at her, tall and she reminded me of

Babs when she was younger. She wore an army fatigue jacket, a white tee, and jeans. I chuckled, "We're going together, if that's okay." I crossed my arms over my chest. She nodded and looked at her checklist, scrawling something.

Maeghan asked us to speak clearly, and adjusted microphones. "Are you are comfortable with the mic's, the headphones? Need anything to drink?" I adjusted my microphone. "No, this is fine. Water would be great if you have it." Maeghan motioned to some shadowy figures in a booth, then the light came on. Steven looked more settled, more comfortable. "Either me or Steven will bring you all some water. Make sure if you drink you move away from the microphones, we don't want feedback." She looked at Steven again, whom put his headphones on and gave her a thumbs-up."

Maeghan put her clipboard under her arm and tightened her ponytail. I wanted to be sure this was indeed Reuben's daughter. I was memorizing her face, looking for any piece of him there. I only saw Barbara. As she walked away, her ponytail began to sway like a pendulum as she walked us towards to the red door putting the Notes *On St. Louis* placard on it. She turned once more to me and Deborah. "Are you all sure you're okay?" Maeghan asked. "Tea. I'd like tea." Deborah asked. Maeghan smiled and went to get tea for her.

We sat on blue stools across from Whitney already perched by her mic and thumbing through notes, as Steven announced from the other side of a glass booth he would go pee and come back. Whitney looked up and smiled again. "You ready, Mrs. Carter?" I grinned, and sighed, "No, but no woman is ready to give birth either." She smiled that compassionate-giving smile again. Deborah snorted. Maeghan came back with her tea, and the introduction music to came on for the show and Steven queued Whitney. "Good Saturday morning, St. Louis! This is Whitney Marshall Brown and I thank you for getting your local history fix from Notes On St. Louis."

She smiled at me as she swiveled in her chair. "I am honored today to bring you all a local artist from the Gaslight District that we have, in earnest, tried to find!" She giggled, still swiveling on her stool. "Due to our powers of persuasion, we have found no other than Ethelyene Gibeaux Carter. Known by those that frequented The Gypsy Hand as Ruby." I took my eyes to the floor and fought back tears. Deborah grabbed my hand, slipped a tissue in it.

"Mrs. Carter, thank you for coming today! The whole staff is so glad you're here!" I smiled at Whitney, thought about what I was doing at her age. Deborah squeezed my hand and I remembered to speak. "Thank you for having me, Whitney." She smiled. Her eyes looked brighter as I spoke. I heard Deborah open her tea as Whitney spoke again. She asked about my childhood, where I grew up, where and when I started singing. "Mrs. Ethelyene, do you prefer to be called Ruby or?" I giggled into the microphone. "I have been Ethylene longer, so Mrs. Carter is fine for this interview." "Fair enough."

"How did you actually get to St. Louis from New Iberia?" Whitney asked, seeming to be on the edge of her seat. "I came to St. Louis, because I wanted more. I wanted to not be in New Iberia anymore." Whitney kept her focus on me. "I had a cousin here, John, and I was going to work at his bar, The Sailor Den, before I went to New York City." I chuckled. "What was in New York City?" She asked, and I laughed again. "Everything was in New York City! The lights, the sounds, people! I wanted to be on Broadway. St. Louis was supposed to be a pit stop not a home."

"I can understand that!" She laughed, made an approving noise, looking over her notes, and ticking off information. She looked up again, clasping her hands under her chin. "How did you get the nickname, Ruby?" Deborah cackled laughing, and I looked at her as if she were Colin playing in my flour. Deborah laughed so that she began coughing. "Honey, chile," she started, and I held my hand. Remembering the story before she began. "It came from Ms. Clairol!" We all laughed. "I'm sorry Mrs. Hamilton, I didn't introduce you properly. How long have your and Mrs. Carter been friends?" Deborah looked at Whitney and smiled. "Thirty plus years. And two husbands and three children." Whitney laughed again. "My son, Jackson lives here, and Mr. Hamilton lives here. I was born Deborah Barnes." Whitney grinned. "Ms. Deborah, you said that her moniker came from Miss Clairol. You remember the shade?"

Deborah considered her question, poised her chin on her upturned fist. "Shimmering Scarlet. She dyed it to change. She said her wanted a change. You remember this, babe?" I smiled at her and giggled. "I wanted a change, and you said my name was so country! I didn't think that the red would be *that* red." There was laughter again. "You put that booster in it and it changed it!" We laughed again, echoing in the room. "So, it was an accident?" Whitney asked, making us remember she was in the room. "Yes!" Deborah and I answered. "She looked in that mirror? Chile, and she looked like a wet dog. Stringy, confused and wet!" Deborah shoved me, kept laughing. I rolled my eyes and told Whitney, "I told her my hair was a ruby red as Dorothy's shoes!" I adjusted my headphones,

"You said that I needed a nickname because my name was so country!" Deborah swiveled from me a little bit. "Girl, yes! It was! You were in St. Louis and we were manless and young! Yes, you needed a nickname! Ruby fit." She and I laughed again. Whitney cupped her face, watching us. "That is so cool!" I looked at her and fanned her off, "Girl, we got all kinda stories!" Whitney sat straighter and looked down at her list. "Well, Mrs. Carter, I only want a couple stories." I swiveled towards her again. "Alright, shug. What do you wanna know?" Whitney looked at me, then at Deborah, and took a deep breath. "The song." I looked at her, echoed her comment. "Yes, the song." Whitney licked her lips. "My Man Made Me. How did you get to sing it?" I smiled, looking at the booth that Steven and Maeghan were in, Steven touching knobs and Maeghan answering phones. Did you want it to sing it and how did it come about?"

I straightened my back and answered her curiosity. "The owner was Mr. Levi Keller. Samuel Robinson, we all called him Jack, because he thought he looked like Jackie Robinson." Whitney sat in rapt attention. "He was a songwriter and looking for a girl to sing this song." I looked at Deborah, knowing the dam was about to break. "This song was given, meant, for another person. Her name was Carrie." Whitney folded her hands under her chin and listened. "Carrie was a daughter of the owner and she thought she was gone be Billie Holiday." Deborah made an approving noise and I continued. "I got to sing the song because I had come over to Levi's house—he was the owner of the club—to drop off some laundry. Carrie was actually sick and lost her voice."

"Really, you were a laundress?" I nodded, told her about my aunt that took in laundry and ironing for folks in Ladue and other neighborhoods Levi was a client. "Samuel heard me humming and asked me to sing this song." I closed my eyes, willed my tears back. "And...I did. Levi was in the room and didn't say anything." I studied Whitney's face, looked for an anchor in Steven, and saw Maeghan writing and on a phone in the production booth. "I was working at The

Sailor's Den, the bar that my cousin owned." Whitney sat in rapt attention. "That is awesome, Ms. Carter!" I smiled at her, and she continued. "Let's talk about the Gypsy Hand. How long did you sing there? What was it like?"

I sighed, Deborah put her hand on my shoulder. "I sang there about two years. It was—amazing." I sighed. "There were always people, and music and," I looked off. "And I found someone I gave my heart to. But I was young, and I don't even know where he is or if he's still alive." Whitney made an approving noise. "What do you miss about it?" I looked at her. "How do you feel when people die?" I closed my eyes, felt a weight settle in my chest. "It's a mourning. It was an incredible time! I met Deborah, I got photographed, and I met some people that I still remember." I dabbed my eyes with the tissue Deborah gave me. "It was great and let me leave St. Louis and do something else."

Whitney ticked off on her list again, before making eye contact again. "Where did you go after St. Louis? Did you make it to Broadway?" I sighed in to the microphone. "No, but I made it to nursing school and got married!" Deborah moved her hand and Whitney spoke again. "Was it the young man that you married, the one you gave her heart to, did you meet him there?" Whitney had a lift in her voice, the same tone my Michelle had when she was determined to be nosy. I swallowed. "No, it was someone else. We got separated." Whitney's eyes widened. "Oh! Why not?" She caught herself and put her hands up, trying to apologize. "Mrs. Carter, I'm sorry. If you want to you can answer." I tapped my shoe on the stool. "No, you're fine. There was a fire and we got separated. We were supposed to get married. He asked me the marry him about two months before the fire."

Whitney looked at me, sat in the quiet and I could see her thoughts spin as to how to go forward in the interview. "Yes, March 1957, it burned down." I felt my eyes itch. "I had left St. Louis by the first of May that year. I had a cousin in Memphis and there was a nursing school there Deborah, me and three other black girls integrated. My cousin Bessie helped me get into the school, and I went. I needed a new start."

Whitney leaned forward, her pen pointing at me as another finger. "Do you remember what caused it? The fire?" I closed my eyes and tried to remember. I opened my mouth and told her what Deborah already knew. "They made boiler gin in the raggedy still. The man, I was engaged to, Reuben Lewis," I bit my lip, wishing I could have stuffed his name back in my mouth, but it was too easy to say it. "He told me to get ready that night to go out of town." I sighed, bit my lip, fighting tears. "I remember that still would kick, and buck and his brother, Nathan, left this liquor next to it. Reuben told him not to. All the time."

I sighed and remembered. "I had done my set, and I went to lie down. I woke up to smoke and screaming. The still exploded." I heard my voice shake, heard a tissue box slide over towards me. "I thought I was in Hell. There was screaming, and smoke and Mr. Levi put this young man in my room. His nickname was Doc, his real name was Richard." I reached for a tissue, remembering that night all over again. "I looked up at him, snotting and crying." I dabbed my eyes and didn't stop the words that were coming fast and bold as water. "I got this blanket and wrapped him up in it and ran him down the stairs. I was in my black gown, and bare footed, and ran." I heard Deborah sniffle, she, too, transported back to 1957 years. "I remember I left him outside and ran back in to get Mr. Levi, I didn't see him outside." I dabbed my eyes. "I saw his jacket on the back of a stool, and thought he was inside."

Whitney reached for my hand, and I let her hold it. "I ran back in, and made sure everyone was gone, and ran to get this blue jar he had given me." I sighed. "I got it, I got it, and flames lapped at that door, and all I could do was scream. That's when the fire department came and got me. I saw Deborah outside, my jar in hand." The tears came, but I determined to will my mind from being that young girl. "But there was a man, Alderman Parker, that said a colored girl had set the fire and they arrested me." I opened my eyes and looked at Whitney. Deborah had her head down, remembering with me. "The alderman lied?" I looked at her, dabbed my eyes. "He lied because, "I sighed, heard Deborah sniffle. "he had enough influence to make my life, as well as Reuben's, or anyone that knew us, horrible". I took a deep breath, there wasn't enough air in the room. "Alderman Parker even visited me in jail, later that night early morning." Deborah cursed quietly. "He even tried to bond me out, with *conditions*". I exhaled and looked for comfort in the celling. "He smirked at me and cursed me out and told me I was his and I could rot there."

Deborah started to hum softly, I recognized the tune as *Blessed Assurance*. "Deborah and her guy, Calvin, got to the precinct. They managed to get the janitors of one of the patrons, who happened get to another patron who was a cop." I knew the dam was breaking, I couldn't help it. "A patrolman that frequented the club, white guy, that had a crush on Deborah." I heard her sniffle, Whitney sniffle. "Together, they got me out." Whitney was dabbed her eyes. "Ms. Carter, that is a lot! That is a whole lot! Do you still sing?" I shook my head. "From time to time I do, but not to the point that I had before. "Do you still remember *My Man Made Me?*" I chuckled and nodded. "A little bit." Whitney perked up, waited for me to sing. "I think I can hit a few notes. Whitney clasped her hands and sat back as if she was going to see Santa Claus.

I took a swallow of Deborah's tea and licked my lips. I looked up at the ceiling, remembering the chords and the melody. I closed my eyes and sang what

I remember:

When he touched me,

All I felt was fire,

My man made me---made me love him like I do.

I opened my eyes, to clapping with Deborah cheering the loudest. Whitney dabbed his eyes again and smiled. "Mrs. Carter, you still got it! I thank you for coming all the way from Memphis to sit down and talk to people whose parent's parents may have remembered you singing. Thank you again." I winked at her. "I enjoyed myself, I thank you."

Whitney gathered her papers and her pen and pushed the button for the sign off message. Steven interjected as Whitney played the sign off. There was a yellow light, and his voice that said. "We have a caller, Whitney." She looked at him through the dual paned glass, quizzical look on her face. She pressed the intercom button. "Okay, get a message for me, Steven." She smiled at him. Steven pressed the intercom again, Maeghan looking paler than she did earlier, her eyes wet-looking. "Okay. But he said his father knows Mrs. Carter."

Chapter 18-St. Louis/July 1998

Lord, I know he'll look just like him! He looks just like Reuben. We sat in a Denny's, looking like the three Chinese monkeys. We sat in this booth, Whitney looking out the window for him, ran to him when she saw him pull up in a red Mazda. Deborah and I hadn't even been able to go back to our room and freshen up. Whitney had called this mysterious person back, come to find out it was Brian, Brian Lewis, Maeghan's big brother.

The three of them spoke in whirlwind tones in the production booth. In hushed whirlwind tones, they arranged a meeting. We sat there like caught catfish, and Deborah spoke first. "I swear to God if it's Finn Parker, I'm going to jail." I looked at her, silent and knowing. We began to talk about who it could be, who it shouldn't be as Michelle came in and put headphones and mics away. Now, we had made it to Denny's in Deborah's car—looking so out of place at this Denny's on Hampton. We had sat there, nursing water and coffee thinking Brian wasn't going to come, and this was all a waste of our time. I could have at least been eating, but I had no desire for food.

Whitney had walked him in, walked him back to the booth where we were sitting. I grabbed Deborah's hand as he walked in holding Whitney's. He was tall, just like his dad. His eyes were that same cobalt bottle blue, and his smile was crooked—just like his Dad. He sat next to the chair that he pulled out for Whitney. "Good Morning, Ms. Deborah." He had spoken to Deborah first as he sat down. He looked down, and took a deep breath, his eyes on the table. I looked at his fresh haircut. I looked at his ironed dark blue Polo shirt. The tops of his ears got red. That was Reuben's tell when he was nervous or anxious also.

He looked up at me, slow and focused. "Ms. Ruby," his eyes were watering. I just looked at him. That's all I could do was look at him. I watched him exhale weights, as his chest deflated from the shoulders down. Whitney rubbed his back, leaned on his left shoulder. "Ms. Ruby," he started to speak again, and sobs came out. He folded into Whitney and stayed there. The same waitress, Diane, came by with her short dark hair, clear brown skin and black uniform to came by to ask if we were still okay. "Shug! The boy is folded up in the arms of his woman! No, nothing is aight. You can brang me," Deborah looked down at the menu. "this chicken salad and her the same thing." I looked at Deborah like she had called her a name. Diane scribbled on her pad, her brown eyes wide, and she scampered away.

Whitney rocked Brian then, his sobs edging off. I watched him, thinking of my own son. I couldn't, didn't know what to do to help him. I wanted to stand up and wrap my arms around him. I reached for my purse and went to the ladies' room. I walked towards the front door where the ladies room was and went to the mirror. I powdered my nose and watched the young girl with her blue dress and walnut brown face and these dark blue highlights in her short hair walk out of a stall as it flushed. I thought she was about Michelle's age, she smiled at me, and washed her hands and left.

I looked in the mirror, smoothed my hair, and looked at my reflection. Reuben's son was at the table crying, barely holding his life together. I was powerless to help him. As a nurse, I knew how to help him, but all those powers were rendered null now. I thought about the night Reuben asked me to marry him, how broken he was, the plans we made after. I willed myself to stay together, baring up on the side of the sink. I fought back tears that traced over my cheeks out of shut eyes. I opened my eyes to look at horizontal mirror. My eyes had a pink tint and I rummaged through my bag for Visine, cursing when didn't find it right away. I had it in my hand as Deborah came through the door like the March Hare. "You okay? We can leave if you want. We can leave right now!"

I looked at her. "No." I felt the tears again, Deborah didn't move, watched me and was quiet. "Okay," she kept her arms crossed, looked at me with her patented nurse look that made the medical residents in our hospital nervous. That same look was known to make nursing black nursing students straighten their backs and made one white nursing student cry. I watched her adjust her cat-eye glasses, she must has slipped them on to read the menu. That same look helped me get rock in my soul to grip when James died; the first time our clinical instructors told us at University of Tennessee she didn't believe 'nigras made good nurses.'

That look, and the look I mastered in return, had kept out friendship from then to now. "You don't owe these folks nothing, shug! You did the show, you came here, and you entertained these white folk," she whispered. "You ain't responsible for them, and you ain't got to mammie Reuben's boy!" She moved closer to me, her heels echoing in the small bathroom. She put her hands on my shoulders, "Ethylene, don't let these folks take you hostage. You made a whole other life for yourself. Had babies, raised a family, got grandchildren. He wants

Ruby, not Ethylene."

She dabbed her own tears away then. 'You made a whole life. You don't have to pretend to be that girl from The Gypsy Hand. You can walk away from this, from St. Louis," she tipped my chin up at her. "And Reuben. If he was anybody worth anything. He'd've brought his ass here himself instead of his son." I looked at her, studied her face, rolled her words around in my ears and head. "I know." I stepped back from her, went back to my mirrored perch. "I am not a mammie," I said to her, eyes front towards the mirror as I reapplied my lipstick. "My Daddy always told me to come from place of power when dealing with certain folk." I capped my lipstick, held it in my hand. "Besides," I looked over at her. "Can't nothing hurt me 'long as I got my war paint on."

I looked back at the mirror, dabbed my eyes again. I went back to the table, Deborah's hand on my back. I counted my breaths as I looked at Brian's head. I counted as his shoulders rose and fell, keeping time with mine. Our stride split as we walk back to the table, back to our respective seats. Our food had come, and Whitney had her third cup of coffee she was sipping. We sat there, picking at food that we anxious to eat. I made it through half my sandwich before Brian cleared his throat.

He put his plate on the empty table and smoothed his face. Putting his palms together, and pointing those hands at me, he closed his eyes. "Ms. Ethylene, I," he stopped again. I fought the urge to call him his father's name, that's all I could see. I kept my hands clasped on my lap, remembered what they teach every new nurse in uncomfortable situations: they told us to default-- see but don't feel. *Your emotions are not your profitable to an anxious situation.* Here, the same. No matter what it hurt, I had to hear him out. I bit the inside of my bottom lip.

"Ms. Ethylene, my father is sick. And he keeps calling for you. The medicine he has, his Alzheimer's medicine, its working, but," he signed, looked down, I saw Reuben again. "The doctors think that seeing you would help. It would help." I sat there, wanting to yell, wanting to curse, wanting to leave, but could only find strength to swallow, and suck my bottom lip like my mother told me not to do. I blinked hard, and heard myself ask, "Where is he?" Brian looked at Whitney then back at me. "What?" "Where is *he*?" I asked, louder, leaning in. Brian sniffled, "At my Aunt Barbara's house. He got into a fight with my mother and threw something at her." He looked at Whitney.

I still didn't reach for him. I fought every ounce of me that ever loved his father I willed to die so I wouldn't touch him. "Is she okay?" Deborah's voice, a whisper. "She got some stitches, but she's fine." He sighed, the weights moving from his chest again. "She, she's not been giving him his medicine the right way, and we think something else is going on". Whitney smoothed his face, dabbed his tears. "I don't know what her issue is, but," his brows knitted up. "I just want my Dad to be alright." He looked at the table, Whitney rubbing his back, as he finished his thought, not looking at me. "I think that you will help him be alright."

His right hand lingered on the table. Deborah put her right hand over it, didn't squeeze it. "Brian," Whitney spoke. "Babe just leave her the letter. Don't, you don't have to say anymore." Brian looked at Whitney, kissed her, moving his hand from under mine and padded his pockets as he stood. He handed this folded white envelope to me. He stood, extending his hand, Deborah and I shook it, watching Whitney's mocha brown face redden and her eyes water. I was grateful for my last years on the floor being in the ICU. I had to get used to mourning, familiar with separation death gives—death had creeped in on Brian and Maeghan. I knew they were trying told hold back the wind.

I took the envelope and sat to read it, determined to remain seated. "Don't worry about this lunch thing, Ms. Ethylene, I'll pay for it." I looked up from opening the letter and saw Brian, Reuben's son, looking back at me. "Thank you." Deborah said. We sat there, me holding this letter like Moses and The Commandments. I was amazed, I was scared, and I really didn't want to read it. I finished opening it and handed it to Deborah. I didn't want to scan it, I didn't want to know. Slurping the last of her sweet tea, Deborah read it softly:

Ethylene-

Brian told me that he heard you on the radio, and I am so glad that he did. I hope and pray that you are well, from the last time we spoke. Brian wanted to meet you to make sure that you were real, and not something Reuben had made up. My brother has been diagnosed with Alzheimer's about three years ago. He has been asking for you, remembering old times, for the better part of a year. If you can, could you—please—consider calling me or coming to see him.

Thank you.

-Babs

I shook my head, gritted my teeth as I rested my chin on my fist, turning my body from her. "What do you want to do?" I kept quiet. "What can I do?" I couldn't face her. "Reuben is alive. Reuben is sick. Reuben's son just told me, the woman he made a life with, isn't taking care of him." Deborah slid the letter back. "You ain't the mammie, Ethie. Don't be this man's mammie!" I turned to look at her. "Dee," I swallowed hard again. "I know you never really liked him." She put her hand up, "No, I was suspicious of him. I wanted to make sure that you were alright. I'm mad that he ain't come!" I stood up. "I can't deal with you right now, Dee!" I grabbed my pocketbook and walked towards her car.

I waited by the locked the door, Deborah unlocked it and got in the driver's seat. We sat in silence, my stomach growled. "Deborah, I asked you to come with me as my friend, my oldest friend, not my mother." I heard her keys dangle in the starter. We sat there, in the quiet, and heard her sigh. "You're going to go see him, aren't you?" She looked at me, that same rock-giving look. I turned my body to face her, mirrored that same look. "I don't know, Deborah. I don't know." I faced the brick wall we parked against. "I'll call Babs when we get back. I need to hear from her what is going on. This man will not a haunt another night."

We drove back to the hotel, in silence and hunger. I thought about the card in the back of my wallet. I had Babs's number. I had left her a message when Deborah had gotten to sleep the first night in St. Louis. I knew she would talk to me, I needed her to talk to me. I wanted to know if the ghosts were haunting Reuben. Deborah pulled back into the same spot we had pulled out of hours earlier, and complained her head hurt. "I'm going to go lay down, Ethie. Jackson and Calvin are taking me to dinner later. You are welcome to go." I looked at her as I got out of the car. "No. But it's good to know Calvin has landed somewhere, seeing that he couldn't stay were you were." Deborah sauntered to the hotel's front door. "Look, we got divorced when Jack was young. And if he wants to see me, I don't mind seeing him."

We laughed as we went through the door, happy to be where we could rest again. Deborah went to the desk to ask for towels, and I made my way back to Room 220. I used my key to open the door and made a beeline to the phone on the nightstand between our beds. Sitting my purse near me, I retrieved my wallet and the Lewis Construction card from it and dialed. "Lewis Construction, Barbara."

My throat was dry. "Hey, Shug." Silence. I was holding my breath. "I'm sorry, who is this?" her tone still professional. I swallowed, looked over at the mirror, my eyes tearing. "Ruby." There was more silence, threatened to swallow the room. "Where are you?" I held the phone to my chest, my breathing crazy. I licked my lips and got on the phone to my ear again. "The Holiday Inn Downtown St Louis, Room 220."

"You alone?"

"No." There was paper rustling. "I have an hour worth or work left here, but I'm on my way. I'm getting Carolyn, and we will be there in an hour." I studied my reflection in the mirror again. "Who is Carolyn?" My tone clinical and dispassionate. "Rube's oldest. See you in an hour." I hung up the phone and wept. I laid on the bed cried. I cried and howled so much when Deborah got back she thought someone had died. "What is wrong?" she knelt on the floor next to me, makeup on the towel she dabbed my face with. "Babs is coming."

Deborah looked at me, dabbed my eyes. "Okay, get your war clothes on." She got me to my feet, sitting on my bed. I told her Babs's number worked, she was at work, and then she was coming over with Carolyn. "Who is Carolyn?" I wiped my eyes. "Reuben's oldest daughter." Deborah sat next to me and hugged me, just held me. I cried, I didn't know where all those tears came from. The phone rang, and she laid me on the bed like I would have Colin and sat on her bed. I heard her speak to Calvin, "Oh, y'all are downstairs in the lobby. Oh, I don't think—" I looked at her, fanned her off, told her I would be fine. She looked at me with the rock stare. "I'll be fine, Deborah Anne." Rolling her eyes, she told Calvin she would be right down.

She hung up the phone, came over to me. "Calvin and Jack are taking me to the Riverfront. I am leaving you Calvin's pager number, and Jack's." Deborah squeezed my hand. "If anything happens, let me know. I'll talk to you when I get back." She put her forehead to my forehead and went to freshen up. As the water turned on in the bathroom, I closed my eyes.

There was knocking, and my eyes opened. I stumbled to get to the door. "Dee, if you left your key—" I snatched the door open and saw him. I heard Babs's voice. "I tried to come by myself, but Keys wouldn't let me." He wore a Lewis Construction shirt and jeans, a young woman behind him with short brown hair. He wrapped his arms around me, and I held him. Just held him, I heard sniffles in the hall. I felt fire all through me, warm and known. As my mouth dried, all I could manage was, "Hey."

*****

There was flurry of information thrown at me from Keys, Babs and Carolyn. Reuben had started the construction company, Babs kept the books and had been a widow for about the same time I was. Carolyn was so soft spoken and sat on the bed with her father and aunt. She held his hand as Babs talked about why they were there. "Reuben and Katherine are getting divorce." I looked at Carolyn, wiping her eyes, her head on her father's left shoulder. I looked back at Babs, Reuben was looked at his sister and the floor. She cracked her knuckles. "Umm, I, we thought he had Alzheimer's, and he was calling for you and…"

"My mother wasn't taking care of him and made everything worse!" Carolyn screamed. She went to the bathroom and shut the door. I stared at Reuben, those cobalt blue eyes on the dark hotel carpet. "Keys?" He looked up at me, smiling. "Ruby?" he answered. Babs spoke again. "Brian and I had been looking to his diagnosis. Some things looked like Alzheimer's, and some didn't." I stared at Babs. "What are you telling me?" Reuben looked up at me. "My head ain't as sick as Katie thought it was."

I stood from the bed, "What the hell is going on!" Babs stood, walked over to me. "I'm saying, we're saying," she gestured to the her sitting brother and niece. "Rube isn't sick, Ethelyene." I felt my brow furrow. "It's his hip." I crossed my arms over my chest, fury making my ears hot. "His hip?" Babs nodded. "He had a dementia episode." Babs dabbed her eyes with the back of her hand. I looked at Reuben, seeing his eyes blink as he nodded. "I fell on a rehab site after I last saw you in Memphis. I had a partial replacement." My eyes went from Babs face and the blue shirt and shorts she wore. "Metal?" They nodded. Babs spoke. "The sealing around a portion of the hip broke down." I looked at her and back at Reuben. "The doctors don't know what caused it, but Katherine was making it no better." I put my hands to my face, covering the scream that scratched at my throat.

I stared at Reuben, not looking at me, looking short in the white shirt and jeans. "I took your advice, Ethylene. I started a business, made legal money." He sniffled. "I tried to make life better." Babs walked over towards the window. "But you got married? You're married? And I ain't about—" he looked up at me. "I can't tell you what it was like trying to live and not think about you." I crossed my arms over my chest, could only listen. "I can't tell you what it was like to worry about you!" I felt that warmth between us crackle as he moved towards me. "It was your aunt that told me you were in Memphis, met a fella and weren't coming back." I bit my lip, felt my chest deflate.

I had only been back in St. Louis right after James died in 1994 to bury her. Stubborn old woman was determined not to come with me, had no children and told me she was 'gon die where she owned the bricks.' Babs read of her dying in an obituary in a newspaper, the St. Louis American. I had seen her at the funeral home, she came to drop off a card. We had lunch, exchanged numbers and condolences at her house, I had yet to clean out. I remember I had only taken her cards, some linen and her mammie jar in her room. This jar that had all her important papers inside, the deed to her house, and the life insurance policy I sent her after I had become a nurse. I remembered it was just enough to bury her, I gave the house on Arsenal back to the bank. I knew I would never keep it, keep it up or want to set another foot back in this city.

"No, I wasn't, Reuben. I'm leaving tomorrow as a matter of fact." He stared at me, Babs stayed at the window. There was flushing from the bathroom. "Dad, whenever you want, we can go." Reuben stood, still tall and walked over towards me. "I made no bones about how I felt about you, devil may care if it was almost forty years ago." He cupped my face, and there was fire again. "I got married yes, and so did you." I kept my eyes to the floor. "We had lives we tried to make and made without the other." He massaged under my ears. "I made the best life I could with the best I had."

I looked at him, offended and crying. "The best you got was a broad that isn't half of me on my worst day." Silence. I looked at Carolyn, she, too, was in jeans and a green shirt with *Zelda's* on it, and short brown hair. He looked me, and I moved my hands to his to move them from my face. "Yes." I looked at Babs, moving towards her. "What am I supposed to do with this? I wasn't a mammie or mistress that long ago, and I ain't about to be one now!" My eyes were burning from trying not to cry. "Y'all can all get the hell out of here!" I pointed to the door. More silence. "Do you love my Dad?" I looked at the direction of the voice. I swallowed and lied. "No." I heard her snort, watched her as she moved back towards where her father stood. "Mrs. Carter, I don't believe you." I stood with my arms akimbo.

"I doesn't matter what you think, I have been me longer than your Daddy or aunt have known me." She stared at me, Reuben's expression on her face. "Mrs. Carter, my father still loves you. I know you are lying, I saw your face. I saw my Dad's face in the company office when he heard your voice on the radio." I turned to face the window. "Y'all…"

Babs wrapped her arms around me. "We aren't saying you need to leave everything and come to St. Louis, we have no right to do that." She sighed. There was warmth behind me. "Know that I didn't forget. I didn't forget."

Chapter 19- September 1998/ New Iberia, Louisiana

I tried to leave as soon as I got the call last week after Labor Day, but there were too many things at work. I couldn't leave, and Deborah was on vacation. When my mother called again, on the 15th, I decided to leave the next day. I had no time to throw no clothes worth anything in an overnight bag. My mama had called me and only told me to 'get my ass home.' She doesn't curse a whole lot, so when she said that, I knew someone had to be dying, dead or broke.

I took the Southwest Airline flight, called into work to angry Mark, the manager of our department, and got there in by the end of the day that Wednesday. I ran over what could be wrong. I thought about the last time I was home--a few Christmases ago with James. We had gotten the flooding damage fixed, James had fixed the front steps and door jamb to the kitchen and back door. He had Moses's son, Kevin, help fix Mama's porch. I replaced the washer and drying in her laundry room. We had even left her some money. I concluded Daddy had gotten sick again.

I sat on that plane, next to a white girl that was younger than Maurice, and she was bouncing a young child on her lap in this blue outfit with a red trimmed bib. He reached out at me, and I cooed at him before going back to my book, *I Know Why The Caged Bird Sings*. A flight attendant came by offered me a blanket. When I told him no, I looked at his name plate. His name? Reuben. As he went passed me, tending to other passengers, I put my light on. When he came back, his blue eyes looking back at me, I said. "Shug, I'm sorry, on second thought. I need a that blanket, and two fingers of Jack Daniels—short glass."

Reuben left the glass on my tray and I was relieved at the heat that came as a slammed the whiskey back. Brian had Whitney call me to touch base once I had gotten home that Monday in July. Deborah had stayed with me that same Monday night. That night was so long, I thought morning was a dream. It all spilled out of me like a kicked milk jug. "Reuben isn't sick. His metal hip mad him sick." She sat across from me on that couch, clad in blue pajamas and her blonde hair in a scarf. "Katherine is crazy as all outdoors." Deborah sat straight on back if the couch. "What?" That was all I remembered her saying. She was almost as bad as a hoot owl. "The dementia was episodic." I had shifted under the heavy white blanket in James's chair. "It was caused by the hip. Babs said they got it replaced, he's living with her and Brian until the divorce is final."

Babs sat that looking like a trout. "He's not sick." I had shaken my head, "No." I smoothed the white shirt I had worn under the blanket and shorts I wore. "Aside from checking in with his physician every six months, he was a healthy as any other sixty-three-year-old man."

We had sat in my bedroom that night of the 20th. We among old photos I had, and whatever Deborah had brought. This pile of paper and photos, we took pen and paper trying to piece together a timeline. From what Babs told me, Reuben and Katherine got married around the time James and I did. Katherine and Reuben married on my birthday in 1961. James and I were married in August of 1961. "So, they were inching towards the forty-year mark." I had birthdays and anniversaries in my head from hers and mapped how old their children were. And what was going on when he and Babs were in Memphis.

Oh, that night in Memphis. He and Babs had come to my house and we talked. On the back of the card I had given her in Hubbard's I left my address. I didn't think they would come by and had no idea why they were in my city! I welcomed them into my home, and Babs and I spoke about things that all old women talk about: kids, money and life. Reuben just chimed in as his name was called.

I had gotten up to go get ice for my tea, as Babs asked where the bathroom was. Reuben looked at me, watched me like he used to when I would get ready to go downstairs and sing. "You still are so gorgeous, doll." I looked at him, smirked as I got my ice. I watched him get up and walk towards me. I was grateful James was dead then, because I knew, I knew that if he touched me, I wasn't going to make him stop.

I set my glass on the sink, I watched him, eyes deep like the ocean I had only seen in books, and he cupped my face, touched my lips and there was fire. His hands were diligent, from my face, to my hips, to my rear end. He just held me and kissed me. I didn't want him to talk. I thought if he spoke, the spell would be broken, and I would have to wake up. I would wake up in this big house, with this big bed, and be alone. He kissed me like I was, like he was home.

Like he didn't have a whole other life to get to or go back to.

He broke our kiss, and held me, walked and we walked back to the kitchen table to wait for Babs. We just exchanged looks over our glasses, sitting on opposite sides of the table. Babs made her way back, and grinned, smoothing her black shirt and pants and she sat between us. She looked at her brother, then at me, and cleared her throat. "Well, to answer the obvious question, we're here on business." I started to laugh. "Damn right y'all are." Babs rolled her eyes and giggled looking at the floor. "No," we all laughed then. "My husband, Thomas, works with us at Lewis Construction. Business was a little slow and he told us there were a chance to rehab some houses here." I sipped my water, stared at Reuben.

"This was unexpected. We had just left Thomas's friend, Calvin Hamilton, when we saw you." I remember coughing, not saying anything about them knowing Calvin. "If not for the red hair…" she giggled and sipped her water.

We talked into the night, too late for them to drive off into a hotel in a city they weren't familiar with. I offered Barbara the downstairs bedroom, it was clean and quiet. I was more relieved I wouldn't have to sleep in that house by myself for just one night. I got up leading her to the room, and the bathroom in it. James used to call it the small Master bedroom. He had put the half-bath in for me. "Towels are all clean," I started, showing the bathroom and the bedroom. "There's an alarm clock and the bed linens are clean." Babs grinned, thanked me and laid down, turning on the television. I closed the door and shut off the light. I knew Babs would asleep in no time.

I went back to the kitchen and saw it empty. I saw Reuben leaning at the sink. He was sniffling. I went over to him and stood across from him, leaning against the stove. "Katie, my wife, she's sick." I sucked my teeth. "Sorry to hear that." He looked up from the floor, looked at me. "And found out she cheated on me, with her principal, I guy I grew up with." I looked at him, my mouth turned up. "She's a teacher." He turned and faced the window, watched the night outside. "Okay, but people mess up, Reuben." He turned to face me. "They been at this for almost two years. That's not a mess up, it a decision." His chest heaved, moved towards me. "He wanted to leave his wife for her." I looked at him, wondered why he was telling me this.

"I would have never known if Maeghan, my youngest," he wiped his face with his left hand, smoothed his graying hair. "Umm, he called and thought it was Katie. Maeghan heard everything." I gasped and hated this woman whom I had never met. "Are you going to leave? Does Babs know?" He was silent. "I don't know. I know if I stay, nothing will be the same, and she definitely can't go back to teach at that school she's at!" I stayed in my position. I let him keep talking. I offered to keep talking on the deck, walking to the sliding doors.

I knew it was after midnight because my neighbors where pulling in, a young married couple that works swing shift. They were always home about midnight or one. I heard flushing and footsteps then. "Where did the party go?" I heard Babs's voice. She saw me and her brother on the deck and said nothing, going back to her room. I waited for her reaction and there was none. She smiled, watching us, before going back to her room. I listened to Reuben talk, heard about his kids being grown, how could she do this to him and the like. I had wanted Babs to break in to this moment. I thought she would drag him away from me like an angry mother: berating him about being married, his life together in St. Louis-- I waited for the sanity to break in. Instead God blinked: no one saw us. No one. "You can sleep with Babs, or the room—Maurice's old room". I went to back in, waiting until he passed through the open door, before I shut and locked it.

He followed me upstairs. I heard his footsteps behind me, his eyes on me, memorizing and checking what my body was and is now. I don't know how it happened. I was at the linen closet upstairs, between my room and Maurice's old bedroom. I gave him a blanket to stay warm, and then he was next to me, touched my face, then his hands were in my hair, looking at me as if I was the pearl of great price.

He didn't say anything, he buried his face in my neck, and I held him. I remembered his eyes, the relief and regret I saw in them. The same look he had when I told him that Alderman Parker was still after me, that I had to leave. This is the same look he gave me when I told him that night, was our very last one. I told him the Alderman was trying to frame me for the fire. It was the fire marshal that told him and Nathan, it was the still that caused it. The fire marshal didn't believe the club belonged to Mr. Levi.

I wasn't sure if he was with or even knew of Katherine then. I held him in the dim hallway. Kissed him and felt peace I hadn't touched since or before I married James. *I be damned,* I had thought. *That old witch was right.* "I love you, I have never not loved you. I will never stop." It was that same scruffiness to his voice that had soothed me so many nights before, in the life before. "I have never not loved you, Reuben". I dropped the heavy blanket. Kissed him, nipped his bottom lip. "Even after, even after this, when you leave again, you never take your ghosts with you. You leave them here to haunt and love on me." I giggled in his ear, "What I tell you?" he said, kisses over my left ear. "You can't shake me, babe." He kissed me again, hands on the nape of my neck, massaging it. "Let me stay where life is, babe. Let me show you how much I still love you."

He took my hand, made it to our bed, and it happened as it did the first time we were together. Reuben knew he was my first. I was nervous all over again. He knelt at my feet, kissed and licked the heel of my left foot. He smirked at me, before pinning me to my bed. He kissed me, touched me just where and just right, leaving fire wherever as he touched. My head on his shoulder, kisses over his lips and we undressed. I had bought this bed the week James died, that Monday in May I was married, bought a new bed that Wednesday. That Friday, they delivered it and set it up—that evening he was gone. He held my hand, squeezed it. There was no friction of rings as our hands melded.

I was that girl again, on that day bed, pretty and all his. I was her, and it was as if there was no other time had passed. There was only James after Reuben, I couldn't give myself away again, I couldn't think of doing it a third time. Among sheets and the memory of my hands to his body, and his to mine, it was our first night again. All I could remember as his lips and hands were along my thighs was how could I ever give him back? Why would she have him?

The morning after, he woke me up my kissing my shoulder. My ear, before pulling me on top of him again. "Home. You have always been home." My body relaxed accommodating his passion and girth again. "Sing." He whispered, his hands in my hair. I heard the scale come from my throat, his thrusting as insistent, his hands greedy and they were before when the world was just he and I. I clenched around him and took him over the edge with me.

Reuben touched my shoulder with my blanket, taking my empty glass. My eyes opened, searching for Keys. I focused on his eyes and brown hair and his Southwest shirt. "Ma'am the plane will be landing in about twenty minutes." I took my blanket and wrapped it around me, shuddering. I prayed my brother would be at Acadiana Regional, at Gate 7 so I wouldn't have to worry about renting a car and being alone with my thoughts. I closed my eyes again, tried to reach back for Reuben. I wanted to touch him again. I wanted to remember what loving him, being loved by him was like. I asked Airplane Reuben for one more drink and shot that back as well.

I heard the captain's voice come over the loud speaker, instructing us to put our trays up, and brace for the landing. I looked at the woman next to me, and then out of the window across the aisle, greeted by sparse building and grassland. I closed my eyes for the last time and thought. "Southwest flight 451 is now landing at Acadiana Regional Airport. Please remain seated and listen to the instructions of the flight attendants. Thank you for flying Southwest!" I looked out at the window, watched the bustle of the airport workers and the mobile walkways to the main terminal. I thought about what could have been wrong with my Daddy; Oliver was too mean to die, but he still got sick.

I got my purse from the overhead compartment, and headed to Gate 7, relieved I wore comfy clothes, sweatpants and a one of James's old shirts. I went to the baggage area, waited on the carousel that would bring my overnight bag. I sat on the bench in by the baggage claim, after calling Frank and by way of our mother's phone number. He sounded so tired, so ready to leave when he told me that he would be there in 'just a few.'

I saw people going and coming, the young and in love hugging hello and good-bye. I saw this young couple, swinging their son with between them as they walked. As I moved to grab my bag, the caramel tone of his mother, struck me, along with her red hair. As they walked past me, I saw his father and grinned: olive complexion and blue eyes. "Yep, I'm home." I giggled and watched the small child in sandals, a red shirt and blue shorts. "More Daddy!" the child yelled. I smiled at them as they walked in front and then past me. I could only smile as I followed behind them towards the Arrival/Departure lot.

I looked for Frank through the gate and saw him parked in the Arrival/Departure lot leaning against his red van. He hugged me, and I nuzzled his neck, and he opened the door for me. He smiled, wearing his overalls and dark gray shirt, his hair thinning and closely cut, just like he had while in the navy. "Hey girl! Still moving good, by God!" he said. I grinned as I as put things in his sliding door of his red van. "Yeah, I ain't dead yet!" I got in the front seat, and he pulled off, looking in the rearview mirror. I looked for my couple again, and their baby, so perfect and whole.

I smiled as Frank turned on the radio and the Temptations played. I still racked my brain as to what it was my mother had called me for, what she had wanted? I knew Daddy was sick, but I knew that she had fallen soon after he got diagnosed with dementia. What more could I do, should I do, about all that was indeed set before me to do? Esther lived in Tunica, Frank had moved back home from Chicago with Nola. "It's good to be home, cher." He said, speeding down the interstate. "I moved to makes sure they would be okay." His time in the service making his life there bearable, his pension made New Iberia easy.

I took off my blanket, leaving it in his van. I was starving and ready for whatever rations my mother had in her house. It was almost 11, so I knew it was going to be some kind of grits, bacon and eggs. I knew that she would be shuffling through the kitchen, half cursing, but busy. She'd fuss at us about not helping or having all the energy of the dead. I chuckled as Frank drove, putting on my sunglasses and closed my eyes. I smiled listening to the song *Home* on the radio as we continued on the interstate and towards the little house on Fulton Street.

We talked about his recent retirement, Chicago and as we turned towards the house, he talked about our parents. "Daddy, gon have to go to Nawlins. Mama, since her fall, she really can't look after him." I looked at him. "Okay," I looked towards him, taking off my sunglasses. "So, what do we, what does she want us to do?" We kept bumping along that paved, then dirt road to our mother's house, and as I watched her white fence come into view, Frank said, "We gon have to put one or both of them in a home. Nola don't want her in Chicago." I looked out the window, exhaling. "Nola got our own grandkids, and you in Memphis and Esther still down here."

Frank's loud van pulled in our parents' driveway. I left my bag in the back of Frank's van and I held my head as he parked with my door facing her front gate. "Mama," I couldn't muster up the other words, so Frank just echoed it. "Mama." We got out the van and he went to grab my bags. I helped taking my toiletry bag, and my purse from the front seat. Walking with him and we got through the gate, up the groaning stairs and into the front door. "Mama!" Frank yelled. I set my bag down by the door and went looking for her. "Mama!" I went down the short hallway and heard crying. I followed the sound, and saw our mother, her black and gray hair French braided into her crown, on the side of the bed she shared with my father for all of my known life, crying and praying. "Father, Father, Father! Let me bare it! I can't do it 'less you help me!" I stared at her. I watched to see if she needed help to get up but watched her through from the door.

I turned around and my mouth was dry. "Frank!" I ran down the hall, forgetting my age, and looking for my father. "Daddy!" I went back up the hall, screaming. "Daddy!" I sucked in more air to call my brother again. "Frank!" I checked the kitchen, living room, and looked on the front porch. I screamed from the front porch, making my hands a megaphone. I walked down the porch, "Daddy!" saw Frank come up to the gate again. I went to the gate, mouth still dry. "Frank, I can't find Daddy! Mama in there praying, and cryin' and I can't find Daddy!" Frank sighed as he opened the gate, shook his head as he went past me. "He at Esther house, Ethie." I stared at him, grabbed his shirt. "What the hell you mean? Esther lives a mile up the street. Our father is almost eighty-five, Frankie!" I looked at him, shook his arm like a child to look at me. "Franklin," he didn't look at me. "Frankie!"

He walked past me, is shoulders in his gray shirt slumped and stooped, with most dust gathering on his overalls, he looked like he did when he was little and would have to tell our parents he broke yet another window playing baseball with those 'treacherous chil'un' our mother named his friends. He left me at the gate, watched him, with his hand on our parents' door. "Daddy at Esther house. He always go to Esther house. He looking for you and Reuben."

I stared at my brother, watched him walked through the door. I looked down the road and looked at the door. I went up the stairs and went to my brother. I found him looking in the new refrigerator we had gotten our mother the year before. I sat at the table, right after he shut the door. "Is that how Mama fell? Is that why she called me?" Franklin didn't answer me, didn't turn to me. "Franklin!" He turned, mason jar of sweet tea, and eyes looking towards me and past me. "She fell, trying to keep him in the house. He thought he heard Reuben and you coming to see him. He got Bessie Coleman and went outside." He sat down, slammed the jar. "She fell down them damn front steps, trying to stop him. I shoulda fix them damn steps when she asked me."

I looked at him. "He had a gun, looking for me and Reuben?" Franklin didn't answer me. "Esther so happened to be coming home from her job at her dress shop, you know she a manager at Yvonne's now, and saw him coming up the street." He put his face in his hands, sighed. "So, Esther told Mama, where he was?" Franklin started to cry. He gathered himself, turning to put his drink on the counter. He wiped his face with a red bandana. "Mama called you last week, and a few days ago, because she almost fell again when he pushed past her to go see you."

My chest got tight, and the room spun. I sat down, listening to the decline of my father. "He thought you were hiding outside under the washtub." I leaned back in my chair. Franklin moved towards the table, sitting across from me. "How long has this been going on?" Franklin sighed, resigned to my questioning. "Shug, it's been going on for almost two years."

I sat slumped forward in chair, heard my mother humming in the hallway behind me. "Babies, yall in here like someone died!" She laughed and went to the bowls on the counter she had covered with a red checkered napkin. She sat in the chair nearest me, and began to snap the green beans, throwing the ends in the bowl her green beans were nested in. I watched her blue house dress accommodate her bowls. I looked at her French braids and the ruddy patches on her face. I reached over to her bowl, started snapping beans next to her, turning my chair to face her. "Mama, are you okay?" she chuckled. "I'm as okay as the Father let me be."

I smiled over at her, Franklin screeched his chair from the table, walked towards the front door. "Mama, Imma go to Esther house, since we bout to eat." The door slammed behind him. I faced my chair to her. "Mama, where you wanna live?" She snapped beans. "Right here with Daddy." I smiled, she still didn't look at me. "Mama, but you fell." She snapped her beans, I noticed that her bowl of beans was larger than I thought, and her right hand had a wrap on it. "As long as you get up, don't matter how ya fall, baby." She looked at me again, her eyes were red, I smiled. "Daddy just need some help, Ethie. Just a little help."

She wiped her hands on the towel, and then her face. "There's this place where he can go, it starts with a—no, it's Maison Deville Nursing Home." She dabbed her right eye, still red with the back of her hand. I looked at the bowl, sniffling. "That's a long-term care facility in Nawlins, Mama." There was more snapping, the bowls she balanced not wavering.

"We went there, me and Frank and Esther." Her voice wavered. "It's clean, the folk are nice and there's a colored girl that runs the place, her name is Diane." I made an approving noise, made a note to look at the place myself and curse out Frank and Esther. "Daddy just need a little help. Just a little help, this ain't forever." I looked at her face, "I know, Mama. He just need a little help." She looked at my face. "That's right. Daddy just need a little help." We finished the bowl, and she got up to start the beans. She got her salt pork and potatoes from the refrigerator. I got up to go back outside, saw the red pack of Lucky Strikes and lighter on the window sill. I lit it, started to inhale, needed the burn in my chest to cancel the stinging in my eyes. I sat down in one of the two lawn chairs under the kitchen window.

I saw Franklin driving back, Daddy in the seat next to him. They got out, Daddy pushing off Franklin's help and he saw me. He smiled so big. "Ethie, I been waitin on that white boy to get down here." He laughed, slapping his hands off his overalls, his yellow shirt shiny in the sun. "I told Bessie Coleman, we might not have to get him, he might be alright. Ain't you gon get married and leave this place?" I smiled at Daddy, too tired to lie, and watched him walked past me.

"Mae! Where you be girl!" He called my mother's name and told her he was hungry, and I shook my head. Franklin sat next to me, under that same kitchen window, our parents inside. He took a cigarette out of the pack. He had started smoking before he went into the Navy. He exhaled, and looked out to the houses across the street, and told me, "Just because they say these things'll kill you, don't mean they ain't medicine."

Chapter 20- October 1998

After Labor Day, I took my father to Maison Deville Nursing Home. My mother didn't go, said she didn't need to. "Whatever spirits in dat building, ain't about to get on me!" A week later at work, I told Deborah over a coffee break, I needed to go see Reuben. I didn't care what it meant, how it looked, and who would call me a mammie. I was a woman. I was entitled to peace to closure and, and to be happy.

I rented a black Mazda, and we trekked back to St. Louis, that same Holiday Inn in downtown St. Louis at a weekend rate for the second weekend of October, the 8th. I had talked to Brian, and had talked to Babs, and we were going to meet her, Brian and Reuben at Babs's house. I had planned to go alone. I thought I needed to go alone. Deborah tried to convince me her presence was needed. "What do you think stopped you from going back? He got married like, what, two years after you left St. Louis?" I nodded, smoothed my hair in the car's vanity mirror. I looked at my clothes again, the violet wrap dress, and the black slippers I wore.

"What peace would his family give him? What life would we have had?" I had looked at her in parking lot of the Memphis Enterprise Rent-A-Car, exhaled deeply. "His ugly Daddy called me a shake-dancer at a Christmas dinner!" I shut the vanity mirror on the driver's side quick, facing forward, arms shut over my chest. "Nall, they would not have let him have a life with me."

We rode in silence up I-64 East, and the radio keeping my thoughts company. It was like I had lived two lives, been two people, I had to have been two people to love these men like I did. As we drove, I remembered how I talked to my mother about how I felt about Reuben, even while I was about to marry James. "Are you sure about James?" she asked me. "You sure you want to go through with it?"

She had cupped my face on this visit to James's mother's, Eula's, house about six months before the wedding. He had already proposed and his sister, Naomi, was making my dress. In his mother's sitting room, she cupped my face, and stood in front of me. She dried my tears as I spoke. "I don't know, Mama. I haven't stopped thinking about him, dreamin' bout him and I promise I see him when I wake up like morning fog." I was crying more, words like an open hydrant. "I think I wanna go see him, find him—we had planned to—" My mother had kissed the top of my head. "Nall, baby. He got the keys to the Kingdom. You gon have to learn to live without him." I cried and held on to her apron.

Mama used to say that tears are seeds. "The ain't never wasted, just planted in the word soil. Some people ain't worth your tears and shouldn't know you ever cared for them." I thought what I would even say to him if I had found him then? What could I have said to him?

****

We got to the Holiday Inn at three in the afternoon. It took us so long because I thought that I might pass out as we left Tennessee, crossing through Illinois. We stopped at this truck stop, The Flying J, and went to the bathroom. "Don't follow me." I told Deborah. I looked in the mirror and splashed water on my face. I started praying. I prayed the car wouldn't crash. I prayed that I wouldn't have to clown at Babs's house. In the mirror, I saw back in time. I saw the night I left him. I saw the night I thought I lost our baby. I saw the night he came to my Aunt Linda's house, and how she swung at him with a stick until he told her who he was. I remembered how warm he was when he held me, remembered how he told me we could still leave. I was too weak then to go, I couldn't go. *I couldn't go.* I left after my cousin whom was a nurse, got me into her school, University of Tennessee.

I thought I would die without him, but I didn't. I wasn't going to die now. If I saw him, I would still be me. He didn't own the story, we did. That meant I had right to him, right to closure and get questions answered. When we checked in, I plopped on the bed. Deborah stood over me, arms akimbo, sunglasses on top of her head. "I can't believe you're about to do this." My eyes were shut. "I am. I am." Deborah chuckled and went to unpack her bag. "Well, let me change clothes and get this war paint on because we gon have to be like Bette Davis." I opened my eyes and looked her back, met her eyes over her shoulder. "Oh?" She made and approving noise. "This is about to be a bumpy night."

I had Deborah call Brian and got his address. He gave us specific directions, including landmarks, and I was so happy. Now was not a time to get lost. I heard her repeat the specific directions back to him. "Is your father there?" Deborah asked, her cat-eye glasses slipped down her nose. She shook her head, that blonde bang of hers shook as she put notes on blank hotel paper. She hung up the phone and the smoothed the pink shirt she wore, looked down at her jeans and bare feet with red painted toes. "Reuben is on his way. Babs is with him." She kept talking, looking at her feet. "Brian said Katherine might be there." I exhaled in the door, shrugged and freshened up.

We arrived at Brian's house in this suburb called Hazelwood. There were all these trees that lined it on this cul de sac. We pulled in the driveway on the 620 Tesson Park Court, this beige stone house and sat as Deborah parked behind what might have been Brian's blue pickup truck. I thought better of it and parked in the curved driveway rather than the street. Deborah grabbed my left hand

and looked me in the face. "If you wanna leave, cher, just say so." I exhaled, the kind of breath the tell you to take before you give the last push to give birth. "I'm ready." I closed my eyes, exhaled got out. I walked around the back of the car, opting to keep my violet wrap dress and fall boots, I figured the slippers would not have played well. I walked ahead of Deborah and up the stairs to the red door. I held my breath as I knocked and hoped no one was home. Deborah's hand was on my back, steadying me.

There was a lock that turned, and Brian answered the door. He spoke, and stepped aside to let us in. Whitney sat in the living room, feet tucked under her, wearing a big white shirt, crucifix and jeans and bare feet. She had long curly her brow- blonde hair in a ponytail. Brian walked us towards other chairs, overstuffed and blue, asking us if we wanted anything. Deborah asked for a Pepsi and I asked for coffee. As he fussed about the kitchen, Whitney spoke. "Brian was so excited this morning when you called." She untucked her feet and sipped her cup. I smiled at her, and Deborah stood and went to look out the window.

I stood and went towards the kitchen where Brian was. I looked at him from the door. He wore this baggy sweatshirt, and shorts and sneakers he poured coffee near the sink and looked me and smiled. "I can't believe you're here, like really here." He said, putting all the drinks on the red tray. I grinned, "Can I help you do anything?" He shook his head no, walked towards the living room as he looked at me, smiled as he went past. "I'm not Carmen Jones, shug, as much as I loved Dot Dandridge." I giggled as we crossed the hardwood floor of the foyer of the door, as the knock sounded.

I met eyes with these blue ones on the side panel of the door, unable to move, not wanting to move or speak. The eyes looked at me, didn't move. "Coming!" I heard the clatter of the tray to the table and Brian jog to the door, backwards ball cap. sweats and a white shirt. In walked Babs, I would know her anywhere. She walked in, red Mia Farrow haircut, running towards me hugged me. "Ruby!" she screamed, held me and jumped up and down. I smoothed her tears, hugged and rocked her. "Hey, Dad." Brian's voice was muffled as Deborah saw Babs and we all hugged, talking like teenyboppers again.

Our eyes met again, fire went through me. His voice raspy like I remembered, and he stood still at his full height. He looked healthy, and strong and walked over to me. Deborah kept speaking and I didn't hear it. "Hey, Shug." He said, he held my hand, and cupped my face, nuzzled my cheek. I felt Deborah pull away from me. My arms pulled from my sides and around him. His warmth pulled me in, held me to him. There as a slamming of the front door and I saw Carolyn, hair all over her head, red shirt and jeans. Her jacket was barely on. She was washed in sweat and leaned against the door. "Brian, please call the police!" Brian adjusted his ball cap, puzzled and upset. "What the fuck are you talking about?" Carolyn took him in the kitchen, scurried like mice. Deborah, Reuben and I sat in the living room with Whitney. She picked my brain about nursing school, Memphis and life in the Gaslight District.

There was knocking then, and a screaming white woman on the other side of it. "Goddammit, open this door Brian! I know he's in there, I know she's with him! Open this damn door." I looked at Reuben who looked at Deborah. "Babs!" she screamed, "I think Katherine is outside!" Deborah ran to the kitchen, calling 911 again. Babs came from her spot in the kitchen and looked at Brian. "Are you sure it's final, you sure she brought it?" she asked him. Her and Brian looked at each other before coming towards Whitney on the couch. "Call the PD, babe. Now."

I looked at Whitney, followed her to the kitchen where the phone was. "What is going on?" I asked her, tone low. Reuben followed me wrapping his arm around me. "Ms. Ethylene," she shook her head. "Brian's mom is not taking the divorce well. It got finalized last month. She's been coming around here every so often trying to make Mr. Reuben come back to her." She went on to tell me, with Reuben's arm around me, holding me up and to him she was obsessed with getting Reuben back. "The lawyer Babs found made sure she had no access to the money and the house is still his" I looked up at Reuben, desperate for what she said to make sense. I heard Babs from the kitchen, cutting her thought in half. "I cut her off, because she tried to kill my brother! She didn't need anything but to leave him alone!"

Babs walked in front of me, adjusted her glasses with a stapled document in her hand. "My brother was almost murdered by his wife, and I wasn't going to stand by and watch her steal his money or his life!" The knocking and screaming out louder. "Fuck her!" Babs pointed to the door. "She was never interested in what we were building, only what she could buy!" Reuben kissed the top of my head, and I turned to face him. "It's final?" I asked, my eyes watered. He nodded. "I couldn't do it anymore. She---" Deborah came in the living room where we all still stood. Barbara went to the door, cracking it. "We've called the police. You cannot be here, and you no you can't." I heard Babs shouting. She was definitely arguing with a woman. "I want my damn money, Barbara! At least give me that!"

I watched as went to the door, Whitney fiddled with her necklace, pulling the charm back and forth. Her mouth was moving and her face paled. I felt my hands and feet get cold. Brian's voice, calming and reassuring to his mother. She was crying and screaming. "I am your mother! How can you let them do this to me! To me!" I walked towards the front door, watched her go back towards a red Mazda. She was holding some papers at an odd angle and I went outside, seeing this woman go in the car. I heard the car start, stood next to Barbara who was tense. Brian was leaning in the driver side window, Katherine was crying, beating the steering wheel. "Brian! Don't let her do it! Don't let her do it!" This woman was crying, inconsolable. "That's Katherine." Babs muttered, like she drank vinegar. "That's the woman that damn near killed my brother. Who kept him drugged up and fought Brian and I about getting him a new diagnosis." I looked at her, studying the shape of her face. The only thing that changed on her were the lines on her face, proving she, too, had lived life a little harder than I thought.

I stood next to her, shoulder to shoulder, looking at Brian walking back towards us. As Brian walked towards us, I heard fireworks. I looked at the direction of them, and heard Babs screaming. "Katherine!" I saw the glint of what she carried in the opposite hand as her paperwork. "I cannot believe it. I cannot believe you would do this to me, Babs! He is my husband! He is my damn husband!" Brian walked towards her at the end of the lawn. "Mom, go home! Put that up! Go home!" He was closer to her than he was to us, with his arms outstretched like Jesus.

Katherine craned her neck around her son. "Why on God's Earth is this harlot here!" There was this woman, white blonde hair almost, with rage tears on her face, and I thought I smelled gin on her from where I was. "Reuben! After everything! This is how you repay me! Adultery with this negro bitch!"

More fireworks, and I watched Brian run back towards us, smothering us in the concrete and grass, and I felt something warm and wet on me, before I passed out.

Chapter 21- Late October 1998

Brian, poor Brian! His own mother shot him, three times in the back. Maeghan and Carolyn had managed to get the gun from their mother, and Maeghan sat on her until the police got to Brian's house. I had come to when a paramedic had asked me if I was hurt. There was blood on my dress, and I had a cut on the back of my head. Babs was still out next to me. I looked around for Deborah, who was with Reuben on the front step. He was screaming and pounding the brick. I couldn't get up; my body was jelly.

I was processing all that I saw. I heard the sirens of a police car, and saw Brian loaded behind the ambulance along with Whitney, crying and cursing his mother. "Ma'am, do you know where you are?" I stared in the direction of the voice, the sun dazzling off his badge. I nodded. He asked me my name and birthday, who the president was. He asked if I could stand, I shook my head no. He helped me up, dizzy and bleeding, took me to the other ambulance. As the two medics treated the cut on the back of my head, I saw Babs moved on to a stretcher, oxygen mask on her. I stood from the bumper with the medic's help, and they took her in the ambulance.

"What hospital?" I asked, I didn't recognize my own voice. "Barnes, ma'am." They were bagging her as the door shut. I fell to the ground and cried. Aside the small cut on back of my head, some scratches but I was okay. Deborah had run over to me, in disbelief and astonishment and we sat there and cried. There was warmth behind me, and Carolyn's voice. "Ms. Ethylene are you okay?" I looked at her, sun giving her brown hair a halo. I couldn't speak, didn't want to speak. "Maeghan and I are taking Dad to the hospital. I don't know if you were wanting to go." Deborah helped me stand, and we went back to the house. I heard Carolyn's voice again. "She shot at Dad when he came to where you were." She seemed not to be able to process her mother shot at and almost hit her father.

I bared against Deborah as we went through the house, past a crying Reuben on the front porch. Once I got back to the kitchen table, "Please, someone, anymore, get me some water?" With a clank, a water glass was in front of me, and Maeghan's dark hair and UMSL shirt smiled at me. "I need someone to tell me what the hell just happened!" I moved the water from in front of me. Maeghan sighed, put her face in her hands. The door shut, and Deborah had brought Reuben in to the couch, he was still crying. "What the hell!

She should have just shot me! Just killed me!"

He was still cursing God and Katherine when Maeghan blurted out what I thought was impossible. "My mother got a gun weeks before the divorce was final! Really, does anyone know how long she had it? Checked on her to see if she was stable enough to have it!" Silence answered her. "She saw some mail here to Aunt Babs, and saw your name and was," she put her head in her hands again. "My mother shot my brother because she was aiming for you." She looked at me as if I didn't believe her.

Deborah came and sat next to me at the table. "So, Katherine, your mother," Maeghan nodded. "Has been waiting on her," she pointed at me, "to get here, or Reuben to get here, so she could hurt one or both of them?" Maeghan put her hands up, resigned to what just happened. Deborah got up from the table, walking towards the front door. "Carolyn has already gone to Barnes-Jewish Hospital to meet Aunt Babs and Brian. She's supposed to touch base when she knows more." She started to cry. "Brian got hit at least three times in his back!" Maeghan got up, headed to the front door and through it with a slam.

It was the three of us again, Reuben was crying on the couch, Deborah slapped the front door. "That woman tried to kill you or both of you, and almost killed her own son!" I went over to her, had to make sure she and I had seen the same thing. I nodded and heard Reuben cry, "Brian! Brian!" We looked at him, sullen and head in his hands, sitting upright on the couch, "My son, Brian, my son!" I looked at Deborah. "We can't leave him like this." She said, not meeting my glance. "If he hadn't lost his mind before, this would take him there."

We decided we would stay the night at Brian's, and head to the hotel in the morning. We found linen to cover Reuben up in the couch. Deborah and I decided to find a bedroom upstairs to find a bed. I was scared to leave Reuben there. I was scared that he would do something silly, like go to where his ex-wife was. He couldn't claim he was crazy if he went over there and got her, but no one would blame him.

After a quick take out dinner, we made Reuben join us with our feast to Mexican food, before we all went to bed. There was no need to talk. Carolyn had called early that next morning, the day before Halloween of all things. "Thank you for staying with Daddy." She was crying again. "I am so sorry for what my mother did, tried to do." There was silence and then she hung up. Maeghan called when Deborah and I were making coffee as Reuben slept. "Brian is in intensive care. Aunt Babs," she sniffled hard. "She might've gotten hit and had a heart attack. She's still unconscious." The microwave in Brian's kitchen read 9:03am in unwavering bright blue.

Sleeping became a nuisance hours earlier. I went to my bag at the door of the guest room Deborah and I had shared. I didn't fight her when she said she was going to the hotel for our things. I showered and put on my trusty red robe and went downstairs, sore from the violence of yesterday. I found my neglected coffee in the kitchen and Reuben on the back porch, sitting, watching the grove of trees. I wasn't sure if I needed to speak to him. I ventured out with him through the sliding door. He looked up at me, still in yesterday's clothes. I stood there, next to him, and he spoke first. "I am so sorry about this, Ethylene. I had to get away from her, so overdue. I never thought she would," I put my left hand on his right shoulder. "She tried to kill me too." I looked at him, he still looked out at the trees. "Why did you stay?" He didn't move. "I, I can't tell you how I was locked in my own head, and she had the key." He wiped his face with his whole hand again. "She had the key, and every time I thought I could break out, she'd give me more medicine. Always medicine."

I went back inside, needed coffee, needed not to be where he was. There was a door sliding. "She tried to kill me, because I couldn't shake you!" I spun to look at him. "Reuben," he walked over to me, cupped my face and kissed me. "No, no. This is what I want. I wanted this life with you. I fought to remember you." He kissed me again. "I don't know why God didn't let me die with her, or," he looked at the floor and then up at me. "just let me remember something else." He kissed me again. "Don't put me away, doll." He was searching my eyes. I shook myself free of him, moved to the coffee maker on the counter. "Look what happened! I caused this!" His arms were around me, face in my neck. "No, Katherine did this! I did this!" He held me, breathed me in as if I would vanish. "The divorce has been final for months, not just last month. I have been living with Babs since before then. She saved my life, doll."

I turned to face him. "We aren't kids, Reuben. We're talking about a real start over." He kissed me, bold and slow. I wrapped my arms around him. There were more kisses, caresses under my robe. "A real start over. We will see." As I moved to kiss him again, Deborah barged in. "Babs is slipping, and Brian is awake." We stared at her, and I headed to our borrowed room, and changed. Deborah and I had to storm Barnes-Jewish Hospital for Brian, praying for Babs.

The traffic was brutal going from the directions Carolyn gave us. We made it to I-70 East, going to the Kingshighway exit. I found the parking garage, and parking further down the street. I don't know how we all got across the street and to the Information Desk so fast. But I managed to tell the older red-headed receptionist with the librarian glasses on the other side of the sliding door we were looking for Brian Nathaniel Lewis and Barbara Lewis Redding. Barbara was on the 8th floor, and Brian on the 11th.

Deborah and I decided we would see Babs, and Reuben go see Brian. "Get to your son, go see your boy." Deborah said. Following the directions of the receptionist, we took the Central Elevators, one floor up by the Gift Shop, and Reuben was to go the same way but past the same gift shop to the Rand Johnson elevators. He was to go to the 11100 division and see his son.

I held Reuben's hand up the escalator and going around the banister towards the elevator, grateful for the signs towards the appropriate ones. At the Central Elevator, he squeezed my hand, kissed my cheek. I saw his eyes water as the doors opened. "Start over." He whispered. I went through the door, with Deborah, leaving him to the wilderness of the crowded hospital. I turned my gaze to Deborah, still silent and worried, looking at the mirrored doors. "8300 ICU. Let's see our girl. The lynchpin as always."

We stepped out of the elevator, and when the doors opened I pushed the large square button to open the unit. Deborah stayed out the unit going back towards the elevators, almost like she was dropping Jackson off at the first day of school. I was welcomed by beeping, and the hum of monitors. "Can I help you?" There was a male nurse in his blue scrubs, and short dark hair and eyes, sitting at the desk. I reached deep and pulled out my nurse voice, cool and unpanicked. "I am a friend of Mrs. Redding, I was told she was on this unit." He looked down at a sheet, and then lead me to a room three rooms down from where I stood.

I walked with him, my sneakers matching his stride, and my comfy sweatpants and sweatshirt showing how comfortable I was in this setting. I saw his badge before I went in, his name was Michael of all things. I grinned remembering he was the angel that kicked the Lucifer out of Heaven. I pushed the blue curtain back and I saw her. "A few minutes please, we really want her to rest." I nodded, not looking at him. I sat next to the bed in one of the chairs, under the barrage of monitors. I tied a small knot in the sheet at the foot of her bed. I held her right hand, assured by her warmth. "Always gotta make a splash, don't you?" I giggled. "You better not leave me," I squeezed the hand I held. "I may need a bridesmaid." There was the ring of monitors again. "Reuben told me he wanted to start over. I'm thinking about it. I really am." There was more of her breathing, the simple rise and fall of her chest with the non-rebreather mask on. I scanned the monitors and remembering their numbers, translating their meanings. "Babs, I know you can hear me. Get up and come home. Brian is going to be fine, and I know Thomas doesn't want you with him yet. Wake up, Shug, wake up!"

******

The ride back from the hospital was somber. Reuben and I sat in the backseat, holding hands, unsure and trying to comfort one another. Deborah broke the silence, "Maeghan said their mother is out on bail. Carolyn and mother's friends bailed her out." I said nothing. "They are charging her with either assault or attempted murder." We got on the interstate from the hospital, headed towards Brian's house. Brian was up and talking, sore, and the three bullets from his mother's gun missing his heart and spine. I sighed, closed my eyes again as if it was Maurice that was hurt.

There was warmth around me again, it was Reuben. He kissed the top of my head. I listened to the sounds of the radio and being soothed by his presence. I fell asleep to his heart, just like before. We reached Brian's house again, happy he was okay, no funerals to plan. Deborah decided to go and check out of the room at the Holiday Inn, there was no use for it. "Girl, clearly we have a home right here! You got the car rented, I got the room reserved, so let me go save gas and money."

She gave me the rock look through the rearview mirror. I smiled and unlocked the back door, both of us heading towards the front door. Reuben wrapped his hand around my waist and unlocked the door with the key Brian gave him. He locked the door behind him, and we walked to the deck again.

We sat in beige wicker deck chairs, happy in the silence. He reached over to me again, staring. The heat from his hand pulling my gaze towards his, all his youth coming back to his face in a flash. "If we start over, it's on my terms." He said. "Let me stay where life is." I looked at him, watching the sun go over his face. I thought the world had stopped. I watched him get up from his chair, towards me, cupped my face and kissed me. And there was fire, all over again. When I caught my breath, I opened my eyes and said, "Our terms." He made an agreeing noise, before taking me from the chair and held me to him. I melted into him, and the world fell away.

Epilogue

St. Louis, Missouri

2000

August 2000

St. Louis, Missouri

Lauren Bacall said nobody had a better romance than her and Humphrey Bogart. I disagree. I knew my brother loved Ruby. I think I knew before he did! There was something that she had Katherine wanted to mimic yet hated her for having. She couldn't compete with that. Like I said, Alzheimer's was the best thing that ever happened to my brother. The absolute best thing! I was glad to know he was misdiagnosed.

After my week in the hospital in October 1998, I woke up. I wasn't aware

I was shot, even that Katherine had shot me. It was Maeghan and Brian whom me about Reuben's hip. It had been in a partial replacement, from a fall from a rehab site maybe a few months after he saw Ruby in Memphis. The metal in that hip tried to kill him. After my time in the hospital, Brian told me what happened to his dad and what was being done to help him. "He's gonna have to get a different hip part, Aunt Babs. This almost killed him."

He needed to be with someone that loved him, all of him, and when he saw Ruby again in Memphis, I knew I had my brother back. The year 1998 ended with my brother sane, and above ground. Carolyn's bullet had punctured my lung and broke my left shoulder. But, I made it—I don't know how, but I made it. The next year was a whirlwind.

I got home to a paperwork from Katherine's attorney, her best friend Ruth Bright, which I was prepared for. Katherine had been sending me orders and motions for the better part of a year, almost two. There was alienation of affection, she tried to sue me for a portion of the company she didn't help build. There was no way I was going to give her anything, especially with what she was going on with Reuben. I was suspicious of the medicine, his behavior and why she wouldn't let anyone else go to the doctor's appointment with her.

Brian helped me get a lawyer through the practice of Stevens & Mueller to defend Lewis Construction, and stop this campaign Katherine was waging. We got medical records, letters, and a report from Dr. Miller about Reuben's care before and after being with Katherine. She had even found out where Ethylene worked at Methodist University Hospital and had her served with alienation of affection paperwork! She called her at work and sent a restraining order to her house in Memphis. It was incredible.

When I checked on Brian Christmas of 1998, when he was strong enough to talk about what happened to not just me, but him. I felt horrific after his mother shot him—trying to protect me and Ethylene. Katherine had joked about getting a gun, and I never thought she would! Brian could have died. Katherine even called Reuben, whom was living with me, while he healed from his second hip operation. Whenever she would call, we would record it, sending it to my lawyer at Stevens & Mueller. It was Richard Stevens; the little boy Ethylene had saved from that fire was the Stevens in Stevens & Mueller. Ethylene had called me on New Year's Day in 1999, that Katherine had called her, probably drunk, calling her names, blaming her for ruining her life. "This is all your fault, you bitch. All your fault! I wish I had hit you and not my boy!"

One of the reasons why I loved Ruby like I do because she was smart! She saved all these messages, even the ones at work, got a lawyer *herself* and sued her for harassment, stalking and emotional distress. The money Katherine did have from the company through the divorce settlement was eaten up with attorney fees—even with her friend Ruth representing her! While awaiting trial for what she did to Brian, she complained of chest pains to Maeghan while she was visiting her for Mother's Day. The chest pain turned into a fainting spell. At Barnes-Jewish Hospital, with a chest X-Ray, her cancer had returned in the same the same spot and different lobe of her right lung.

I never liked him with Katherine. She couldn't stand when things weren't about her. Ruth had spoken to the St. Louis County Prosecutor Davidson with the attempt to have the charges dropped to assault, rather than attempted murder—they claimed, and I quote, "Katherine was provoked by heart break and thought the stress of the divorce threw her into a psychosis'.

Five years. This is what she got for the four and five times she shot me and Brian. She would have to be driven to Arnold for chemotherapy treatments. Maeghan visited her mother all the way out there, to ask about the house and what she wanted to do. Oil and water, those two. On one visit, Maeghan and Katherine fought in the Visiting Area! The conversation almost came to blows! Maeghan was then asked, Johnathan in tow, to leave.

Katherine didn't stop smoking, wouldn't stop smoking. Carolyn was the one that got the letter in the mail from the jail detailing her mother had died either in her sleep in the therapy room at affiliated with the prison. Carolyn called me hysterical—losing her mother and having a living father. "She is your mother. Bury her next to her mother, your grandmother Zelda in Oak Grove."

Reuben had stayed with Brian since the shooting, making sure he was okay. Brian making sure his father was okay after his hip surgery. It was still so amazing to have the light come back in his eyes, to see his head unfog. All three kids made their way to Memphis to visit Ruby and her kids for all of 1999 before Reuben proposed to her after her birthday in May last year.

It was perfect! We all were in on it. Her oldest son, Maurice barbecued, for the Fourth of July of 1999, and we all traveled to Memphis. Ethylene was inside being distracted by Deborah, and her Reuben had called Maurice in June to finalize everything—from consideration, to ring to her surprise. When he said, "Mama, come outside!" Reuben produced and ring with Scarlet and Colin holding a sign that read, *This is serious.*

I was so glad I was there. Reuben, in true fashion got on his knee and asked her, "Can we do this your way now?" She cried and screamed but said, "Yes." We all cheered, and her daughter Michelle got it all on video. They decided to get married on his birthday the following year, this year. Really simple, quiet. All five children had attended, everyone staying at the house on

Mayfair.

Ruby was stunning in this long ecru colored off shoulder dress, her hair still shimmering and red, and she had grown it out for the wedding. Reuben's hair greying a little at the temple but when he saw her come down that aisle? He stood as straight as he could. I cried, oh, I cried! The garden at my house shimmered as the sun set and Pastor Williams married them, putting life as it should have always been for them. They had written their own vows, with Ethylene going first then Reuben. His read, "I held onto you. I fought to remember you. There you always were, lovely and open. You have had my heart longer than it was ever mine."

Maurice had been standing behind Brian, whom was behind is Dad, smiling at his mother. I prayed that smile was God's way of telling Ethylene everything was okay now. Ethylene read hers, she dabbed her eyes, her calla lilies to her best friend, Deborah, whom shimmered in a violet summer dress, and short blonde hair. She had decided to stay in Memphis rather than move to St. Louis. "Someone has to make trouble." she said. Ethylene took a breath and said something I thought only Steven could have uttered. "I loved you as best I knew before. I can and will love you better now. Let us set the suns."

When Pastor Williams, pronounced them man and wife, I watched the care Reuben took as he cupped her face to kiss her. There was this warmth that chased through me as I stood behind Deborah whom was her Matron of Honor. I watched the goosebumps on her shoulders when he touched her. I smiled, remembering what she said about that 'fire' Reuben gave her, that she clearly kept for him. The six-month neurological checks didn't deter my brother. Reuben was determined to have his mind and health back. The third visit, the first one of this year, came back clear: No metal poisoning, no dementia. check-ups came back clear. "I'm gonna have my life back and with her." he said.

They walked down the aisle, amid cheering and Scarlet and Colin were strewing grasses and flowers. Reuben scooped up Michelle's son, Colin, with Ruby's help, as Johnathan ran to Ruby. I watched them look at each other again, holding all their secrets tight.

Carolyn and Michelle wrapped their arms around Ethylene, then their father. The Honeymoon was going to be in Hawaii, so he could show her the ocean. Carolyn and Jason decided to spring for their trip at the last minute. Carolyn had given a red envelope to her father before the ceremony, tickets inside.

They were going to leave the next morning. Ruby looked back at him like she could never be without him. When she kissed again, the yard cheered. Colin opened the door for his new grandparents, whom walked right through. I watched them walk towards the back door, this regal walk from yard to porch. Maeghan gave me a tissue, helped me dab my eyes. "What's wrong Aunt Babs?" She whispered among the cheering, radiating in the lavender dress Ethylene and Michelle picked out. I looked at her, smiled through tears, "Nothing, Maeghan. Nothing at all."

THE END

ABOUT THE AUTHOR

Jennifer Harris is a wife mother and is a lifelong St. Louis, Missouri resident. She still resides in St. Louis with her husband, Phillip. A storyteller all her life, she began writing at age 8, at the confident insistence of her third-grade teacher, Ms. Constance "Connie" Kelly.

In addition to her love of words, she enjoys traveling, cooking and the occasional Netflix binge. Her current projects include being at the helm of two blogs: The Ideal Firestarter (founded in 2016) and JBHarris Writing Services (founded in early

2018). Her Patreon was launched in 2018 and can be found on patreon.com/shewhoisalwaysnamed.

She is also a contributor to the blogs A Write To Live and CONTEMPTOR.

Beginning in 2018, she has started a writer's workshop called In The Lab Writers' Workshop for those interested in writing. She is in process of finishing her BFA in English at the University Of Missouri-St. Louis.

Follow Jennifer on Social media!

IG-@authorjpharris/@theidealfirestarterofficial

Twitter-@theladyofharris

Facebook –http://www.facebook.com/thephoenixalsorises

Patreon-http//www.patreon.com/shewhoisalwaysnamed

Current works:

Love Songs Of The Unrequited (Volumes 1-3)

Lullaby

Bend Blank Pages, Volume 1

A Lamp Unto My Feet

Not All Are Samuel

WriteLife

Future Works:

Rosary

The Alpha Code

The Deacon's Girl

•

Made in the USA
Columbia, SC
14 March 2019